MonSterS

Monsters

DONNA M. YOUNG

Published by Donna M. Young
P O Box 76, Lawton, IA 51030
dmywriting@wiatel.net

Author photo by Elizabeth Rose Kahl

Book Cover and Layout by Christina Hicks Creative
www.christinahickscreative.com

Published in the United States of America
soft cover: 978-1-947143-10-4
E-book: 978-1-947143-11-1
Fiction / General
Fiction / Christian General

http://www.donnamyoungwriting.com

Monsters

Day brings safety through banished shadows.

Laughter resounds all 'round, but never within.

Secrets cover much, making truth forever hollow.

Little one's dreams might as well never have been.

Nighttime, stomach clenches, soon bedtime will follow.

Not all who should protect will care enough to intercede.

Not all monsters appear as monsters, but all in darkness go.

Donna M. Young

"For anything that becomes visible is light. Therefore it says, "Awake, O sleeper, and arise from the dead, and Christ will shine on you."

Ephesians 5:14

CHapter 1

Nightmares are peculiar things, sometimes pure nonsense, but often comprised of an element of fear and another of inner, early warning system. And, sadly, the ones that are embedded deep in our psyche, way down where our most profound terrors reside, don't haunt us only when we sleep.

Marie had been blessed, or probably more accurately, cursed; with dreams that actually and frequently, moved into the realm of divination; some good and some bad. She was never quite sure in advance, which ones would manifest and which ones would just fizzle away like so much mist on a foggy summer's morning. But, because so many of her dreams had come to fruition, she'd feared this particular day for a very long time.

The night terrors, foretelling today's events, had always been shrouded in a dark haze. Not clear enough to prepare for in any significant way, but there, somewhere, lurking in the not so far-flung future. Dread that was very real and oh so present ate away at her gut and the furthermost reaches of her mind every day for years. The realization of that made her feelings of guilt even more intense now. After all, if she'd always known somehow that this was her fate, why hadn't she done more to keep it from happening?

Her migraine, a common symptom of her dislike of people in general along with her extra high level of current anxiety, was growing worse by the minute. Pain pulsing in her temples, till she felt her head would explode, was causing her eyes to tear up and her stomach to churn with enough acid to dissolve metal.

Standing on the threshold of the ornate, double doors; afraid to step over the sill into the heartache of her new reality; Marie suddenly felt ridiculously, hopelessly unprepared for this moment, and her lower lip began to quiver. She hadn't wanted to come, but her husband Jake and his mother, Dorothy, insisted she put her selfishness aside and do what they considered to be the only appropriate thing. Appropriate thing. What did she know of propriety, especially in this kind of situation? She'd never felt so lost or alone.

The greenish-blue, polyester pant suit she wore was uncomfortable to say the least. Three sizes too big, it hung from her slight frame like an turquoise colored tent. The high, white, starched collar, excruciatingly scratchy around her neck, made her skin raw and red, but the pain kept her grounded, and even helped her feel as if she were somehow paying penance for her inability to stop the seemingly inevitable. The inevitable that was probably all her fault.

They'd persuaded her that none of her own clothing was suitable for the occasion. The ill fitting suit came from her mother-in-law's vast, and age appropriate, closet. She didn't care though. How could anything be less important today than her own comfort, or appearance? She, for one, had only the devastating business of the day on her mind.

Watching streams of comings and goings through the fancy, front parlor, filled to capacity with mingling bodies; in pricey, dress up clothes; she noted the event certainly appeared to have drawn a large crowd. Of course this was all due to the efforts of her socially connected mother-in-law. Marie was sure she didn't know a single soul in the place; except of course for those in her husband's exceedingly odd, extended family. Finally, forcing herself to step over the doorsill into the milling crowd, she shuddered and walked through what should have been a somber gathering, and heard instead, snippets of light banter and bursts of laughter. Many of the comments were so far off today's obviously solemn theme, she couldn't imagine they would ever be considered proper under these, or any other similar circumstances.

Those present must be Jake's friends and those of his family, she reasoned. They carried on much as if they were attending a merry holiday event; or perhaps an elaborate dinner party; though admittedly there was a meal planned for after, and if she knew Dorothy it would be grand.

Vegas' social elite, compared to other who's who lists in more culturally refined areas of the country, was comprised mostly of comparatively new money. Those who'd recently 'hit it big', some stars and starlets involved in local headlining shows, and then those who owned casinos, whether mobsters or entrepreneurs. There were a few old money families in the community, such as Jake's, but they were the minority. So, the room was mostly populated by the horridly, socially inept and those devoid of simple good manners.

Marie thought it ironic that many who'd been treated poorly by others who had money, when they had no money of their own; who then came into vast, fast wealth; could suddenly begin treating others in the same rude and demeaning ways they'd been treated, and not realize their own transformation to the dark side at the end of it all.

Confident that most of these guests were here for the social status their attendance afforded them, or perhaps worse, the free food, made her angry. People sickened her, they and their inconsiderate, selfish ways annoyed her and over the years had caused her to be a bit of an introvert. She didn't intend to talk to any of them today even though her mother-in-law had given her personal diktat to mingle, "And be sure to thank each one for coming". Why in the world would she want to thank a room full of complete strangers for coming to witness her private pain? Her personal preference would be to scream at the top of her lungs, ordering them from the premises. All she wanted now, was to be left alone. To be as isolated physically, as she already felt emotionally.

Making a B line for the far corner of the room, managing all the while to avoid looking into anyone's eyes, she chose a large wing backed chair; upholstered in an attractive floral, burgundy and gold material; in which to sit. From there she could watch the better part of the goings on, without the need to be in the middle of any of it.

With throngs of people between here and there; she was

in a practically perfect position to escape looking at the far side of the cold, larger space for at least a little while longer.

She was pretty sure she'd seen her mother-in-law talking to Nicolas Cage earlier. She was, after all, friends with most of the famous names living in the area, but he was gone now. He'd probably come to pay his respects, as the woman was widely considered early Vegas royalty and one to be respected.

Attempting to occupy her thoughts Marie noted the room was impeccably decorated, from the plush burgundy and gold carpet, to the rich maroon, navy blue and gold wall paper. Elegant, imported chandeliers hung from the ceilings. Stunning art pieces graced the walls and tables. And the marble, grand fireplace was lit to take the chill off the place on this chilly January day.

Marie hadn't signed the guest register, and didn't intend to, instead walking right by the small art nouveau table, which held a long, plumed pen and open, parchment paged, visitor book. She wasn't trying to insult her mother-in-law, who had really done a bang up job of pulling this whole thing together by-the-way. It was rather that she didn't want any reminders she'd ever been in this cold elegant place, on this devastating, terrible day.

Sitting motionless, so as not to bring undue attention to herself; well, no more attention than her huge aqua tent suit already had: as she rested in her wing backed, flowered, hiding place. She watched her husband talking to, and laughing with, a beautiful young woman dressed, from her earrings to her stiletto heels, all in red. She couldn't hear their conversation, but didn't need to, to know he was flirting. The body language was all there; the intimate touches, her overly exaggerated laughing through blood red lips, and the hooded eyes of those whose hormones have gotten the better of them. They would likely be in the sack together before the night was out. That was the way of it, the way it had been since day number one in their union. It didn't really bother her. After all if he was chasing another female, he would most likely leave her alone for the evening. So, she hoped the other young woman would fall handily into his grasp, or he into hers, whichever would free her from his bed for another night and hopefully for as long as possible.

The woman in red's giggling attempts to lure Jake, however unnecessary they might be; grated on her already frayed nerves and she began in frustration to pick at a loose string on the arm of her flowered chair, unraveling an embroidered flower and then looking up to see if anyone had witnessed the destruction. "How rude" she mumbled, as she tried to pat the mangled flower down, "how horribly, terribly rude of them both, especially here, especially today". Another series of tittering giggles caused her such irritation she got up and wandered toward a door to the long outer hallway, in an effort to stay busy and to perhaps find a much needed restroom. She already knew from previous experience that no 'wifely look' across the room would cause him to behave himself and do the right thing. Though one look from his mom could straighten him up pretty quickly.

She was all too aware he'd never loved her. Theirs was a marriage in name only. It was her older sister he'd been after that dreadful night a year and a half ago, so she understood perfectly. It never occurred to her to be jealous of his frequent indiscretions, since she absolutely did not love him either, and wanted nothing more than for him to stay occupied elsewhere.

Marie was painfully aware she probably deserved this day, and all the pain that came with it, for what she'd attempted to do when she'd discovered her predicament; and let's face it, for all the other evil things she'd done in her life without much urging. Her sins were great and she'd used them not merely for survival, but also in order to seek revenge on some. This was simply the universe's way of returning evil for evil. She was sure of it. Karma had a way of coming back around to visit those who willingly placed themselves in its grasping hands.

It was all too clear to her that her life had come down to this one painful point. Sitting in a room full of strangers on the worse and loneliest day of her life.

The woman in red didn't realize she needn't waste so much time enticing Jake; and Marie was tempted to walk right up and tell her so. Perhaps it would save the girl some of the energy involved in completing the boring and unnecessary mating ritual. She was all too aware her husband would go with any bimbo who looked at him twice, and some who didn't exert even that much effort. Then, realizing she wasn't the only witness to his lack of discretion she decided to clear the way, and leave things in the very capable hands of his mother who was currently headed quickly in his direction.

Dorothy didn't like Marie, she was abundantly aware of that. Marie was nothing more than a constant reminder of her son's biggest, and most tragic, blunder; in what was actually a very long line of previous drunken blunders; but she would step in quickly enough if her own stellar reputation might be jeopardized by his constant lack of good judgment. Dorothy's husband thought she should allow Jake to crash and burn, "It might teach him a lesson", he said. But it wasn't likely she would let that happen at one of her own social events.

Out in the hallway, tasteful, though sumptuous, golden granite tiles led Marie to a serene, plant filled, atrium. A place of peace in the midst of so much loss. Informative signs, carved from polished cherry wood, which read, 'Gentlemen' and 'Ladies', hung from the ceiling. Following arrows on the signs she pushed past a handsomely carved cherry wood door, and entered a beautifully appointed lounge. She nodded approval as if to recognize the carefully designed and well maintained space; after all, she saw no paper on the floors, no 'out of order' signs on stall doors and no obvious filth, as was constantly present in restrooms at the local public park, and other places she was more likely to frequent.

Stunning bouquets of flowers, in gleaming white vases, were placed appropriately about the room; and lovely pearlescent, porcelain dispensers, filled with a delightfully scented soap reminiscent of orange blossoms, decorated the long marble topped vanity. She ran her hand along the cool stone of the vanity top, and then grabbed a handful of paper towels to wipe up a few drops of water that might dry and leave marks on the otherwise perfect surface.

She seldom approved of public restrooms, being more than a bit of a clean freak, *"but"*, she thought, *"this one certainly passes the mom test"*. "No, but, wait", she contemplated out loud as her voice echoed back to her in the large marble room, "I'm not even a mom anymore, am I? Don't you have to actually have a kid to be a mom?"

The sudden, and all encompassing, revelation of her new condition, like a lightning bolt to her heart and a slap to her face, caused her to gasp out loud and wrap her arms around her middle as she staggered backward a few steps into the polished marble wall. She entered a stall, slumped to the impeccably clean floor and cried. Not a delicate damsel in distress kind of cry, but a full blown sobbing, snot inducing, ugly cry. It wasn't fair. None of it was fair; and she didn't want to be part of the bitter finality of it all no matter who that might put off or offend.

When she finally felt cried out again, she pulled wads of toilet paper off the roll and blew her nose, twice. Then, remembering why she'd come, she sat and took care of business.

After wasting as much time as possible looking at paintings in the restroom's enormous lounge and then playing with the automatic hand dryer for a few minutes more; hopefully, without alerting her personal decorum police to her absence; she washed her hands one last time. Watching the hot water overflow her cupped palms, oblivious to the fact that the temperature was so hot it left her hands lobster red; she observed the whirling liquid as it swirled around the perfect, pink, basin, and launched a plume of steam into the air, that bathed her face in moist warmth. This sent a small shiver clear down her spine and to her feet. She was tired. So tired.

When she finally stood up straight and looked in the mirror; a young woman she barely recognized looked back. Dark circles from crying until she felt she couldn't anymore, virtually blackened her eyes. And her usually bronzed, healthy looking skin seemed pale as a ghost's. Strange was the visage staring back, she thought, and she wondered when she'd begun to look so old and haggard. How was this even possible?

At barely seventeen years old; her birthday came months

after her son was born; she'd certainly seen her share of heartaches, but this was no mere girl gazing back at her. The misery in her eyes was deep and abiding, as ancient as the desert sands surrounding the city, and as real as the profound pain of an unnatural loss such as this. Nine months old. It wasn't fair. How could any entity in the universe think that nine months was a full life? He never had a chance to run and play, or even to have a puppy. And, she'd promised him she'd get him a puppy someday.

Without much sleep these past few nights, old nightmares had reawakened as they often do in times of stress. To top it off, she hadn't bothered with applying makeup. What was the use of that? It would only wash off with the tears she knew could begin again at any moment. So, it was no wonder she looked such a mess.

Bending over she splashed a little cold water on her face, it felt refreshing, but didn't help her appearance, so she patted her face dry with a paper towel and tucked her long auburn hair behind her ears. With a sigh she pulled open the door and stood facing the hall for another long moment.

Wandering back out to the atrium, and then the longer hallway, she approached the dreadful room again only to be confronted by the sight of Jake carrying camera equipment into the parlor. "I suppose they think that's appropriate?" She muttered to herself. The room felt cold, even colder than before, she imagined that was for reasons only the mortician could understand. This was certainly a lovely funeral home, she thought, not that she'd had many experiences with funeral homes. She glanced over at the far side of the room for the first time since arriving that day and felt her heart tighten in her chest.

A tiny white coffin on a gold stand against the back wall, surrounded by dozens of flower arrangements on ladder racks, filled the space. She wondered absently who could have sent all those flowers. And then knew instinctively it was her mother-in-law. The casket pulled at her, but she'd sworn to herself she wouldn't look. They could force her to come, but they couldn't force her to look at her dead child.

It was bad enough that the last picture burned forever in her mind of her baby Johnny was the way she'd found him when she came home from work very late that fateful night. Jake was charged with watching the baby while she worked, but, as usual, he'd called a sitter the moment she left the house, to go do who knows what with who knows who, and he still hadn't made it home by the time she'd arrived back from her job at the nursing home in the wee morning hours. The sitter hadn't checked in on the baby even once, but only because Jake told her he was down for the night and a very good sleeper.

After paying the girl and sending her home Marie went to check on Johnny as was her custom to give him a peck on the cheek and tuck him in. As she stood in the doorway of her baby's room she felt a deep and penetrating chill. Due to the cold, or perhaps some other innate feeling, she found herself frightened to enter. There was something wrong, something terribly, terribly wrong, she could feel it in her bones, but she also knew instinctively there was nothing she could do about it. She entered slowly and crept to the side of Johnny's crib only to find him lying with his eyes wide open and his tiny arms held forward as if he was reaching out to be held. His eyes were dull. The spark that was Johnny, had already flown back to the universe. But that didn't stop her from thinking there might be something that someone else could do.

Snatching him up and checking for breath, or pulse, she found none. Cradling him in her arms; she heard a cry of despair, emanating from somewhere deep in her heart, escaping through her mouth. It sounded primordial to even her own ears. Frantic, she ran from the house with her child clutched tightly in her arms, screaming for help. Her cries woke the neighbors. One of them called the police and an ambulance and tried to comfort her until help could arrive, while another tried to gently relieve her of her small burden; but she would not release her hold and she would not be comforted. She rode to the hospital, in the cab of the ambulance with the driver, because no one was able to find her errant husband. 'You Are So Beautiful to Me', gratingly sung by Joe Cocker, played loudly, over and over it seemed, on the radio.

At the hospital she was directed to a room in which to sit and wait. Posters of internal organs and their varied bodily functions plastered two walls of the room and other flyers dedicated to the prevention of spreading disease by covering one's mouth, with one's elbow, when coughing, or sneezing, decorated another. The last wall was fitted with a huge dry erase board, she assumed for teaching small seminars. A large polished wood table and eight sturdy, wheeled chairs were the only furniture she saw in the semi-dark room.

Because she was the only one in the place, she chose a

chair nearest the door and sat rigid, waiting for someone to come talk with her.

"Where's my baby?", she questioned a nurse who walked into the room. Assuring her someone would be in shortly to answer her questions, the nurse turned on additional lights; which only managed to aggravate her already ensuing migraine, and made her tired eyes burn; and asked if she needed a cup of coffee or glass of water. Marie shook her head. When the doctor did finally enter with a police officer and a Department of Human Services worker in tow, he started by asking questions; lots and lots of questions including where her errant husband might be located. It seemed they believed she or Jake might have something to do with her little boy's death. And though they allowed her to leave the hospital when they were done with their lengthy interrogation, she was told not to leave the city, and that the officers wanted to speak with Jake and the babysitter he'd hired as soon as possible. An officer, they told her, would be in contact after the coroner had an opportunity to compile his findings and after all other parties had been questioned.

They were treating her like a criminal, and she didn't know whether to be angry, hurt, or frightened. So instead, she let the pain of heartbreak rule. Her baby was gone. How could this be?

She'd played with him right before she left for work; covering his little tummy with raspberries, making them both laugh till he farted, which made her laugh all the more. She'd kissed him and left him in his play pen with his favorite stuffed bear, as she walked away wiping tears of joy from her cheeks. She always felt so guilty leaving him, because she knew Jake didn't care, didn't play with him, and didn't seem to feel a connection with him at all.

She took a cab home from the hospital, arms and heart both wretchedly empty, but didn't remember much of the long ride. First filled with the flash and glitz of neon signs on 'The Strip', and then the semi darkness of her residential neighborhood, occasionally interrupted by a street light, or porch light on a neighbor's home.

When she entered her front door she collapsed into the nearest chair, numb with pain and loss, and sobbed for what seemed like hours. Blowing her nose, she tried catching her breath. It was all her fault, she reasoned, because she knew Jake didn't care about their baby. She should never have left her son with a man who didn't care. This was most certainly punishment for the way she'd felt when she first discovered she was pregnant all those months ago. She finally fell asleep where she sat and napped fitfully for a few hours, until she woke with her legs and left arm numb and tingling. She stood and tried to get the feeling back in her limbs, but, she reasoned, nothing would ever put the feeling back in her heart.

When Jake arrived home later the next day, with no explanation of where he'd been, and a complete lack of any visible emotion over their baby's death, Marie felt she'd had enough of this cheating, gambling, lazy, good for nothing man. Not only did he not seem the slightest bit sad over the loss of their child, she thought she even detected an air of relief in his attitude. She wondered if Jake had indeed had something to do with Johnny's death. Could that be why he'd told the sitter she needn't check on the baby? Or maybe Johnny had woken up crying and the sitter had taken extreme measures? She'd heard of people shaking babies until they died. Oh, why hadn't she been with her son? She had no one to blame but herself and she knew it.

Marie never wanted to marry him. That was the base commander's insane idea, coupled with her step dad's desire to get rid of the delicate problem of having to save face.

Jake was almost nine years older than she and they certainly had nothing in common. Jake, like every other soldier on the base, where her step father was currently stationed, was simply head over heels in lust with her older sister Anne; the sister that caused heads to turn everywhere she went.

One Saturday after work, just a couple months past her fifteenth birthday, Marie headed down to the basement of the apartment housing unit where she lived with her family, to wash the third load of laundry for the night. Jake had been drinking with friends most of the evening and was out of his mind mooning over the elusive Anne; who had so many boyfriends among the ranks she simply wouldn't give him the time of day. In his anger and lust he didn't see the grave mistake he was about to make. As Marie approached the bottom of the cellar stairs she was tackled and dragged into a nearby storage room.

She screamed, but no one heard. She kicked and fought, but wasn't strong enough. She didn't know it yet, but in his drunken state, he'd thought she was her sister, Anne. He held her down, covered her mouth, and raped her on a pile of dirty, canvas tarps. When he finished he got up, yanking at his pants, and staggered toward the door; stopping outside in the corridor just long enough to relieve himself of some of the quarts of beer he'd drunk earlier that night. Even in her dazed state, she could still distinguish the sound of wet splattering on the concrete floor. Though she was bruised and bleeding she managed to turn her body over, and as he lurched toward the stairs she clearly saw his face framed in the faint light there.

Marie, frightened and ashamed, wondered, had she fought hard enough? Why had he chosen her for his evil needs? Perhaps she had done something to bring this on herself? This certainly must be her fault. Her whole life she'd felt less than, and this event sealed her opinion of herself once and for all. She sought out her sister Anne and shared with her the whole sordid tale. They didn't report him to the authorities, which was Anne's idea. He was part of the military police unit on base and the girls were painfully aware that military police stuck together, always covering for their own. In fact, her sister actually suffered a rather embarrassing run in with them in the very recent past.

When thirty days passed since the attack and Marie hadn't begun her monthly cycle, she knew something was wrong. Anne had all the answers. Being promiscuous, as she was by any sane person's standards, caused her to be prepared for any contingency. She offered Marie a solution.

She obtained two bottles of castor oil, which she told Marie to drink very rapidly, and then she plopped her into a tub of water hot enough to boil lobsters. This was supposed to cause her body to abort the baby. It made her so ill she wished for death several times over the next forty eight hours, but it didn't work.

When Marie missed another cycle the girls went to their dad and mom to confess the secret they'd been carrying. Dad, in his drunken state, was so furious he beat Marie within an inch of her life for her carelessness, punching her repeatedly in the stomach. "Why couldn't you be as smart as your sister," he railed, "at least she doesn't bring her problems home to me." She'd never known him to be this angry with her, or anyone else in the family for that matter, and it broke her heart; to think he'd actually yielded up and extinguished the last spark of compassion he had; for the daughter he used to lovingly refer to as his shadow. Now, after so much heartache, it was finally and positively confirmed, she really didn't know him at all any more. He'd become just one more monster in her life.

When the beating didn't have its desired effect, and his

rough treatment hadn't forced a miscarriage, he went to the base commander to demand justice. The authorities on base gave Jake an ultimatum; he could do considerable years in the brig for statutory rape, or he could marry Marie; he chose what he believed to be the lesser of two evils, but what choice did she have? No one asked her what she wanted out of all this. Jake vaguely remembered the night of the rape, but commented during his hearing he'd never intended to go after the kid, he was only interested in her sister who'd ignored all his previous passes. He was drunk, he explained, and was only trying to, "Get even with the stuck up b-t-h".

Completely and totally against her will, but at the insistence of her parents and base authorities, Jake and Marie were married in an impromptu ceremony before a Justice of the Peace. Marie wore her sister's lemon yellow, floor length, prom dress, from the previous year's dance, and carried a limp bouquet of Shasta daisies. Her sister Anne stood as her witness. Jake wore his dress blues and an angry frown which engulfed his entire face. One of his drinking buddies, who looked at Marie with a distain she couldn't understand or fathom; after all, she was the victim here; stood for him. The only guests were her few family members.

Marie, sobbing; and still confused as to why she was being punished for the wrong done to her; packed up her few belongings and moved to Jake's small apartment off base.

Her husband's appetite was insatiable and Marie had no way, or desire, to fill it. Frankly she couldn't have if she'd tried, especially in her condition. When Marie's sister Anne began spending more and more time at their apartment she didn't mind a bit. Anne's presence kept Jake so busy trying to impress her he didn't have time to molest Marie so she was content to let her sister carry the brunt of that burden. And, according to the frequency of nights in which she'd heard noise coming from the spare room across the hall Anne seemed to be entirely okay with that too.

It was odd to Marie that Anne held no interest in Jake until he was married to someone else. She was strange that way. It seemed almost a game with her to prove she could get a guy interested in her, even when he belonged to someone else. In Marie's case it was a blessing, so she would be the last to complain.

As Marie's belly grew Jake became more disgusted with her. That was fine as far as she was concerned. But his abuse grew exponentially as well and she had all the bumps and bruises to prove it. His gambling problem escalated and his drinking grew worse. There was no money for food and when she wanted to find help, Jake warned her not to seek it through the base commander, social services, or his family. No one on the outside was aware of their situation; until she was forced to beg food from her mother's cupboards in order to feed their small family. She'd sworn to herself she'd never be indebted to her drunken, abusive mother; so her contempt for a husband who couldn't, or wouldn't provide for his family grew. Jake never wanted her and he certainly hadn't wanted the baby she carried, she was reminded of that relentlessly.

Orders came for a change of duty assignment for her dad and her family was moved to the middle of the country. Anne, stayed behind, being of an age to make that decision. She enjoyed the atmosphere in Vegas, and had no intention of giving that up for some Podunk town in the nether reaches of North Dakota.

Marie was desolate without her family. As much as she'd resented her mother's abuse toward her when she was a child she had to admit the woman had been at least minimally sympathetic toward her since she discovered she would be a grandmother. Marie especially missed her siblings. She'd been their caretaker and surrogate mom for so many years;

as her mother wallowed in self pity and alcohol; that she wondered how she would survive without their presence now. Over and over again she contemplated ending her life, and her strange nightmares continued.

"Hear, O Lord, when I cry aloud; be gracious to me and answer me!"

Psalm27:7

Chapter 2

Due to her youth, and perhaps the circumstances of her arrival into their culture, Marie had no close friends in the women who were wives and girlfriends of Jake's co-workers and friends. As a matter of fact, a couple of the women even had children who were about Marie's age. At the division softball games she sat alone, garnering stares and off putting looks from the other spouses and significant others. Most of them knew the story that had landed her in their midst, and yet they felt no compassion for her. Instead they, along with their husbands and boyfriends, were angry with her for caging 'poor Jake' up like a prisoner. As if any of this mess had been her idea, or her fault. They all knew their wayward friend as 'the life of the party', and felt he'd been dealt an overly harsh hand by the base commander.

When the time eventually came for her to give birth, no one was able to find Jake; and a neighbor, though reluctantly to say the least, drove Marie to the base hospital where she labored quite alone, frightened and ashamed. Due to reports she received from the same neighbor who drove her to the hospital, Jake arrived home the next day; but she was painfully aware he didn't come to the hospital to meet his infant son. She held the tiny, warm bundle in her arms and cried. Rocking her baby gently; as her tears fell on his blue, bunny print, receiving blanket; she spoke softly to him. "Well Johnny, looks like it's just you and me buddy. Don't worry little guy. Mommy will take care of you. You don't have to be scared. Nothing will ever happen to you. I won't let it. I will protect you forever. Just you and me baby boy."

The bond was instantaneous and powerful. Marie had never felt so loved, or so loving, as she did in that moment. Looking into her son's face, and seeing his blue eyes; which would transform into a beautiful, dark hazel over the next few months; looking intently back into hers, changed all feelings of fear and anxiety into ones of protective motherly pride. Her heart swelled with love for the little boy she held. She would do anything to keep him safe and well. And, she would do whatever it took to be sure he had everything he needed. Suddenly she felt awash with guilt over the thoughts she'd had when she'd discovered she was pregnant. And, she felt especially ashamed about her attempts to abort her little miracle. Truly, if there was a God in heaven, He must despise her for that.

It seemed forever before the coroner finally notified her, through an officer of the court, that her child's cause of death had been ruled 'death by natural causes'. The officer informed her that her Johnny died of S.I.D.S., Sudden Infant Death Syndrome, and her heart broke all over again. She'd never heard of S.I.D.S. and couldn't imagine how many parents had suffered this loss as its cold, uncaring hand reached out to ravage their families. How could anything which stole the life of an innocent child be called 'death by natural causes'?

The coroner could find no evidence of illness, or foul play. Johnny had simply slipped into the night. When the coroner's office at last released Johnny's small body into the arms of his family, they were able to plan his funeral. Jake's mother had taken over at that point, but Marie didn't care about that. She walked through the next few days in a fog too dense to penetrate by any of the insignificant members of Jake's family, and couldn't have taken care of the necessary details on her own to save her life. "How had this happened", she wondered, "Why my baby? No, I don't really have to wonder, do I? I know this is my punishment."

Was it so obvious to the universe that she couldn't take care of herself, or her son? Whatever, or whoever, it was that ruled the cosmos, if there was indeed anyone out there; had to know she'd tried every venue available to her to find a job, but being sixteen years old in Las Vegas wasn't conducive to finding gainful employment. It seemed that even restaurants and grocery stores sported slot machines in this neck of the woods; so a girl didn't have a chance at a position until after she became twenty one; what was she supposed to do?

Throughout the months of her son's life, she'd agonized over Jake's unwillingness to supply her with money for food and diapers. When, after much thought and preparation, she'd confronted Jake again about his drinking and gambling and voiced her concerns about the welfare of their child, he'd looked down at her with contempt and said, "I don't care what happens to your damn kid. I hear whores make pretty good money in this town. Why don't you try that!"

As much as the idea of prostitution frightened and disgusted her, the thought that this might be her only option filled her mind, as she persisted in her search for work with no luck. Would that seriously be the only way she could take care of Johnny? Surely there must be another way.

Now, as her son lay in a cold white box in the fanciest room she'd ever seen, she couldn't help thinking, was she being punished for having tried to abort her baby all those months ago? Perhaps she was being castigated for having even the thought of taking the despicable route of prostitution back when she didn't know where to turn?

Even worse, was the thought that maybe, just maybe, the universe was striking her down for not having been brave enough to sell herself, or whatever else might be necessary, if it was the only way she could take care of her baby.

When Marie finally tracked down a job as night janitor at a local nursing home, she was relieved. Jake, on the other hand, was livid that she would take a demeaning job which might shed a bad light on him as a husband and his ability to provide. But she was done listening to him, because how his friends and family perceived him was not her concern. He was afraid his mother would find out his wife was scrubbing toilets for a living and be angry with him, which might further widen the gap between his mother's money and his pocket. He was also irritated over the fact that if he wanted to go out and party now; since Marie's hours were seven in the evening until three in the morning, Monday through Saturday; he would be forced to secure a sitter to watch her damn kid until the old ball and chain arrived back home.

Eventually Jake's utter contempt for Marie had grown by such degrees that it colored his every thought and action. He felt trapped in their forced marriage and blamed Marie for his imprisonment. Thoughts of doing her harm were frequent imaginings. He often wondered why he hadn't killed her; using some inventive accident as a ruse; before the kid was even born. Daily new ideas and plans to rid his life of them both at once danced through his mind more frequently than many would imagine.

He knew he was violent with her when he drank, but he had no love for the girl and hoped his mistreatment of her would serve as warning that he alone was in charge. If he could only manage to get her to leave him. As long as it was her idea, they couldn't punish him for that could they? His mother couldn't find him to blame if this little girl took off on her own, could she?

When he was brought up on charges, after Marie discovered she was pregnant, his base commander didn't give him a choice in the matter. He had to marry her, or spend time in jail and he'd decided then and there he wasn't about to do time over this one lousy mistake.

To be honest, if they actually knew how often he'd gotten away with the same sort of thing, and worse, with no repercussions, they'd likely be pretty surprised. Well, everyone but his mother, of course.

Jake was pretty sure of himself. He'd always had good luck with the ladies. He knew women wanted him and he felt he was doing them some kind of a favor when he was with them, so why this worthless kid reported him to her dad was a mystery he couldn't fathom. She could have gotten rid of the baby, nice and simple. He'd even offered to pay for the whole thing, and they would have all been better off. Jake was so self absorbed he figured Marie should have been flattered he even looked in her direction, accident or no accident. She sickened him with her enormous pregnant belly and swollen ankles and, all through the whole ordeal, he hadn't known how to get out of the fix he was in.

Her sexy older sister Anne was a tease, in his mind she'd been coming on to him for months prior to the attack.

He'd been after her that night, but he'd had too much to drink and things got out of control with the kid. He still couldn't figure out what the big deal was. People make mistakes. They should all just get over it. And now that his mom was involved, he was on her list for sure.

Jake knew if he left Marie he would be in bigger trouble than that which his commander could dole out; his mom could cause him much more pain than the Air Force could ever imagine, and she was a staunch believer in facing responsibility, and in avoiding bad press as much as possible, so he would stay for now. As a bonus, he was getting a little face time with that gorgeous, whore of an older sister. He would take advantage of that as long as it was available to him.

Before joining the Air Force Jake lived with a silver spoon in his mouth. His whole life had been about getting whatever he wanted, exactly when he wanted it, without any actual effort on his part. So, being put in a position of responsibility, especially the responsibility of taking care of another life, was not his niche. His father died of a heart attack when he was very young and left his mother extremely well off with millions of acres in property and vast holdings which could be traced back five generations, including gold mines in Nevada. She'd eventually remarried and his step father, Mark, gained an instant dislike for the grasping young man. Her new husband was wealthy in his own right, and had worked very hard to achieve this status, so he expected as much from Jake. But, when he looked at his new wife's son, he saw nothing more than a lazy, entitled, brat.

Where Jake's mother, in her years of grief, had seen a constant, though admittedly grasping companion; her new husband, Mark, saw a user, and a con. Jake knew very well he'd taken advantage of his mother's loneliness to gain access to her money, and without a guilty thought or moment of regret he'd lived a life of parties and virtual ease for as long as he was able.

Flunking out of every private-institution in which his mother managed to secure a space; spaces which only money could buy; Jake thought he had his future of ease all wrapped up. "They can't make me go to school if no school will take me", was his mantra. And though he wasn't by any means a stupid young man, it finally got to a point that no reputable college was willing to offer him an opening, since he'd proved himself to be not only an academic lost cause, but a constant source of serious trouble just waiting to happen.

Once he'd reached a more than appropriate age and after much debate with her husband; his mother insisted he either join a branch of military service, or get some other real job, promising to cut him off from all other financial help if he did not comply. He was indignant and angry at the suggestion that he should actually have to work for a living, but was forced to acknowledge that she was serious this time.

After he'd been charged with raping Marie and threatened with court martial; his mother and her husband all but disowned him. He was only slowly getting back into their good graces; as the baby's arrival became more imminent; so this time he didn't dare rock the boat. The idea of a grandchild is enticing to people of all societal stations. A legacy, if you will, and he'd hoped to gain back some of the favor he'd lost with his mom upon the impending birth.

Marie did not fit into his family's idea of a socially acceptable partner and they had therefore treated her with scorn upon their few brief meetings. Marie felt more and more like she was paying the price for Jake's lack of self control. After all, she hadn't wanted any of this. But as time went on Dorothy became a bit kinder and started to treat Marie in a friendlier manner. She was, after all, the mother of their grandchild.

Jake had told her, before they left home for the funeral, she really should see the baby in his casket, "it'll give you closure", he said. Well, from the looks of all she'd seen earlier in the day he had all the closure he needed. He'd obviously recovered and moved on. Would she ever be able to do the same? While she was agonizing inside he was flirting and partying. But, what was new? She really couldn't say she expected anything else from him. After the visitation they would necessarily trek out to the cemetery and Marie wasn't sure she was up to that; but she was positive her feelings wouldn't make a difference to Jake and Dorothy.

There'd been a tugging at her heart all day and she finally gave in to the pull. She began to slowly draw near the place where her son lay. As she approached and gazed into the face of her baby dressed in his satin christening gown, and wrapped in the beautiful quilt her grandmother made before she passed away a few ago, she was struck by the fact that he looked to be only sleeping. Her little guy tucked in to layer upon layer of crushed satin looked as if he might wake at any moment, to look up at her with his impish hazel eyes and dimpled, magical smile. She imagined him reaching out with his tiny, grasping fingers begging to be held. The idea she would never hold him again; never nuzzle his neck or breathe in the wonderful powdery, baby smell of him was more than her wounded mind could fathom. She reached in to the casket to touch his small hand and found his fingers icy, and then his face waxen, then the tears began again to flow in earnest. There was no question now. Her tiny broken doll was nothing but an empty shell.

Grateful someone had placed his favorite stuffed bear with him in the casket, she tucked the toy into the blanket closer to his unmoving chest. Then she saw a flash of white light through her peripheral vision and turned to see her husband taking pictures of their son in his satin lined coffer. Disgusted with his behavior Marie turned and walked back to the flowered chair in the corner, fists opening and closing in frustration. She would have liked to hit him, to punch him full in his uncaring, selfish face, but what would that accomplish?

Chilly; and fully encompassed in a fog that seemed to separate her from reality as she stood waiting in the cemetery; Marie absently pulled her bulky sweater more tightly around her shoulders. Wispy white clouds, like strands of wayward cotton, moved slowly through blue skies. Causing the sun to play hide and seek with those few rosy cheeked people standing below. And creating pockets of frigid air, or warm, depending on where they were positioned near the open grave. She thought it copiously unfair that the world continued to spin relentlessly around the sun, and that people still smiled, and laughed, and continued to live their lives in that fickle sunshine.

Why was it that so many continued to hold those they loved, while her own arms were so miserably empty. Today it should be raining, and that complete with thunder, lightning and hail. How dare the sun shine, creating this obscenely beautiful day in which to bury her son!

Shadows came and went on rows and rows of granite headstones catching the corner of her eye like ghosts of decades, and centuries, past. Making her ever more aware of the finality of this last earthly act involving her little child.

Very few had come along from the wake to the burial and Marie was grateful this moment wouldn't become an occasion for interlopers to invade her heartbreak with their own tedious agendas.

Sitting in chairs under a large, flapping, green canopy, the family didn't cry, or try to comfort one another. The tiny coffin, closed now, lay upon a mound of earth covered by faux grass. Flowers from the funeral home covered the casket, which to her mind looked even smaller now next to the huge, gaping hole in the ground where it would be placed. The priest from Dorothy's church was droning on endlessly. Dorothy insisted he come to the interment to say a few words, though for the life of her, Marie couldn't understand why. None of them went to church while they were alive, so what they thought would be accomplished by this phony charade after death escaped her.

Did her baby simply cease to exist, she wondered? Or would he become one of the elusive shadows dancing among the grave markers on days such as this? The droning ended and someone handed her a flower. Two men in coveralls took hold of the lines on either end of the small coffin and began lowering it into the ground. A panic strong as that which had overcome her on the night of Johnny's death overwhelmed her and she screamed. She tried to run, to throw her own body into the opening where her baby lay, but hands grabbed her, held her down and then someone slapped her, hard. She looked up to see her husband's sneering face above her and she loathed him now, more than ever.

She hadn't been back to the nursing home since the night of Johnny's death, but her employers had sent flowers, and enquiries, and she couldn't put them off forever. She liked the company of the elderly patients who lived there and knew they liked her too, so she was prepared to immerse herself in the act of taking care of people who needed her until she could save enough money to leave Jake.

He didn't want to be with her any more than she wanted to be with him, but he had an image to uphold and when she approached him with the idea of separation shortly after the funeral he exploded. "Nobody leaves Jake!" he shouted, speaking of himself in the third party, "You were never good enough to be with me you little slut, and you sure as hell aren't good enough to walk out on me! My mother has the idea we should stay together for at least a year to mourn the damn kid and you will do exactly what she says, or I will make your life a whole lot more miserable than it already is!"

She couldn't understand the reasoning behind her mother-in-law's orders, but she was terrified of Jake and his threats and she really had nowhere else to go. She would continue to work and save and when she got ready to leave they wouldn't be able to stop her. Her days were filled with futile attempts to avoid Jake when he was around, or to try to help Dorothy only to have her well intentioned actions shot down. Her attempts to please the woman most usually went wrong. She'd not been raised knowing the socially acceptable way to do most things and was typically more of an embarrassment than a help to the elegant lady Dorothy. At night she cleaned at the nursing home and chatted with some of the ancient, lonely folks who resided there. Most of them had met her Johnny. She'd brought him in on several different Sundays, and they fawned over him like he was their own. Their hearts broke as one for the lonely girl.

Three months after her son's funeral she came in from work at three thirty in the morning to find Jake in their bed with his latest easy conquest. She turned and walked back out to the living room only to be grabbed from behind by her very naked and very drunk husband. He yanked her hair and threw her to the floor kicking and punching her until he was too tired to strike another blow. He went back to his paramour and completed his business then promptly fell asleep.

Marie woke later to a cool cloth on her face, applied by the still naked woman who had recently shared her husband's bed. The woman was engulfed in the distinct odor of sex and body odor, and Marie turned her head slightly to avoid the aroma. The girl murmured, her voice soft and soothing in Marie's ear, "You poor thing he really went to town on you. I'm so sorry. I guess you really riled him, poor, poor thing." Marie climbed on to the sofa and while the lady with the soft voice crawled back in bed with Jake she rocked and cried herself to sleep.

In the morning Jake shook her roughly by the shoulder and when she rolled over he looked genuinely surprised at the bruises on her face and neck. Gruffly, he told her to sit up and when she did he tossed a manila envelope into her lap. She opened the flap, pulled out the pages, and gasped. The contents yielded several shiny eight by ten photographs of her dead baby in his small white casket. She dropped them to the floor as if burned by the images, and he laughed. He laughed until tears ran down his face. He laughed until he had to sit down, or risk falling over from laughing. His paramour looked shocked' and while he had his back to her, she shook her head in disbelief, completely confused by the strange arrangement.

Marie hated him with every fiber of her being. He had proved himself to be nothing more than a monster in every definition of the word. And she would get away. She had to. She knew her life and sanity depended on it, and now she was more determined than ever.

"Some wandered in desert wastes, finding no way to a city to dwell in; hungry and thirsty, their soul fainted within them. Then they cried to the Lord in their trouble, and He delivered them from their distress."

Psalm 107:4-6

CHAPTER 3

Marie never knew her birth father. Her mom thought that information something to be tucked away in dark, secret places. The nearest she could figure, from snarky comments proffered by nosey neighbors with smug looks on their faces, was that each of the kids in her family had a different father. She longed for a dad like the ones her friends at school bragged about. Someone to spend time with, to play with, and to tuck her into bed at night.

Her mom brought home all manner of men while she was growing up, each with the distinct look of predator in his eyes. When she entertained the possibility of monsters in her closet, or under her bed, they generally had the faces of those leering men.

It seemed every man who darkened their doorstep had ulterior motives. And some had, much to Marie's detriment and horror, achieved their evil intentions. However, she'd learned the hard way that she was on her own and couldn't expect any help from her mother to thwart their plans. By Ten years old she was very jaded, but also pretty self sufficient. Her new found, and well rehearsed instincts soon taught her to keep her distance, and to protect her siblings from these evils at all costs.

However, she found herself, for all her high and mighty thoughts of independence and self sufficiency, still plagued by recurring nightmares caused by these heinous monsters and the wickedness they'd perpetrated in her life.

Wondering why she'd been singled out so many times; and now convinced that it was somehow her fault, something she'd done to encourage their malevolence; she tried very hard, as much as she was able, to erase those terrors from her mind, and to take precautions that would keep incidents of that kind from ever happening again.

Ten years old was certainly young to be so cynical, but Marie had begun to think there were no honorable men left in all the world. That fairy tales were just that, fairy tales. That all men were monsters. Her personal experiences certainly proved the truth of that claim. That is, until her mom brought home an Air Force Sergeant, eight years her junior, who would successfully break that awful mold.

The sergeant was an elite 'Special Operations Weatherman'. His sixty one weeks of training and unique missions skills had earned him the right to wear the distinguished 'Grey Beret'. Special operation's weathermen were among the most highly trained personnel in the United States military; though, for now, in a time of relative peace, he'd been assigned to the weather base in northern California. He'd never married, and never had kids of his own. And, as their new romance flourished Marie could see that this man might not only be good for her mom, but good for all of them; a stabilizing force where none had existed before. He could also potentially be someone she would be proud to call Daddy.

Most of their subsequent 'dates' were such that they included the children, and Marie thought she'd never seen her mother smile so much. It was kind of funny how a smile could transform a face and, for that matter, even a personality. Being in the same room with her mom didn't make her stomach hurt so much anymore, at least when their soldier was around. He really made a difference. But, it was a tenuous difference for now. One that she could tell might be easily shattered if something happened to remove him from the situation.

Day trips to the park; cookouts, featuring his 'famous'

homemade burgers and potato salad; swimming in the river; capturing fire flies, in old pickle jars, to use as lanterns in the dark; singing around bon fires roasting marshmallows; and going to drive in movies, complete with blankets and big paper bags of homemade popcorn; became some of her new favorite things. He taught the kids to fish. They ventured off to go panning for gold in the area's creeks and streams; and took tours of the base where he worked, meeting many of his comrades along the way.

Above all else, his patience was never-ending. Marie hoped with all her might that they might keep him. Her eleventh birthday was the best she'd ever had. Daddy made her a cake, and when she blew out the candles she wished for this man to be her dad forever.

It wasn't long before the young sergeant proposed, down on one knee, with tears of joy streaming down his cheeks. He had the blessing of every one of the family's children, who couldn't wait to be his 'real' kids, and they stood together in the wings waiting for her reply. She said yes, much to the delight of the cheering crowd, and with a bit of preparation they all participated in a small, but charming wedding ceremony at the local Baptist church.

Each of the children had a function, from ring bearer,

to flower girl, to reception hostess, and so on. Marie's mom wore a cream colored two piece suit on her attractive, but slightly gaunt, frame; and carried a bouquet of her favorite daisies. A cream colored hat adorned with short, stylish veil, over her newly coifed, dark auburn hair, completed the ensemble. Marie had never seen her mom look so beautiful, or, frankly, so sober.

Daddy; she loved the warm feeling that word invoked; wore his dress blues, a daisy in his lapel, and the somewhat dazed, though thoroughly pleased, look of a man who was about to become father to five children in one fell swoop.

Spice cake, with cream cheese frosting, was their choice of wedding cake, Daddy's favorite. The masterpiece was designed by a neighbor, and was crowned with a topper picturing a couple surrounded by five small children (where in the world she came across that gem was anyone's guess). The towering work of art was the centerpiece of a large buffet table.

Surrounded by the usual wedding punch, nuts, and mints, it was also accompanied by pot luck dishes happily supplied by Daddy's co-workers and friends from the base. Marie noticed how many friends her new dad had, compared to the one semi-reluctant neighbor who represented the sum total of her mother's acquaintances, if you could even call it that. It might be that the neighbor was present simply because she had been paid to make, and set up, an elaborate wedding cake.

Thirty pounds of crusty, juicy, beautiful, beef brisket was set up in a place of prominence for the wedding feast. Daddy smoked it for a full twenty four hours before the ceremony began, and it was so tender it fell apart at the mere suggestion of being touched. It smelled downright heavenly, and filled the church basement with its heady fragrance. In close proximity were sweet buns; Daddy's homemade barbeque sauce; pickles; onions; and a spicy coleslaw, which her new dad liked to use to top off his brisket sandwiches. Friends brought a variety of salads, relish trays, deviled eggs, and various other signature dishes; including her new favorite, a pink fluffy one with tiny marshmallows; until there was so much food Marie wondered how they would ever eat it all. They ate and danced and celebrated well into the afternoon.

A surprise honeymoon began immediately following the celebration, and after a quick change of clothes. And, much to the excitement of the children, was planned as a whole family affair. A camping trip to the mountains. The kids were fairly leaping out of their skin with anticipation. It would be a time to learn more about the man who'd stepped in and changed their lives so dramatically, and for him to get to know them better too.

Making their way up the slopes of Mount Shasta, the kids noticed patches of white stuff. They'd never seen snow up close, so Daddy let them get out of the car to jump on the hard patches of ice until they were soaking wet and tired; but laughing, and filled with childish joy.

The mountain air was crisp and cool, and smelled of damp earth, and pine trees. Marie breathed in the clean scent until it seemed to wash away years of pain and ugliness. The family arrived at a perfect spot to set up camp, and all went to work, a tent for Daddy and Mommy, and one for the kids. They dug a fire pit, surrounding it with stones collected from the area, and made it complete with supports and grills to hold Daddy's frying pan and coffee pot. A lake, sapphire blue and so crystal clear it took your breath away, lapped at the shore a mere hundred yards from their tents. And, as the sun began to set in the most beautiful sky Marie had ever seen, they could hear fish leaping in the distance. Daddy showed the kids how to build a camp fire, and they set about preparing supper. "Tomorrow, our dinner will be all the great fish we're going to catch. How does that sound?"

"Yaaaaaaayyyyyy!" The kids yelled. They'd never fished in their lives until Daddy came on the scene; and they loved everything about it, except for the worms.

Marie had to admit to herself that clear up until the moment of the wedding she'd had a deep seated fear that something might happen to take this wonderful man out of their lives. After all, her mother's track record hadn't been so great up to now. And, let's face it, even at her young age she knew there weren't many men who would take on a woman with five children. A huge weight lifted from her shoulders when the last "I do" was said.

For the first time in her life, Marie went to bed that night without a knot in her stomach. Something she'd always assumed was just part of her natural makeup. She laid in the tent warm and content; with the sleepy sounds of her siblings all around; being lulled to sleep by the rhythmic melodies of rustling leaves, crickets and frogs.

Waking to the smell of coffee and bacon, Marie made her way past the tent flap, to the chilly morning beyond.

Though it was summer the mountain at this elevation remained cold. Breath escaped her lips in small frosty puffs, as she wrapped her blanket tightly around her shoulders. She looked to see her mom sitting across the open expanse and in front of a blazing campfire, wearing Daddy's military parka. With her thick auburn hair pulled back in a neat pony tail, lips painted red, and a smile that traveled all the way to her usually dead eyes, she looked surprisingly like a regular person today, even this early in the morning. It appeared the joy of the day before had not worn off. Marie approached the normally unapproachable woman, and was surprised to see her arm lift in a welcoming gesture, indicating an invitation to sit close. Her face lit up, and she scurried to the rock where her mother relaxed, all too aware that this could quite possibly be a once in a lifetime opportunity.

Daddy was busy frying bacon and dropping eggs into holes made in thick slices of sourdough bread, which had been toasted lightly in butter until it reached a lovely golden brown. He called them 'gas house' eggs, and he proceeded to show Marie all about how it was done. He smelled of aftershave and campfire smoke, and she decided that was her new favorite combination of smells. Marie was in heaven. She had a dad.

He'd brought orange juice along from town. It was being kept icy cold in a crevice dug into a icy snow patch nearby. Pouring Mom a big mug of hot coffee, he brought it to her along with a lingering kiss. Marie blushed, but her heart went wild with happiness at the obviously loving exchange. Maybe, just maybe, this would all work out and they would get to keep their new Daddy forever!

That night they sat around a roaring blaze, preparing fresh caught fish in Daddy's ancient, seasoned, cast iron pans, on their very own campfire. The feast was made complete with crispy, fried potatoes, biscuits, and a big bowl of coleslaw brought from home in the dented red and white cooler. After they cleaned up from supper they huddled close together and sang dozens of campfire songs fresh from their new dad's repertoire, and roasted marshmallows on sticks that Daddy had whittled into spears. Daddy smoked a pipe that night, filled with what would turn out, upon asking, to be his signature cherry blend tobacco, and Marie added that fragrance to her new list of favorites.

For a whole blissful week they played and fished; with prizes for biggest fish, smallest fish, most fish, least fish, prettiest fish and ugliest fish, a sure way to see that everyone was recognized. They sang around fires, told ghost stories and jokes, and learned to make smores. Daddy owned a rather extensive rock collection, and while they were on the mountain he employed the efforts of the children to bring him any interesting examples they might find on their hikes and expeditions. They learned to recognize animal prints, and spent time tracking some of the mountain's smaller creatures together. Daddy also taught them the names of local trees and many types of vegetation, including poison varieties. The time flew by much too quickly, but she was happier than she could remember ever in her life, and grew quickly to love this man more than anyone else in all her small world. This was all she'd ever wanted, someone to look up to, to feel safe with, a man who wasn't a monster like all the rest.

The family arrived home from their vacation, laughing and joking, to a manila envelope that would change their lives forever. Daddy had orders to deploy to Viet Nam. He'd been given five months to put his affairs in order and show up for deployment with his unit, clear across the country in New York. In a state of fear and confusion, they sat in their small living room and just stared at one another. How would they survive?

Marie was terrified that with Daddy gone things might go back to the way they were before he came into their lives. What a cruel turn of events. She'd never been one to pray, and none of them had ever been much for going to church, but she prayed. Not quite sure how, or even particularly to who she should pray, she just cried out to the universe and begged. Begged for her daddy's life, begged for her family, begged for the intervention of a god, any god, to help in this horrible chain of events that might tear them all apart forever.

Plans were made. They would make the most of the next five months and do as many new and exciting family things as possible together, making as many memories as they could in the short time they had. They even made lists, letting the little ones come up with their own ideas for family adventures. Then, when it was time, they would drive across the country to New York, which was Daddy's home state. He thought they would be better off in his absence with his family in close proximity. They really didn't have relatives in California to speak of, so it sounded like a good plan. Having family around for once might really be a good thing, or so they thought.

Marie stuck to Daddy like glue for the next five months. She'd been mostly self sufficient before he came into their lives, and could cook well enough to keep the family from starving, but he taught her how to cook, really cook, and to make his special Sunday morning cinnamon twist braid. It was one of the best things she'd ever tasted, warm and dripping with a sweet maple glaze. "Is this enough cinnamon?"

"Add just a little more. Cinnamon is one of those things that's hard to overdo."

"Okay. Who taught you how to make bread, Daddy?"

"My own daddy taught me when I was even younger than you, Marie."

"How old were you?"

"I was only six when I learned to make bread. You're practically a young woman, so there's a big difference. It's about time you learned some of these things. You'll be out on your own someday."

"I don't ever want to leave you. I want to learn everything you'll teach me. And, when you come back from the war I will cook for you."

"You promise?"

"I promise. But, why do you think the rest of the kids don't want to learn how to cook?"

"Not everyone has a knack for cooking, and even fewer for baking. You're lucky."

Marie felt lucky. Having more interests in common meant she could spend more time with her favorite person in the world. He taught her all of his 'signature' dishes, like: bean with bacon soup; potato and leek soup; his secret hamburger recipe, complete with homemade fries and milkshakes; pot roast with loads of succulent potatoes and vegetables; firehouse chili and cornbread; French toast with home fries and bacon; and Dagwood sandwiches. There was so much more and she soaked up the information like a sponge. They loved setting the table for meals, in Daddy's tiny trailer where they all lived now. They used the nice dishes to serve their specially prepared meals. And, when supper was ready and they called everyone to the meal, Daddy held Mom's chair for her and gave her a kiss. She went on and on about how delicious everything was, and Marie felt proud as a peacock being his special chef's assistant.

For five months they played board games and told stories, climbed trees and conducted science experiments. He was so smart, the smartest man she'd ever known, and he taught them so many magical things. Marie couldn't wait for the kids at school to meet her new daddy. After all, they'd tormented her all the way through grade school and seventh grade when she didn't have a dad. So, she wanted to rub their noses in the fact that she had the very best one now. Eighth grade was a big deal. And, when Daddy offered to take the whole class through the weather prediction hangers where he worked for the Air Force, she was ecstatic!

Arrangements were made with the school, and on the day of the class trip they loaded all the eighth graders on to busses to make the short journey to the base. While they were there Daddy explained the process of sending weather balloons into the atmosphere and, much to their amazement, even demonstrated the launch of a balloon for them; they were all allowed to breathe helium gas, to alter their voices, and everyone laughed and had a good time; he loaded them, a few at a time onto lifts that went clear to the top of the hanger, and they were astounded with the enormity of the buildings.

Marie watched the reactions of her classmates. And

as she saw the growing respect for her dad in their faces she was proud. She knew they were all a little jealous that she had this handsome, smart, strong soldier as her new dad; and she was glad; though she felt just a tiny bit guilty about that part. The girl who'd been her biggest nemesis all throughout grammar school. The one who'd called her the worst names and made her feel the most ashamed that she didn't have a father present in her life, came up to her before they boarded the busses to head back. "Your dad is really great."

"I know."

"Do you think he'll let us come back again?"

"I don't know, but I don't think so. He has orders to go to war, so we'll be moving to New York in a few weeks."

"New York? Are you scared?"

"Not really."

"But you won't know anyone there. You won't have any friends."

"I didn't have any friends here until today, so I think I'll be fine."

"I'm sorry we've always been so hard on you. If I'd have known you were so nice I would have been your friend."

"Thank you for that, but I haven't changed at all. I was

just as nice in grammar school. So, do me a favor, okay?"

"Sure, what is it?"

"When someone comes behind me to fill my seat, please don't be as mean to her as you were to me. invite her in and help her get to know everyone. I'll survive wherever I go."

"I will. Are you scared for your dad?"

"Yeah, I am. And I'm going to miss him like crazy too, but we're trying to make the best of things before he goes."

"Maybe we'll have a party for you before you go. Kind of a going away thing. I know everyone had a great time today."

"That's not necessary. If it's okay with you, I'd rather go quietly. No one ever made a big deal about me while I was here, and I think I've gotten used to staying in the background."

"Well, if that's what you want. I am sorry about before."

"I forgive you. We've all done things we weren't very proud of. I probably could have tried harder to fit in too."

"So, are we okay?"

"Yes, I think we're fine." Looking back, Marie guessed that was the best school day she'd ever experienced. But, she wouldn't be sad to go.

Daddy owned a colored television, which was something fairly rare during the mid-sixties. They didn't own a television at all before they met him, so when they moved from their tiny apartment to the tiny trailer on the two acre lot filled with trees, after the wedding, they were amazed at the presence of this magical device. And, though they didn't watch much of it, on Wednesday evenings when 'Lost In Space' came on, they were all parked in front of the 'Boob Tube', as Daddy called it, with their homemade burgers, fries and milkshakes. This was an especially rare treat, as they'd always been expected to sit at the table in the kitchen to eat their meals. These were memories Marie would hold close to her heart for the rest of her life.

Those last weeks before departure to New York were bittersweet. Every night after supper Daddy sat in his recliner, in the trailer's miniscule living room, and smoked his pipe with the family gathered around. He told stories of his youth, and each was more funny or exciting than the last. An ordinary evening would resound with children's voices clamoring, "Tell us a story, Daddy, please." Then for the next couple of hours they would sit rapt, as he wove his tales of childhood escapades. They would gasp in all the right places, then they would laugh, and cry with the ebb and flow of the story. Those moments would be remembered among Marie's favorite times. Sitting at the feet of her hero, listening to the melodious rhythm of his baritone voice, the light fragrance of after shave and cherry blend tobacco in the air.

Marie and her new Daddy spent some additional time over the last month on a building project. They made a great team! The family's only vehicle, since Mama didn't drive and never had, was the red El Camino pickup truck that was part of the package when they married Daddy. And; though it was great for drive in movies before the world got serious about seat belts; getting seven people from point A, to point B, in it might be a bit of a problem. So, Daddy had decided, sort of last minute, to build a topper on the back of the pickup. The project turned out pretty well, even if Marie did say so herself, and Daddy told her she was the best helper he'd ever had. The wooden unit was roofed with actual roofing shingles, and inside the camper unit was complete with sanded and padded, wooden benches on each side, Plexiglas sliding windows, and a door in the back that latched.

Since they would be traveling in December, and the

topper had no heat, every blanket they owned was loaded into the place the children would inhabit for the duration of their trip. Most of their earthly belongings were put onto a military moving truck, which was to follow them to New York. Those items would presumably take up residence at Daddy's parent's house, where they would be staying until he returned from Viet Nam.

The morning of their departure was exciting, and frightening all at once. They'd never met their new relatives, or for that matter, even talked to them on the phone. She couldn't help but wonder how they might be received. It would surely be a whole new world. But she trusted her new dad. And, if he came from these people, they had to be good too, didn't they?

As the family packed the last of their travel items into the back of the El Camino, they also filled the dented, red and white cooler with lunch meats, cheese, and fruit. Marie was eagerly stocking as many apples into the cool depths as she could, when she noticed a six pack of beer buried beneath the ice. Instantly, shocked and dismayed, she looked up from the container. Her eyes locked with her mother's steely gaze. She didn't want to make more of a deal out of it than it was. And, she certainly didn't want to be confronted with that threatening glare again, so she didn't say a word. Her mom had been doing well since she married Daddy, and she'd never known him to take a drink, ever. Perhaps it was just a little something with which to wash down their bologna sandwiches on the trip. All she could do was hope.

Each of the kids was allowed a pillow and their favorite stuffed animal, along with all those blankets, and Marie was feeling especially protective of them as they loaded into the back of the home made camper for the long trip.

It was cold in the wooden topper, because it was the beginning of December. But complaining would have left Daddy feeling bad, so the kids buried themselves in layers of blankets and snuggled together as much as possible to try to stay warm. This journey would take a week. They would stop at rest areas along the way, to use the facilities, wash up a bit, and eat their bologna sandwiches. The cooler stayed up front, in the cab, with Mama and Daddy. But Marie was encouraged when she didn't see them drinking beer with their meals. Maybe she had been worried for nothing. They couldn't afford to feed seven in a restaurant, so sandwiches and fruit would be their staples for the whole trip.

At a store along the way, while restocking their supplies, Marie's hopes were dashed when she noticed the six pack at the bottom of the cooler was gone, and was now replaced with a twelve pack of whatever local beer was cheapest. She didn't need to look up in order to feel her mother's defiant stare boring through the back of her head; daring her to say a single word. Instead, she stacked the fresh packages of lunch meat and cheese on top of the slowly melting ice. They hadn't bought apples to replenish their fruit supply this time. Supposedly there wasn't enough money, and they would have to be satisfied with sandwiches or go hungry. She rightly guessed that the fruit money had been spent to purchase beer.

Now she was very worried, because, if they weren't drinking the beer at meals, where the kids could see them; they must be drinking it in the cab while they were driving. It wouldn't be so bad if she knew who was drinking. Mama wasn't driving, and as much as she hated the thought that she'd slipped back into old habits, perhaps out of worry or fear of her husband going off to war, at least that wouldn't cause an accident. The bigger concern was that maybe, just maybe, she'd convinced her new husband that a few beers would make the going a bit easier, you know, take the edge off. Marie had a hard time sleeping that night, and not just because of the cold. That familiar old knot was back, and her stomach was hurting pretty badly.

The next evening her worst fears were confirmed, when from the inside of the camper the kids could hear the sounds of horns blaring all around them. Marie pushed aside the curtain covering one of the Plexiglas windows and was horrified to see cars all around them going in the opposite direction. Somehow, her parents had gotten onto the wrong ramp, and were driving against traffic in a heavily traveled area. She lunged to the front of the camper and began pounding on the window there. Sadly, that window didn't slide, and there was a gap of four inches between the camper window, and the window of the cab. She could see her folks drinking beer, and they seemed oblivious to the fact that hundreds of cars were coming directly at them. Soon a police car cut them off and directed them to the side of the road. The kids were crying, and hysterical, but Marie hushed them. And, when the officer knocked on the camper door, Marie opened it. He seemed angry when he saw the five children, and stood watch over them until another car and a tow truck arrived on the scene.

"The Lord is your keeper; the Lord is your shade on your right hand. The sun shall not strike you by day, nor the moon by night."

Psalm 121:5-6

CHapter 4

S itting in the police station, Marie and the kids were terrified. Dingy grey walls, concrete floors with dubious stains of various colors, and flickering florescent lights didn't help the mood. Daddy was locked in jail for the night, and would have to see a judge in the morning. That Judge would decide what was to be done with a man who drove drunk with five children in the back of his truck. Mother was in another room talking to a lady police officer. Marie could tell by the way she'd walked into the station that she was pretty drunk too, and was worried about what would become of them if they locked her up. Surely they could smell the alcohol on her breath.

The kids stayed huddled together on a bench, jumping every time anyone walked past, sincerely afraid they would be locked up as well. Eventually, an officer asked them all to come with him. Marie's stomach was shaking so badly, she feared she would vomit. They were shown to a room and told to wait. Soon, a middle aged lady, wearing a frayed two piece suit and scuffed pumps entered the room. A haggard face and deeply sad eyes spoke to the probability that she'd seen way too many domestic tragedies and abused kids. She spoke mainly to Marie, since her older sister appeared to be off in her own world, and the others were all obviously much younger. "So, are you Marie then?"

"Yes ma'am."

"Do you know why the police officer brought your family here this evening?"

"Yes ma'am. My parents were driving on the wrong side of the road. I tried to stop them. I was banging on the window, but they didn't hear me."

"Marie, you are not in trouble here. However, your dad and mom will be spending the night at the station with the officers, until your dad can see a judge in the morning. We didn't think it was safe to send you out with your mother either." At this the younger children began to sob.

"It's okay you guys. We'll be okay. Can we at least have someone take us to our truck? I can take care of the kids if we're back at the truck."

"Well, that is where we run into a bit of a problem, Marie. Your dad's truck has been impounded and he won't be able to retrieve it until he visits with a judge tomorrow morning. And then that will depend on what the answer from the judge is after that visit."

"Well, what are we supposed to do? Can we stay here? We won't be any trouble, I promise. the kids aren't a problem, and I will keep an eye on them every minute."

"I'm afraid we can't allow that, Marie. We have a nice couple, the Millers, who have graciously offered to let you stay at their place until things are settled tomorrow. They should be here at any time, if you would like to see that the children gather their things?"

"How do we know they will bring us back in time? I don't even know these people. How do I know I can trust them around the children? We are all supposed to be going to New York together before my dad goes to Viet Nam. That's the only reason we are driving all this way. I don't know if it's such a good idea for us to leave. My folks won't know where we've gone. I don't want to worry them."

"My dear, I'm afraid we don't have another choice. It's nice of you to be concerned for your parents. It would've been very nice if they'd been equally concerned for all of you children. Perhaps then we wouldn't be in this situation. But, things are what they are. Now, please get your things together, so that you will be ready when the Millers arrive."

Angry at her mother for the predicament they faced, Marie set about collecting the kids and their belongings. The littlest one was shaking so badly that all the hugs and reassurance in the world didn't seem to help. And, though they'd all believed her thumb sucking habit to be in the past, this series of events had placed that calloused digit securely back in its old familiar resting place. "Oh well, we'll just have to work on that again when we get where we're going." Marie thought with a sigh.

Marie wasn't mad at her dad. Confused, and a little, well, maybe a lot, disappointed. But she was furious with her mom. She knew deep down inside that it had been at her mom's urging that he'd drank the beer and, in turn, put the kids in danger. She didn't believe for one minute he would have ever done that on his own. She was sure he was terrified about the idea of going to war, though he tried hard to pretend otherwise. And she knew her mother well enough to know she'd probably played on that fear to get him doing something completely out of character, just so she'd be comfortably back drinking again. Marie hoped the judge would see Daddy for who he really was, and not be too hard on him. As far as she was concerned, if they wanted to leave her mom locked up for awhile, that was fine too.

The Millers were actually really nice people. They took the kids with them, to their lovely home, just outside of town. They had plenty of clean beds and bedding. Mrs. Miller helped Marie give the little ones a bath. "Have you always taken care of your brother and sisters, Marie?"

"Ever since they were born, ma'am. Diapers, feeding, bathing, the whole works."

"Well, what about your parents? Don't they help?"

"Ma'am, I don't know who my father is. None of us do. Our mom is sick a lot, and she's always counted on me to take care of things at home."

"Sick? Well, what about your dad?"

"Well, Daddy hasn't been with us for very long. He married my mom about six months ago, and now they're sending him to Viet Nam. I think he's scared of leaving us and going so far away. He's been the best thing that ever happened to us in our whole lives, and now they're taking him away. I know that's the only reason he made a mistake and drank the beer. He never does that. My mom is a different story. But, he's a great dad, and I'd dare anyone to say different around me."

Once the kids were all tucked in, Marie laid her head down on the softest pillow in the universe, and spent most of the night staring at the ceiling. Morning couldn't come quickly enough.

Mrs. Miller was up at the crack of dawn. Marie listened to her rustling around the kitchen, readying breakfast for the crowd that would invade her table shortly. Not being used to anyone waiting on her, she decided to check with the lady of the house to see if she could help. The other children were still fast asleep when she crept from the room.

She looked over at her older sister and shook her head. She'd wondered for a long time if there were drugs in Anne's life. She didn't seem to have any interest in anything, and removed herself from family as often as possible. At fifteen she thought she was old enough to run her own life, and took offence to anyone trying to help her or give her advice. She wasn't opposed to Mom marrying their new dad, and she didn't have a problem benefiting from his hard work, but she was bound and determined not to take orders from anyone. She would be a problem for all of them, in ways they couldn't even imagine.

"Good morning Mrs. Miller."

"Well, good morning, Marie. How did you sleep?"

"Fine." Marie lied. She didn't want to hurt the nice lady's feelings.

"Good. I'm making pancakes and bacon. Would you like a cup of hot chocolate, or a glass of juice?"

"Well, I mostly came to see if there was a way I could help you. I'm kinda used to taking care of most of this myself. Except for these past few months. My dad makes great French toast, and I like to help him."

"It sounds like you've grown very close to your new dad since he married your mom."

"Yes ma'am. I believe he's my favorite person in the whole world. It's like he came in and saved our lives. That's why I said before that this is the first time I've ever known him to drink. It just isn't something he usually does. And, I know he feels bad. Especially if he woke up this morning wondering where we are."

"What about your mom? Don't you think she'll wonder how you are?"

"I'd rather not talk about it, ma'am. May I help you?"

"Sure, Marie. Why don't you go over to the fridge and get the eggs and milk. We'll get the batter all mixed up while the bacon is sizzling away in the oven. Do you think the little ones would like some hot chocolate?"

"Well, they've never had it, but I'm sure they'd try it. It sounds good."

"Oh, it's delicious! And, we'll add a little cool milk so they don't burn their mouths. Let's get all this taken care of, and then you can go in and wake them up."

"Okay. Are your kids usually up by now?"

"Well, we don't have any children, Marie. God never blessed us in that way."

Marie had never heard of children referred to as blessings before. "So, why do you have so many rooms?"

"Now, I never said we didn't want a house full of children. But, God had other ideas. We've been able to help out many times over the years, to be a safe place for young ones such as yourself. If we'd had a houseful of our own, we wouldn't have been able to do that."

"It must be sad to have this big old house that you wanted to fill with children, and have it be empty all the time."

"That would be sad if it were true. Situations arise more often than you think, and we've had some children here for months. Sadly, there seems to be more and more of a need all the time, for safe places that kids can go."

"Well, I want to thank you for taking us in. I don't know what we would have done last night if you hadn't helped us."

"Oh, don't even mention it. It truly is my pleasure. My husband is out feeding the chickens and the dogs. He should be along any minute. Shall we get things ready?"

"Yes ma'am. Just tell me what to do."

Marie couldn't help but think about the fact that here was this kind woman, who wanted a house full of kids, and couldn't have any. And then there was her mom, who didn't want the kids she had. If there really was a god out there somewhere, how did he get that one so screwed up? She wondered how many other kids were in families who didn't want them, and how many good people wanted kids and didn't have any. This world really was a mess. And, now they were taking her dad away. The dad she'd hoped for all her life. He was going to war and might never come home. It might almost be better to never have known him, than to lose him like this. No, she had to take that back. She wouldn't trade her time with him for anything in the world. These last months had been the best of her life.

She woke the kids and they all sat down to a breakfast of pancakes with butter and warm maple syrup, and crispy bacon. Mugs full of warm chocolate and glasses of fresh squeezed orange juice were sitting at each place, and if she could just get her sister's thumb out of her mouth, they would all have a great meal. But first, Mr. Miller wanted to say grace.

"Thank you Lord for the food we are about to eat. Please let it give us the strength to do those things you have set before us to do. Thank you for loving us, and giving us the chance to know you better. And, thank you for this fine company."

The kids didn't come from a praying family. And, they all sat still until Mrs. Miller finally said, "It's okay. Time to eat now."

What a strange prayer. Marie wondered what Mr. Miller meant by saying that God loves us, and that He gives us the chance to know Him better? Where was this God he prayed to? She certainly had never felt any love from Him. Everyone ate their fill, and after cleaning up it was time to head off to the courthouse. Marie's stomach was filled with butterflies trying their best to escape. She hoped she wouldn't throw up in these nice people's car.

Mom was sitting in the courtroom. She'd slept in a cell, but hadn't been arrested, and she was angry. Mad as a wet hornet was more like it. Marie could see it in her eyes. She didn't look at all excited to see them, and even less like she'd been worried about their welfare throughout the night. A bailiff brought Daddy in, and the kids ran to him. They held on to him like a life raft on the open sea and cried; and as he knelt down to their level, his own face wet with a million tears. He just kept saying, "I'm sorry guys. I'm so sorry." Over and over again. The bailiff didn't try to stop the contact. Everyone there witnessed the sweet exchange, including Mother. And, Marie watched as the woman's eyes grew darker, as the malice built. They would all pay for this moment. She would have to keep her eyes open, because mom was smart enough to bide her time until there were no witnesses.

The judge took the time to listen to Daddy's story, and took into consideration the upcoming deployment and recent marriage. He berated both parents for their lack of judgment and the fact that they'd put their children in so much danger. Daddy apologized multiple times to the court, just as he had to the children, but Mom just sat and glared.

Marie saw several in the courtroom shake their heads in obvious scorn of this woman who had so little regard for the safety of her own children, and so little respect for the sitting judge. But, the judge was lenient, due to extenuating circumstances, and soon, after payment of tickets and fines, they were on their way over to retrieve the El Camino from impound. The moment Daddy wasn't looking, Mom pinched Marie on the back of her neck. She pinched so hard that she drew blood, and still that wasn't enough to satisfy her need for revenge. Before she let her loose she wrapped a clump of hair, from the nape of her daughter's neck, around her finger, and pulled until the hair came away from her skin. Marie knew better than to say anything, so she simply dealt with the pain and counted herself lucky it was only her and not one of the little ones.

Back in the truck; minus the beer, and quite a bit of badly needed trip money; they were on their way once again. Sandwiches would now consist of bread and cheese, to conserve as much of their dwindling funds as possible. They needed the money for gas, and the ticket and fines had eaten most of that. Mama was in a foul mood the rest of the journey, and Daddy clearly wasn't prepared to see this side of her so soon after their nuptials. He must have apologized a million times for his carelessness, not understanding that she was more angry over the lack of beer, than at any of the events of the past few days. Marie and the kids knew to stay clear, so he was on his own.

They were a day late arriving at their destination, for obvious reasons. There wouldn't be as much time as they'd hoped for, to settle in before Daddy was expected to deploy. As they made their way through the charming town, to his boyhood home, tension inside the vehicle became palpable. Daddy seemed especially jumpy, and Marie thought that odd.

They pulled up in front of an old Victorian style home with all its peeks, gables, and period colored paints. the kids were excited at first, because the house was large and looked a little like what their idea of a mansion might be. The yard was neatly mowed, and hedges and bushes trimmed, but as they got closer, Marie could see that the outside of the house was badly in need of new paint. One of the windows on the front of the house had a crack right down the middle, and was mended pretty well with clear packaging tape, so that it was hard to see unless you were close, and the boards on the front porch groaned when stepped upon, causing concern that perhaps they shouldn't stand so close together. She tried to settle the little ones, so as to make a good impression on their new grandparents, and they all stood wide eyed with hearts beating overtime in their chests.

Daddy didn't walk in, but stood on the front porch and rang the doorbell. This was more puzzling still. After a few moments the family began to look sideways at each other, in obvious wonderment over what could possibly be taking so long. Certainly they were expected. Daddy rang the bell again, and after a few moments more, the front door opened slowly. An elderly man with a pronounced limp answered the door, and when he saw Daddy a smile proceeded to spread over his ashen face. "Son. It's so good to see you."

"It's good to see you too, Dad. I wondered if anyone was home."

"Well, I don't move as fast as I used to."

"Isn't Mom home?"

"Well, yes, but she hollered at me to get the door. She must be busy in some other part of the house. So, this is the new family is it?"

"Yes Dad, I'd like you to meet my wife and kids."

"Very happy to meet all of you. Please come in. It's cold out there. Just put your things down by the stairs and we'll get you all settled in. This will be the first time in a great while that having so many rooms will be a good thing."

Marie liked him right away, and could see where her new dad got his gentlemanly tendencies. She imagined they would become great friends. "I'm pleased to meet you Grandfather."

"Oh, little one, you can call me Pops. You are actually our first grandchildren, and I always wanted to be called Pops, just like I used to call my granddaddy."

"Yes Sir, Pops. We're happy to be here, and we will try to stay out of your way and be as helpful as we can."

"Well, thank you for that child, but don't make it so quiet that we don't know you're here. It's been a long time since small footsteps rang out in these halls. It'll be a nice change."

"That one is Marie, Dad. She's a big help."

"Well, thank you for that, Son. I will likely put her to good use around here if she likes to help."

"Daddy says I'm the best helper he's ever had."

"Good, I can use a good helper. I'm sure we'll find plenty for you to do while your dad is gone. You're probably going to miss him."

"Yes I will Sir, I mean Pops. He is my best friend."

At that, Marie looked quickly sideways, and saw her

mother glaring at her. If looks could kill, she'd probably have fallen to the floor in a heap at that very moment. She could see that her mother was angry, but more than that, she was also anxious. She was nervous about staying with Daddy's parents. She'd heard her husband's conversation with his mother shortly after their trip to the mountains, when he was asking if his new family could come to New York and stay while he was deployed. From the sounds of it, his mother had objected to the fact that his new wife was so much older than he, that she had five children, and that they needed a place to stay. Mom hadn't told him she'd overheard the conversation, but really didn't have many options as far as a place to stay while he was gone, so there was no use bringing it up now. After the night they'd spent in jail and the last days of their hurried trip, she was just tired.

About that time Marie heard a noise from the second floor and turned toward the stairs. A tiny woman with a shock of white hair, a small beak like nose and huge dark eyes, behind extremely magnified glasses started down the steps. Marie thought she looked like an owl, an angry owl. Her look was not one of welcome, but of annoyance. She barked some orders at her husband, who scurried off to do her bidding, and walked up to Daddy. "Well, looks like you made it."

"Yes Mother, we made it. Good to see you too. I'd like to introduce you to my family."

"Your family? You mean the family you took in."

"This is my wife Mom. And these are my kids."

"Your kids? You mean her kids?"

"Mom, please. For me, can we not do this? Just for me?"

At that, Marie stepped forward and said, "I'm so glad to meet you. May I call you Grandmother, or is there a special name we should use?"

"Do not ever call me 'Grandmother', I am not your grandmother. I'm not even old enough to be your grand-mother. I will never be that old. I am Peter Pan. Do you understand me? Peter Pan. You may call me Bernice. If any of you think I'm going to be taking care of you, you have another thing coming. You are only here as a favor to my son, and he was stretching it to ask even for that."

"I promise you, Bernice, we will try very hard to stay out of your way, and we won't expect you to do a thing for us. As a matter of fact I am a pretty good cook, so I'd be proud to cook for the whole family. And I will keep the kids quiet. I promise."

"Good. See that you do." As Bernice walked past the

crowd in her front hall she looked them all up and down, but spent an especially long period of time assessing Mother. At the end of it she shook her head, made 'tsk, tsk, noises, and started back up the stairs."

Marie felt as though she'd had acid thrown in her face. Perhaps this was going to be a bit harder than she'd hoped.

"I'm sorry guys." Daddy shook his head. "I'd really hoped she'd mellowed a bit. Now you can see why it was easy for me to take a position in the Air Force so far from home. I felt bad leaving my dad here alone, but I thought I'd go crazy if I stayed a minute longer."

"Well, then, thank you very much for bringing us here husband." Mother spit out with as much venom as she could muster. "I'm sure we'll be much better off with your family than we would have been in California."

"It will be okay Honey. Mom can be a little cantankerous, but she'll get used to having you all around and she'll grow to love you as much as I do."

"Oh yes, I'm sure she will. Children, we need to figure out where we will be sleeping. I'm hoping someone will show us around." Her mother's voice was filled with spite, and Marie shuddered at the thought of being trapped here with her mom, and Bernice, both under the same roof.

At that moment Marie looked over at the rest of the kids. Her older sister had a look of pure distain on her face; and as usual was doing as little as possible to be part of the conversation; while the littlest one had her thumb back in her mouth. She closed her eyes for a second and took a deep breath, then opened her eyes just in time to see Pops coming around the corner to show them their rooms. She made herself a promise. She would stay as far away from good old Bernice as possible, and make sure the woman didn't have any more reasons, than she already did, to want them gone.

Before they knew it the time had come to see Daddy off at the airbase. Pops drove them to the base, while Mom and Dad held on to each other in the passenger seat like they were glued together. Marie felt sick, and the little ones were crying. Her older sister had chosen to stay at the house, and said her curt goodbyes from the top of the stairs. No one knew where Bernice was hiding. Marie was trying not to cry. She didn't want to make Daddy feel any worse than he already did. At the airstrip they unloaded his duffle bags and lined up for their last farewells.

Once again her parents embraced and kissed for a long time. After that Pops and Daddy shook hands, and after a brief hug Pops told him to watch his back and not to take any wooden nickels. Such an odd exchange. Then Daddy hugged each of the little ones and reminded them to be good, promising to bring them a present when he returned. When it came time for Marie to say goodbye, her lip began to tremble. She buried her face in her daddy's chest and breathed in deeply of his cologne. They hugged, and Daddy grabbed her by the shoulders, looking her in the eyes. "Marie, I'm counting on you to help Mom with the kids. She's going to be very stressed and afraid. You know I would never leave you all alone if there was anything I could do about it. I will be thinking of you guys every day."

"I promise, Daddy. And we will be thinking about you too. Please be safe. If I write to you, can you write back?"

"I don't know how things are set up yet. It could take a very long time to get anything back and forth."

"But, you're going to be gone so long."

"I know. Take care of your mom for me. Promise me."

"I promise. I'll do my best to take care of everyone."

Then he was off. Climbing aboard the troop carrier with his gear. They watched the enormous C-130 Hercules taxi and take off, staying on the tarmac until the aircraft was nothing more than a speck in the sky. The little ones clung to her and her mother's face clouded over in an old familiar way that scared her to the depths of her soul.

Pops looked sad, his eyes glazed with unshed tears. Marie would find out, through many later conversations with her new grandpa, that he had his own war stories from time spent in Germany and France during WW2 and then Korea. He hated the idea of his son heading off to face the demons of battle, and wondered if he would ever see him alive again.

Marie knew her own heart was breaking, but Mama just looked angry, clear down to her core. Thank goodness the house was large and, perhaps, Marie would be able to stay out of her way until she cooled down a bit. The biggest problem there was that this had been her mother's mood for most of Marie's life, so she could not be assured that any cooling down would indeed take place. She wasn't sure she could stay out of the way for all the months Daddy would be gone either. And, to top it off, there was another force loose in that house, Bernice. That woman might actually be able to give Mama a run for her money in the cranky old lady department.

When they entered the house and hung their coats by the front door, Bernice's angry glare met them at the bottom of the stairs. She hadn't wanted to see her son off, as she was sad to see him go; but now that it was too late, she was angry at herself for not having said goodbye. And, similar to Mama's skewed rational, she would now take her hurt feelings out on everyone in the house to try and make herself feel better. She barked some orders to Pops, and he scampered off to see to her demands. Then, she snapped at Mama, who simply glared back at her with the same venomous gaze. Mother pushed past the old woman and walked up the stairs to her room, where her eldest daughter had fallen back asleep the moment everyone departed for the airstrip.

Marie looked at Bernice and saw the irritation in her eyes, knowing she'd better calm the elderly woman down before she went into a rage.

As 'Peter Pan' continued barking orders at the kids, Marie organized work brigades. Soon she was cleaning bathrooms and scrubbing floors, while she had the younger ones dusting and doing their best to fold laundry. The long day concluded with Marie doing dishes from the delicious meal she'd made for the family. Bernice was certainly getting her money's worth. As the kids slowly ascended the stairs for baths before bed, Marie wondered how she would keep up with this hectic pace in this big house once they were enrolled in school. She was about to find out.

"As for you, you meant evil against me, but God meant it for good, to bring it about that many people should be kept alive, as they are today"

Genesis 50:20

CHapter 5

The Sergeant arrived at Da Nang air base, on the Eastern shores of South Vietnam, on a cold winter's day. Da Nang was located midway between Hanoi and Ho Chi Min city on the coast of the South China Sea. He made his appearance during a thirty seven day pause in bombing by American troops, as the U.S. was attempting to enter into a negotiated peace with the North Vietnamese. This lull in the action was the second since 'Rolling Thunder' began on March 2nd, 1965. and successfully gave him a very skewed vision of the Vietnam he would be witness to later in his deployment. 'Rolling Thunder', America's attempt to keep North Vietnamese supplies from making their way through the Ho Chi Mihn Trail, which was supposed to last eight weeks, managed to continue, with negligible consequence, for three long years.

Soon the North Vietnamese would denounce the bombing halt as a 'trick' and continue Viet Cong terrorist activities in the South. By the time of the sergeant's landing

U.S. troop levels in Vietnam had topped one hundred and eighty four thousand. This was following the desertion of an estimated ninety thousand, so called allied, South Vietnamese soldiers, while approximately thirty five thousand soldiers from North Vietnam infiltrated the South via the Ho Chi Minh trail. By this time up to fifty percent of the countryside in South Vietnam was under some degree of Viet Cong control. The constant bombing proved to be of little effect, as the damage caused by bombs dropped from American jets, was efficiently cleaned up each day by female Vietnamese construction crews. America lost over five hundred jets to that trail, and never managed to slow the transport of supplies and troops.

After the sergeant and his crewmates stowed their gear, they were invited out to the beach where a huge cookout was taking place. It was cold, as it was the first week of January in Vietnam, but the bonfires helped. Someone handed him a cold beer and told him, "The food will be ready pretty soon. Sit down and relax man. Nobody's going anywhere." He settled right in with the guys, and by night's end they were playing cards back in their quarters. He missed his family, but if this light duty was what he could expect from his deployment, things wouldn't be nearly as bad as he'd envisioned they might be in a war zone. That first night was followed by a couple dozen more just like it. During the day he worked on the battalion's planes, getting their radios up to specs, and then repaired the base's communications gear as well. Then, every evening at sunset he hung out with the guys. Drowning his loneliness for his family in cards, and a few nice cold beers.

After two weeks of acute depression, following her husband's departure, which caused her to take to her bed with covers over her head; Mama began waiting for Bernice to fall sleep at night, and sneaking off for destinations unknown. Marie wasn't sure where her mother was going, but if the sounds of stumbling and tripping as she ascended the stairs later each night were any clue, her best bet was a local bar. Marie wondered how she was getting back and forth, since she didn't drive and they were quite a distance from the downtown area. So, watching out the window one night she saw a car pull up at the end of the block and then observed her mom, in a dress and high heels (click, click, click, click) run down the sidewalk to climb, giggling like an errant teenager, into the vehicle waiting there.

Marie could only hope the old woman wouldn't find out, knowing she'd probably flip her lid. But, she could tell Pops had already figured out what was going on, and the sad looks he was giving Mama weren't going unnoticed by his new granddaughter.

Pops' bedroom was a small space at the bottom of the stairs. Marie figured it was probably originally intended to be a storage space, or closet of some sort, since it didn't even have a window; but he had everything he needed: a bed, a thirteen inch black and white TV, and shelves for his books. He used the bathroom downstairs. This way he wouldn't have to navigate the long flight of stairs to the second floor in the middle of the night. Due to his location, he would also be privy to the comings and goings of anyone using the front door.

Bernice had a large, lovely room upstairs, all done up in shades of purple and lace, with a king sized bed and her own bathroom. Mama and Marie's older sister were sharing a bedroom, and Marie was bunking in with the three younger ones. They all shared a bathroom, so Marie waited and showered in the mornings before school.

It only made sense for her to stay in with the younger children, so she could make sure their homework was done, and their baths were taken before bed. She often played board games with them, or read to them, even though she was exhausted from her own schoolwork and all the house work and cooking that was now expected of her.

And, yes, she had started school at the large, local junior high. At eleven she was the youngest student in the eighth grade class. Her new teacher embarrassed her upon introduction to the rest of the students, and practically ensured that she would be the new school pariah forever. "Oh class, I want you to meet Marie. She comes all the way from California, and she is very smart. She's skipped two whole grades when she was younger, and I'm sure she would be very happy to mentor anyone who needs help in math or English, once we have her up to speed with where we are in our current books." Marie could tell, from the empty, and in some cases defiant, stares around the room that there weren't too many who were interested in becoming her new best buddy, or, for that matter, in experiencing her mentoring prowess.

With a heavy heart she claimed her seat and set her mind to the task at hand. She'd never been popular, so this wouldn't be hard to get used to. But, she was a pretty smart kid, and she decided (just as she had in her previous school), that if she couldn't join them, she might as well beat them.

The sergeant lay in bed, separated from his loved ones by thousands of miles, wondering how his little family was doing in the same house with his mother. He knew how hateful and distant she could be, which is why he'd sworn to himself that if he ever had kids of his own, he would try to be a light in their lives, instead of an anchor to their souls, as she had proved to be for most of his life.

The only reason he'd insisted his new family move in with his old one, was because he'd already had a couple of brief glimpses, very early in their union, of his new wife's alcohol problem, and he didn't want her getting out of hand, especially with the kids. He'd been able to keep those instances secret from Marie and the other children, as her drunken episodes had happened after the kids were in bed. He knew she had party buddies back in California, and thought it best to get her as far away as possible from those influences. Perhaps living in an alcohol free house, without access to her old friends, would help her stay clean. He could only hope. If he'd had another choice he would have taken it. He loved them all and just wanted them to be safe. In fact, just that morning he'd sent off a letter informing them of an address where they could send mail, and he hoped to be able to send encouraging letters to his wife and kids. The only problem was that it could take weeks for correspondence to get from point A, to point B.

He was discovering that he didn't need to be out on a mission, to be in danger. Snipers were everywhere, and even a reconnaissance gig could turn out to be fatal. The country was filled with handmade booby traps, and mine fields, set to take out the enemy (him), or at least separate victims from as many body parts as possible

Recently he'd been reacquainted with an old friend from his high school days, and they'd become fast friends all over again. Ralph Miller was helping him adjust to life so far from family, and he was glad for the friendship. He grew tired of his bed, and the worrisome thoughts that took him to the family he'd left behind to fend for their own. Maybe he'd go find some of the other guys. A nice cold beer, and a hand or two of poker, sounded pretty good right about now.

Constantly exhausted these days, from a combination of school, homework, housework, laundry, cooking and kids, Marie knew this life style was wearing her out. She didn't dare ask Bernice for help, for fear of upsetting the delicate balance of things. Asking her sister for help garnered a laugh, and at her sincere request her mother gave her a look that could quite possibly shatter mirrors. So, she had no choice but to forge on.

She knew for sure her mom was drinking again, even in spite of the sounds of her stumbling up the stairs when she arrived home. She knew because just like in all the scary, bad years, before Daddy came along, the smell was back. She hated that smell. The excessive alcohol permeated her mother's system, and she reeked of it. Body odor and alcohol. It was her least favorite smell in the entire world, and it haunted her dreams again when she was able to fall asleep at all.

Mom was sleeping in pretty late these days, but it didn't really bother Marie to be able to get the kids out of the house without negative energy being bantered about. She could tell though that Bernice was getting more annoyed by the minute. Marie was doing all she could to keep the old lady calm. Feeding the kids breakfast, dressing them and getting them off to school. But only after she cleaned up the kitchen and started a load of laundry.

It was a difficult task, to get it all done before she was expected to arrive at the junior high school in the mornings, especially without any help. But, she thought her new grandmother might be starting to figure things out. After all, she'd have to be five I.Q. points short of an idiot not to see what was going on right under her nose. However, Marie thought, if she could just keep them apart, and keep Bernice happy, maybe things would turn out okay.

Marie loved school. Though she had no friends to speak of, she was an excellent student and was trusted implicitly by all her teachers. They saw she was a good kid, and most of them could also see how important it was for her to have their approval. Getting out of the house where she felt she was a prisoner of everyone else's needs was essential to her sanity, and felt a little like a vacation of sorts. Honestly, while she loved her siblings very much, she had to admit she wasn't looking forward to the advent of summer vacation in just a few months. A time when she would be expected to keep the kids entertained and out of her mother's hair, as well as Bernice's.

Pops tried to help Marie as much as possible, without accruing his wife's wrath. Marie understood. She didn't like being on the receiving end of Bernice's tirades either. Mama didn't seem to care what the old woman had to say about anything, and continued to push the envelope. Eventually, Marie started making a habit of getting the kids into bed, and going downstairs to talk to Pops. He was an extremely smart man, even though he'd only made it as far as eighth grade in his schooling. So, especially on Friday and Saturday nights, when she could let the children sleep in a bit the next morning, she would sneak down to the room under the stairs and visit. It was clear that Daddy got his patience and good nature from his dad. Goodness knows, it certainly wasn't from his crazy mom.

After the war, Pops was an engineer for the New York Central Railroad (NYCR) for several decades; until an accident caused by another railroad employee took his legs. He was awarded disability and an early pension, so he and Bernice didn't have to worry about bills and daily expenses. In addition, if he ever passed away before Bernice, she'd be left with a nice income. He had interesting stories galore about his life and adventures, and just like Daddy, he could really spin a yarn. At times Marie was forced to clamp her hand over her mouth, while she snorted with glee and tears spouted from her eyes, because he would have her laughing so hard at his escapades. She could tell Pops liked her company too. It was nice to have a friend and ally in this difficult place.

He'd been left alone for so long, and her heart broke for him. Like an old horse put to pasture, he'd clearly suffered greatly from lack of meaningful contact. Considering that his wife's idea of communication was to bark orders at him and call him terrible names, he'd been withering away from loneliness for years, and it was good to see a sparkle in his eyes when she would enter his room. Throughout their stay Marie could actually see his color and mood change for the better. He seemed excited to get up and out for the day, and, as of late was making use of his ill fitting prosthetic legs, often limping along with Marie and the kids clear to the bus stop at the end of the block.

It wasn't hard to tell that Bernice resented the time Pops spent with Marie and the kids. After all, if he was with them he couldn't be there to leap at her every beck and call.

It made Marie feel angry to see that perfectly able bodied, angry woman treat him like a lowly servant.

It wasn't until later, during an especially somber discussion with her grandpa, that she would find out Pops had suffered from his own journey through anger and alcoholism after he'd lost his legs. Their marriage had come close to falling apart, and indeed went through some pretty bad times before he straightened out. The old woman never forgot those times, and had clearly never forgiven him. He felt it was his duty now to try to 'make it up to her', for the pain he'd put her through. It was hard to imagine this quiet, patient man as an angry alcoholic, but she was abundantly aware what a difference a few drinks could make in an otherwise relatively normal person. She was glad her instincts told her to give him a big hug after his confession. They both cried and it seemed they were even closer than ever after that heartfelt exchange. Marie decided that her new grandfather was her second favorite person in the world, right after Daddy. And, she would spend as much time with him as she possibly could.

That same night, Pops passed away in his sleep. Marie thought it odd when she and the kids got ready to leave for school that he didn't come bounding from his cubby hole to join them. She knocked on his door and got no answer, so, thinking he might be sleeping in she made her way off for the day.

They saw the ambulance and police car the moment they stepped off the bus returning home. Marie hurried the kids and they ran to the big house as quickly as possible. Bernice and Mama sat on opposite ends of the sofa. It seemed Bernice had slept in and didn't need Pops for anything until early afternoon. When she called his name and he didn't answer, she grew angry and began to shout. Mother came out of her room and told the old woman to "shut up"(it was transforming her hangover into a migraine), which produced a melee the likes of which most people have never seen. It began with yelling, and evolved into slapping and hair pulling. Bernice actually tried to push the younger woman over the stair banister, without success. Once they were through trying to kill each other, Bernice stomped downstairs, huffing and puffing, to demand Pops throw the ungrateful tramp out of her house. Opening his door, she saw him lying lifeless on his bed, and took several steps backward until she tripped and fell.

She walked calmly to the phone and called the ambulance. "I believe my husband is dead", she proffered. "No, I didn't try to give him CPR. It looks as if he died sometime in the night. I didn't think it would help. Would you just please send someone?"

"What do you mean? He's dead? How do you know if you didn't even touch him?"

"Listen tramp, I don't need any comments or advice from you. The hospital is sending an ambulance now, and they will check him over." Bernice walked to the front door and opened it a crack to give the emergency workers access when they arrived.

"We need to make some phone calls. His son needs to know."

"We aren't calling anyone. My son is in a war zone, and I won't have him upset in battle, where any distraction could get him killed. Why would we call him anyway, when he would only worry. There's nothing to be done about his father now, so I won't have him jeopardized in the process."

"You didn't even care enough about him to come to the airstrip to say good bye. How can you pretend to be concerned about him now? He'll be devastated if he finds out his dad is dead and no one told him."

"It is what it is. And I will handle the aftermath, just like I have his whole life. I've kept more things a secret about his dad than this, just to shield him from the truth. Don't tell me how to handle my relationship with my son."

"You have no relationship with your son. His dad is the only one who ever tried to reach out to him. He hated you. You've never been anything but mean and horrible to him."

"Get out. Get out of my house. Go upstairs and pack your things, and when your filthy brats get home from school, take them and go. I don't ever want to see you again. Do you understand me?"

"Yes, I understand you. You old witch! You never wanted us here, and you've made that clear from the moment we arrived. Don't you think for one moment that your son won't hear all of this when he gets home."

"Oh, I have plenty of my own to tell him, you slut. Do you think I don't know you've been sneaking from the house every night? Out drinking. I can smell it on you from here. And whoring around. I can smell that from here too, as sick as it makes me to say it. I promise you he'll be a whole lot more interested in what I have to say, than anything that comes out of your lying, cheating mouth."

At that, Mama streaked across the room and leapt on Bernice. They were actively rolling on the floor pulling out handfuls of each other's hair, when the officers and ambulance attendants arrived. The officers separated the two clawing, spitting women, and sat them on the couch, just before the children came running through the door. "What's going on? Why are the police and ambulance here?" Marie asked.

Just then the attendants rolled out of Pops' room and past the family with a gurney. On it was a body, covered in a pure white sheet. Marie stepped forward and touched the cloth. She looked into her mom's face, then into Bernice's, and then stepped back, dropping straight to her butt on the floor where she sat in a state of shock for a full three minutes. Then, remembering their sweet conversation from the night before, she burst into tears, stood, and ran up the stairs to throw herself on her bed. "No, no, no, not Pops. Why couldn't it have been one of them? Why Pops? He was the only one who cared."

Her mother approached the girl from behind and slapped her on the leg. "Get the kids together and pack all your things."

Turning around, she sat, and then looking suspiciously at her mother she rose to her feet. "Why? What did you do?"

The hand that came swiftly to leave a red mark on her left cheek was too quick to avoid. "Don't you dare make this about me. You know that old witch has been out to get us all since we got here."

"She found out, didn't she? She found out you were sneaking out and drinking, didn't she?"

That time she managed to duck before a closed fist could connect. But, before she knew it her mom had her hair, and pulling it, threw her to the floor. She scrambled to her feet and ran down the stairs. "Bernice, Grandma, please, you can't throw us out. Where will we go? We don't have any other place."

"That's not my concern child. Your mother has made her bed, and yours too, for that matter, so you'd best be packing your things. I'm not going to be changing my mind."

Police were still in the living room, and they watched the scene taking place before them. One of them stepped forward, "Is there anything we can do here. It seems there's a dispute?"

"No officer. My son is in Vietnam. He left his whore of a wife and her children here to stay until he got back, but she's been stepping out on him since the beginning of his deployment and I'm not going to stand by and watch it any longer. I've invited her to leave."

"What about the children, ma'am. That will leave

the children without a roof over their heads. It's winter out there."

"Not my concern officer. She should have thought of that before she started her drinking and tramping around. I refuse to let this be my problem anymore."

The officer shook his head and looked toward his partner, then toward the girl. "Child, what's your name?"

"Marie, Sir."

"Why don't you do as your grandmother says and go upstairs to pack. Tell your mom we'd like to speak with her."

"I am not her grandmother. Do you hear me? Do I look old enough to be her grandmother? I assure you I do not! I am Peter Pan!"

The officers looked sideways at each other. "Go ahead child. Get your mom."

Marie ran up the stairs and gave her mother the message, ducking another badly aimed slap. She ran into her room and began repacking the bags and boxes they'd arrived with less than a month and a half before. Her little sister sat on the bed with her thumb back in her mouth and tears streaming down her cheeks. Meanwhile, the ambulance attendants were finishing downstairs, getting Bernice's information and choice of mortuary. Mom walked slowly down the stairs, watching Bernice and trying to stay clear of the angry old lady.

"It sounds like you have no place to go, ma'am?"

"That's right officer. The old witch is kicking us to the curb, while my husband is overseas serving our country."

"Oh, yeah, whore. You really care about my son, who is serving our country, don't you? Then, tell me this, why are you out drinking and whoring around every night? Tell me that!"

"Shut up old woman, or I'll..."

"Or you'll what, you tramp!"

"Ladies, we're just trying to come up with a solution so these children won't be out on the street. There is a shelter in town that can put a roof over your heads, at least for a couple of nights, until you can figure something else out."

"Thank you officers. We have no way to get there. I don't drive."

"We will wait for you to get your things together. I'm going to call a van, and we'll be able to get you there safely, before they close their doors for the night. They have some resources at the facility that might be able to help you find something more permanent."

"We'll try to hurry. I promise you I can't get away from

that woman fast enough."

"Well, that makes two of us, tramp, and good riddance!"

"Ladies, ladies, the children can hear you. Okay, if you could head back upstairs ma'am and finish getting your things together, we'll get that van out here."

Marie could hear most of the conversation taking place downstairs and her stomach began to churn. She was angry with her mother, for her reckless behavior, but also knew she was right about Bernice. That woman hadn't wanted them living in her house from the moment she heard her son was married and that he would be leaving soon for the war. Of course her mom hadn't made anything better by her drinking, lying and cheating; but, this was bound to happen eventually. Her stomach was in knots, a familiar feeling, but she knew she had to protect the little ones from whatever stupid plan her mother might come up with next.

The officers were great and got them all to a shelter where they could stay for a couple of days until another way was found. There were no tearful goodbyes with Bernice. They made sure they took everything they'd brought with them. There would be no way to retrieve their belongings, which had arrived later by moving truck, from Bernice's basement until Daddy arrived home. She'd made it very clear that she never wanted to see them again. As she walked past Pops' empty room, on her way out the door, Marie's heart broke a little more. No more visits, no more stories, no more laughter. Perhaps she would never laugh again. What was there to laugh about anyway? They didn't even know when or where the funeral would be held, and Bernice made sure they never received that information, so Marie felt like her farewell would never be complete. Perhaps it was better this way. She would dry her tears and be a shield between her mother and the children, as she'd always been.

The kids didn't attend school during their days at the shelter, which was filled with other women and children who were homeless as they were. There was a place to shower, so she made sure that she and her siblings were clean; but her stomach disorder became worse, by trying to eat the food so graciously provided in the shelter's cafeteria. Her older sister spent the entire three days sleeping, and her mom clung to her cot with her blankets over her head, as was her habit during any turmoil.

On their third day in the facility, a woman from the

office came to talk to mother. It seemed there might be a place for them. You see they had an advantage that the others in the homeless shelter didn't have. Daddy had set up a bank account before he left, and most of his biweekly paycheck was being deposited in that account. Marie had been unaware that her mother was spending money from the joint account on her own selfish desires. But, there was still enough left to cover the deposit and first months' rent on accommodations that might be suitable for the family. Arrangements were made to take them, and their belongings, to the small trailer they would be renting on the following day.

Bombing resumed. The U.S. government launched 'Operation Masher', a name that was later changed to operation 'White Wing'; due to pressure caused by American opinion polls; from January 28th to March 6th, 1966. The name change was almost comical. As if an operation could become more or less deadly by the name it was given.

This forty two day operation was a combined undertaking through the 1st Cavalry Division and 1st Calvary Airborne, and included members from all four branches of service. These troops were engaged in search and destroy missions to root out Viet Cong from towns and hamlets all throughout the Bong Son Plains, clear to the Coast of South Vietnam. Small towns and hamlets in the hills, brush, and jungle had become striking points from which the Cong could attack U.S. and South Vietnamese forces. The typical huts (or hootches), in these small hamlets were often covers, protected by Cong sympathizers, that housed tunnels, weapons caches, trenches and bunkers for Viet Cong activity. These sweeps through heavy brush and elephant grass were treacherous, as the enemy had ample cover in which to hide and inflict casualties on the combined U.S. troops.

These were the circumstances the sergeant and his troops found themselves in after previous weeks of virtual inactivity, and the shock of the change was complete and overwhelming. Being the most knowledgeable communications NCO in the command, and the assigned squad leader for his recon group, he would be in the thick of it every day going forward; until he left the country, if, by the Grace of God, that happened at all.

They moved their modest belongings to a shabby trailer, in an even shabbier, mobile home park behind 'Frank's Full Service and Gasoline Station'. The small mobile home village consisted of a half dozen old, rusty, rental trailers and another small building that contained coin washers and dryers on one wall, and locked mail boxes for each tenant on the opposite wall. The grounds of the mobile home village were nothing but gravel. No grass, or places for the children to play. Each trailer had a cement slab on which to park a vehicle, if you were lucky enough to own one, and a set of wobbly wooden steps that led to the home's front door.

Once inside the trailer they were met with a sour smell that seemed a combination of years of filth and perhaps pet urine, well, hopefully pet, but, whether from pets, or people, they didn't know. Marie's nose wrinkled at the foul odor and she glanced over at the kids to see the same look on every face. The carpet was stained and dirty, the kitchen was actively making scratching and crawling noises that Marie was sure belonged to undesirable pests, and she hadn't even walked down the hallway to the bathroom yet. It was obvious she would have to scrub at least the bathroom and kitchen before they attempted to sleep tonight.

A discolored sofa leaned crookedly against one wall in the living room, and a small dinette with three mismatched chairs stood in the kitchen, but there was no other furniture. No beds, no dressers for their clothing. The small master bedroom had a tiny closet, but the one other bedroom in the place didn't even have that. She'd thought her mother said the place was furnished, so obviously there was a misunderstanding.

It appeared that someone, perhaps in a fit of anger, had put their fist through the particle board wall halfway down the hallway, and Marie could feel a draft coming through the hole, so she assumed the walls had virtually no insulation, and wondered what else might make its way into their space through that opening.

"Well, I'm going out. My ride should be here soon."

"Going out? Mother, I'm going to need some cleaning supplies, and there is no food here to feed the kids. Where are you going?"

"That's none of your business. And, you'd best remember who is the parent here missy, so I don't want to hear any more sass. I got us a place to stay. I swear, nothing I do is ever good enough for you."

"Well, it would be super nice to be reminded of who

the parent is every now and then. I don't know how you expect me to take care of everyone with no supplies and no money." Once again, the slap was swift and she didn't duck in time. Her left cheek would carry the new mark for several days. Perhaps it was good that this was Friday, so there wouldn't be any curious looks from teachers or classmates upon her return to school.

"Fine, I'll leave you a little money for cleaning supplies and some food for the kids." Mother said in a dramatically sacrificial tone. "See that it lasts you. I only have so much out of each paycheck, and you can't expect me to do without."

"Do without what, Mother. I don't ever see you do without much." This time she ducked the swing, leaving her mom glaring at her. "Well, do you at least want to tell your eldest daughter to help me with the cleaning? There's a lot to do around here just to try and get the smell out."

"Did you hear that? Help your sister get this place in shape."

Mother left twenty dollars on the table and ran outside to catch her ride. No sooner had she vanished than her sister headed for the door. "Hey, you heard Mom. You're supposed to be helping me for once."

"Yeah, right. Good luck with that. See you later."

Marie felt as though she carried the weight of the world on her shoulders. At least she could be thankful there was no school the next day. In fact, she didn't even know where they would be expected to catch the bus on Monday, so that discovery question was high on her list of 'to dos'. There were many things that needed to be handled, and she figured she'd better get on it since there were only a few hours left till dark.

She took the kids with her to Frank's. Outside the front entry door was a pop machine that contained assorted bottles of ice cold soda. A small bell dinged when she opened the squeaky door, and once inside they were met with a thick cloud of cigarette smoke which seemed to be emanating from the far side of the room. Behind a small desk in the corner sat a middle aged man; with a bulbous, red nose, bushy eyebrows that seemed to have a life of their own and watery, yellow tinged eyes; that she figured must be Frank. Something about him, and the way he looked at her for a very long time, gave her the creeps. Trying not to choke on the thick smoke she said, "Hello Sir. I'm hoping you can help us."

"You're the new kids aren't you?"

"Yes Sir. I was wondering if you could direct me to a place where I might pick up some cleaning supplies and groceries. The previous tenants didn't leave the place in very good shape and I'd like to do a little cleaning before we try to settle in."

"Oh, they left it a mess did they? I didn't know."

Marie was quite sure he knew exactly how disgusting his horrible trailers were, but she would let it go for now, as long as he could help her. "I also wanted to know if you had a vacuum cleaner. The carpets are very dirty, and I'm sure you know there are no beds even though the advertisement claimed the place was furnished. So, before I let the kids sleep on the carpets, I'm going to try to get them as clean as I can."

"Yeah, yeah, I got an old one in the back you can use. I'll want it back though.'

"Of course, but I'd like to use it every week if I might. At least you'll know someone is keeping one of your little trailers clean."

"Sure, we can do that. I'll just go in back and get it."

As they waited for Frank to return, Marie took in her surroundings. The office/ store area had a counter and cash register positioned right in front of the back wall. In the glass case beneath the register she saw a collection of snack items; candy bars, potato chips, etc., and several brands of cigarettes with matches and lighters. On the walls behind the counter hung assorted engine belts, filters and other various car parts. On another wall, tires in a variety of sizes were displayed. On the counter top stood a rack which held scented tree deodorizers to hang from your rear view mirror. She leaned forward and sniffed one, only to find it smelled more like cleanser than trees, which left her with a wrinkled nose and a swift and painful sinus headache. The windows were dirty and didn't let in much natural illumination, so even with the overhead lights on the place seemed dingy and dark. When the door to the back opened again, she briefly glimpsed a large shop designed for car repair, but didn't get a very good look.

The vacuum cleaner was ancient, and had more than its share of dings and dents. But, if it worked that was all she cared about. "Great! I'll take good care of it Sir, and I'll bring it back tomorrow afternoon, if that's alright."

"That's fine. I'm only here till four on Saturday."

"I'll be sure to have it back by then. Thank you. Now, if you can direct me to a store, I'll drop the vacuum back at the trailer and go to get some supplies."

"Well, the closest store is a little Mom and Pop shop about two miles up the back road. You gonna try to walk all that way with those little ones?"

"Unless you have a better idea Sir, I don't have much of a choice."

"Well, where's your mama, girl?"

" I have no idea. Now, I really need to go, so we can try to get back before dark. I'll be sure to bring the vacuum back by tomorrow afternoon."

"Okay. Watch yourselves on that back road. It curves and winds around when it's following the river. Drivers don't have a clear view, so you have to stay clear on over to the side, or you'll be road kill in no time."

"Thank you. We'll be careful. Oh, I forgot to ask. Do you know where we will be expected to catch the school bus?"

"Yeah, as a matter of fact that's about a half mile up the main road going north."

"I apologize. I don't know which direction is north."

"When you get out to the main road, turn right. It will be right after the fancy gas station with the tiger on the sign."

"Thank you again. You've been very helpful. I'll see you tomorrow afternoon."

Marie half dragged, half carried, the vacuum back to their trailer, locked the door, and headed up the back road with the kids in tow. She only had twenty dollars to spend, so she knew she had to be thrifty with her purchases, but she was sure she could get the things she needed if she was careful.

Two miles was a long walk with little ones, and the two youngest whined and fussed the whole way. To their case, it was much colder in New York than it had been in California, so their clothing wasn't well matched to the climate, and it was getting late in the day. Throughout their trek Marie alternated between trying to calm the children, and worrying about where her next twenty dollars would come from. She needed beds for the children, but blankets on the floor would have to do for now. She also needed coins for the laundry, and was very grateful she'd done laundry every day at Bernice's, so they all had a few days worth of clean clothing.

Knowing her mom didn't care about all the mundane day to day things, like; how would the kids be fed; how laundry would get done; and where they would catch the school bus, was disheartening, but at least she knew where they stood on the woman's priority list, so they would manage somehow.

They finally arrived at the quaint grocery store, and walking in Marie took a look around.

"Can I help you young lady?" The woman behind the counter asked suspiciously.

"Yes ma'am, we are new in the area and I need a few things."

"You said new? Where are you from girl?"

"We've moved into the small trailer park about two miles down the road."

"Oh, that place?" She looked down her nose at them, making Marie feel almost dirty by association.

"Yes ma'am. And I need some cleaning supplies, and a few food items."

"Do you have any money? We don't do charity here, and we won't let you buy your supplies on credit either, you understand?"

"Yes ma'am, I have money for the things I need, and I will keep the other in mind for future purposes. Can you direct me to the cleaning supplies?"

"Yes, they're right over here." Marie chose a good cleanser, dish washing liquid, ammonia, a bottle of bleach, and a large bottle of vinegar, along with some sponges, a package of cleaning cloths, two bars of bath soap, a small bottle of shampoo, toothpaste and a package of toilet paper. Having used half of her money on non edibles, she had to choose wisely for her food purchases. Two loaves of bread; a large package of bologna; peanut butter and grape jelly; a gallon of milk; several packages of Kool-Aid, two pounds of sugar; and a large bag of apples, were all the supplies she could manage out of the meager funds her mom had left her. But it should be enough to last a few days, even for six people.

After all her purchases there was thirty seven cents left from the original twenty dollars, so she allowed the children to choose from the penny candy counter. This seemed to please them so much that as Marie and her eight year old sister struggled to carry bags of groceries two miles to their destination, the two youngest didn't whine or fuss a bit. After all, candy was a rare treat indeed. Marie was exhausted and shaking, having taken on most of the load herself, once they reached the trailer. But, the stress was not caused only from the walk.

Frank had been right about the traffic coming down the back road. Drivers couldn't see around the bends and curves of the river road, and even staying clear over to the edge of the trail all the way home, they'd had a few close calls. She would have to try finding a wagon in which to transport the little ones. It would not only be perfect for carrying the kids back and forth, but she could load the groceries in there too. But, that was one more thing for which she would need access to money she didn't have.

Marie made bologna sandwiches for supper. After searching all the cupboards she'd discovered there was no pitcher in which to make Kool-Aid, or cups with which to drink it. She made a mental note to make another note, when she found her school supplies, of all the things they would need since all their household supplies were in Bernice's basement. No pots and pans would make it very difficult to cook. And meals would be nearly impossible without dishes, glasses, and utensils. She'd found a small plastic container that, after she scrubbed it clean, they used to share some milk with their sandwiches, then she allowed them each a small apple. "I hope you are all full enough, because this food will have to last a couple of days." They all agreed that they'd had plenty to eat, so she scooted them off to the bathtub, admonishing the oldest to watch the two youngest; and proceeded to vacuum the heck out of the carpet in the smallest room. Adding up in her head all the things she needed to purchase left her dizzy with worry, and she knew she'd have to figure out a way to make some money, and fast.

"Whoever receives one such child in my name receives me, but whoever causes one of these little ones who believe in me to sin, it would be better for him to have a great millstone fastened around his neck and to be drowned in the depth of the sea."

Matthew 18:5-6

cHapter 6

Operation 'White Wing' continued, as U.S. troops attempted to root out Viet Cong infiltrators to the South. The sergeant is terrified every time he embarks on a 'search-and-destroy' mission with his men. He doesn't ask the others how they feel, because the dread is evident on their faces; though he knew no one would admit it out loud. War is a strong man's game, and they wouldn't have their comrades think them weak, or cowardly. Generally, as the squad heads out to new coordinates, there is no sound but the whir of engines, while the soldiers are inbound to a battle zone; except for sporadic, softly mumbled prayers and an occasional newbie vomiting out the chopper door from a sudden bout of air sickness or uncomplicated abject fear.

Dressed in combat fatigues, flak jackets and helmets, and loaded for bear with M-60s and grenades, they file on board the waiting Hueys.

Helicopters transport them to each day's starting point,

throughout the operation's duration. Where they will leap six to eight feet from still airborne choppers with all their gear, and proceed to the nearest village or hamlet. Radio gear is heavy, usually a PRC-25 with RC-292 ground plane antennae, and the sergeant knows it takes the edge off his radio man's speed. So, he lingers to grab the troop's pack strap, to help him off the ground if the weight takes him down. Hopefully it won't slow him too much when it really counts. They've found out on numerous missions that Cong snipers inhabit spider holes around every village where sympathizers are located.

As they approach the next assigned village, children scatter, and women rush in out of the fields to the protection of their huts. As squad leader he relays orders to search every dwelling for embedded Cong and hidden weapons. The panic on the faces of village children is especially hard to take. He knows they are frightened and he thinks of his own kids at home.

Moving from hut to hut he hears gun fire break out in a nearby dwelling. The entire squad converges on the sound. His men have found a cache of weapons under floor mats of a nearby hut and the huge haul of ammunition will be confiscated. Meanwhile, the two VC hiding in with the weapons have been shot as they tried to escape. A family is on their knees in the village center, with rifles pointed at their heads. He calls for the interpreter.

"Ask them where the rest of the soldiers are hiding."

"Yes Sarg. Nhung nguoi Linh an nao o dau?"

"Chung toi khong biet nhung nguoi linh o dau." "He says he doesn't know where any soldiers are."

"Tell him we know he is lying. There were two under his floor."

"Yes Sarg. Chung toi biet ban dang noi doi. Co hai duoi san cua ban."

"Neu toi noi voi ban ho se giet gia dinh toi." "He says if he tells you they will kill his family."

"Tell him if he doesn't tell me we will burn his village down."

"Yes Sarg. Neu ban khong hoi voi chung toi chung toi se dot lang cua ban."

"Anh ay biet." "He says he knows, Sarg."

The sergeant orders the village evacuated. "Do you want us to search for hold outs, Sarg?"

"Nope, we don't have time for that if we're going to stay on schedule. if they didn't heed the evac. warning, they can live, or die, with the consequences."

A call to air support, and coordinates for the village they'd just searched, brought F-4s roaring to their location, with a hail of white phosphorus bombs raining down on the huts of those who were helping the enemy, and those who were not. The bombs also brought two more gooks out of hiding, as their skin burned from contact with the deadly phosphorus. Their screams could be heard for miles. The troops set fire to the village's fields as well, sending the crops they'd been caring for up in a plume of smoke that could be seen for miles. Other than the two Cong who'd been found under the floor mats, no one was shot; but the shocked faces of the children who would now be left without a roof, or food, gnawed at him. Orders were orders, and if they didn't destroy obvious weapons cachets and punish sympathizers, this war would go on forever. He just wanted to make it home to his own wife and kids.

After several more hours of fighting their way through elephant grass and brush to clear the perimeter, the sergeant called for a ride home. Back at the base he couldn't drop his gear and head off for the NCO club fast enough. The thought of those children's faces continued to haunt him, like ghosts wandering in a fog. Maybe a few beers would dull the image in his mind.

Mama didn't come home that night, or the next, and when she finally got back to the trailer on Sunday evening, staggering drunk, Marie confronted her. "I don't know where you've been, and frankly, Mother, I don't care, but I'm going to need more money for food soon."

"Don't you lip off to me girl. I don't have any money for you. Your dad's check won't get deposited till next week, that's why they call it biweekly!"

"So you spent it all? On what? What did you think I was going to feed the kids with for another whole week?"

"Knock it off Missy! I'm tired, and I don't need your sass. I'm going to go lay down. Keep the brats quiet, or else."

"Tired? What are you tired from, Mother? It certainly isn't from cleaning, because I did all of that without you, and without your oldest daughter for that matter. You know she hasn't been home all weekend? You didn't even ask if the kids are okay. Just, "Keep the brats quiet, or else", or else what, Mother? What are you going to do? Hit me? Not feed me? Make me clean your house? Not allow me to have my own life, while you take off and party? Sorry, but you've already worn out your arsenal of 'or else's'." Marie turned to walk away, and the blow to the back of her head knocked her forward so fast that she staggered and fell into the wall. The children began to cry again, and, dizzy, she picked up and held the littlest one while she shushed the bunch.

"It's okay honey. I'm fine. She can't hurt me."

Her mother glared at her from across the space and went back to the master bedroom to sleep off whatever she was on. Marie had purposed half the blankets they'd used in the truck's camper to cover the floor in the small room where they'd all been sleeping. Though she'd vacuumed and scrubbed all the carpets and floors in the trailer, she wasn't able to make much of a dent in the years of built up filth. So, she hoped the blankets would act as a barrier until she could come up with another solution. They used the other half of the blankets to cover themselves.

Her mother didn't say a word as she slammed the door behind her. "Oh well", Marie thought, "Let her sleep on that filthy carpet. She doesn't deserve anything better." She refused to even ask if she'd like a blanket. And, from the immediate snoring heard through the door, the alcohol seemed to be keeping her warm enough.

Her older sister still hadn't made it home from her

weekend, and who knew what that consisted of, but she wasn't going to concern herself with that. She would have all she could handle getting the younger kids to school the next day, and explaining to teachers and principals where they'd been over the past week. She didn't expect any help from her mother on that, or anything else for that matter.

Walking into the elementary building on Monday morning, she went straight to the office. She explained to the secretary that she didn't have notes for the children's absence, but that they had been moving and things got a little hectic. The secretary gave her a sympathetic and knowing look, and Marie figured that people must be talking about her mom already, just like they did in California. She assured Marie that she would speak to all the teachers, and that everything would be fine. Marie was aware that the lady was doing her a great service in not calling social services, so she thanked her and set off for the junior high building to settle her own situation.

Walking into the office at the junior high building, Marie was practically set upon by concerned administrators. "Oh Marie, we've been so worried. When you didn't come to school we called your grandmother's house and she said she had no idea where you were."

"Yes ma'am. Things were a little distressing there between her and my mom, after my Pops died, and we had to find another place. I've been moving us in. I'm really sorry. I don't have a note, and I know that is required after an absence."

"No, no, don't worry about that. Your teachers have all been worried sick about you and they will be so happy you're alright."

"We don't have a phone yet. And, to be honest, I don't know if we will be getting one. But, if we do I will bring you the number."

"That's fine. Is there another way we can reach you if you're absent again?"

"I guess, if there's an emergency, you could call Franks Service Station during the day. We're living in a trailer out back of his business."

The look, on the face of the secretary, was one of pity; and she didn't think she liked that look any better than the one of scorn she'd seen on the face of the store owner last Friday. She was bound and determined to do the best she could, and to take care of her brother and sisters, no matter what anyone thought. For the rest of the day she got the distinct impression her teachers were treating her a little differently than they'd ever done before. Like something delicate and fragile. And, it was a feeling she didn't much like.

On the way home from the bus stop, she stopped, with her younger siblings, at the big Esso service station on the corner to talk to the owner. The station boasted eight gas pumps and four service techs, if you included the owner. They did small repairs, oil changes, and service with a smile that meant fill ups and window washes. Marie was there to inquire about a job. The owner took one look at this slight, almost twelve year old girl, and laughed. But, she didn't give up. "You're laughing, but I can do things that you and the rest of your guys don't want to do. It would free you up for the more important things like repairs, oil changes and fill ups, which are the things that really make you money."

"So, let's say I give you the time of day, to tell me how you can help me; what can you do that would save us so much time?"

"Well, as we were walking by I noticed you had two men out in front of the pumps spraying the area down from gas spills. I could come every afternoon and clean the bathrooms, your office, and spray the pump area down. Those are all jobs that I'm sure you wouldn't mind giving up. I also noticed you struggling a bit with your books when I walked in. I'm pretty good at math, and I think I could make short work of those books for you."

"You're that good at math? These are business matters, for adults."

"Yes Sir, I am that good at math, and I'm very well aware that this is a grown up business. I'm sure I can handle it just fine."

"So, how much are we talking? I'm guessing you'd want to be paid."

"Well, of course I would. I think ten dollars a day would be fair. It would only take me a couple of hours a day to do the bathrooms and your office, along with spraying down the pump areas and emptying the trash bins by the pumps. I could do the books on Saturday, which would be an additional hour, so I think fifteen dollars on Saturdays would square us."

"So, minimum wage is a buck twenty five, and you want me to pay you five bucks an hour?"

"Yes, and it can't be reported either, because I'm underage."

"What makes you think you're worth four times the minimum wage?"

"I think I'm worth whatever I ask, because I'm willing to do the things none of you can, or want to do, and I can free you up to do things that will make you a lot more money in the long run. Face it Sir, none of the guys likes cleaning the bathrooms, so they don't get cleaned correctly, am I right? You're tired of your office looking like a tornado hit it. You have to fight the guys to spray down the pump areas and empty the trash; and I watched the look on your face when you were trying to figure out your books. I think I'm worth every bit of five dollars an hour, or maybe more. Why don't you check with the guys to see if they would each be willing to pitch in a buck or two a week, so they wouldn't have to do the chores they hate. I'll bet you pay them a percentage of the repairs they do also, so they'd make more money too, and they wouldn't have to scrub toilets. I'll bet if you verify with them, they'd be willing to pitch in. Go ahead and ask them. I'll wait."

The owner left the office and talked to the guys, who were whole heartedly in favor of hiring help to do the least savory chores.

"It looks like you were right. They are all on board. They

had one request. None of us likes dressing up as the Esso tiger on Saturdays and passing out lollypops to the kids. The costume would be big on you, but we could probably make it fit somehow. If you would be willing to do that for an hour on Saturdays we would give you an extra five dollars."

"Okay, but I have a request too. I have my three younger siblings that I'm in charge of. I need to bring them with me. They're good kids, and I can have them sit on the floor in your office doing their homework, and coloring while I'm working. If we can agree on that, then we have a deal."

"I'll agree to that if you can promise me you can control them. If they mess up, or get into anything, then I can't have them around, is that understood?"

"Yes Sir! If you'd like I can start today. I could really use the money."

" I don't usually pay my guys till Friday."

"Well, I've got to feed my brother and sisters, so may I have one day's advance on my pay? Then I'll make it last till Friday. If that's okay with you."

"Yeah, I can probably make that work. But, hey, I have a question. Where are your parents kid?"

"Marie is my name. My dad is in Vietnam, and I never know where my mom is. That's why I take care of the children."

"Then sure, you can start today. Sorry your dad is gone. I hope he'll be okay. And sorry about your mom."

"Yeah, me too, but I'm used to it I guess."

Marie sat her brother and sisters on the floor in the office doing their homework, and admonished them to be quiet and not to move a muscle until she came back for them; warning them that if they caused trouble she would lose her job and they wouldn't eat. She was shown the cleaning supplies and got to work. The bathrooms were a definite challenge, and had never been so clean and shiny as they were when she was done. The office and windows fairly gleamed from her ministrations. When she finished spraying down the pump areas and emptying the waste bins, she was tired, but a ten dollar bill in her hand made it worth it. Now she could pick up a couple of food items and the kids wouldn't go hungry.

It was a long walk to the small grocery store from the service station, but when she arrived she noticed an old, beat up wagon on the side of the building. She approached the lady who treated her so badly on her previous visit and got her attention. "Hi there, I came in to pick up some supplies, but I noticed an old wagon on the side of your store, is it for sale?"

"Well, everything is for sale for a price."

"How much would you take for it?"

"How about five dollars?"

"Oh, I haven't got that much if I'm going to feed the kids. What about two dollars?"

"I can go as low as four dollars."

"I can't go any higher than three, so I guess I'll have to look somewhere else."

"Fine missy, you can have it for three. Now, what supplies do you need?"

"Marie."

"What?"

"My name is Marie."

"Fine, Marie. What can I get for you?"

The trip home was a breeze, now that the two little ones could ride, and she didn't have to carry groceries. It was one of the best purchases of her life so far."

Her routine fell into a pattern. School, work, supper, homework, baths and sleep. Marie did laundry after she put the little ones to bed, and usually somewhere around midnight she fell into a fitful sleep, filled with images of Pops, her Daddy, and another man in the distance that she didn't recognize, but who seemed to beckon her to come to him. Upon waking she felt puzzled at her dreams, but tucked them away in the corners of her mind.

She didn't know if her older sister was going to school, it was hard to keep track of her, though she'd come home occasionally to eat, shower and change clothes if nothing else. It was clear she wasn't showering anywhere else, by the smell of her filthy clothing. Marie was sure there were drugs and alcohol involved, but what was she to do. After all, she saw her mother about as much as she saw her sister, and when her mother dropped by the trailer, she smelled every bit as horrid as her daughter.

Marie didn't ask her mother for money. She didn't need her now that she had a job. The strange thing was that her mom never asked how she was buying groceries and household items. She just spent the money deposited from Daddy's pay, and didn't think about anyone else's needs. Marie was grateful that at least the rent, water and electric was paid, so she didn't want to push her luck asking for too much else.

The morning's recon mission would be an especially

dangerous, but equally important, one. Intel told them that the village they had on their radar was filled with Cong sympathizers. They'd actually gotten word through local communications channels that one family in the hamlet was loyal to the South, and they were worried for their lives if the NVA found they'd leaked information. Their mission today would be to root out the insurgent Cong, search for weapons, and get the South Vietnamese loyalists to safety. There would be a lot going on, and the sergeant was concerned that he couldn't be everywhere at once. He'd already decided he would keep his friend Miller close. After they had the village tied up, and the loyalists safely away from danger, he would call in air support and wipe the place off the face of the earth, without any guilt whatsoever. He was getting tired of the North's never ending bullying of those in the South. He wanted the damn war to be over. He just wanted to go home to his family and be done with this place.

As squad leader he had complete autonomy, and therefore complete responsibility, on their daily search and destroy missions. The troops exited their ride about a mile from the village and were making their way to the hamlet when all hell broke loose. Cong snipers had dug themselves into spider holes all around the perimeter of the village, and the only thing between them and the sergeant's men was elephant grass. His soldiers were dropping like flies. "Miller, with me." He shouted to his friend, thinking if they stayed together he could keep his friend safe. Just as Miller gained his side, a sniper's bullet ripped through his helmet. The look of complete surprise on his face, as his head disintegrated before the sergeant's eyes, would haunt his friend's sleeping, and waking hours, for the rest of his life. He would just never be the same. He leapt from his semi protected position and walked toward the hidden snipers as if invincible. And perhaps, at least for that moment, he was. For no matter how many bullets whizzed around and past him, from the constant rat a tat of dozens of AK 47s, the enemy could not seem to penetrate the field of rage that surrounded him. Those that remained of his men followed in his wake, as he took out sniper after sniper, gaining ground on the Cong entrenched village.

Once on the outskirts of the village he took his fury from hut to hut indiscriminately killing any and all who were before him. Two of his men found the loyalists and rushed them to safety, as the rest of the squad, in a spree born from pure hatred, murdered every last man, woman and child in the hamlet. Once they were done, the sergeant, breathing heavily, shaking and drenched in sweat, looked around and realized the indiscriminant slaughter surrounding them. He called for an airstrike, as much to cover the carnage, as to be sure they hadn't left any living Viet Cong behind, and walked away devoid of any feelings at all on the matter.

As they vacated the area he gathered his friend; his men rounding up the other dead and wounded; and slung the limp body over his shoulder. Running toward the arriving Huey, with blood from Miller's lifeless form soaking through to the skin on his back, he repeated over and over in his mind, "Leave no man behind". A call to Air Command for 1st Cavalry sent F-4s screaming to their location, and before their transport was out of sight, the whole village and all surrounding fields were a roaring inferno. That night they drank to Miller and the others who'd given their lives, and the sergeant didn't remember how he made it to his bunk.

Marie made a very loose and lumpy tiger, with various alterations done so she wouldn't trip on the costume, but she really enjoyed that hour on Saturdays. If truth be told, she would probably do it for free if she didn't have the kids to think about. Passing out lollypops and hugs to children, and seeing the smiles of grateful parents, without having to show anyone who she really was, turned out to be a very rewarding way to spend time.

The guys at the station loved Marie. Their jobs were much easier with her, kid or no kid, in their lives. The boss was amazed. A job he'd given, in part, to a poor kid who seemed down and out; truthfully, to help her out because he felt bad for her more than anything else; turned out to be one of the best business decisions he'd made in his working career. The bathrooms were so clean you could practically eat off the floors. The office was spotless. The pumps were clean and trash was emptied fastidiously.

There were also no more problems with the accounting books, Marie even made out the guy's paychecks, and took care of accounts payable and receivable, getting all checks ready for the boss's signature. And, everything in the place was organized. She was well worth every penny they paid her, and more if she ever decided she wanted a raise. The younger kids did as they were told, and she seemed to have everything under control.

No one knew how tired she was. There were moments when she couldn't remember where she was, or what she was supposed to be doing next, and that worried her because she was responsible for her family. But, at least until her daddy came home, she didn't know what else to do. And, the kids were safe. That was all that really mattered.

She finally had enough money for some used beds she'd had her eye on at the antique furniture place down the road. The owner would even deliver the items in his truck, which was a huge help. They weren't anything fancy, and she would definitely be scrubbing the mattresses before she covered them with sheets and let anyone lay on them, but it was a start. She'd been picking up some household items one by one, and they now had some cook ware, dishes and several utensils. She was making good use of the local Salvation Army store, so nothing she purchased matched, but it would all serve its designated purpose. She'd even put a down payment on a used vacuum cleaner that would soon be hers. She'd grown very tired of the way Frank looked at her, and his lingering touch on her hand, when she picked up and returned his vacuum. It would be fine with her if she never had to deal with him again.

Anti war protests were being held in New York, Washington, Chicago, Philadelphia, Boston, and San Francisco. It was no longer safe for Marie to tell people that her dad was in Vietnam. A pack of teenage boys at school had even cornered her in the hallway one day and beat her badly, punching her and kicking her over and over, screaming at her the whole time, "Your dad is a baby killer!" She wasn't sure what they meant, but the idea anyone could hate her dad so much, without even knowing what a kind, wonderful man he was, broke her heart.

Her teachers wanted her to tell who the culprits were, but she wouldn't give them up. She'd seen what kind of repercussions a snitch could expect.

When she showed up at work that day with a black eye, and covered in bruises, the guys from the station wanted to head off to the school and mop the floor with the whole bunch of them. It took her a half hour to calm the men down, and talk them out of their revenge rampage. "It's okay guys. I'm alive. I don't think they damaged anything necessary. Besides, the police wouldn't think a bunch of grown men beating up teenagers is such a good idea. I don't want to get any of you in trouble."

"Marie, you shouldn't have to deal with that kind of bullying," they told her.

"It's fine. I'm used to it, and I think they got it out of their systems."

One of the men gave her a pocket knife that she refused at first, but then, decided might come in handy. She would tuck it in her jacket in case it was needed later.

Fridays were slowly becoming her favorite day of the week, even though it meant not seeing her teachers for two whole days, and having to put up with possible face time with her mom. After all, a whole week's pay meant groceries, paid bills, another chance to pick up a few things they desperately needed for the trailer, and even the possibility of indulging the children to some small treat. At the Salvation Army store she found a couple more kitchen items she'd been wanting, and some small colorful baskets that would fit in perfectly with the surprise she'd already planned for her brother and sisters. And, while the kids were looking longingly through the toy section of the store, she had the sales clerk quickly bag them, so as not to give away the secret.

She'd talked to the owner of the grocery; who, by the way, was much more respectful to her these days; about purchasing chocolate bunnies and a few other candies. The candies would be wrapped up when she arrived to shop today, so the kids wouldn't have a clue, and the package would be inserted in with her regular grocery order. Marie was sure the store's owners were grateful for the regular business she brought them week after week in recent months; since most of their former customers had succumbed to the lure of variety and selection, and started driving to bigger stores in the area. With their new clientele purchasing only one or two items per visit, and some constantly bothering her for credit, they'd grown to appreciate this little girl who shopped so carefully and always paid cash.

She was excited to do something special at Easter for the kids this year, as most religious holidays were usually, widely ignored in their household. She had to admit, at least from what she'd observed in general, this particular holiday confused her. At school she heard students and teachers alike talking about their new Easter outfits, and the special services planned by their churches for the holiday. They seemed excited about the day, and what it represented.

Some referred to 'Good Friday' services at their churches, though all she really knew about that was they got the day off from school, plus the whole next week as well. She heard some say that 'Good Friday' was the day their Jesus died, so she wasn't sure why it would be considered 'good'. After all, didn't their religion revolve around this Jesus character? Well, she couldn't make much sense of it, and maybe never would. Especially odd was the way the guys at the service station made a big deal on Saturday. She showed up to work with the kids in tow and when she took them into the office, her boss handed her an envelope, and each of the kids a brand new coloring book and box of crayons, exclaiming, "Happy Easter everyone!"

"The children were excited for their gifts, and each gratefully answered, "Thank you, Sir." When Marie opened her envelope, a puzzled look covered her face and she looked up. "I don't understand, Sir. You paid me yesterday. Why would you be giving me twenty dollars?"

"Call it an Easter gift, or a bonus, Marie. Having you and the kids here has been great. I've never met a harder worker, and the guys and I just wanted you to know how much we appreciate you. God bless you."

Holding back tears that threatened to spill from her

eyes at any moment, she muttered, "Thank you, Sir. You have all been so kind, and I couldn't ask for a better boss, or a better place to work." A piece of her wanted to know more about this God her boss spoke of, but another part of her was afraid to expose her sensitive underbelly to one more thing that might, figuratively, rip her guts out. She was tired of being hurt by those who were supposed to care and protect.

At that, she collected her cleaning supplies and went to work. And though she always did her best work, no matter what, that day she did it with a sense of gratitude that had not been so strong in the weeks before. Being appreciated wasn't something she was used to, and she discovered she really liked the feeling of satisfaction it gave her. After her cleaning chores she donned her tiger costume, and though the weather had been turning a little warmer as of late, and the suit was a bit hot and uncomfortable, she passed out lollypops with all the vigor she could muster.

Though Mom and her older sister didn't bother to show up, the little ones woke to Easter baskets filled with candy treats. The littlest one began to cry, and when Marie asked why, she said, "I always knew there was an Easter Bunny, but I guess he just didn't remember where we lived before."

Marie made spam and mashed potatoes for lunch, and the children spent hours coloring in their new coloring books.

New intelligence showed growing concern for attacks on Tan Son Nhut Air Base. The sergeant's unit, and several others, were transferred in to shore up defenses.

White House orders include the use of B-52 bombers against the North, for the first time since the beginning of the war. Each bomber can carry up to one hundred bombs, and when dropped from six miles high, they begin to make a dent in the number of power facilities, war support facilities, transportation lines, military complexes, fuel storage complexes and air defense installations the enemy has at its disposal.

The very next day sirens erupt and troops scramble into defensive positions as Tan Son Nhut Air Base is attacked by Viet Cong. The sergeant, new to the base, is terrified, but controls his emotions and rallies his men. One hundred and forty American troops are killed on base that day. Five of them are from the sergeant's unit. His rage against the enemy is almost beyond his control as he hears about the loss of life. They've also lost twelve choppers and nine other aircraft. That night the base observes black out conditions, so the men get together and drink in the dark.

New intelligence reports suggest that the Viet Cong are infiltrating the South at a rate of forty-five hundred per month. The sergeant and his men are chilled to the bone at the revelation. He wonders, "Will this madness ever end? I just want to go home."

With enough money, finally, to make the very last payment on her own used vacuum, Marie waited until the children were sitting at the dinette table with their coloring books, and then left the trailer to return Frank's cleaner for the last time. It's so heavy that she was forced to half carry and half drag the darned thing to the service station yet again, relieved that this would be the end of that annoying scenario. As she walked in through the front door of the station, she was once again assailed by clouds of cigarette smoke emanating from the corner where Frank sat. "Hi there, Frank. I am proud to announce that this will be the last time I have to borrow your vacuum!"

"Oh, is that so, Missy? You've decided vacuuming ain't your thing?"

"No, not at all. I've just saved up enough to buy my own vacuum, so I won't need to use yours anymore."

Rising and moving closer to the girl, Frank's face took on a nasty leer with which Marie was all too familiar, considering events which had transpired in her childhood years. He reached for the vacuum, but grabbed her arm, and rubbed his hand against her breast instead. She tried to twist her arm away, but he pulled her close and rubbed his body against hers. "Let go of me. I mean it! Right now! Let me go you monster!"

"Oh, now I'm a monster? I wasn't a monster when you needed something from me. I'd say you owe me, wouldn't you? I'm just taking my due." He kissed her, hard, and the smell of his breath, the closeness of him, made her gag. She brought her knee up, and connected with his groin in a way that brought him swiftly to his knees. Collapsed on the floor he groaned.

"That's it, you little brat. You and your whole family are outta here. You hear me?"

Backing up, Marie hissed at him, "If you even try to kick us out, I will report you for attacking me today. You can't get rid of us that easy you dirty old man. And if you ever touch me, or anyone in my family, again, I will kill you."

Still holding himself he began to rise, and as his face twisted into a mask of hatred, he snickered evilly. "You think anyone is going to take the word of a poor little gutter rat over a respectable business man?"

"If they don't, I have friends, lots of them, who will come down here and tear you limb from limb. Do you hear me you monster? You may have gotten away with things like this before, but never again, Frank. You are finished, do you hear me?" She turned and ran, stumbling into the fresh air. Would he follow through with his threat to evict them? She couldn't tell if her own threat had caused him to rethink. Perhaps she would tell her boss about the assault when she arrived at work on Monday. Just for a small degree of insurance. She would ask him not to act on it, at least not yet, but it could make the difference between a roof over their heads or not.

When she went to bed, she couldn't sleep, knowing Frank most likely had a key to their trailer. Nightmares, filled with the stench of his breath, and the actions of every other monster she'd encountered in her life, plagued her until morning light. there were moments in her life when she really longed for an adult in her life who could protect her. If only Daddy were home.

The war raged on, and the sergeant's only relief was in the welcome forgetfulness of alcohol. He and the troops he led did their duty by day, and drank away the memories of their missions by night. On occasions where they conducted night maneuvers, tracer bullets made their way to the snipers in their sights. Day melded into night and into day again, and he felt he was slowly loosing what remained of his fractured mind.

Marie couldn't let it go. Her anger over the sexual attack from Frank haunted her. She'd told her boss about the incident, and just as she thought, he and the other guys wanted to beat the crap out of the service station owner. But, she held them off. If he were put in jail, there was no telling what might happen to his disgusting little trailer park. As long as he minded his Ps and Qs from now on, she didn't need to see him dead. Anyway, she really didn't want her friends to get into any trouble for what they might do to him. No, it was better for him to wonder. The fellows did come to talk to her in front of the service station one day.

And, with Frank watching warily out the front window, they talked and looked in his direction. She was sure that would most definitely put a fear in him.

But, as time passed, she found that wasn't enough. She was so furious over the whole incident she just couldn't get over it. Finally, she devised a way to exact some revenge. A way to make him pay, at least a little, for what he had done to her. And, for that matter, what he had probably done to many others before her. In her experience, once a pervert, always a pervert! She waited till the children were fast asleep and snuck out of the trailer.

Dressed in black clothing and gloves she made her way, nervously, to the back of the service station. It was dark. Not even a sliver of moon to light the way. Locating a window, low on the rear wall, she covered it with an old towel and hit the glass with a rock, shattering it quietly. Removing jagged pieces of glass from their frame she crawled inside and located a flashlight. Her first job was to look around and see what she might exact her vengeance upon as a substitute for Frank. She didn't want to destroy anything that might belong to a customer. Those people hadn't done anything to her. The longer she was inside, the more nervous she felt, but her anger kept her motivated.

She finally decided not to do any damage to cars in the service bays, as those were most probably the property of customers. But, as she walked through the back, she picked up a lug wrench from his work bench. Making her way to the front office she took a look around and then proceeded to smash the glass on the display case, throwing candy and chips out of their comfortable little space. Pulling packs and cartons of cigarettes out of the cabinet, she opened them and crushed them into the floor. She drew her knife and cut every single belt hanging on the wall. Opening bottles of 5-30 and 10-30, she poured them all over the office, covering car parts and food items alike. Then she dumped Frank's full ashtray on top of the mess. For good measure she opened a can of spray paint and scribbled "Pervert" across the back wall and then slashed every tire on the far wall. Her fury abated somewhat, she hefted herself up and through the back window, and slunk back home without being seen. She'd left no witnesses, and no evidence, but for the first time in her life she felt a smidgen of justice had been meted out. She wasn't an idiot, she knew what she did was illegal, and even morally wrong somehow, but she didn't care. Tired of being a victim, she vowed that she wasn't going to take it anymore. No one would ever again use or abuse her!

The next day, as she and the children were walking to the bus stop, she saw police cars in front of Frank's station. And, when she showed up for work after school, her boss told her that Frank's had been broken into and vandalized over night. "I know, I saw the police cars this morning."

He looked at her and smiled. She smiled back, but didn't say a thing.

When they got home, Mother was there. "Where have you been?"

"What are you talking about, Mom? We were at school."

"School's been out for hours. Where did you go after school?"

"I was at work."

"Work? What are you talking about?"

"Work, Mom. You know, that thing people do to make money?"

"Who would hire you? You're ten years old. And what do you need money for? I give you money."

"Okay, first of all, I'll be twelve in a couple months. And, the last time you gave me money for food was months ago. Did you think twenty dollars bought groceries for two months? Didn't you notice that when you show up occasionally there is always something to eat? And where did you think the furniture and kitchen supplies were coming from?"

"Listen, don't you sass me brat. I've had a hard week. My boyfriend dumped me."

"Your boyfriend? Have you forgotten that you are married? You mean that while your husband is off fighting for our country, you are cheating on him with a boyfriend? And let me guess. Your boyfriend didn't have any money, so the funds you were supposed to be giving me for groceries went to him. Am I right?" She ducked just in time.

Mother went back to her room and slept for several hours. Marie fed the kids and helped them with homework before baths. After they were tucked in bed, Mom got up and showered. A bit more sober, she noticed that there were clean towels in the bathroom and plenty of shampoo and soap. As she came out of the bathroom, wrapped in a clean towel, someone knocked on the door. Marie looked suspiciously at her mother, "You're not expecting anyone, are you?"

"Who would I be expecting?"

"Oh, I don't know? Your boyfriend maybe?"

"I told you we broke up. Just open the door."

"Are you going to the back, or are you going to stand there naked?"

"Oh for god's sake. Just open the damn door!"

Marie opened the door to see her sister, disheveled and filthy, with a middle aged man. The man was holding her by her upper arm, and when the door opened he pulled out a badge and flashed it. "Is your mom here?"

"Yes Sir." She answered, as her mother, wet hair, dressed only in a towel came forward.

"Hello officer. What can I do for you?" The officer blushed and looked down at his shoes.

"Ma'am, I am Vice officer Lieutenant Owens. Your daughter was found quite out of it, in a known drug house. I checked, and she didn't have any prior arrests on file, so I thought I would give her a break and bring her home." Batting her eyelashes, Mother leaned over to show as much cleavage as possible, and smiled at Lieutenant Owens.

"I appreciate that so very much officer. Get in here girl!"

"If you think you can control her, I will leave her in your hands. I don't like to see kids in trouble, unless there doesn't seem to be any other alternative. If you need anything else, or think I might be able to help, please call the precinct."

"Thank you Lieutenant Owens. I am most grateful. I

can't tell you how much this means to me."

After the door was closed Marie turned to her mother. "Do you think you poured it on thick enough? I can't believe you Mother. You were practically doing a strip tease for the guy."

"Shut up, Marie. He was a nice looking man, and he did us a huge favor. I just wanted to express my gratitude."

"Oh for Pete's sake. Okay, Mom, I'm sure he got a good look at your gratitude." She stepped sideways just in time to miss the slap intended for her left cheek.

Marie saw a copy of the June 4th, 1966 New York Times on her boss's desk. In it was a three page anti war rant signed by sixty four hundred teachers and professors from the state of New York. She stopped to read the article, and noted that some of her own teacher's names were on the list. It was summer, but when school began in the fall, she wasn't sure how she would face those instructors. She thought they liked her, that they were friends. But, every one of those teachers knew her dad was in Vietnam, and the things written in the article made it sound as if our soldiers; the men drafted into service and yanked away from their families, fighting for our country; were nothing but a pack of murderers. How could she ever look any of them in the eye again?

With summer came more freedom. Her mom and sister were gone most of the time, so they had no one to answer to but themselves. Marie worked a few more hours per week, and was able to take the kids, by city bus, to the park and the town's swimming hole. Sometimes she would make up a sack of peanut butter and jelly sandwiches, and they would buy ice cream in the park. But, a couple times she let the kids buy hot dogs from the vendor there. They looked at her as if she were a hero, and if she had to be honest, she didn't mind the feeling. Most of the time she felt so bad about herself. Due to things done to her, and all the terrible things she'd done. Anything to feel a little better about who she was helped for a short while.

She was scrimping and saving to buy school supplies and clothing for herself and the children. She would be twelve, in less than a month, and going into ninth grade. Boy oh boy, ninth grade, a high school freshman. She was already much younger than her peers, and figured it wouldn't hurt to have a couple new outfits. She honestly didn't know if she could pull off cool, but it might be worth a try.

These care free summer days, without school or time consuming homework, were filled with endless hours of liberation. Even with work at the service station, and household chores, she managed to spend time with the kids outdoors. They explored the woods a couple miles from the trailer park and found a beautiful hidden glen complete with a fresh water stream and a dozen varieties of wild flowers; built a small structure under a tree in the farmer's field out back of Frank's, calling it their barn, and adopting a stray cat to feed that they named Gertrude; and made numerous trips down the main road to the antiques store and the Salvation Army shop. Her kitchen was pretty well stocked with all the utensils and cookware she needed, so she'd been working on the rest of the house. An additional chair for the dinette set in the kitchen, two chairs and a coffee table for the living room, dressers for the bedrooms, and a couple of folding chairs for the concrete slab in the front of the trailer. The managers of both places had been great about delivering her items. She now owned a broom and dust pan, along with her used vacuum; a plush cushion for the old wagon, which they hauled everywhere;

and most of the necessities of life.

Marie liked it much better when her mom wasn't at home to berate and belittle her and the children, but something inside her longed for someone, anyone, to care about what happened to them. It was scary when one of the kids got sick, or something broke down. She'd had to call Frank once, to come fix the toilet in the trailer, and she felt terrified the entire time he was in their place. She also felt he knew it was her who'd trashed his place, but he never said a word about the incident. She was pretty sure he knew he'd had it coming, and he was careful to stay away from all the kids while he was in their home. His careful actions, and quiet demeanor caused her a few moments of guilt, but only a few.

Citing increased infiltration of Communist guerrillas from North Vietnam into the South, the U.S. began bombing oil depots around Hanoi and Haiphong, ending a self-imposed moratorium.

The U.S. has been very cautious up to now about targeting the city of Hanoi itself over concerns for the reactions of North Vietnam's military allies, China and the Soviet Union. This concern also prevents any U.S. ground invasion of North Vietnam, despite recommendations by military planners in Washington.

A Cong sniper who successfully made his way to Tan Son Nhut Air Base, by hugging the bottom side of a supply transport vehicle, was poised to do his worst.

Things were more dangerous by the minute, for U.S. troops still in Vietnam. And, as they were battling Cong, the elements, and in some cases their own constantly wavering government; media in America were hanging them out to dry with one scathing article after another; and this, happening several years before 'Hanoi Jane' began her treasonous actions against America and its troops, to turn public opinion even stronger against those brave fighting men. Public opinion in the U.S. about the war had taken a downward turn from practically the beginning, but polls were more sharply negative after American media made account of the over twenty thousand acres of food crops that had been destroyed around Viet Cong sympathetic villages; and then, not long after, 'Hanoi Radio' reported that captured American pilots were being paraded through the streets of Hanoi to jeering crowds.

The sergeant and his squad were set to leave on perimeter guard and recon, when the embedded sniper let loose a volley of bullets that sent all those within earshot running for cover. The attack killed four of his troops, and wounded three others, before the enemy was located and put out of commission.

Seeing those dead soldiers, his dead soldiers, was pure agony. And, of course the sergeant blamed himself for the loss, with so much blood on his hands. No one knew the extent of the sergeant's mental instability, as he seemed to be in proper control at all times, but the loss of four more of his men put him one more declining step closer to a meltdown.

Back in his quarters that night, he cried. He cried for the loss of his men, but he cried for his family too. He knew they must miss him as much as he missed them, even though he still hadn't received any answers from the multiple letters he'd sent. Perhaps the government was having a hard time keeping up with the guys who'd been transferred out of Da Nang. He wanted to go home so badly, but the faces of men under his command who'd given their lives for this worthless, stupid war, and would never see their families again, swam before his eyes. He felt completely responsible for the loss, all of it. How could he go home and enjoy the rest of his own life when those men would never hold their babies, kiss their sweethearts or hug their parents again. All the booze in the world couldn't fix this, but he'd take a shot at it anyway.

Marie was an early riser, she always had been, but on this particular day just two days from her twelfth birthday she awoke even earlier than normal, to a feeling of panic. She rose and checked on the kids. Her brother was missing, and the front door was wide open. She woke the girls. "Hey, hey, wake up. Where is your brother?"

"He's in his bed."

"No he's not, and the front door is wide open."

"I'm not sure, but last night when we were trying to go to sleep, he said he wanted to go get candy from the store. We told him it was bed time and he'd have to wait till morning."

"How did he think he was going to get there?"

"I don't know. We didn't really take him very seriously. Besides, you're usually up before anyone else, so we didn't think about it."

"Okay, I need you to get up. I'm going to have to go

find him. Will you two be okay if I leave you here with cereal and milk?"

"Sure, but don't you want us to come with you?"

"No, you'll only slow me down. I'm going to borrow the neighbor's bike, so I should be able to make good time." At that she ran to the kitchen and got down bowls, spoons, cereal and milk. "Now, you two take care of each other while I'm gone." The little one was crying and her thumb was right back in her mouth. "Oh honey, everything will be alright. I'm just going to be gone a little while. I need you to be a big girl, so I can go get your brother. Can you do that?"

"I'll try."

"Okay, I'll be back as quick as I can." She dashed to the neighboring trailer and asked the boy there if she could use his bike. He went quickly to unlock the chain, and she took off like a flash. Not having experience on bicycles she was a bit wobbly, but she was also making better time than she would have made walking, or even running.

A mile up the back road she found her little brother scared and looking a little lost, but determined to get his candy. "What are you doing? You scared me to death."

"I was going to get candy. The girls said I had to wait

till morning."

"Well, you're too little to be out here on your own. This is too long a walk for you, and what were you going to buy the candy with?"

"I was going to trade them my sheriff badge."

"Honey, they don't want your old sheriff's badge. Now, we're going home."

"But I didn't get my candy."

"I know, and you're not getting any candy today. You will have to be punished for leaving the house without permission, so we aren't going to go anywhere today except work."

"Nowhere? Then the girls are going to be mad at me."

"Yes, they might be. But I need you to learn how important it is for you to always be where I can find you. You're too little to take care of yourself yet."

"I don't want to always be where you can find me. I hate you." Her heart broke. Her little brother had always looked up to her. But, she couldn't have him running off and getting hurt, so she would deal with his stinging words for now.

"Alright, you hate me. Now, get on the back of the bike. We're going home."

Starting back down the road toward home, she noticed the steep grade of the hill was much more noticeable on a bike than it was when walking. The bike began to gain speed and a car came careening around a bend.

"See that you do not despise one of these little ones.

For I tell you that in heaven their angels always see

the face of my Father who is in heaven."

Matthew 18:10-11

CHapter 7

Still no letters. The sergeant was beginning to worry now, on top of everything else he had on his mind, about what was going on with his little family. Many of the other guys had gotten mail from home since arriving at Tan Son Nhut, and his own mail had gone out with theirs. He couldn't imagine what the problem might be, but he hoped his new wife hadn't started drinking again. There'd been some concern before he left. He'd seen her with a few too many drinks in her a couple of times, and watched how she was with the kiddos, especially Marie, so he didn't want anyone hurt. It broke his heart that he couldn't be there to mediate and set things right.

He missed his wife more than he ever imagined possible, flaws and all. After all, he was hardly perfect himself. And, yes, he knew she was older than he, but what did age matter if you really love someone? They'd hit it off right away, when they met at a USO sponsored dance on the air base in California, where he was stationed at the time.

She'd come with a group of her friends and he noticed her immediately, even from clear across the room, tapping her high heeled feet to the music. She was quite the looker, with a quick smile and a personality full of vinegar. She even seemed to get his jokes, which was a rarity in the women he'd met along the way. But, the clincher was those great kids. Something that would have scared most men away was the final figure in the equation for him. He'd always dreamed of being a dad, and this was instant gratification at its best. They seemed to really love him too, especially Marie. They'd developed a fast friendship and shared many interests. So, it was especially hard to believe that even she hadn't answered any of his letters yet.

Noticing his hands shaking quite a bit lately, he wondered if it was the stress of battle and all the drinking he'd been doing. He began spending more time drinking in his quarters and less time drinking with the guys because of it.

This took him back to a time when he was young. After his father was badly hurt at the railroad yard and couldn't work anymore. Back when Pops began acting strange and his parents were fighting all the time. It made him uncomfortable to think about those days. Mom had kicked Dad out of their bedroom and sent him to the cubby hole under the staircase like a bad dog being punished for piddling on the floor. For a long time his dad kept to himself, ignoring his son. But, after his hands began to shake uncontrollably, and the sounds of crying in the night grew more frequent, coming from his tiny room under the stairs, he made some drastic changes and slowly got better.

When the sergeant was a young man, he'd wondered considerably about that period in his family's past, and guessed alcohol might have had a great deal to do with those tumultuous years. Eventually, after Pops had done much healing, he developed a good relationship with his son and they spent some great years as buddies. Often fishing together, or spending hours talking about everything under the sun, tucked away under the stairs in the cubby hole; they even cooked and baked bread together. But, it seemed as if his mother grew more distant from him as he grew closer to his dad. Sometimes, as they sat together around the supper table, you could almost cut the tension with a knife.

When he graduated from high school, he signed up for military service right away, and left for basic training only a week later. It was good to be away from the stress of his parent's problems and anger, but he'd felt bad leaving his dad home alone with his mom. Who knew what might be left of him as she spent hours a day cutting him to the ground with her vitriol.

He knew the booze probably wasn't good for him either, especially after seeing what it did to his dad and his family, but he also knew he had it under control for now, and since it was really the only thing keeping him sane some days, he'd take care of it after he got out of this hell hole.

Faster and faster she flew down the winding road, unable to control her speed. Attempting to slow the bike she tapped on the brakes and realized there weren't any. Horror filled her mind. Her brother was hanging on tight, crying, and she didn't have a clue as to how she would stop the hurtling metal. So, she focused instead on staying to the edge of the pavement, knowing that to venture onto the gravel at this speed would be disastrous, yet to get to far out onto the road might be worse. The car rounding the corner, at a high rate of speed, didn't see her until it was too late. It veered too far over to the edge of the road and hit her back bumper, hard, before swerving madly in the other direction. Sending her flying over the handle bars, over the railing, and down two hundred feet of river embankment.

She vaguely remembered hearing her brother scream somewhere in the distance, before hitting the packed dirt and rock surface, plus every root and stunted tree on the way down. Laying at the water's edge, small waves lapping at her now shoeless foot, she tried to open her eyes. When that didn't work she attempted to lift her arm to check her face, and discovered that wasn't working either. A tear worked its way out through one of her swollen eyelids and down her face, salt stinging open wounds as it made a path through blood and embedded gravel. Trying to move her legs, she discovered she no longer had control of those and tried to sit, also futile. Where was her brother? She attempted to cry out his name, but the gurgling sound emanating from her mouth didn't sound even remotely human.

Suddenly her brother was beside her, crawling in the sand and gravel. He touched her face and she could hear him crying. "Marie? Marie? Are you okay, Marie? I don't know what to do. I'm scared."

Marie had no idea how far she'd flown, or fallen. She only knew she needed help. Mustering every ounce of strength in her body, she croaked, "Honey, get help." She wasn't aware that her very small brother had made his way down the two hundred foot drop by holding on to bits of scrub brush, stunted trees and protruding rocks. He would now make his path back up the same way. Once he arrived up top he stood on the side of the winding road, scared, crying, confused and trying to figure out a way to help his sister. She was everything to him, a mom, a friend, and the only one who cared enough to take care of him. And, he recalled, the last thing he'd said to her was, "I hate you."

Scanning the road in every direction he suddenly had a nudging that caused him to look up. On the other side of the road, where the mountain continued to rise; Almost hidden in a large cranny in the rock, and surrounded by fir trees, was a small cottage. It didn't look like there was an access road on this side of the cliff, so there must be a way up on the other side of the mountain. But, he didn't have time to investigate, so he proceeded to access the house the same way he'd gotten down and up from the river's edge. He began to climb by holding on to any piece of protruding vegetation he could get his hands on. It took him a full ten or fifteen minutes to reach the homestead. Once there he ran to the door and knocked. An elderly woman of about eighty or eighty five answered the door, and his heart sank. He was young, but he wasn't stupid (well, he had sisters who might disagree). How would this old woman be able to help?

His story came tumbling out in a torrent of sobs and tears. The old woman held him and said, "It's okay my dear. We will help your sister. Stand right here while I call the police and an ambulance." So he did. She made her phone calls and grabbed her sweater as they went through the door together. It turned out that the road leading to her house was very close to where he had climbed the rocky cliff, so they used that instead. Across the road they looked over the railing and down the embankment to where Marie lay. "Alright my dear. I'm going to have to make my way down to where your sister is, but I want you to stand right here. Stay in the gravel, away from the road, right here next to the railing, do you hear me?"

"Yes." He sobbed.

"Listen, little man. I know you're frightened, but someone has to stay here and wait for the police and the ambulance. Can you do that?"

"Yes, I can do that. I just want her to be okay. I told her I hated her when she came to get me. I shouldn't have left the house, but I did, and now she's hurt and it's all my fault."

"No, no, no my love. None of this is your fault. The fault is with a bicycle that had no breaks, and a car that came flying around the bend and then took off. I will take care of your sister. I don't want you to worry, okay?"

"Okay. But how are you going to get down there? You're old and it's a long way."

"I may be old, but God will see me safely to where I'm going. My name is Angela, little man, and I want you to know that God loves you. Everything is going to be fine. The Father has many things left for your sister to do, and great plans for you too." At that, the woman swung one leg over the railing, followed by the other, and proceeded down the embankment foot by foot until she reached the bottom.

Once she arrived at her destination she brushed the hair from Marie's face, and covered the girl with her sweater. "Marie, Marie, I'm here to help you."

At the sound of the woman's voice the girl moaned, "Who are you?"

"I am a friend. Your brother found me and I'm here to help until the ambulance comes. I want you to know that God loves you very much and thinks you are very brave." From that moment forward, each and every time Marie felt as if she might begin to cry, the woman's words claiming that she was very brave stopped her.

"What's your name?"

"My name is Angela, and God has sent me to see that you are safe and cared for. Don't worry my child. The police and ambulance will be here very soon."

Struggling to make sense of the conversation, and also to convey her fears to the lady, she gasped, "I don't know where my mother is. I can't go to the hospital. Who will take care of the children?"

"Now, I told you not to worry. Everything will be fine. The police are stopping by to pick up your mother and the other children before they arrive here."

"But, how."

"Now, I told you not to worry. You will be safe and your mother will be there to care for the children until you are healed. Believe me child, God has many plans for you now and in the future. Know that He loves you and will take care of you. You can trust that."

Marie didn't know what to make of Angela's claims. She'd never really seen evidence of a loving God in her life, and certainly not in this situation, but the woman sounded so sure. "Just please, don't leave me."

"I won't leave you child. And God will never leave you or forsake you either."

They could hear the sirens as emergency vehicles approached the site of the accident. Pretty soon an ambulance attendant was by her side, then another, and within minutes they had slid a board under her, put a strap and foam cushion around her head to hold it steady and lifted her into a basket, which had been carefully lowered down the side of the embankment. She was strapped in tightly and then raised a few inches at a time to the top.

She saw her mother, clearly staggering drunk, but with a look of concern on her face. "Is she going to be alright? Why is she shaking like that? Why do you have all those straps on her head? Where are you taking her?"

"Ma'am, the shaking is most likely due to shock. The straps are to keep her neck stationary, until we know if there is damage to the spine; and we will be taking her to West Point. The military hospital is located there and they have the best E.R. in the state. The police will follow us there, and I'm sure they will let you ride along. Is there anyone you need to call?

"No, my husband is in Vietnam. The kids and I are all alone here. I don't drive either. How will we get home?"

"I'm sure the officers can arrange something for you."

"Mom? I didn't know you were home."

"I wasn't Marie. The officers came right to where I was, like they knew where to find me, and then they drove right to the trailer to get the kids."

Riding over the winding road, even in an ambulance, was painful. And, before they were down the mountain Marie had passed out. In her pain filled nightmare she saw a light and longed to head toward the inviting warmth of it, but something held her back. Angela's words, "God has many plans for you now and in the future", echoed in her mind.

Arriving at the hospital in a blaze of flashing lights and sirens, emergency room doctors and nurses met the ambulance outside the doors and began work immediately. Marie wondered where Angela was. And, now that her eyes were able to open to narrow slits, she looked around the E.R. as far as possible without moving her head, searching for her new friend. X-rays showed two hairline fractures in her neck; an arm broken in two places and a leg with two broken bones; as well as three cracked ribs, a cracked collar bone and a fractured pelvis. Her other wrist was sprained, as well as her other ankle, and they hurt worse than the broken ones. There was a plethora of gravel imbedded into the skin of her face, arms and hands; and it appeared the impact had lifted her completely out of her shoes, as they were nowhere to be found. She was heavily sedated and when she awoke some time later she was sporting a halo vest to stabilize her neck for the time being, and plaster casts which covered two of her limbs from A to Z. Breathing hurt, due to her cracked ribs, but the dressing wrapped tightly around her chest helped. Sitting with a fractured pelvis would be impossible for now, so she would be imprisoned here, in these sterile confines, for quite some time.

The children weren't allowed in ICU, but her mother made an appearance after the anesthesia wore off. "Well, it looks like you'll live. I hope you know that I won't be able to come up here all the time since there isn't anyone to watch the kids."

"I know Mother. That's usually me, remember?"

"I also want you to know that I'm stuck at the trailer until you get out of here, so you need to make that as soon as possible."

"Yes Mother, I'll try to take care of that right away. Do

me a favor, okay?"

"What?"

"Please don't take all this out on the kids. It's not their fault and I'm sure they're scared to death as it is."

"What kind of a mother do you think I am?"

"We won't go there for now, Mom. But, please make sure you remember to feed them three times a day, and see that they get baths every night. There's a full coffee can of quarters on the far kitchen counter, and the laundry soap is under the sink with the cleaning supplies. You do have to go to the mail building to do laundry, but during the day there aren't many people using the machines, so you've got the place pretty much to yourself. The vacuum is in the hall closet with the broom and dustpan, and I just went grocery shopping, so there should be plenty of food for the week. I'm sorry I'm in here, and I will do my best to get out as quickly as possible."

"Fine, but I don't know why you're telling me where the cleaning stuff is, because I don't plan on spending all my time cleaning."

"That's great Mother. I'm sure it will be easy as pie for me to get all caught up once I get home with casts and compression wraps on all my arms and legs. But, don't worry about it. I'll take care of it all, the same as I always do."

"Okay. That works for me. Someone will have to call me when they are ready to send you home, so I can make arrangements."

"I'll make sure they call."

The nurse, who'd been in the hall listening to the whole exchange between Marie and her mom, entered as her mother was leaving. Forcing herself not to glare at the woman as she passed, she was trying very hard not to follow her down the hallway to give her a piece of her mind. But, she'd be sure to anger her superiors if she did that, so she chose to mind her own business.

Marie was in a significant amount of pain, but didn't like the way the heavy medications and pain killers made her feel, so she told the nurse she was comfortable and chose to live with the consequences. "You are a very brave young lady. And, from the sounds of it, very responsible too."

"People keep telling me that today. I just do what I have to. That's why I'm in here I guess. Can you tell me, have you seen an elderly woman around? Her name is Angela, and she would be asking for me."

"No, I can't say as I have, but I can ask around for you to see if anyone else has."

"Thank you. I'd appreciate that very much. She was there by the river after the accident, and I'd like to thank her for staying with me."

"I'll see what I can do. I filled your ice water. Would you like a drink?"

"That would be great. It's kind of hard for me to reach for anything."

"Well, I'm going to put your call button right here in your hand. If you need anything, even a drink of water, please don't hesitate to call and we will be right in."

'Thanks. You're great. And thanks for being patient with me.

Out in the hall the nurse had to stop, close her eyes, and clench her fists to gain her composure before going on to the next room. She wiped an angry tear away with the back of her hand. Hearing that mother talk to her own daughter that way had her blood boiling and she didn't want to take that anger on to the next patient. She had a daughter of her own. Little Faith was only three years old, but she couldn't imagine ever treating her like that. This made her want to look out for this eleven year old slip of a thing even more. She would take care of her as if she were her own daughter. Didn't every child deserve that?

When Marie didn't arrive for work, the guys at the station knew something must be wrong, so the boss showed up at the trailer to ask about her. "Hi Ma'am, I'm the owner of the Esso station where your daughter does some work for us. She didn't come in to work today, and I wanted to know if she's alright. It isn't like her to miss a day."

"So, you're the idiot who hired an eleven year old girl? I thought she was crazy when she told me, but now I can see you are even crazier than she is. So, how's that working out for you?"

So, this was Marie's mother. He hadn't liked her even before he met her, due to the red marks frequently seen on the young girl's face, but now he saw what a prize she actually was. "Actually, Ma'am, Marie is probably my best employee. I'm sure you know that she is a very hard worker, very smart, and the most loyal and dedicated young person I've ever met. If I had any answer for you, other than that, I probably wouldn't be here checking to see if she was okay. Is she here? I'd like to talk to her?"

"No, actually she isn't here. She's at West Point Hospital."

"At the hospital? What happened?"

"She was out looking for her brother this morning, after he ran off, and she was hit by a car. Ended up thrown over the river embankment, and laying down by the river's edge."

"Oh my gosh. How badly is she hurt?"

"Bad enough I'd say. She's got a neck thing on and casts on her arms and legs. I don't know when they'll be letting her come home, and I'm stuck here with these damn brats until they do. So, if you think you have it bad, walk a mile in my shoes."

"I'm sorry Ma'am, but aren't these all your kids?"

"That isn't the point. Oh never mind. You wouldn't understand."

"If you'll excuse me Ma'am, I'm going to call my wife and run out to the hospital to see your daughter. She must be scared to death."

He walked away from the trailer shaking his head and wondering how Marie put up with her situation as well as she did. He was committed now to doing whatever he could to help Marie and her brother and sisters. How could that woman be so cold and uncaring? He couldn't imagine himself or his wife treating their children that way. Some people shouldn't be allowed to have kids.

At the hospital Marie was tolerating the pain with effort. Still wondering where Angela might be, she knew she wouldn't really have any visitors to break up her day, so she went over math equations in her head, in an effort to distract herself from the obvious. Her nurses came in to check her vitals and give her drinks of water, but other than that, she was on her own. Lying in this hospital bed might just do what her mother, as yet, had never successfully accomplished. To drive her absolutely stark raving mad.

She was worried about the kids. Were they being fed? Would they be traumatized by all of this? She knew for sure that her brother was terribly upset, and she could imagine the littlest one with her thumb in her mouth. Mother hated that and was likely to do something extreme to stop the habit. Just then, she looked over and saw Angela. "Hey Marie, do you feel like company?"

"Boy do I ever. I kept asking everyone if they'd seen you. I wanted to thank you for staying with me by the river. Where did you go?"

"I thought it best to let the doctors and nurses do their work before I stuck my big nose in where it didn't belong. Is there anything I can get you?"

"I'd love a sip of water if I could?"

"Sure." Angela grabbed the ice water mug and sat in the chair nearest to her friend, in order to allow her to drink. "Are you in much pain?"

"It hurts, but nothing I can't handle. I've kind of gotten used to a certain amount of pain in my life."

"I'll bet you have. I'm sorry that life hasn't always dealt you an easy hand, but you are learning more about yourself with each new trial along the way."

"Well, if you don't mind, I'd rather learn the old fashioned way, if you know what I mean."

"Agreed. I hope you know that God loves you, Marie."

"Actually, you keep telling me, but that is a hard one for me. I have lots of questions, and I feel very angry about many of the things that have happened in my life. If He loves me so much, why does there have to be so much pain and unhappiness?"

"I hear that question often. I guess the short answer would be, how could you ever know what great joy was, unless you had first suffered great unhappiness? I know it can be hard, Marie, but know that He truly does love you, and He is with you always." Suddenly, it was as if all the air had been sucked from the room and, dizzy to her core, she took in a huge breath of air. Noticing that Angela was gone, she looked around frantically for her friend.

"Marie?"

"What? Oh, hi boss.?"

"My gosh, Marie, what happened?"

"I had a bit of a run in with a car on the back road up the mountain. I'm sorry I didn't make it in to work. I had no way to call you."

"No, for heaven's sake, don't worry about that. When I told my wife what happened to you, she told me to spend as much time as I needed to make sure you're alright."

"That was nice of her, but I don't want to keep you from your family. I'm getting pretty tired. And, listen, I don't have any idea when I'll be able to get back to work, so I wouldn't blame you if you need to hire someone else."

"No one could replace you, Marie. The guys and I will go back to taking care of the bathrooms and pumps until you're better. Though, I can't promise anything about the books, you know what a mess they were before you took over, so you'll probably have a mess to clean up when you get back. I brought you some flowers. They're from all of us. Where do you want me to put them?"

"Just put them on the table please. Thank you. That

was very nice of you. And, I look forward to the mess, if it means I get to be out of here and out of all these casts and wraps."

"Good, because I'm sure you'll have all the mess you can handle. I have to ask you. Were you adopted?"

"No, why?"

"I met your mother."

"Oh, sorry for that. I wondered how you found out I was here."

"Yep, I made it over to your trailer home, and there she was. You're just so different, I had to ask."

"Well, thank you for that. It was one of the best compliments you could give me. I'm just glad she was there and hadn't left the kids alone. I've been worried sick about that."

"No, she was there, but already complaining about being stuck at home with them, so I'm not sure how long she'll last."

"I know, that's what scares me. I need to get out of here as quick as I can."

"No, you need to heal and get better, or you won't be any good to those children or yourself and we can't have that."

"Did you see an elderly lady around anywhere when you came in?"

"No, just you. But, it did sound like you were talking to someone when I came down the hall. Why, are you missing someone?"

"My friend Angela was in here right before you arrived, and then she was gone. She stayed with me by the river until the ambulance came."

"If I see her when I leave, I'll tell her you were looking for her. I'm going to let you get some rest now. I'll tell the guys you said hi, and know that my family and I are all praying for you."

"Thank you. So, you are a Christian?"

"Yes, I am. My wife and I had been praying for your situation, even before I met your mom. I'm sure we'll be praying even more, now that I've met her."

"Thank you. Maybe we could talk sometime?"

"Any time, Marie. I'll come see you again."

"Oh, you don't have to. I don't want to inconvenience you."

"Don't be ridiculous young lady. I'll say something to the guys, and I'm sure you'll get more visitors too. Just do like the doctors tell you, and you'll be right as rain in no time."

Attacks against the base had doubled. The sergeant was overwhelmed with repairs to aircraft radios and communications equipment, but at least it was keeping him, and his men, out of the field. A much appreciated respite. The U.S. had intensified bombing along the Ho Chi Minh Trail winding through Laos; and Marines and South Vietnamese troops launched Operation Hastings against more than ten thousand NVA in the Quang Tri Province. This was the largest combined military operation in the war so far. Only days later the U.S. bombed NVA troops in the Demilitarized Zone. He can't get the sounds of gun shots and exploding bombs out of his head. The only thing that quiets the noise, even a little, is the alcohol. Still no letters from home, and every time mail call is announced he is disappointed again. His heart is broken. And, a broken heart is not a good thing for a soldier's morale. His guys are really beginning to worry about him. The fact that they didn't become more worried, earlier, speaks to his enormous degree of self control.

"I don't know how your sister puts up with you brats! You're driving me nuts. Why I ever thought it would be a good idea to give birth to any of you is beyond me. And, if I had it to do all over again, I'd never go through with it!" The children stood before her in a line, shaking and terrified. Their mother had gotten meaner by the day, and was punishing them by whippings and missed meals for infractions such as; taking too long in the bath; not folding a towel properly; asking to go outside to play; and thumb sucking. Now, the little one stood, knowing it was her fault that they were all being punished, because she couldn't keep her thumb out of her mouth. And, all she wanted to do was close her eyes and put that darned thing right back in there. Last night when she was caught sucking her thumb again, her mother put hot sauce and red pepper on the calloused digit and shoved it back in her mouth. When she tried to pull it out, her mother held it steady, until she began to cough and vomited. Then she was forced to clean up her mess before she could go to bed. Today, everyone would suffer for her inability to do as she was told, and tears ran silently down her cheeks.

Since she was youngest, she'd never really known her mother as care taker. In her lifetime it was always Marie feeding them and taking care of them. Marie wasn't cruel like their mother. She didn't know why Marie left them, why she wasn't here to take care of them, but she hoped she wouldn't stay away too long. With her sister gone they were hungry and afraid.

Mom blamed their brother for the accident and for Marie being gone, and she beat him pretty soundly when they got home from the place where the police car took them. After the beating, when he went to bed crying, the littlest one crawled right into bed with him and snuggled. All she wanted to do was comfort him, and without Marie a snuggle was the best thing she could come up with. Whenever Mother wasn't looking she slipped her thumb in her mouth, just for a minute, because it was the one thing that gave her a feeling of comfort. And, now that she was caught again, they were all going to pay for it.

"Well, isn't this lovely. You can all blame your sister for this. Once again she can't keep her thumb out of her mouth, as if somehow she is being nourished by sucking on that thing. If her nourishment is coming from the thumb, then why would she need food? Well, if she can get by without food, I don't see why all of you can't do the same thing! There will be no lunch, or supper, today. Perhaps she will think twice about putting that nasty thing back in her mouth if she can see how it is affecting her brother and sisters."

"No, Mama. Please don't do this to them. They didn't do anything wrong. You can take my food away, but don't do this to them, please. I'll try harder."

"It's already done. No lunch and no supper. You might as well go to your room, so I don't have to look at your faces." Once the kids were in their bedroom, the little one broke down in tears.

"I'm sorry. It's all my fault. I'm really sorry."

"Don't worry about it honey. We've been hungry before. It's not your fault, she's just mean."

"I wish Marie was here. She wouldn't starve us. I hate Mama."

Her sister shook her head. "Join the club. But, you can wish all you want. I don't know when Marie will be back. She was hurt pretty bad, and they have to keep her at the hospital until she gets better."

Then their brother admitted. "Yeah, that's my fault. If I hadn't run off to get candy she would've never been hurt."

"Nobody's mad at you. You already got a bad beating from Mom, that's punishment enough. You didn't know it was going to happen, and you weren't driving that car, so quit kicking yourself. I heard Marie's boss from the service station come to the door the other day. He was worried about her. I hope he went to visit her at the hospital, and I hope she hasn't lost her job. I really like it there."

"Me too. Especially on Saturdays when she gets to be the tiger. I miss her so much."

"Me too."

"Oh give thanks to the Lord, for He is good, for His steadfast love endures forever! Let the redeemed of the Lord say so, whom He has redeemed from trouble and gathered in from the lands, from the east and from the west, from the north and from the south.

Psalm 107:1-3

cHapter 8

Marie graduated from a halo vest to a cervical collar. Now that her neck fractures were stabilized, the danger of a spinal break was no longer a threat, and it allowed her more freedom of movement. With her new freedom came a regular room, instead of a cubical in ICU. Her room was sparsely furnished, besides the normal nurse's equipment for checking vitals; just her simple, adjustable bed, a small side table and a chair. An abstract painting hung on the kakis colored wall directly in front of her bed, she assumed to take the eye's focus off the awful kakis color. But, other than a small window, which gave her a lovely view of the neighboring building's roof, a clock, and a chalkboard near the door for patient information, there were no other decorations or distractions.

Four weeks in the hospital would have driven her insane, if it hadn't been for the kind nurses, and visits from the guys at the service station. They took turns coming and brought flowers frequently. She was so worried about the kids she could hardly sleep or think, and the doctor promised he would minimize her casts at four weeks, as long as the x-ray results were favorable. Getting around with crutches wouldn't be easy, but nothing in her life was easy these days, and she desperately wanted to be home. The nurse came to wheel her bed to radiology, and her heart leapt for joy. Soon, she was sure, she would be getting partial casts and be heading out the door.

Results came back and the doctor entered her room. "Marie, I know you were looking forward to your partial casts, so you could return home, but I'm afraid it will be another week before I can do that for you. Your bones are healing, but not quite as quickly as I'd hoped. Obviously we can't minimize your casts if the procedure would leave you with insufficient support. In the full casts, you just wouldn't be able to get around. Besides, the extra week will help your fractured pelvis, and make it easier for you to stand and sit once you're released."

"But I've already been here for four weeks. I really need to get home. My brother and sisters need me."

"My dear, you wouldn't be any good to any of them in the condition you're in. No, I'm sure things will look better in a week. We will take more x-rays then."

"Okay, Doc. But, please don't make me stay any longer than that. I really need to get home."

"We'll see what we can do, Marie. Until then the nurses are taking good care of you, aren't they?"

"Oh, yes, I couldn't be happier with them. It isn't anyone here that is making me want to go home. It's fear of what the children are going through without me."

"Do I need to have one of the nurses call social services, Marie? I mean if you are sincerely frightened for your siblings, perhaps we should have someone go out there and check on them?"

"No Sir. That won't be necessary. I'm sure they'll be fine." Marie knew that if a worker from social services were to visit their house, to check on the kids, with her mother in charge, they would likely be taken from the home and put into foster care. How then would she ever find them again? She wasn't even an adult, so she would have no authority. Under her breath she muttered, "Hang in there kids. I'll get there as quick as I can."

The doctor interrupted her. "We will do the best we can, Marie. Stay strong and think good thoughts. We will check again in a week."

The guys continued to visit and saw her getting better

by the day. Angela never came back, and Marie hoped she was okay. Perhaps she'd go to the house on the hill when she was released from the green halls and linoleum floors of West Point hospital. Maybe her friend needed her. At any rate, she wanted to thank her one more time for her kind words and comforting protection.

Horrors continued in Vietnam. Two villages are mistakenly attacked by U.S. jets; killing sixty three and wounding over one hundred others. More South Vietnamese are becoming sympathizers to the NVA, as U.S. mistakes pile up. The sergeant is relieved that the amount of repair work needed for upcoming bombing raids is enough to keep he and his troops occupied on base for the time being. Nightmares about the death of his friend are growing worse, and sleep is almost non-existent. He continues to write home, unaware that all his letters are going directly to his mother, and are not being forwarded on to his wife and kids. He has no idea that Marie is as heartbroken about the lack of communication as he is. The shaking in his hands, from alcohol dependency, is getting worse and making it harder to do his job; but the only thing that calms them down at the end of the day, is more of the same poison that's causing the problem in the first place.

Reports from the latest x-rays are good. The doctor will be in momentarily to cut her plaster casts down; creating a walking cast for her leg, and a lighter one for her arm. They will leave the compression wraps on her other arm and leg, as the sprains were very severe and may take longer to heal than the breaks. She'll have to wear all of those for two more weeks, but they should be off before school starts right after Labor Day. Her boss has offered to drive her home, to save her mom the hassle of trying to find her a ride, and she has gratefully accepted.

So excited to leave, she can hardly contain herself. She's missed the kids more than she ever imagined she would, but also wonders how they will act upon her return. After all, they're so young. Have they perceived throughout these five weeks that she deserted them, or even, heaven forbid, doesn't care about them anymore? Hopefully not, but she'll cross that bridge when she gets to it. For now, she just wants to get home.

Very disappointed that she wasn't able to make any extra money over the summer as was her plan, because that was the vehicle by which she'd planned to buy school supplies and clothes for the children and herself. She quietly determines that they will just have to make do with what they have for the first couple of weeks until she can get a little set aside for school and winter must haves.

It will be good to get back to work. She probably won't be able to get much cleaning done until the plaster casts come off, but she could straighten out the books, and that would be a relief for her and for her boss as well.

The doctor and her nurses entered. "Well, young lady, are we ready to do this?"

"I'm way past ready, Doctor. And the quicker the better!"

"You know we're really going to miss you around here, don't you?" Her nurse looked as if she might cry.

"I will miss you ladies too. You've been so good to me, and I can't thank you enough for all the special attention. I know you went way out of your way for me."

"It was a pleasure, Marie! You are a special young lady, and we were happy to do it. We also have a small gift for you."

"Oh, that wasn't necessary. You've been so wonderful to

me already."

"Don't be silly. We all chipped in. It's just a little something." The head nurse handed her a bag, which upon examination revealed a bevy of delights that any young girl would find exciting. And, for the most part, that she would never have spent money on for herself: a hair brush and comb; lotions; a lovely bottle of cologne in a light, fresh scent; deodorant; a manicure and pedicure set; two tubes of lip gloss in light pink colors; scented bath soaps; pretties for her hair; her own razor; and a beautiful scarf of many colors. Tears filled her eyes and she began to sniffle. "Oh, please, Marie, don't cry. We did this to make you happy, not to make you sad."

"I know. It's just that I'm not used to people making a fuss over me, much less spending money on me. You are all so kind."

"Well, we found out you had a birthday a few days after your accident, and none of us knew about it at the time. So, we figured a twelve year old young woman, going into high school, which is a huge accomplishment on its own, could use a few things to make her feel pretty. Enjoy. You deserve it. And, we want you to know that we all believe you will do well in whatever you decide to pursue for your future."

"Thank you so much. Please tell everyone else thank you for me too."

"Well, there's one more thing." The nurse held out an envelope and Marie took and opened it. There was a card inside, signed by all the staff that had been involved in her care during the five weeks of her stay. Inside the card were ten, twenty dollar bills. Two hundred dollars! She gasped.

"I, I can't take this. This is too much!"

"No, this is exactly the amount we wanted to give you. We know you work to make extra money for your family, and that you haven't been able to do any of that during this time in the hospital. We hope this will help you with the things you need to start school."

Now Marie really began to cry. "You have all been so kind to me already. How can I thank you?"

"No need for that. Once the doctor finishes with your casts, we will help you get your things together, and help you get your bearings straight on the crutches you'll be using until you get the casts off in two more weeks. It will be a bit tricky at first, because of the cast on your arm, but we all know that you'll figure it out in no time."

The doctor finished his work, and the nurses gave her a crash course in the use of her crutches, laughing with her as she clomped about in her giant white boot. They also gave her some large plastic bags with elastic closures that she could use to cover her casts while she showered. Life would be a bit of a challenge for her the next couple of weeks, but honestly, when wasn't life a bit of a challenge?

When it came time for her to leave, she gave and got dozens of hugs and well wishes. Her boss was there to carry her collection of 'get well' gifts: balloons, stuffed animals and flowers; along with her personal belongings; and he gave her an encouraging smile as he helped her navigate the front seat of his Chevy truck. "My wife sends her love, and well wishes."

"Please tell her thank you for me. I would like to meet her sometime. I'd also like to come back to work tomorrow if that's alright."

"Oh Marie, maybe you ought to be resting. I don't want you to overdo."

"I know I won't be able to do much cleaning with these casts on, but I can at least catch up on the books."

"In that case, I'll come and get you and the children. I know it's not very far, but it will seem like miles with those casts and crutches, and you surely won't be pulling a wagon anytime soon."

"Okay, it's a deal. I have one more favor to ask of you. And, it's okay if you say no, since you've already done so much for me."

"Sure, what is it?"

"Once I get these casts off I'd like to go up to Angela's house and thank her. I have a feeling it will be awhile before I have many long trips in me, at least if I'm traveling on my own."

"I'd be happy to take you, and I know you walk with the kids to the market every week too. Until you are feeling more able, I'd be happy to drive you there as well."

"I know it's a huge inconvenience. Are you sure you want to take that much time away from your family? Your wife has been so patient."

"Oh, I won't take time from the family. I'll do it during work hours and have the guys keep an eye on everything while I'm gone. How's that for power and control?"

"I would say that is very powerful and controlling, but I don't want the guys to be upset with me either."

"The guys won't be a bit upset. They all love you and have been excited to get you back. They'll be fine."

"Then, I accept your offer. Boy, I can't believe how much I've missed the kids. I hope they are alright. I feel like I've really let them down."

"I'm sure they're fine, but we'll see them soon at any rate. I have something for you. It's a little something from my family, and the boys at the station."

"Oh Boss, you don't need to do anything else for me. You've already been so great."

"No, my wife and kids insisted, and the guys all wanted to chip in. I won't take no for an answer." He pulled a folded envelope out of his pocket and handed it to her. Her hands were shaking as she opened the flap. The envelope was filled with twenty dollar bills. Four hundred dollars worth of twenty dollar bills to be exact. Her mouth dropped open and she looked up into his smiling eyes.

"I was hoping to get that reaction."

"I can't take this. No, really, this is too much. I can't."

"I already told you that I won't take no for an answer. You will take it and get the things you need for school, and the things the children need. If you won't think of yourself, at least think of them. I'm sure you know I'm right. So, just say thank you."

"Thank you. I will work hard and make all this worth it for you."

"You already do that, Marie. You are the hardest working employee I've ever had, and you're just a tiny slip of a thing. I can't imagine you doing more than you already do, and this is just a small sign of our appreciation for the way you've whipped the station, and all of us guys, into shape. It will be good to have you and the kids back. Do you want me to pick you up tomorrow, or do you need a day to settle in?"

"Well, I won't be able to do much at the trailer, so I'd rather get the books caught up. I'm sure the kids will be anxious to get out of the house as well. I doubt they've seen the sunshine since I left."

When they arrived at the trailer Marie saw the curtain at the front window move, and heard loud squeals coming from inside. The door flew open and kids, filthy dirty, thin, battered and bruised, came tumbling out to fall on Marie as she was being helped from the cab of the truck. They practically climbed her, and then covered her with hugs and kisses. She looked them over, and with a set jaw and steely glare, looked over at her boss, who was shaking his head in dismay. She couldn't wait to get inside and give her mother a piece of her mind, no matter what it got her in return. However, when she got inside, with her boss following close on her heels, as he didn't want her to run into more than she could handle with her mom, her mother was nowhere to be found. "Where is Mom?"

"She's not here." Came the reply from the oldest of the three.

"Well, I can see that, Honey. But where is she? Is she doing laundry?" The trailer looked as if a tornado had lit on the premises, and it smelled like sour milk, body odor, feces and other indistinguishable horrors she didn't dare put names to. Once she looked around, it was clear no one had done laundry, probably since she'd left. But, most of the quarters were missing from the can in the kitchen.

"I don't know where she is. When Sis came home she left in a car with a man and we haven't seen her since."

"Do you know how long ago that was?"

"I'm not sure Marie, but it's been a long time."

"Well, if she left Sis here, where is she?"

"I don't know. She left a few days ago. Some of her friends were here. They were all drinking, and smoking out of a big glass thing with water in it that one of the boys brought. After awhile they all just got up and left. She said she'd be back later, but she never came back. I hope you're not mad, but we bought snacks and pop from Frank's since there wasn't any food left."

"No, no, I'm not mad at you guys at all. I'm glad there were quarters in the can. Why are you so dirty? And, what are the bruises from?"

The littlest one popped up. "It's all my fault, Marie. I kept sucking my thumb and everyone got punished. I tried to stop, but when I was sleeping it just kind of snuck back in my mouth. I'm sorry."

"No little one. None of this is your fault. Well, we're just going to have to get you all in the tub, and see about cleaning up some of this mess. Then we'll go pick up a few groceries." The last part was said with a look of pleading on her face toward her boss.

"We can't take baths, Marie. There's no water. We haven't had water for about a week. We've been drinking out of the water jugs you had in the refrigerator." Marie walked to the kitchen sink and turned the cold water tap. Nothing happened. Then she walked back to the bathroom. Clearly the children had continued to use the toilet, even though there was no water with which to flush, and some of the worst smells in the trailer were emanating from that room.

Marie's hands began to clench into fists, and her face turned red. "I can't believe him. I want you all to stay right here for a minute. I have to go talk to Frank."

"No, Marie, don't go. We don't want you to leave again!"

"I'll be right back. I promise. I'm not going anywhere ever again."

"I'm coming with you."

"You don't have to, Boss. I can take care of this."

"It never hurts to have backup."

"Fine, but come quick before I lose the desire to kill this jerk. I want him to know exactly how angry I am!"

"Yes ma'am!" They marched to Frank's front door, and as usual, were met with a cloud of cigarette smoke as they entered there.

"How dare you. How dare you shut off the water to our trailer with children inside. What kind of monster are you?"

"Hey, I have the right to shut off the water if your payment is late."

"I paid the water bill right before I was injured, and the kids said the water has been off for a week. So, even though I was in the hospital, and had no way of getting here to cover that bill, you shut the water off. What, the next day after it was due?"

"That's my right to do. That bill is supposed to be paid every four weeks. If it's not paid on the due date, I can shut off the water."

"Well, now you've created quite a mess for yourself. You see, the children, through no fault of their own, have continued to use the toilet, the entire time you had the water off. I am paying the water bill this instant. Now, I have to go to the grocery store, and I need to bathe the children before I go, so turn the water on this instant. When I leave for the store I will inform you, and I want the toilet fixed and clean before I return, do you understand me?"

"Hey, you can't come in here and....." Her boss stepped forward and stopped Frank's rant dead in its tracks.

"Oh, Frank, I forgot to introduce you to my boss. I believe I told you about him. He's the fellow I confided in about our incident, and I believe he and the rest of the guys have been waiting for an opportunity to tell you how they feel about that. Now, turn the water on. And, if you ever do this again, I can't promise you won't get a visit from my friends."

"Fine. I'll go to the back and turn it on. But, you're paying it right now. Agreed?"

"Agreed. And you will get the mess cleaned up the moment I'm gone. Are we agreed on that? I have enough other messes to clean up, and as you can see, it's going to be difficult for me as it is. Not that you would care about that one way or another."

"You're right. I don't care. But, I'll get the toilet running, as long as you keep your friends off my back."

"They will stay off your back as long as you treat us fairly and keep your hands to yourself."

At that, Frank's face turned a bright shade of crimson and he nodded.

Marie paid the bill from the envelope in her pocket, and headed off to clean the children up as best she could under the circumstances. When they returned from the grocer, who was genuinely pleased to see Marie and the kids again, the toilet was working. She opened the windows, to help air out the trailer.

"I'm so sorry to have caused you all this trouble, Boss. Thank you for all your help."

"I was pleased to help cart you and the kids around, but you did all the rest of it yourself."

"No, you proved that it is good to have backup. I believe Frank was positively intimidated by you, and that helped a lot!"

"Okay, maybe that did help some, but I wouldn't want to be on the wrong side of you in a dark alley. You were absolutely fierce."

"Thank you. I was shaking like a leaf inside. It helped to have you standing behind me."

"Well, you are welcome. Do you want me to hang around and help for awhile?"

"No, you go on to your wife and kids. We'll be fine here. I'm going to get the kids to help me with a few things until I'm able to do more. It won't hurt them to learn a little. As long as I'm watching them, it will be a good life lesson. The first thing we're going to do is gather all the dirty clothes together. The reason I bought all those quarters at the store, is so that I could get caught up on laundry."

"You sure? They'd understand. They know it's your first day home."

"Nope, I'm fine. But, we'll see you tomorrow at nine?"

"Yes ma'am! With bells on. Like I said before, it will be good to have you back, and the guys will all be excited to see you."

Marie and the kids spent the afternoon and evening going back and forth between the trailer and the laundry. She made spaghetti for supper, with assistance from the kids. They actually wanted to help, and had a great time, but mostly because it was Marie they were helping and they'd missed her so very much. Once they were done with the chores they'd decided to tackle the first day, they settled down in bed, in clean pajamas, on clean sheets, and Marie read them stories. Mother never came home, and neither did Sis. But, that was okay with the children. Marie was home and they were safe again.

The sergeant woke up screaming, completely drenched in sweat and gasping for air, as he has done most nights now for the past few weeks. He isn't perspiring as much from the heat of a late August night in Vietnam, as he is from the nightmare which still holds him in its steely grip. His dreams have gotten worse. Visions of his childhood friend walking toward him with hands outstretched and questioning eyes. Eyes that not only question, but plead and beg. They seem to say, "Why didn't you save me? You say that you kept me close to keep me safe, and yet your decision was the very thing that killed me."

His nightmares are filled with the blood, and gore of all the many men he's lost. The men whose families will never see their husband, son, brother, or dad again. His hands shake almost constantly now. And, his recurring headaches are becoming just short of unbearable. He's taken to keeping a bottle next to his cot, and wakes up several times a night to relieve himself into a bucket, and take a couple shots of hot, bitter whiskey. He savors the burning sensation from his mouth to his stomach, as his headache dims just a bit for a short while. And then he uses his sheet to wipe the sweat from his face and chest. His gut has been bothering him more lately, and he knows the alcohol is probably burning a hole right through something important in there, especially since he switched from beer to the hard stuff a while back. He's miserable and lonely, and he just wants to leave this place and go home.

Waking in the morning, still shaking, with a brand new splitting headache; that is ripe and ready to accompany his almost constant gut ache; he heads to a mandatory daily briefing and discovers his unit is being called to do search and destroy missions, once again, in nearby villages. Panic, that he must hide from the brass and his own troops, sets in.

Fidgeting as she waits, Marie shushes the kids for the hundredth time, while also perfectly understanding their impatience. She's impatient too. Nurses who'd tended to her during her five week stay in the hospital walk by; and when they notice her they smile and wave. She waves back and tells the kids the names of each one. The casts are coming off today, and she couldn't be happier. Her boss is chauffeuring her around once again. She would have to come up with a way to thank him for all the sacrifices he's made.

Marie finally met his wife, Sharol, and his two small children. They were invited, as a family, to a cook out just last week. He grilled juicy hamburgers and hot dogs, and she made potato salad, corn on the cob, and a yummy gelatin dessert with tiny little marshmallows. Their house was beautiful, and the littlest one piped up with, "This is a mansion. Your boss lives in a mansion!". The comment caused her great embarrassment, as she remembered his visit to her own filthy squalor behind Frank's service station. Sharol was wonderful, a beautiful blond with kind, twinkling eyes and a sincere smile. When Marie watched how she interacted with her children, and the loving glances she gave her husband, she could see why he adored her so much, and her own heart hurt a little that she would probably never know that kind of love.

The sweetness of it all caused tears to well up behind her eyes, and she had all she could do to not cry in front of these people who had been so good to her and certainly wouldn't understand her sadness. She was forced to wait until the children had played with their hosts for an acceptable period of time, and he seemed ready to release her back to her destitute life style, before she could ask to be ferried home. "Is everything alright, Marie?"

"I'm fine. I think I just got too much sun. I have a headache and I should get a few things done before work on Monday. You know I'm getting my casts off on Tuesday, right?"

"Yep, I can't wait. And, not just because my service station bathrooms will sparkle again. Sharol and I wanted to invite you and the kids to church with us next week. Would you consider coming?"

"Maybe. I'm not sure. I'll have to think about it. I'll let you know." Marie had no intention of going to his church, as she was sure it would be filled with rich people, just like these, and she would feel just as out of place there as she had at his beautiful house today.

For now she would humor him. He had been so good to her that she owed him at least that much. Seeing his house and the way they lived made her question the existence of this God of his, or any god, more than ever. Why do some have so much and others so little? Why were her brother and sisters subjected to the horror that was their mother, but these children had a loving, caring mom? If there was a God, why didn't He step in and step up for once? She was tired of feeling lost and forgotten by the universe, or whatever they wanted to call it. Where before she'd thought about having a discussion with her boss about this God they worshipped; now that was out of the question. Of course he would see a loving God in his life. His family had everything. He couldn't possibly see things from her perspective.

That night, as she lay in bed, contemplating life and the unfairness of it all, she heard a car door open and close outside. She crept to the window, expecting to see her sister sneaking in from days of partying. Instead she heard the familiar click, click, click of her mother's high heels on the cement slab in front of their door. The same sound she'd heard at her grandparent's house that night so long ago. The window was open to usher in the lazy summer breeze. And with a full moon, even through the darkness of her hiding place behind the curtain, she could see perfectly.

The fragrance of her mom's perfume wafted through the air and made her catch her breath and sigh, as she closed her eyes and savored the heady aroma. Mom set a bag on the top step that led to the trailer, and when she looked up her beautiful face was captured in moonlight. She was so lovely with her perfect features and red lipstick. It was no wonder she never lacked for male company. But, most puzzling of all, was that she looked so happy. That fact was of great concern, and great confusion to Marie. How could she look so happy when her husband was thousands of miles from here, in harm's way, and she hadn't seen her children in weeks?

Just then she turned, and hurried back to the car, click, click, click, where a man waited behind the steering wheel. Marie strained to see who had driven her, and when the door opened and the light switched on, she could clearly see that it was the vice officer, Lieutenant what's his name, who had brought her sister home months ago. So, that's where her mother had been spending her time. It was so sad that Marie could hardly stand it, and she had to fight with herself not to call out.

The most heartbreaking part of all was that she looked just as pretty that night in the moonlight, as she did while she was attempting to win Daddy's heart. A lump swelled in Marie's throat. A lump so large it threatened to choke her to death as she thought of him, her daddy. Off fighting a war that made people call him a baby killer, for what? So his wife could cheat on him? So they could all go through the hell that was their daily life now? So he could someday come home to this, this nothing, and find his father dead and his wife in the arms of another man?

How could there possibly be a God? Because if there was a God, and He allowed this to happen, then He was no more than the angry old man in the sky that she'd envisioned on the rare occasions that she pondered Him at all. Just another in a long line of monsters. But, what then did this line of thinking speak of Angela, and all that she'd said? Soon she would have her casts off, and then she would seek Angela out, wherever she might be. Perhaps her friend had answers for her.

Heading for the showers with tunnel vision, he was already trying to erase this day's events from his mind. They'd dropped from their transport as usual, into six foot elephant grass, to begin a vital search of nearby suspected Charlie hideouts. Women and children scattered and hid, while the interpreter gave orders for everyone to make their way to the village center. Again, because they were slow or reluctant, he ordered everyone to file into the village center. Slowly and hesitantly, some of the villagers made their way, but others remained in the shadows. The sergeant's troops were getting antsy, knowing through reliable sources this was a Cong holdout, and held a massive weapons cache, but not knowing how many of the 'civilians' might be dangerous as well. Two by two the men began to search huts and storage buildings.

In short order there were shots fired, followed by a fair amount of shouting. The sergeant made his way to the ruckus and attempted to sort things out. There was blood everywhere, and upon investigation, the body of a young woman and a small child. The men had indeed found two VC and multiple weapons under the floor mats of the home, but just as they were securing the site, the mom and child entered the hut. One of his men, stressed and frightened, opened fire and killed the mother and her little one without a second's thought. Now he stood, with tears streaming down his face, shaking uncontrollably. "What happened here?"

"I don't know, Sarg. We came in and lifted the floor mat. The gooks put their hands in the air right away, but when the door swung open I thought it was a trap and I shot. I killed them. She's just a little girl, Sarg. What do I do?"

"Go on out of here. Get to the village center and guard the prisoners. I'll take care of this."

"Okay, Sarg."

The sergeant looked at the twisted, bloody body of the child and shook his head. What a tragedy. But, if the woman lived in this hut, obviously she was a Cong sympathizer and knew what was hidden under the mat. She got what was coming to her, didn't she? The girl, that was the tragedy, another story all together, but nothing could be done about it now. With shoulders sagging from the weight of his upcoming part in this, he gave his other soldier a look, and his man tied the hands and feet of the two Viet Cong combatants, including stuffing gags in their mouths so they couldn't scream for help. Witnesses to his trigger happy troop would disappear with the seized weapons they'd been guarding, as soon as he ordered an air strike.

If he could possibly keep his soldier from undergoing an internal investigation, he would do whatever he had to do. These men had already suffered enough. He already had plenty of blood on his hands at this point. He called for the air strike as he and his men were loading onto the transport that would take them back to the base. Another village will be burned to the ground, and civilians will be left without food or shelter, but the weapons, and witnesses will be destroyed as well.

Soaking in the shower, hot water running in rivulets down his face, he broke down and cried. He knew deep inside he couldn't take this much longer, but he also knew he had to stay strong for his men and for his family.

They were taking city transportation today. The town connection point was only a block further than their regular school bus stop. It would be a busy day but, potentially, a very fun one. The biggest trick would be keeping the little ones from becoming too tired without a wagon to ride in for the trip. Marie was going to try and outfit everyone for school; clothes, supplies, and new shoes plus winter wear, all in one day. It would be exhausting, especially since she'd only been out of her casts for a couple of days. But, school was starting next Tuesday, so she didn't have a choice. They didn't have much time to sort things out and get ready for the big day. She was especially nervous, because it would be her first day of high school, and she wanted to make a good impression.

She'd spent two whole days catching up with her cleaning at home and at work, and she was feeling pretty good about how much she'd gotten done in so short an amount of time. The trailer no longer smelled so ripe, and her boss seemed very pleased with the gleaming bathrooms and office at the service station. The exercise was good for her, and was helping her get her strength back. Strength she would need to get through the days to come.

Frank hadn't given her any more problems. As a matter of fact, he avoided her at all costs. She was sure her big strong boss had sufficiently frightened him, and was grateful for the reprieve.

The money gifts she'd been given at the hospital, and by the guys at work, would be enough to purchase everything they needed, even after the twenty two dollars she'd given Frank for the water bill. The children were excited, in part because she'd promised they could eat their dinner at the little park by the court house, and then their supper at McDonald's, an experience they'd never enjoyed before. She was feeling rather magnanimous as she herded the little ones onto the uptown bus. The sun shining through the enormous bus windows felt good on her face, and she smiled as she watched kids on bikes, and grownups in cars going along on their busy ways below her. Today, she wasn't a poor kid from a trailer court. Today, she had money in her pockets and she was going to treat the kids to the biggest shopping spree of their lives. She could get used to this.

At the park they bought soda pop from a vendor and sat to eat their peanut butter and jelly sandwiches. The littlest one, who hadn't put her thumb in her mouth in days, was jabbering a million miles a minute, and Marie laughed. "Hold on, Honey. You're talking so fast I can't keep up with you."

"Sorry, Marie. I'm just succited."

"You're succited? I know, Honey. We all are. So, should we buy our school supplies first, so we can make sure we have everything we need?"

"Yes. Can I pick my own folders? Since I'm going into kindergarten I will probably need real folders like the big kids."

"Well, if I'm remembering correctly, you will need crayons, paper, pencils, glue and scissors, plus a pencil box; but if you're really good, I will let you pick out a couple folders too. We will all get backpacks as well. Then I want to go to Connor's Department store and get new underwear, socks, and a week's worth of outfits for each of us. I think shoes and winter coats should be last, since those things will be the heaviest. We'll have to carry them to McDonalds for our supper, and then home on the bus too. What do you think?"

"We will all help carry!"

"Good, then let's get on it, okay?"

Off they went, and not a one of them could ever remember having such a grand time. They got all the items they would need for school, and loaded them in their new backpacks for easier carrying. Then they bought clothing. New dresses for the girls, dress pants and shirts for her brother, and even some pretties for their hair. Underwear and socks for everyone, plus bras for Marie, and some stylish items to begin her high school career, including a pair of very fashionable bell bottomed pants and a paisley print shirt. Last, but not least, winter coats, shoes, and boots. Happy, but tired, they made their way to McDonald's, where they unloaded all their purchases, folded them neatly, and packed as many as possible into their backpacks. Leaving much less to carry in shopping bags. Then they ordered cheeseburgers, French fries, and chocolate milk shakes. It was getting dark by the time they climbed the stairs of the bus back home. Huddled together in one seat on the bus with their bags piled in front of them, the kids, tired as they were, couldn't stop talking about how wonderful the day was. Marie, watching the town go by outside the window, noticed her own smiling face reflected back at her in the darkened window. "I love you, Marie."

"I love you too."

"We all love you, Marie."

"I love you guys too. You are my life."

"I wish you were my mom."

"I don't have to be your mom to love you."

"I know, but if you were my mom then the other mom wouldn't live with us. I don't like her. She's mean and she scares me. Is Daddy ever coming home?"

"I hope so. But I don't know when."

"I miss him."

"Me too."

Once all their purchases were hauled home, and tucked safely into their bedroom away from possible prying eyes, she loaded everyone in and out of the bath and into clean pajamas. Two stories was all it took to send them off to sleep, before she could get in the bathroom to take her own shower. Tomorrow, after work, they would make a trip to the grocery store and stock up on staples before school started on Tuesday. Maybe, for the Labor Day Holiday on Monday, she would make Daddy's cinnamon twist bread with maple icing. She'd need yeast for that, and maple flavoring too. Perhaps she'd even teach one of the kids how it was done, so the tradition would live on.

Arrangements were already made. Sunday, after he was done with church, her boss was coming to take her and the kids to Angela's house. She didn't know what she might find there, but hoped with all her heart that her friend was well.

Walking through the front door he sees his wife and kids, but it seemed no one recognized him. He tries to put his arms around his wife and she begins to scream. He looks down and sees that he is covered in blood. Suddenly his children are backing away from him in fear. Crying, they begin to scream, "Baby killer. You're a baby killer." He gasps for air in the sweltering heat of his darkened quarters, and awakens, covered in sour sweat. He lays on his cot, attempting to calm his breathing and slow his heart beat. The never ending nightmares are becoming worse.

Later that day, as he walked through a perfectly normal looking field toward the mission's target, unfocused and exhausted, the soldier directly to his left stepped on a powerful land mine. It happened so suddenly that every soldier behind them stopped dead in his tracks. At first he thought the wet substance on his face might be sweat, but lifting his hand to his cheek he found the blood of his brother there. It took him a moment to remember who'd been walking beside him. And, he would need to remember, as it didn't appear there would be enough of the man left to identify. They wouldn't dare try to scour the field looking for dog tags, for fear of losing more troops to mines. He halted his unit. They were in the middle of a mine field, and he had no earthly idea how they would get out. He signaled his soldiers to follow in his footsteps, and they carefully moved to follow directly behind him. Looking around for signs of snipers, who might use this opportunity to pick them off one by one, he proceeded slowly forward. By the time the squad accessed the far end of the field, the sergeant was shaking like a leaf. He wouldn't discover, until later, that his fatigues and back pack contained various bits and pieces of his fallen comrade. He vomited until his ribs hurt, and then he cried.

Marie hasn't been this excited about anything for a very long time, not even shopping. They are going to see Angela today. She woke everyone early and fed them a hearty breakfast of pancakes, bacon, eggs and orange juice. Once the kitchen was in order and the dishes washed, she dressed them all in nice clothes and brushed everyone's hair until it shone. Even letting the girls wear some of their new hair pretties. Once her boss arrived they loaded into the extended cab of his truck. "Are we ready to do this?"

"I believe we are. I'm so anxious to see Angela again. I know you haven't ever met her, but she's a wonderful lady, isn't she buddy?"

"Yes, but she's old. I don't know how she got down to the river that day. She is very, very old."

"Anyway, you will all like her. She was so good to me, and continued to visit me until the guys started coming. It was like she didn't want me to be alone. And, she kept telling me that God loved me, whatever that meant. She made me want to be brave. I just hope she's okay. I don't know why she stopped coming, but I can't wait to see her again."

"I'm sure we will all like her, and I can't wait to meet

her. Everyone settled in?"

When they arrived on the back road they searched out the street that ascended the mountain to Angela's house. The street was called, ironically, 'Mountain Road', and was practically hidden by trees and brush, to anyone using the back road to the grocery store. The road was steep, so they traveled slowly, winding around to the back of the house's rear property. Once there, they piled out of the truck and walked around to the front of the house. To their surprise they found the front door and windows boarded up, and posters declaring that the property was 'Condemned' nailed to every access point. "I, I don't understand. Why would her house be boarded up?"

"I don't know, Marie, but these boards and signs have been here for quite some time."

"Hey, Buddy, I thought you said this is where you found Angela?"

"It is, Marie. She was right inside when I knocked on the door, and none of these boards and signs were here, I promise. This is where she called the police and the ambulance."

"Well, that's hard to believe, because the phone lines aren't even attached anymore, look." At the side of the house were wires and cables, that had been pulled from their necessary connections, frayed and useless now.

"I don't know what to tell you boss, but she came to me, down at the bottom of the embankment. How do you explain the police and ambulance? There aren't any other houses for miles. What phone did she use to call them? I'm telling you she came to me. And, she stayed until the authorities brought my mom. How do you explain that?"

"Well, there's obviously no one here now. I don't know what is going on. I have no earthly explanation. I'll tell you what. Tuesday, when you come to work after school, we will call the county court house from my office, and see what they have to say. Is that good for everyone?"

"Yes, I can live with that. I'm more confused now than ever, and I really want to know what happened to her."

"Okay, then it's a deal. Should we go?"

"If it's alright with you, I'd like to look around the property a little."

"I guess that's okay. I didn't see any 'No Trespassing' signs anywhere. Just don't go in the house. We could get in trouble for that."

"I won't. I just want to walk around a bit. You kids can come with me, but don't get too close to the edge of the cliff. I'll see you in a few minutes, Boss."

"That's fine. Take all the time you need. I'll be waiting in the truck."

Marie walked slowly, around the side of the house toward the back. The area was large and the grass was tall, but she could see various wild flowers intermingled with the grass, and even some evidence of long overgrown flower beds filled with choked and crowded perennials. There were a couple of dwarf apple trees, almost ready to harvest, a clothes line, and an old wooden chair. A pole held a couple of handmade bird feeders that, though they were badly weathered, were still useable. A window on the side of the house had been broken, and when she peeked in, she could see that animals and weather had badly damaged the interior.

Walking back around to the front of the house she made her way to the edge of the cliff; to examine the view that could be seen from the road. The house was almost hidden from below, but her view from the top was expansive. She could see for miles in every direction, and for a few minutes she stood, watching river traffic as it navigated the mighty Hudson. She wasn't able to see the bottom of the embankment from this position, and after a couple deep breaths of the sweet mountain air, she made her way around to the back of the house where her boss waited. She'd almost forgotten the children were with her, as they'd been so quiet and respectful while she investigated. "I wonder if it would be alright to come back and pick apples? Is there someone we could ask?"

"We could certainly check on that when we call the courthouse. Are we all set?"

"Yes, I'll just have to wait until Tuesday to find out. Thank you for bringing me."

"Anytime, Marie. I should get you kids home, so I can head out. My wife has plans for the holiday tomorrow, and I'd better not be late."

When they arrived home, Marie and the children found a sack on the top step leading into the trailer. In it was a loaf of bread and a gallon of milk. She picked up the sack, knowing who'd come by in secret, and headed in the front door shaking her head. Did the woman truly believe that a loaf of bread and a gallon of milk was enough food for all these kids? Especially when her offerings only arrived every couple of weeks or so?

He watched them go, and wished there was more he could do. Knowing that to call Social Services would mean the children would be separated, he could never do that. Marie was doing a fine job of caring for her siblings, and still managed to be an honor student and an exemplary employee, even through all the additional crisis of the summer. He was blessed to have an understanding wife, who knew him so well. Enough to know he had to help where he could.

"Do not neglect to show hospitality to strangers, for thereby some have entertained angels unawares."

Hebrews 13:2

CHapter 9

The first day of school brought with it both excitement and fear. The little ones were tickled to be able to wear their new outfits, and to use their new backpacks and school supplies. Seldom had the kids in their family begun a new school year so prepared, and Marie felt very good about being able to do something about that. But, after she dropped them off at the elementary building, she would be venturing into a whole new world of her own. In the high school building she would not only be an underclassman, but she'd also be the youngest person in the school. A twelve year old amongst mostly fifteen to nineteen year olds. Taking a deep breath she made her way to the front office to claim her locker number, and class schedule. Locating her locker, she memorized it's exact position relative to her first morning class, and attached her new combination lock to the door. Her first day would be filled with navigation and logistics, introductions, and a large assembly which would give the school's administration personnel a chance to let their students know what was expected of them. As she walked into the gymnasium after lunch, Marie could feel hundreds of eyes on her, and hear snickering and giggling from some of the gaggles of girls. Immediately she was embarrassed and uncomfortable. Wondering if she'd chosen the wrong outfit, or the wrong way to wear her hair, her face turned red and she wished she could disappear into the bleachers. She'd never really had the ability to fit in anywhere with people who were close to her own age. Tending to stand out like a sore thumb, except at the service station, and with her family. It was reasonable that her only friends would be grownups. Her peers seemed to be intimidated by her good grades and youth, so it looked like this would be another year of the same. Once again, if she couldn't join them, she might as well beat them.

It was also evident from the way some of her teachers fawned over her that her reputation preceded her. It wouldn't be long before she could tell which ones were truly concerned for her best interests, or only in making themselves appear to be teacher of the year due to her stellar grades and performance. Her goal would be, as usual, to do her best.

After school she hurried the children from the bus stop to the service station. When she arrived she got right to work, getting her chores done quickly in order to have time on the phone with the court house. Speaking with the county records department she discovered that an Angela Winters had indeed lived at 101 Mountain Road, until her death eleven years prior. She debated their knowledge of fact with them until a supervisor came on the line and told her in no uncertain terms that Ms. Angela Winters; who had never been married or had children; was indeed deceased as of eleven years ago, and that her house had been standing vacant since. That, in fact, the house was condemned and, as far as she knew, devoid of electrical power or phone service. Though if Marie wanted to she could call the phone company and power provider to be sure. "Have a good day, Miss."

The county had tried to reach out to a sister in another state, but had never received a reply from any living relative. Normally the county would have confiscated the property by now, but the land at the top of the peak above the river wasn't of much use to anyone, and had remained mostly forgotten until her call today. At some point the house would be torn down if it wasn't claimed, but no one could give her a time table on that possibility, and those in charge of such things had plenty of other things on their plates.

Marie sat dumbfounded. How could any of this be true? Who then had come to her aid? She didn't believe in ghosts. She also didn't believe she'd been seeing things, in part because her brother had seen the same person. Then her little brother asked, "Do you think she was an angel, Marie?"

"What? No, certainly not."

"Why? Why couldn't she be an angel?"

"Well, for one thing, I don't believe in angels."

"I do. I believe in angels. And, I think Angela was an angel. How did she call an ambulance from her house when there aren't any phones hooked up? Maybe God really is looking out for us."

"That's just nonsense. If God actually sent an angel to look out for us, where is she now? Why wouldn't He want us to see her now so we could believe?"

"He sent her when we needed her the most. You saw her then, so why do you have to see her now?"

"Okay, that's enough talk about this for now. Let's get finished up so we can get home. I have laundry to do." But, she had seen. And now she wondered. Was there a God? And, did He really care? It would probably take more than one coincidence to convince her of any heavenly involvement in her life.

The heaviest air raid of the war, to date, occurred on September 12th, 1966, when five hundred U.S. jets attacked NVA supply lines and coastal targets. Two days later America launched 'Operation Attleboro', involving twenty thousand U.S. and South Vietnamese soldiers. They successfully completed a search and destroy mission fifty miles north of Saigon near the Cambodian border. During the fighting an enormous weapons cache was uncovered in a hidden base camp in the jungle. One hundred and fifty five Americans were killed, while four hundred ninety four more were wounded. North Vietnamese losses in the military engagement totaled eleven hundred and six.

With so many jets flying in recent missions the sergeant's men were busy with radio repairs. So, at least for that day, they would survive. However, they were soon pressed into service as the wounded began arriving by chopper, back on home base. They spent most of the day carrying stretchers filled with moaning, weeping, screaming young men. Men crying out for their wives and mothers; men who were missing arms, legs, eyes, and significant amounts of sanity; to designated, temporary hospital tents and buildings. At the end of the day, covered with blood and gore, they met back in the hanger, exhausted physically and emotionally, to share a beer. The sergeant's hands were shaking so visibly that he tried, unsuccessfully, to hide them. He vowed to himself to get something stronger to drink when he got back to his quarters. Maybe that would help.

It's been almost nine months since the sergeant arrived in this god forsaken country, and he still hasn't received a letter from home. He's given up hope that his wife is still waiting for him, and wonders if she's in the arms of another, which is pure torture for his aching heart. Now he's just going through the motions. His men are worried about him, but they know it would be detrimental to his career to say anything to the brass, so they shut their mouths and remember that they will all be going home in a little more than three months. As it stands, they will watch his back out in the field and hope for the best. He's the best platoon sergeant any of them ever had.

Marie overheard a couple of students talking in the hall. Their parents are forcing them to go to a tent revival that will be held on the upcoming weekend. The revival will take place just outside of town, in a farmer's field. As the date moves closer the town is abuzz with excitement. She began to wonder if this might be a way to learn a bit more about the 'God' her boss has tried to introduce her to, without making a public spectacle of herself. In a large tent full of people, she should be able to blend in and keep her anonymity. Her curiosity was at least peaked enough to convince her to give it a try.

School has been going great so far this year. As usual, her grades are stellar. Though she still hasn't made many friends. There is a ninth grade boy, from her English Lit class who's been nice to her. His name is Jeff, and he's kinda cute, but he's also very shy. Some of the other kids have made fun of him for hanging around with Marie, and she's wondered what kind of effect it will have on their friendship. She rises early in the mornings to get the kids dressed and fed, so she will have a little extra time to do her hair.

When he's near she gets a little tongue tied, but he has

actually carried her books twice now, and she thinks she might really like him. However, she is only twelve, and possesses abundant common sense, so she knows dating is out of the question at her age. Or, at least she believes Daddy would say so if he was here. Oh, how she misses him. She wonders continually why he has never written as he promised he would. And it makes her heart ache to think about what he might be going through so far away in another land.

On Sunday she and the children made their way to the tent revival. It was a long trip. The tent was packed with people she didn't know, and a few familiar faces she would try very hard to avoid. The service began with music. There was a band on stage and everyone in the place except her, and the kids, seemed to know the words to all the songs. She clapped along as best she could, and while she clapped she felt a sweet stirring in the air that made her smile. The preacher spoke of Jesus, and the sacrifice he'd made on the cross, in a way that touched her heart as never before. He talked about admitting one's sin, and turning to Christ.

He also spoke of backsliding, and rededicating one's life back to the Lord if you'd wandered away. Then, the subject of damnation and the hell one would experience if your life was filled with sin, really got him going. This topic seemed very crucial to his point, and she listened intently. She couldn't help wondering why anyone would choose to leave this seemingly terrific relationship, if it was as great as the preacher made it sound.

Speculating how one would know if they'd truly confessed all their sins, especially if those sins were considerable in scope and number, weighed on her. And, since this God had never so much as made Himself known to her in any real way that she knew of, perhaps her own sins were far too great for Him to forgive. How would she ever know?

When the preacher offered an alter call, and the music began to play, "Just as I am....", she felt a tugging on her heart she couldn't resist and rose from her seat. The children followed her to the front, where the minister placed his hand on her head and squeezed as he offered a prayer. She and her younger sister asked Jesus into their hearts that day, but she wondered if He'd accepted the invitation into hers, until the tears of joy began to flow.

For the moment she felt new. As if a weight had been lifted from her shoulders. The pastor told her to wait until the service was over, as he wanted to speak personally with her, and then he told the folks in the tent that God wanted to restore them, all of them, to wholeness. Marie and the children took their seats, and watched in awe as one person after another, with crutches, and wheelchairs, canes, and blind eyes, went forward to be healed.

By the time the healing service was over, Marie was convinced she'd witnessed many true miracles and she was excited to begin her new walk with the Lord. Only then, after the time of healing was accomplished, did the preacher take up an offering. His ushers hauled up eight buckets, filled to the brim, with the hard earned money of the community. Including ten dollars from Marie's pocket.

It was a long way home, but Marie was walking on proverbial air the whole way. When they arrived back at the trailer she hummed as she bathed kids and fed them supper. The minister had shared with her that he would be remaining in the area for an additional week or two, to conduct more services. She planned to attend another meeting the following Sunday.

The United States government reveals that jungles near the Demilitarized Zone are being defoliated by sprayed chemical agents, including 'Agent Orange'. These are chemicals that will later leave many American soldiers with agonizing symptoms that the government will deny for decades.

The U.S. Air Cavalry Division conducts 'Operation Irving', with planes, choppers and radio equipment repaired by the sergeant and his men, to clear NVA from mountainous areas near Qui Nhon. Along with the help it is already receiving from China, the Soviet Union announces it will also provide military and economic assistance to North Vietnam, to help repel U.S. troops.

Will this useless war ever end? This isn't what he signed up for. When he joined the military he wanted to protect his country. The South Vietnamese didn't even want them here. They were pretty clear about their overall hatred of the U.S. forces.

He simply had to keep what remained of his men safe for the remainder of their deployment. It was the least he could do. Would he ever be able to get the sound of bombs exploding out of his head? He didn't know.

Mother came home to pack a few things. The children ran to stay out of sight. "You probably won't see me for awhile.”

“So, what's new?”

“Don't be fresh.”

“I'm not being fresh. We've only seen you a few times in the past few months. But that's fine. We've been doing just peachy.”

“My fella is taking me on a trip down the eastern sea board. You know how I've always wanted to track the changing fall leaves.”

“No, actually, I didn't know that. But, I have seen your lame little bags of bread and milk on the top step. You do know you can't leave milk out in the heat, don't you? I've had to throw out every bit of the milk you've left. I don't know if you've noticed, but since I started working we haven't needed your help with groceries. I'm sure you're fine with that. More money for you and all. Can I ask you a question?”

“What?”

“Why do you leave the bags only when you think we're sleeping, or not here?”

“I didn't want the kids to make a fuss. I know they probably miss me.”

“Well, in fact they don't. As long as you continue to

allow the rent and utilities to come out of your bank account, we'll be just fine."

"Well, good. I'm glad you're back to normal. I'll leave you to it then."

"Yep. Have a great time. Oh, by the way. Have you heard anything from your oldest daughter? I haven't seen her in a while, and I don't think she's been to school at all this year."

"Yes, I have heard about her. She was caught in a drug house again and the judge sent her to a facility for troubled girls. She'll be there for six months. She will probably be out in February."

"Did you ever plan on letting me know about that? Kids at school have asked about her and I didn't know what to tell them."

"It didn't come up, okay? Now, I've got to get going. He'll be here any minute."

"Does it ever make you feel bad?"

"Does what make me feel bad?"

"Knowing that you're cheating on your husband. That he's fighting for our country while you run around on him."

"Don't start that again, Marie. We all have our crosses to bear, and I don't want to get into it with you again."

"Crosses to bear? What is your cross, Mother?"

"Well, you damn kids for one thing. I told you I don't want to get into it with you."

"Do you even know when he will be home? Your husband I mean."

"He's due home in January. I mean if he's still alive. I've never had an address for him, because the only address he had for us was his mother's. If he's written, his mother has the letters. And, no, Marie, I don't feel guilty. He knew who I was when he married me. He knew I couldn't be alone. And then he brought us here, to that hateful woman, to try to get along without him. I've been angry with him since he got his orders. He should have known what would happen with his mother. He should have made better plans for us."

"So, if he'd planned things out better, you wouldn't be cheating on him?"

"Stop Marie. My ride is here. I'll see you around. I should be home within the month."

"Take your time."

As mother closed the door behind her, the children came out of hiding.

"It's okay kids. She's gone now. And, I guess we have the

trailer to ourselves for a month."

"Yaaaaaayyyyy!"

"I mean that the heir, as long as he is a child, is no different from a slave, though he is the owner of everything,"

Galatians 4:1

CHAPTER 10

Marie had been excited about the upcoming tent meeting all week, and she wasn't a bit disappointed when they arrived on Sunday, as the place was packed and music already filled the air. Her boss was leery about the revival and it's unknown preacher; probably hurt that she hadn't attended his church first; when she related her experience to him last Monday after school. But, he was pleased she'd asked Jesus into her heart, and wanted to encourage her in her new walk.

Practically exploding with glee, Marie and the kids looked for four seats together and then began clapping and worshipping with the congregation. She looked around her, and noticed smiles on every face; candles burning on the altar; tent flaps up on two sides, due to a particularly warm fall day; and several body guards standing by the place where pastor would be entering. She couldn't help but wonder why there would be a need for armed body guards at a church service, but continued to clap anyway.

Once again the congregation began to sing, but this time she remembered many of the words from the pieces they sang. She was actively teaching the children as they joined in, and they were all having a wonderful time. Soon the music stopped, and the band leader introduced their minister with fanfare worthy of a Vegas show. He began again to speak of Jesus, the remission of sins, and the joys of heaven; followed immediately by the sad state of the human soul, and the punishments of hell due to all those who would back slide in their faith. She hoped she would never back slide, but wasn't exactly sure what that meant, so she was pretty sure she'd have to watch herself pretty closely.

Again, the preacher offered an altar call, and then a healing service. Marie settled in, to watch the miracles, as dozens of people with ailments and symptoms of every kind filed forward. As the service was concluding, and Marie was feeling warm and fuzzy, her brother suddenly needed to go potty. And, no, he couldn't wait to get home, as that would be a long trip. So, Marie decided to take him around to the back of the tent and let him relieve himself. She admonished the girls not to move and to wait in their chairs for her return. Then, making her way out the open side flap, she directed the boy around the nearest corner.

Halting their journey, due to yelling coming from a large group of people gathered behind the tent, she stopped to see what was going on. Positioned where they were, she had a perfect view of the scene, without being visible to the quarrelling group. Marie strained to hear the conversation and discovered they were fighting with the minister about promised payments. Then, she realized who these people were. Some held crutches, or other implements commonly used by people with disabilities, but they all had angry faces. "You still owe us for last week too."

"Now, I told you I would pay you dependent upon the amount of offerings we received."

"We saw how much money you collected in those buckets at the end of the service; last week and this week too. They were filled to the brim!"

"You will all be paid. I promise. You will just have to be patient."

"You said that last week. If you don't pay us right now we'll go to the newspaper. They can let everyone know what a criminal you are and you'll never be able to come back here again. How much is it worth to you to keep your con a secret?"

"Now, now, let's not be hasty. You'll all be compensated

fairly. Wait right here. I'll be back in a minute."

Marie walked forward. Her brother following close behind. "Aren't you all the people that were healed in the service?"

"Hey little girl, you're not supposed to be back here."

"Why is the pastor paying you? Why were you threatening to go to the newspaper?"

"I said you're not supposed to be back here. Now scram." Just then the minister came back through the flap with a handful of money.

"What are you doing back here, Marie?"

"My brother had to pee. But I should ask you. What are you doing back here?"

"You wouldn't understand dear. Now, go back inside, and I will come talk to you in a moment, after I'm finished with these people."

"No, I think I've heard enough of what you have to say. You're nothing but a crook. I can't believe you would do this to people who believed in you."

Marie grabbed her brother's hand and stomped back inside to collect her sisters, with her brother holding his crotch and whimpering the whole way. "Just hold on. We'll find a place for you to go in a minute. Now stop your whining."

"What's the matter, Marie?"

"Nothing. Just grab your things. We're leaving." All the way home Marie fumed. "Why would God allow people like that to con the people who believe in Him?" It didn't make sense. She was more confused than ever before.

"So, let me get this straight", she thought, "I'm supposed to try being perfect every day. I'm supposed to not to commit any sins, not back slide, whatever that means , so that God will continue to love me, while this con man fleeces the very people that have gathered to worship Him?" No, she wasn't buying it. There had to be more to this religious thing than that. Back at work on Monday she told her boss of the double cross she'd witnessed in back of the revival tent. He wasn't surprised. "I'm sorry, Marie. I wondered when you told me about the tent revival if it was on the up and up. Believe me when I tell you that it happens more than you might realize. But, also believe me when I say that not all traveling evangelists are bad guys."

"It was just so impressive when he prayed for healing for all those people, and they were healed. It made my heart feel so good to see that."

"Well, in my church we've been taught that those types of miracles don't really happen anymore. That was something that happened during the 'Apostolic Age', and isn't for today. Today we don't have to see miracles to believe that Jesus exists."

Marie knew there was something erroneous about her boss's statement. It just felt wrong. She knew Angela had prayed for her, and after they'd discovered her friend's boarded up house, Marie had come to the conclusion; without sharing her presumptions with anyone else; that Angela was her angel. It was comforting to believe she had someone watching over her. Especially because she'd felt very alone most of her life.

"I'd like to invite you to come to church with my family on Sunday. Would you consider that?"

"Thanks, Boss, but I think I'll take a rain check on that. I'm not feeling very open to church at the moment. I'll let you know if I change my mind." She really didn't want to hurt his feelings. But, she didn't think she wanted to be part of a church that didn't believe in miracles. It seemed to her that from what she'd heard about Jesus, He was all about miracles. If she was ever going to believe in anything, and she had a long way to go on that one, she'd have to do a little checking around. Maybe she'd read the Bible she received when she gave her heart to Jesus at the first revival meeting.

As she walked through the gravel to her trailer, the boy next door approached. "Hey, I saw you at the tent revival, didn't I?"

"Yes, I was there. But if they come back I won't be going."

"Why? I thought you looked like you were having a good time."

"I was until I discovered that the pastor was paying people to pretend they were being healed."

"Oh, don't take that too seriously. These preachers that come through town do that kind of stuff all the time."

"Then why do you go? I mean, if you know they're just a bunch of crooks."

"Well, it doesn't cost me anything, because I don't put anything in the buckets when they come around. I don't know. It's exciting with all those people there. You know. Small town. It's just something to do I guess. And, I really love the music."

"Well, I believed him, and it was a bit heartbreaking to find out it was all a lie."

"You could try the church I go to, if you want. A bus comes by on Sunday, and stops in front of Frank's. That way you have a ride there and back. Some of the kids from school go there too. You're welcome if you want to come."

"I don't know. I'll have to think about it. Thank you. What time does it stop, if I decide to go?"

"Nine in the morning. That way you're there in time for church school too. There's classes for your brother and sisters too."

"Maybe we will. I'll decide before Sunday. Thanks for the information."

"Any time. See you at school."

"Yeah, see ya."

"Hey."

"Yeah?"

"My name's Richard."

"Hi, Richard. My name's Marie."

"I know."

In all the time they'd lived side by side, this was the first time her neighbor had taken time to talk to her. He'd lent her the bicycle without brakes, as soon as she'd asked, and she'd always wondered if he knew the brakes were bad. But he seemed nice as she spoke to him now. And, as far as she knew, he'd never gotten his bike back, so perhaps they were even on that score. She'd have to think about it some more, but maybe she'd give his church a try. It certainly couldn't be one of those uppity churches filled with rich people, if that was the church these neighbors attended.

The sergeant lay in his cot, sweat pouring from every pore in his body. It was no longer hot in Vietnam, as fall had kicked in a couple of weeks ago, but abject fear will do that to a guy. He's just awakened from another bloody nightmare, screaming. After watching so many die, or completely lose themselves to the horrors of shell shock in this damned war, the dreams seem to be a permanent part of his psyche now. Will he ever be able to get the terrible visions and sounds out of his head? It's too exhausting to think about. And, perhaps there are better ways to silence the screaming.

Sadly, he almost can't remember what his kids look like, and that makes him very sad. He brought a picture of his wife with him the day he left, you know, in one of those pin up poses that most guys like. She loved dressing up for that, or down would be more like it, and couldn't get enough of him after it was taken. Though, admittedly, he seldom pulls it out of his wallet anymore. It makes him too sad to look at her now, since he hasn't heard from her in such a long time.

Who knows what she's doing these days, or if she ever thinks of him. But the kids, that's a different story. He'd give anything to see them now. Though, he was sure they'd all have grown considerably after almost a year had passed, he hoped they might still remember him, considering that their time together had been so short before his deployment. The thought of losing them made his heart hurt.

Halloween was coming up at the end of the month, only a few weeks away. He remembered trick-or-treating in his old neighborhood as a kid, and wondered what the kids would come up with for costumes. Their mom, sadly, wasn't very interested in anything to do with the children, he'd discovered that forlorn fact after they were married, but Marie was pretty creative and had a way of making do with almost nothing.

Still no letters. He couldn't figure it out. Even if his wife had found another man, it was hard to imagine Marie wouldn't have written. It had seemed they developed such a close relationship before he left. At least he hadn't heard anything derogatory from his mom, so they must be tolerating each other's company.

Sunday arrived and Marie had the children scrubbed and dressed neatly, as they awaited the bus which would take them to Richard's church. They were already standing by the road when he walked out from behind Frank's service station. "Well, hi there!"

"Hi to you too, Richard. These are my sisters and brother."

"Yeah, I've seen them around. The bus should be here any second. I'm glad you decided to come."

"I thought I'd give it a try. We'll see."

"You'll like our church school teacher, she's pretty cool."

"You said they have classes for the little ones too, right?"

"Yep, I'm sure they'll like it. Lots of fun things to do, and snacks too. The people there are all great."

"Good, that makes me feel better. I've been reading a little of my Bible. The one I got when I went up to accept Christ at the revival. So far, God just seems like an old mean guy in the sky. The Old Testament is very confusing.'

"Well, you're doing better than me. I have to admit, I've never read my Bible. It's in my room somewhere. Maybe that's something I should think about doing sometime."

"It's a little chilly out here. We might have to break out the winter coats soon."

"It will warm up later. The beginning of October is always a little tricky around here. But, you'll need to dress warmer by the end of October. Speaking of that. We usually have a Halloween dance at school. Are you going with anyone yet?"

"No, and I probably won't, sorry. I'm usually taking care of the kids. You know I'm only twelve, right?"

"Actually, I don't think I did. But, you're a freshman, aren't you?"

"Yes, I got skipped ahead a few times."

"Oh, one of those smarty pants girls, huh?"

"Hey, watch it."

"Okay, okay, I just meant you seem way older than that. If you change your mind, I'd still like to take you."

"Thanks. We'll see. Oh, I think I see the bus coming."

"Yes, that's it. Let me help with the little ones. The first step is a whopper."

At the small church her new friend helped her find classes for her sisters and brother, and then led her to the high school room. Once there she was met with stares from the other girls in the room, and whispers among the groups.

She felt uncomfortable. "Hey guys and gals, this is Marie. She lives next to me at the trailer park. Everybody say hi."

Marie recognized at least two of the kids from school, but she didn't know everyone in the upper grades, so she was sure they all attended. "We know Marie, Richard. But, isn't she only twelve years old? Maybe she belongs in one of the elementary classes?"

"No, I brought her to our class, because she's a freshman in school."

"Well, perhaps you should check with Ms. Peters first, before you start deciding how the class will be run?"

"Listen, I don't want to make trouble. I'll just leave."

"No you will not, Marie. We'll check with Ms. Peters first, but I'm sure you'll be in this room. The placements are according to grades, not age. And, girls, since we're sitting in a church school setting, you might want to act like Christians. Just a suggestion." Marie winced at Richard's last remark. She knew he was only trying to protect her, but the look on the girl's faces was one of pure hatred, now that he'd pointed out their obvious lack of charity.

This would probably go over about as well as when teachers pointed out Marie's IQ to other students, and asked if they wanted to be tutored by this little girl who was obviously more intelligent than they were. She closed her eyes and sat down, grateful that at least this time she had a champion by her side. He would most likely take lots of flak for this when they returned to school on Monday.

Of course Ms. Peters insisted Marie stay and participate in the high school class. And, afterward she commended Marie on the well thought out questions she's posed during their open discussion on the book of Exodus. Most of the girls in class were clearly there due to their parent's insistence on their attendance. Because, it was obvious to anyone listening that they hadn't read the lesson, or their Bibles, and only wanted to disrupt the conversation long enough to wait out the end of the week's class time.

She saw the same thing occur often in school when students hadn't bothered to do their homework, or study for tests. It was one of the oldest tricks in the book. It made her want to come back, with more real questions, to get real answers. And, it made her respect Ms. Peters all the more. She knew her teachers in school were paid to put up with insolent teenagers. This woman did it for nothing more than the joy of teaching young people.

The sanctuary of Richard's church was painted white. The East and West walls were lined with tall, opaque windows, etched with scenes from the Bible. Simple chandeliers hung from the center of the high arched ceiling. Pews had been removed and replaced with padded, white chairs, which could be stacked to the side of the room, when the sanctuary needed to be pressed into service for any number of additional purposes. The dais was carpeted with a light grey, indoor, outdoor carpet, and the podium was constructed of acrylic, which gave it a kind of modern look. In each window sill stood a single candle, you know, the kind that run on batteries and have a flickering bulb that resembles a flame. Pastor's Bible was open and set up on the podium, ready for the day's sermon.

Church services started off with music, but thankfully, in this case, there were words printed on an overhead screen, so she didn't have to feel like an idiot. The preacher was young and not too boring, but she didn't get the same sensation of being covered in a warm fuzzy glow that she'd had at the very first revival meeting. After service she walked through a reception line and shook hands with the minister, who seemed genuinely interested in her presence. Richard introduced her and explained to the pastor that she lived in the trailer next to him at Frank's. All in all the experience wasn't terrible. But, she didn't know if it was worth the hassle she and Richard would likely endure at school.

All U.S. held bases were on high alert, pending a visit from President Johnson. The sergeant was trying his best to present himself and his men in a good light, so he cleaned up his quarters and stashed the bottles that presently got him through the night. The President met with troops at Cam Ranh Bay, and would be making several brief stops at various other air bases around Vietnam. Perhaps his visit was the precursor to halted U.S. involvement? They could only hope.

Rain, which had persisted for the last month came down in buckets; thoroughly soaking everyone as they lined up for inspection; and chilling them to the bone. This was the season to take care of your feet, or you could end up losing them.

Marie was right. The girls who were rude to her at church on Sunday, were standing in the hall at school, right between her and her first morning class. "Excuse me."

"Excuse you? Why should we excuse you? There's no excuse for you." The leader of the pack shoved her and grabbed her books, throwing them all over the hallway and scattering her impeccably completed homework assignments. They pulled her hair, slapped her repeatedly and pushed her back and forth from one provocateur to the next, picking up and ripping her papers to shreds.

"Please, I don't know why you're doing this, but there's no need. I don't plan to go back to your stupid church if that's what's bothering you."

"You're right. It does bother me that you showed up at my stupid church, but it bothers me even more that you showed up at my stupid school. I don't want you here."

"Well, neither of us has much of a choice in that. We're both stuck here. So, if you don't like it, take it up with the school board."

"Or maybe we'll just settle it here." At that the girl shoved Marie to the floor and proceeded to kick her, prompting her followers to join in punching and kicking at will. When all was said and done, Marie lay in the hallway bloody and bruised, unable to move. The janitor found her and carried her to the office, where a shocked nurse began to tend to the girl and tried to get information about who had beaten her so badly. Marie was more concerned about her books and homework assignments, which now littered the hall. She'd spent her life with a woman who beat her pretty regularly, so she was used to this part. She decided not to attend Richard's church going forward.

Later, her smallest sister cried when she saw Marie. The kids were worried, but her boss was angry. "Who did this to you? They are going to be very sorry."

"It doesn't matter, Boss. It was a group of girls at school. I don't want to start any trouble."

"It seems to me that they've started the trouble. Let me at least drive you home."

"I'm fine. I'll do my work first, but then I might take that ride."

Richard knocked on the door later. "Wow! Somebody told me they saw you like this, and I had to come see for myself. Was it the girls from church?"

"Richard, I don't want any trouble."

"It looks like they started the trouble. Did you tell the principal?"

"No, I know how this works. If I tell, then they will simply wait for me to be alone again, and again. They're bigger than I am, so I can't beat them. That's why I said I don't want any trouble."

"You don't seem like the kind of girl who will just let something like this slide."

"Don't I? Well, if this was one of my sisters, or my brother, then no. But, people have been knocking me around my whole life, and I know from experience it isn't worth the hassle to try to stand up to bullies. I'm just not big enough. I've discovered that if you leave it alone they get bored and find someone else to pick on."

"So you wouldn't mind if those girls did this to someone else?"

"That's not what I mean, and you know it. I just don't want to create more of a problem. And, I won't be coming back to church with you either.'

"So, you're going to let them keep you from coming to church? You really aren't the girl I thought you were."

"I guess I'm not. So, if you'll leave now, I can get back to making supper for the kids."

"Fine. Goodbye Marie." It was better if she didn't get too close to anyone anyway.

Mother came home that night. She was back from her leaf peeper trip. She didn't stay long, just long enough to pick up a few things and drop off some dirty laundry.

"What happened to you?"

"Nothing Mother. I fell is all."

"Well, you always were a klutz. I have to get going, he's waiting for me in the car."

"Of course he is Mother."

Supper was simple that night. She thought she deserved a break. Mac and cheese with hot dogs and peaches might not seem like much, but at least it wasn't just a bowl of Captain Crunch cereal, bologna, or a peanut butter and jelly sandwich, which is what they'd survived on for the first month they lived in the trailer; and the kids seemed to like simple meals the best anyway. As it was, she'd be doing laundry for half the night with all the things her mom dropped off.

The sergeant lay in bed imagining his little ones trick or treating. His neighborhood always gave out great treats when he was growing up; popcorn balls, homemade candies and cookies, and often coins that he would add to the contents of his piggy bank at home. But, the best part for he and his friends was the tricks, oh they had fun on Halloween. And, they never got caught, which made it all the sweeter.

On base that day the mess hall handed out chocolate bars with supper, and he munched on his while he listened to the rain pouring down outside, and as he reminisced about his childhood. Heck, for all he knew there might even still be some of his old Halloween costumes in the attic. He hoped the kids were having a good time, even if he couldn't be there with them. He also hoped his mom wasn't being too hard on his wife. Because, even though he hadn't received a single letter from her, he still loved her more than he could express, and hoped to make things right when he arrived home from deployment.

"The wicked watches for the righteous and seeks to put him to death. The Lord will not abandon him to his power or let him be condemned when he is brought to trial."

Psalm 37:32-3

CHAPTER 11

No trick or treating this year. Marie decided it would be too dangerous in this area. There really weren't any typical residential neighborhoods out here where they lived, and only a few trailers at the park, most with questionable inhabitants. She didn't trust her shady neighbors enough to let the little ones go out and play even under normal circumstances, unless she could be out there to watch them. So, she certainly wasn't going to let these people put candy in bags for her loved ones.

Instead of trick or treating, she made popcorn balls and chocolate chip cookies, which turned out pretty good if she did say so herself. Then they all piled into the living room, and told ghost stories by candle light as they ate their snacks. The children assured her it was the best Halloween they'd ever spent anywhere.

The evening reminded her a little of the week they

camped out on Mount Shasta for their honeymoon with Daddy. What a glorious week that had been. It seemed decades ago, though it'd actually been just a little over a year. Had Daddy really been gone almost a year now? She hoped he was okay. Missing him so much that it hurt, she wondered how he would find them when he got back, if he returned at all.

The sergeant, hunkered down in elephant grass; his men well hidden and scattered throughout the area; was awaiting a radio 'go' signal. The village, like so many others they'd raided on search and destroy missions, was alive with chickens, goats, and children playing. Sounds of laughter, floating through the crisp, fall air made the upcoming raid seem all the more unnecessary to anyone looking on. Men working diligently in the fields were completely unaware of the danger lurking only meters away. And, wisps of smoke rising through exhaust vents in various village huts, carried the smells of something delicious on the wind.

Intelligence received from reliable sources told them that there was a large cell of Cong working out of this village, and the biggest cache of weapons in the area. He hated raiding villages where children were so prominent. And he knew from training sessions he'd attended that the Cong intentionally used the little ones as pawns, to keep the weak Americans from attacking. It was pretty much universally known that U.S. troops were suckers for kids. So, he was expected to do his job as ordered, and ignore the fact that there would likely be collateral damage.

Radio silence broke, and they had their signal. Staying low, until they reached the edge of the grassy area, they rose up and stormed the village. Women, children, and animals, scattered. Men began to run from the fields. Troops started in on the nearest hut, and tore their way through each one, until two different shouts were heard that announced the discovery of Cong soldiers and weapons. The enemy went for his guns and shooting erupted. The sergeant, following the direction of the shots fired, made his way back with his squad. NVA troops lay dead in the dirt outside the hut, and inside two more were trussed up like roasting pigs. In the next hut were four dead Cong laying on blood soaked piles of ammunition and weapons. Two of his men were down. One was dead, shot directly between the eyes, and the other was bleeding profusely from a gut wound. He gave orders for two of the men to take their wounded brother to the pickup site, and two more to carry their dead comrade. "We'll do clean up before I call in an air strike," he shouted to the men.

As they continued to do a quick search of the remaining huts, a surprise made itself known. There was a third hidey hole, under the meat smoking hut, where four more NVA awaited. When the door swung open more gun blasts ripped through the air, and two more of his men fell. He unloaded his weapon into the hut and devastated the four enemy soldiers there, as well as any smoked meat on the premises. Shaking, he ordered more of his men to carry their stricken friends and he headed to the village center. He threw his weapon and put his hands on a pump handle to steady himself. "You okay, Sergeant?"

"Of course I'm not okay. It was as if they knew we were coming!" As he released the pump handle and looked around, he saw the dead bodies of several women and children in among the dead NVA, and he shook his head. "What the hell just happened here? I swear they knew we were in the grass. It's like they were waiting for us, and using the children to draw us in. Do we have any prisoners?"

"Yes, Sarg. They're over here." The two trussed NVA were laying in the dirt, as well as two additional men who were not in uniform."

"Ask them who was in charge here?"

"The Cong won't talk at all, Sarg, but the other two just keep begging for the lives of their wives and children."

"Tell them we can get them to a place of safety, if they give us the information we need. We need to know whose orders they were following; how long the Cong have been here; if they know of any more weapons stashed in the area; and who told them we were coming."

"They said they were just following the orders of the soldiers who were here. Neither one seems to know where any more weapons are hidden. And, a runner came this morning with information."

"Where did the runner come from?"

"They said he came from another village close to the base."

"So we have a traitor. We need to know if he's still here, and if he's not, then we need someone to identify him when we get to the other village."

"They're both scared, Sarg. They say they were only trying to protect their families."

One of the trussed up enemy soldiers began shouting at the two villagers. "He's threatening their wives and children, Sarg. Telling them that if they don't quit talking he will kill them all."

The sergeant pulled out his hand gun and shot both Cong soldiers in the head. "Now, ask them which one is going with us to identify the traitor. Tell them that their village will be burned for colluding with the NVA, but those who are still alive will remain so, unless they give us reason to leave them otherwise."

"The one closest to me will come with us, Sarg, as long as we can guarantee him that his family will remain safe from the Viet Cong."

"Tell him that we will relocate him and his family to a safe place, so the Cong won't know where to find them. That's all I can promise. Now, someone clear the village. I'm calling for an air strike."

Villagers ran into the nearby trees and grass. Women carrying babies, children large and small, old men and animals. The sergeant looked around at the destruction and bodies of the dead, and an anger boiled up in him that he couldn't quite describe. The idea that men would put women and children in a position to take the brunt of the attack; that the ground was littered with the twisted corpses of children who would never grow up or grow old, infuriated him. He wanted to destroy them all. All those who would put their own agendas ahead of these innocent souls. He was tired, so very tired, of the killing and death. He needed it to end. He needed to go home. There wasn't much of his sanity left. When would it all end? He retrieved his weapon and followed his men, carrying the dead from among their brothers, out of the village.

He made his call, and as they approached the tree line he saw fighter jets slicing through the clouds. In seconds the village was ablaze with the inferno created by white phosphorus; followed shortly by fields of crops popping and crackling from the intense heat of the blaze.

Back at the waiting transport helicopters his wounded soldier was carried aboard first, his dead soldiers were lifted on board second, then their prisoner/informant, and only after all else was accomplished, his men who were still moving on their own entered the choppers. This was a bad day. Three troops down. Three men who would never see their families again. How would he ever be able to face their loved ones? They'd been so close to leaving this despicable place, and now they would arrive home in flag draped coffins, to jeering crowds. And, all those dead children. His mind couldn't make sense of any of this, and he just wanted to go home. They would interrogate the informant, and then get him to a new location with his family. He'd told the man, "A safe place", but was there a safe place in this God forsaken land?

The 'New York Times' reports that up to forty percent of all economic aid sent from the U.S, to Saigon, is stolen, or winds up on the Black Market. Protests are becoming more frequent and more violent, as the hopeless war rages on.

Thanksgiving is right around the corner, and Marie is going to cook. She's making a roasted chicken, due to the cost of turkey being just out of her price range. Besides, she reasoned, a turkey for the four of them hardly made sense. She looked up a few recipes at the library, and was feeling confident. Her boss and his wife invited them to attend a large feast at their house, but she lied and said her mother would be there, so she had to stay home.

In reality she didn't know if her mother would bother to show up or not, but doubted it, because her husband might be coming home in a couple of months, and she'd likely be trying to get in as much time with her cop boyfriend as she could before his arrival. She wasn't going to try making stuffing. None of the kids would eat it anyway. But, she would make mashed potatoes with gravy; baby peas and carrots; biscuits, cranberry sauce; and a pumpkin pie. The children would be helping her, and she was excited to share her small amount of cooking prowess and the precious time they would spend together doing something so very traditional for so many people.

At moments like this she wondered how her older sister was doing. It had been a long time. She hoped the facility would be serving turkey. She was well aware that her sister probably wouldn't have helped with the preparation of their meal even if she were here, and likely wouldn't even have been here to share it, if she wasn't already locked up. But, just like Daddy said, Holidays are for family. She hoped he wasn't in danger, and that someone would be feeding the soldiers turkey. Was there even such a thing as turkey in Vietnam?

The mess hall was serving turkey for supper tonight. It wasn't bad, but certainly nothing like the meal he and Marie had prepared last year. Just the memory of it made him smile. She was such an eager learner, and he loved having someone to teach.

Their meal was everything it should be: turkey and stuffing, but not his mother's oyster stuffing, he'd always hated that; mashed potatoes with lots of butter and garlic, and gravy from the turkey pan drippings; homemade yeast rolls, mostly kneaded by his apprentice, as she was becoming quite the bread expert; fresh corn and baby peas with carrots; a yummy Jell-o and fruit salad; homemade cranberry sauce, Marie had watched fascinated as the berries simmered and burst; and two pies, pumpkin and apple. They'd even whipped up a bowl of fresh cream that made the pies more special yet.

They'd used the wedding china and cutlery, and the little ones made turkey place cards from construction paper, feathers and glue (lots of glue). The whole family was involved, well, except for his new wife. He was discovering little, by little that she wasn't a big fan of anything even bordering on domestic. But, she did sit close by, with a glass of wine, smiling at their efforts. That was okay with him. He didn't mind being the one to instruct and lead the children. He'd waited a long time to be a dad, and he was savoring every moment of the experience.

Now, as he sat in the mess hall with a tray that was supposed to bring Thanksgiving overseas to the war zone, he felt a lump form in his throat. The lump grew, and he knew he wouldn't be able to eat the meal sitting in front of him. Instead, he dumped his tray and wandered back to his quarters in the darkness of the cold evening. Back in his room he pulled out the bottle of vodka tucked in his foot locker. He'd be having a simple Thanksgiving this year.

Marie and the kids did a great job of preparing their Thanksgiving feast. The little ones made place cards again, just as they had for their first Thanksgiving with Daddy last year. They even made a turkey card for Dad, and set it up at the head of the table, though Marie noticed they didn't do the same for their missing mother, or their oldest sister. The meal was delicious, and they spent fifteen minutes afterward congratulating each other on their success, before they cut the pies.

Marie sent the youngest two off to the bath, while she and her sister cleaned up from their fabulous meal. Leftovers would make a great lunch tomorrow, and she already had plans to start decorating the house for Christmas.

Though they would wait a bit for a tree, she wanted to begin making decorations for the windows and had lots of ideas to share with the children. She'd missed Daddy so much, today, that she'd had to check herself several times in order to keep from crying in front of her siblings. She just hoped he was okay so very far away.

At school she'd listened to teachers speaking endlessly about the unjust war in Vietnam, and America's perceived aggression. They went on and on about the evils of the U.S., and how we always march into other countries as if we are trying to take over the world. The teachers who spoke so disdainfully about the servicemen and women who were risking their lives, had never served in the military themselves. Marie was grieved by the obvious negative world opinion of American soldiers fighting in this deadly battle, most of whom had been drafted and had no choice but to struggle in a war that would gain the U.S. nothing. So many had been lost, and for what? She knew Daddy wasn't a baby killer, and no matter what, she would stand by him, if only he made it home.

As he moved closer to the hut, he saw a bright glow

coming from the interior of the grass structure and wondered if it was on fire. He approached cautiously and saw five children sitting on the floor inside. They were facing a large cooking fire, which would explain the brightness he'd seen from outside the door. He tried to speak, to warn them that their fire was growing, exploding, and getting out of hand, but no sound came from his mouth.

He fired his weapon toward the vented grass of the ceiling, in an effort to grab their attention, and all five turned toward him as one. Their faces were bloody, with missing eyes, broken teeth and crushed skulls. He backed away and tripped over something on the floor. Looking down, he saw it was the mangled body of another child. The body burst open. Blood and guts covered the floor. He turned to escape, but as he tried to run he slipped on the gore. Trying to rise he slipped again, and suddenly the children were standing over him. They began to descend toward him and he screamed. Waking in his cot, he found himself wrapped in bedding, fighting the scratchy military issue blankets that were supposed to keep him warm. He sat up and grabbed the bottle from under his bed, taking a long draw from its contents. But, even that didn't stop the shaking.

Guilt from the part he'd played in the deaths of so many,

especially the children, was beginning to overtake his mind. He couldn't sleep without being persecuted by the nightmares that sprang up from the depths of his soul, like monsters escaping the darkness of a deep closet. And, drowning in pain and anguish, he was attempting to mask his memories in the alcohol that was slowly taking his health and his life. How could he live with all he'd done? And, even if he made it back to his family; even if they hadn't moved on without him; how could they ever love him again with so much blood on his hands? He cried out to God, but didn't hear an answer to his broken, desperate cries. Perhaps he was too far gone for even God to help him now. Maybe he didn't deserve to be forgiven.

Marie's boss asked her to put up a few decorations at the station, and she was happy to do it for him. She and the children had spent the day after Thanksgiving decorating with handmade angels, and construction paper chains. She and her sister painted a Christmas scene, of 'Peanuts' characters, on the living room window, and decided to leave the curtain open to catch the light through their masterpiece. When the light shone on it, just right, it looked like the stained glass windows of the church.

She would wait a couple of weeks to get a tree, but planned to buy a string of electric lights to hang from the branches when she did. They'd already created the ornaments they would use to decorate their tree, and those sat neatly in a box next to the sofa. The little ones picked them up, gently, to examine and look at them fifty times a day. You could feel the anticipation rising in their hopes and dreams, which compared to many children around the country were simple ones. Last year they hadn't put up a tree, and though Bernice had one, it was not a very welcoming tree. Since Daddy had been leaving they didn't exchange gifts, or put up additional decorations, and the whole holiday had fallen a little flat. Marie wanted to make up for that sad Christmas, and give the children something special.

Marie knew that Christmas was traditionally a time when people celebrated the birth of Christ, but her family hadn't ever really gotten into all of that, and her mom never made a big deal of the holiday. This year she planned to change that in a big way.

At the service station she went into the storage closet and found the boxes labeled 'Christmas'. When she opened them she was a bit confused. One of the boxes contained what seemed to be an artificial tree, in many parts, and made of aluminum foil. It took her a little while, but she managed to put it together. Along with the tree there was a device that plugged into the wall. When turned on the device sent out a light beam that shone through an ever rotating wheel of color. The colors reflected on the aluminum of the tree and made a very nice display. The children were thrilled. "Marie, that's so beautiful! Can we get a foil tree?"

"Not this year guys. Maybe we can save up for one. This year we'll have a regular tree, and that will be expensive enough. But, you are free to enjoy this tree when we're here to work."

"Then we get to have both!"

"Yes, then we get to have both." In the boxes were additional decorations for the windows, ornaments for the tree, and even some garland to hang in the pump area. The kids helped and her boss was thrilled when he saw how great everything looked.

"I don't know what we'd do without you around here, Marie. You've been such a great worker, and a real blessing in our lives."

"Thank you, Boss. I feel the same way about you and

the guys. Thank you for giving a kid a chance, and for being there for us on so many occasions I can't even count them."

"It has been my honor young lady. And, I have something extra for you this week."

"No, no, Boss. You've already done so much for us."

"I insist. All the guys are getting a bonus, and you will get one too. It's a Christmas bonus, and you can't say no! This is from my family, to thank you for all your hard work and loyalty."

"Thank you. I appreciate it very much." When she opened the envelope, she gasped. Inside was two hundred dollars in twenty dollar bills. "Oh, Boss, this is too much."

"No it's not, Marie. I wish it could be more. Your hard work has changed our lives for the better in so many ways. We really noticed it when you were laid up, and we appreciate you more than you know."

"Well, this will make for a really nice Christmas for the kids. Thank you again."

"You're welcome, and have fun with it for once."

"I will. I definitely will."

The sergeant and his men were getting antsy. They

would be going home in about a month, and there were some superstitions that floated around short timers in country. They'd already lost so many from their unit, and the sergeant wanted to make sure those numbers didn't grow during the countdown for home. Christmas was coming at the end of the month, but he wouldn't be spending it with his family, as he wasn't scheduled to depart till the end of December.

Christmas season was magical that year! The only thing that would have made it better is having Daddy home, but hopefully next year. Marie and the kids cut down their own tree, from the wooded area out beyond the trailer park. And, though it wasn't perfectly straight, and was missing a few branches here and there, they thought it was perfect. They put it in a bucket of water, and tied string to the middle of the trunk, anchoring it to a door handle on one side, and a window crank on the other. Once it was standing somewhat upright, they applied the lights, and the box of homemade decorations. Standing back to admire their handiwork, they agreed it was the most beautiful tree that ever existed on the entire planet. That night they made mugs of hot chocolate, and sugar cookies, and sat before the tree singing every Christmas carol they'd ever heard, whether they knew all the words or not. By the end of their sing along, they were rolling on the floor with glee.

Marie managed to make arrangements with the grocery owner to purchase gifts for the kids. Each week when she shopped for food, one or two of the gift items came wrapped and tucked in with her grocery order; hidden until she could get home and hide them from the children. She became more and more excited as the big day approached. Openly admitting to herself that she was having more fun preparing for the surprise, than she ever would have being the one surprised.

Things had finally begun to settle down at school. Richard was once again deeply ensconced with his friends from Sunday school, and all but ignored her ever day. Jeff hadn't talked to her in months, intimidated by the upper classmen who didn't like her for whatever reason. She didn't mind. It made the girls who'd attacked her feel that they'd won some kind of victory, and they were content to let her alone. She knew that in the long run she'd been the winner after all.

When school dismissed for the Christmas holidays, she could hardly wait to get off the bus and see the guys at the station. She and the children had made each of them a gift of cookies and banana bread, wrapped up in pretty packages, and tied with red and green ribbon. And she'd hauled them around with her all day at school; passing out small gifts of baked goods to each of her teachers, school office staff, and her favorite janitor. Along with each gift was a handmade card, signed by each of the kids. The guys were very appreciative, and would later tell Marie that her cookies and banana bread were the best they'd ever eaten, really meaning every word of it. She also left a gift of cookies on the top step of each trailer in the park.

Christmas Eve was extra special. It was okay that Mom wasn't there. She made sure, most of the time, to stop by during the day when they were at school. And then only to drop off dirty clothes and pick up clean ones. Marie did think it was kind of sad that when she got home yesterday for holiday vacation, and found a pile of dirty clothing, there were no gifts for the children anywhere to be found. But, the idea of her being home yelling at the kids over the holidays was much worse than not having her around at all. She was sure her mother's Christmas would be merry, wherever she was.

All would be fine, as Marie had thought of everything.

For supper on Christmas Eve they dined on chili and homemade bread, with a nice fruit and vegetable platter. For dessert there were still lots of cookies and more mugs of hot chocolate with tiny marshmallows. They sang and read 'The Night Before Christmas', then Marie retrieved some wrapped packages that they were allowed to open that night. Inside were brand new pajamas and slippers for each child. She sent them off to bathe and get dressed, and then she tucked them in and admonished them to, "Get right to sleep. Santa won't come until you're asleep, and he always knows!".

After they were off to sleep she made a batch of cinnamon rolls, and set them out to rise, then she got to work. There was no chimney, or fire place, so she'd had the kids lay their homemade stockings on the carpet in front of the tree. She singed some cotton, and attached it to the heating grate in the living room; then she scattered wrapped candy on the floor from the grate to the tree, as if Santa's pack had ripped going through the heating unit. At the tree she laid out two wrapped gifts for each child; something they'd written for in a letter to Santa, and a stuffed animal to match their personality. For one it was a beautiful dolly, complete with several changes of clothing and a wonderful baby bottle that looked like it was being emptied when it was turned upside down; for another it was a beautiful purse and wallet, which; when opened, contained a much coveted birth stone ring; her brother received a collection of heavy duty metal cars, consisting of everything from a hot rod to a dump truck, and a set of army men. Inside their stockings they would find oranges, candy canes, marbles, jacks, yoyos and playing cards; there were also new tooth brushes, hair brushes, and for the girls, pretties for their hair. Colored pencils and new coloring books sat next to each stocking. After baking cinnamon rolls and making icing, she finally crawled into bed at midnight, and still couldn't sleep because she was so excited.

Marie finally drifted off to sleep and dreamed that she looked outside and saw Daddy walking to the trailer. She ran into his arms crying, and wouldn't let go. She was in the midst of that dream when she heard squeals from the other room, "Marie, Marie, Santa came! Hurry, hurry, Santa came!" She jumped from the bed and rushed to the living room to see the children standing with their eyes wide and their mouths hanging open. No late night had ever been more worth it than the last one had been, to see the looks on their faces that Christmas morning.

She made a deal with them. They could search out the contents of their stockings, but then they would eat breakfast before opening their gifts. And even that would be done in an orderly manner, with each one taking a turn, to make the experience last longer. As she heated milk for hot chocolate, she listened to yelps and shouts of joy coming from the living room as they dug deeper into their stockings and discovered one delight after another. "Oh, Marie, we can play cards now! Will you play with us?"

"Of course I will, but not right this moment. First we're going to have some homemade cinnamon rolls and hot chocolate, and then we'll open gifts, how does that sound?"

"Yay, this is the best Christmas ever!"

When the children opened their gifts they were thrilled. "Santa got my letter, and he brought me exactly what I asked for!" The recipient of the birth stone ring cried, because she was so happy, (though in reality she'd figured out that Marie was Santa and she knew how much her sister had sacrificed to give them a nice Christmas). They would all remember this Christmas, for the rest of their lives, as the best Christmases ever.

The littlest one piped up, "But, wait, Marie didn't get anything. Why didn't Santa bring anything for you, Marie?"

"Well, I didn't write a letter to Santa. I'm getting a little old for that. Santa takes care of the little ones, like you."

"Then I don't ever want to grow up. I'm sorry you're too old for presents, Marie. You can have some of my candy, and we can play cards and marbles together."

"Thank you. I'd like that very much. Merry Christmas everyone."

"Merry Christmas, Marie."

Christmas was hugely underwhelming for the sergeant and his men. Some had packages from home and shared stale cookies and fudge with their mates, but the idea that their loved ones were so far away wasn't lost on any of them. They'd be leaving this hell hole in just a few days, and they weren't taking any chances, not after all the loses their unit had suffered in this God forsaken place.

Facing harsh scrutiny from American journalists, the defense department finally admits that civilians in North Vietnam may have accidentally been bombed.

The U.S. mounts a large-scale air assault against suspected Viet Cong positions in the Mekong Delta using Napalm and hundreds of tons of bombs.

By year's end, American troop levels reach three hundred and eighty nine thousand, with five thousand and eight combat deaths and thirty thousand and ninety three wounded. Over half of the U.S. casualties were caused by snipers and small-arms fire during Viet Cong ambushes, along with handmade booby traps and mines planted everywhere in the countryside by Viet Cong. American Allies fighting in Vietnam include forty five thousand soldiers from South Korea, and Seven thousand Australians. An estimated eighty nine thousand soldiers from North Vietnam infiltrated the South via the Ho Chi Minh Trail in 1966.

In the midst of the overwhelming disaster that was the Vietnam war, the hatred and bias of the media, and the daily protests by every day Americans, the sergeant boarded a troop transport with his men. They were heading stateside.

The front door opens and Mother is standing in the light. The children, who were busily playing in the living room look up, and the little one runs to Marie in the kitchen. "Oh, I see you got a tree. Kind of an ugly thing, isn't it?" And so it begins.

Mother, after checking with the base, has discovered

that Daddy will be home in a couple of days, and has told her lover they have to cool it for now. She still can't drive and doesn't own a car, so they won't be able to pick him up from the airport. They will have to rely on Bernice to give him some indication of where they are. And the last Bernice knew, mother and children had been transported, by the police, to the women's shelter in town. That was right after Pops died. Marie wished she could be there for him when he found out his dad was gone. He would be so sad.

Mom seemed to only be concerned that one of the children would have loose lips and tell daddy they hadn't seen much of her in the past year, as she was off cavorting with men she'd picked up along the way. They were all threatened with horrible consequences if they gave her up. What was worse was that she would be home now, until his eventual return. Marie knew it would be in her best interest to keep the kids quiet and out of Mom's hair, so they spent the next few days playing cards and talking in whispers.

After debriefing, and a long flight home, the enormous troop carrier landed at the airfield in New York, the sergeant and his men deplaned to the screams and jeers of waiting protesters. Carrying their packs and bags they walked through a shouting, angry mob. Some of whom spit in their faces as they walked by. It was a sad homecoming indeed, hardly a hero's welcome. And, a far cry from the way soldiers from previous wars had been welcomed home. The sergeant didn't think he could feel much lower, until he looked around and realized he didn't see his wife and kids, or even his dad. From inside the airport terminal, being harassed all the way, he called a taxi and, made his way to his parent's house.

"Hey Mom, Dad, kids, everybody, I'm home."

"Welcome home, Son."

"Where is everyone? I thought at least Pop would be there to give me a ride home. I told you I was coming." He spoke as his mother was slowly, and painfully, descending the stairs. It seemed that shortly after she'd kicked Marie and the rest out of her house, she'd fallen down the stairs and broken her hip and knee on the right side, and had never fully recovered. She now relied on a woman, who came in once a week, to do many of the things Marie had been willing to do for free.

"Well, Son, there is much I need to tell you. Let's sit down and have a cup of coffee." Making her way to the kitchen, where she poured two cups, and added milk and two sugars to her own, she sat and patted the chair next to her.

"Just tell me what's going on Mother. I need to know where my family is right now."

"Well, I might say that I'm the only family you really need, and that's a good thing, because that's the only family you've got right now."

"What do you mean by that? Where's Dad?"

"I'm sorry, Son. But your father died of a massive stroke, in his sleep, shortly after you deployed."

"What? And I'm just hearing about this now? How could you not tell me."

"I knew you were in a war zone, and I didn't want you to be distracted. I was afraid that this kind of information might cause you to do something that would jeopardize your safety. Besides, after he was gone, there was nothing you could do about it, and you would have only taken it badly."

"But you had no right to keep something like that from me."

"It's done now. And, being angry about it won't bring your father back."

"When will my wife and kids be home?"

"I have no idea when they get home. They don't live here anymore. I kicked them out when I discovered that your tramp of a wife was sneaking out every night to party with her friends. I tried to warn you about her, but you wouldn't listen."

"So, you kicked them out? Children, in the middle of winter. You just kicked them out? I left them here with you so that they would be safe. Where have they gone? And, since I sent every letter I wrote to this house, did you even bother to send them their mail?"

"I have no idea where they've gone, so I certainly wouldn't have known where to send their mail. They were doing nothing for you, but slowing your career progression. You should never have taken on such a burden. But you never did listen to me. You were always more likely to be buddies with your dad. Your dad wasn't perfect you know. But, you always left me and ran to his side."

"You have no right to decide what I will have, or not have, in my life. My family is not a burden. And, I know my wife has a drinking problem, just like Dad did for a long time, and just like I probably do now. But, they are my family. Unlike you, they've loved me no matter what.

And, I'm going to find them."

"Well, before you do anything rash, why don't you go upstairs and unpack. I'll make you a little something to eat and you can get some rest first."

"Are you kidding me Mother? Please get the letters I wrote. I won't be staying here. Did you at least send them the things we have stored in your basement?"

"Now, how would I have done that?"

"So, you kicked my family to the curb. And, you kept my letters from them. Plus you left them without any of their personal possessions? Way to go, Mom. I will be sending for our belongings shortly, but for now I need the letters."

"Well, I never."

"I know, Mom. You never. That's the problem we always had. That's the problem you had with Dad. You always thought you were perfect, and that all your thoughts were the right ones. You never listened to anyone else, so we had to band together to survive. You never really cared about me. You just wanted me to be on your side against Dad. I always knew you were mean and heartless, and now you have proved me right. Sending kids out on the streets, with nowhere to go, in the middle of winter."

"That's where you're wrong. The police took them to the shelter downtown. I didn't just kick them out into the streets. They had a place to go. There, I'm not so bad after all. Now, you should apologize."

"Sure, Mom. I'm sorry I accused you of being heartless. Now, I need my letters. I'll be going."

"Well, if that's the way you want it. Never mind that you're leaving your poor old mom to fend for herself. Just run off, like you did before, and be with your tramp of a wife."

"Yes, Mother, that is the way I want it. And, if you are alone, you've brought that on yourself. The only thing that makes me feel badly about the way I left before, is that I left Dad here with you. You killed him a little at a time, with your jabs and sarcastic remarks. He had to die, just to get away from you." The sergeant took his letters, his bags, and his truck, and went to find the ones he loved.

He had at least one hint. The police had taken them to a shelter in town. Perhaps they could give him a clue as to the whereabouts of his family.

Mom was still sleeping, so Marie was keeping the kids

as silent as possible. She'd already done her morning chores. She made pancakes and sausage, fed the children, cleaned up the kitchen and washed the dishes, and then started a load of laundry. They were sitting at the table playing a quiet game of 'Go Fish' when her mother stumbled from the bedroom, still drunk from her excessive consumption the night before, dressed only in a bra and panties. "Mom, the kids. Could you please put some clothes on?"

"Oh, like they've never seen underwear? Where is the bottle I left on the counter?"

"I threw it away. It was empty."

"No it wasn't. That was a half bottle of vodka."

"No it wasn't, Mom. The bottle was empty. It's in the garbage. Look for yourself." The woman looked desperate as she dug through egg shells, and other assorted disgusting trash.

"I swear that bottle was still half full. You didn't dump it out did you?"

"No, Mother, as much as I would have liked to, it wouldn't have accomplished anything. Then you would have just spent more of Daddy's hard earned money on another bottle. I'm not an idiot, and I don't like getting beat. So, no, I didn't dump out your beloved booze." Her mother staggered past and smacked her so hard in the back of her head that her face hit the table, hard. She came up with a bloody nose, and the littlest one began to cry."

"Shut your mouth you little brat, or I'll do the same to you." The little one stifled her sobs, and Marie grabbed a napkin to stop the blood running from her nose, as the angry woman made her way to the back of the trailer.

"Don't worry, Honey. I've told you before, she can't hurt me. Let's just get back to our game."

"I don't want to. I'm scared. I hate her."

"Oh, Honey. You don't hate her. She's your mom. It's okay to not like some of the stuff she does, but don't hate her."

"Well, I still wish you were my mom."

"I'm not even old enough to be your mom. Besides, we'll be back at school day after tomorrow. Then we'll only be home with her for a little bit every day."

"Good. I wish Daddy was home."

"Me too, Honey. Me too."

"His feet were hurt with fetters; his neck was put in a collar of iron; until what he said had come to pass, the word of the Lord tested him. The king sent and released him; the ruler of the peoples set him free; he made him lord of his house and ruler of all his possessions, to bind his princes at his pleasure and to teach his elders wisdom."

Psalm 105:18-22

CHapter 12

e parked his truck under the highway 218 bridge and crawled into the homemade camper in back, shutting and latching the door behind him. He remembered so clearly the week when Marie helped him build the topper, but he'd never tried to sleep in it himself. Now he felt badly that he'd expected the kiddos to bed down in there. He tried padding the bed of the truck with clothes from his duffel bag, and wrapped himself up in two pairs of fatigues and his parka. It was cold in New York. It was New Year's day 1967. But, with nothing to celebrate, besides the idea of being stateside, he'd picked up a bottle of vodka and a couple of burgers, planning on hanging out until Monday when he might be able to get some answers from the shelter where his family had been dumped.

When he left his mom's house he'd gone directly to the police station to question the officers who escorted his wife and kids to a shelter in town. Once there he couldn't locate the officers who'd taken the call on the day his dad died. But, the receptionist told him there was only one shelter in town that accepted children, and she sent him on his way. Since it was the combined Christmas and New Year holiday, the shelter was running with a skeleton crew, and the woman he would need to speak with, Ms. Stellar, was off for the holidays, so he was forced to wait till Monday to talk to her.

His heart was breaking, thinking about what his mother had put his family through. But, he blamed himself. She'd always been mean and hateful, and his wife had special problems of her own. What on earth made him think they would be okay living in the same house together? And now Pop was gone too. Pop had been the extra insulation between his mother and his wife, and truthfully, the only reason he'd thought it might work out to leave them there. He didn't even get to say good bye.

How had his dad stayed married to that monster for so long? It was clear from her actions over the years that she never thought of anyone but herself, and if he found out anything had happened to his family, she would pay.

He woke several times in the night, due to the cold, and from the persistent nightmares that haunted him. And he felt the usual panic rise up immediately. Alone in the pitch black darkness of his camper under the bridge, he couldn't remember where he was, or even that Vietnam was behind him. Or was it? Would the guilt ever subside? Did he even want it to? Didn't he deserve to pay, every day for the rest of his life, for the deaths of so many? There were moments of tears, and moments of anger; but the worst were the moments of self hatred and depression so deep that he considered ending his own life. He knew if he couldn't find his family, and a reason to go on, he probably would.

Drinking just enough vodka to keep the shaking to a minimum was a challenge, so, he was spending time today, in the city park, watching people go by. He expected more activity on a Sunday morning. But, then he remembered the day before was the 1st of January, and there might be lots of folks nursing a hangover before returning to work on Monday.

His home town was set up the way many small towns in the North East tend to be laid out. Right smack dab in the middle of the downtown area was the city square. In the midst of the square was a lovely park, that boasted a gazebo the town could light up for Saturday night band performances and other small town reasons to get together. Nearby, a trio of water fountains next to statues of the town's founding fathers, and some nicely tended flower beds (when the seasons were agreeable).

If you stood in the middle of the square and spun around you would see the Courthouse, Police Station, Town Library, Sandusky's Jeweler, Ferris Drugs (they make the best milk shakes in the county), Millie's Coffee Shop & Diner (great donuts, and the BLTs can't be beat), Roy's Barber Shop (where Pop had taken him for haircuts as long as he could remember), Barbara's Books, Betty's Blooms & Baubles, Best Bakers (the smells that emanated from there were nothing short of heavenly), Miller's Dentistry, Dr. Samuel Harris Family Practice, Candice's Candies, Rudolph's Shoes, Fern's Fashions, Jim and Jan's Groceries, Gent Goodman Attorney at Law, Abe Lieberman CPA, Toys and Memories, Campo's Games, and a number of other small businesses. On side streets, branching off from the main square, were various churches and other businesses big and small. Further back, on the side streets and heading out of town were some of what the town's church groups would consider the less than desirable operations; bars, tattoo parlors, bail bondsmen and pawn shops, among others. All around were residential neighborhoods, and these days, super markets, department stores, a local hospital, a veterinarian, and even a couple of small factories.

Most of the businesses in town were closed on Sundays, but that didn't stop the window shoppers and the lookie loos. Little kids with their noses pressed up against windows, ogling the things they wished had been under the tree this year. And women, young and old, admiring a new dress, or a fashionable pair of shoes. The tree was still up in the center of the square, but would probably come down on Monday, which was the usual custom. He remembered when the tree was planted one Arbor Day long ago, and now it was well over twenty five feet tall. They must have had a cherry picker in here to put the lights on this year. It was beautiful, and reminded him again that he'd missed out on Christmas with his family.

Millie's was open for dinner on Sunday, since she went to church right up the street and hated to miss out on any likely business. And many of the local town's folk stopped in after services for her delicious specials and homemade pies. The sergeant grabbed a sandwich and a cup of coffee to go, but garnered many stares and awkward glances in addition to his lunch. Some may have thought they recognized this disheveled, unshaven soldier, but weren't sure.

Could this be the young man who'd moved to California, more than a decade ago, to serve in the Air Force? Perhaps. But, if so, the war had changed him. He was thinner, and his hair had grayed from its previous dark brown. But, the biggest change was his eyes. To look too intensely into them was uncomfortable. They revealed a recently, deeply, broken man. A man who'd seen more than his share. A man who hovered barely on the edge of madness.

He made his way back to the park and chose a likely bench. With his parka on he was comfortable enough on this January day, but he made sure he was situated in the sun for extra warmth. Sunlight on his face felt good. He finished his lunch, and set his coffee cup on the ground in front of him before he leaned back to close his eyes and savor the quiet of the day. Right about then a couple walked by and the gentleman dropped some coins in the empty cup. He opened his eyes and caught a look from the woman. He recognized her from high school. But, if she recognized him she gave no indication. Her look was one of pity, and he decided to move on. He headed back to his truck. Perhaps he'd spend the rest of the day out of sight. He'd seen a McDonald's as he headed into town. A few more burgers for his supper later were probably as fancy as he'd get tonight.

Monday morning couldn't get there quick enough for Marie and the kids. The last few days with their mother had been fraught with yelling, cursing, and lots of physical altercations. Marie always felt very protective of her sisters and brother, so when her mom started in on one of the children, she tended to step in the way and take the brunt of the abuse. Today she had several scratches and bruises, and even a black eye, to show for it. The kids were nervous wrecks by the time they went to bed on Sunday night.

Marie spoke softly to them, and reassured them that she would wake them quietly in the morning. They would eat breakfast, dress, and leave, before Mother was awake. This way they wouldn't have to endure more of her torture. They all thought that was a very good idea. In the morning, all was going as planned, until just as they were going out the door. Mother woke to use the bathroom, still drunk from the night before and still wearing just her bra and panties, and began to berate and belittle them all.

"You kids go on ahead. Wait for me in front of Frank's. I'll be along in a minute."

"I don't want to leave you, Marie. She'll hurt you." The

littlest one cried out.

"What have you been telling these kids about me? What kind of lies are you filling their heads with, you ungrateful brat?"

"I haven't said a thing. Now, we have to go or we'll miss the bus. Why don't you go back to bed and sleep it off?"

"Don't you tell me what to do, Marie. You're treading on thin ice. Now, what did you say to them." At this point she began to slap Marie, and got a handful of her hair. Twisting the hair around her hand, she pulled, and yanked Marie to the floor in front of the open door.

Kids were crying, and the insane, angry woman had Marie down on the floor in a choke hold, when Richard and his brother exited their trailer to make their way to the bus.

"Hey, hey, lady. What are you doing? Let go of her."

"Mind your own business."

"I mean it lady, let her go, or I'll call the police."

She released Marie, and stomped her way to the back room. Marie did her best to straighten her hair, and wipe the tears from her face, as she was hurrying the children to the bus stop. "Thanks Richard, but now you'd better stay out of her way, or she'll figure out a way to get you back."

"I'm not afraid of her. I had no idea, Marie. Is she like this all the time?"

"Only when she's here and awake. She's been gone most of the year, so we didn't have to deal with it. She got word that my dad is supposed to be coming back from overseas soon, so she figured she'd better hang around to make it look like she's been the dutiful wife and mother. She's going to be pretty angry that you stopped her, so I'm sure I'll get it when I get home."

"I'm sorry, but I couldn't just stand there and let her kill you. If you're afraid after school, I can see that you get home safely."

"Oh, she probably wouldn't have killed me. Who'd watch the kids and do the laundry if she did?" Marie let out a nervous laugh, and continued walking to the bus stop. Richard walked beside her shaking his head. Everything made sense now. No wonder Marie didn't want to stand up to those who were bullying her. She was very tiny, and probably found it difficult to defend herself against people who were larger than she. And, no wonder she didn't ever want to go to dances, or anywhere else for that matter, without her siblings. She was afraid that her mother would kill the kids if she wasn't there. And, he could even understand her questions about God now. It would be hard to believe in a loving, kind God if you had people in your life treating you like that all the time. He felt bad about the way he'd talked to her.

At school she was sent to the office, and the nurse looked her over. "Marie, is there anything you need to tell me?"

"No Ma'am. I'm fine."

"Marie, there's no way I can help you unless you tell me how you got all these bruises. There have just been too many instances of injuries, and we need to know who is doing this to you. We want to help."

"I'm fine Ma'am. Really. May I go back to class now? I don't want to miss the lecture, or the assignment."

"Yes, you may go. But, Marie, if you ever need anything, you know where I am." Marie knew that to admit she was abused by her mother, would mean being relegated to foster care, and the chance she would never see her dad again. Besides, what were the chances that she and her siblings would be able to stay together? No, she would just suck it up. There was no other way.

After school, when she stopped at the service station for work, her boss hit the roof. "Oh my gosh, Marie! Did she do this, or was it those girls again? I'm calling the police."

"It was our mom." The littlest one piped up.

"That's it, Marie. I'm calling the police, or social services, or whoever I have to call. She is not going to do this again!"

"No, please, you don't understand."

"Then, help me to understand. How can you continue to live like this? Why won't you let me help?"

"Because it wouldn't help. We've gotten word that my dad should be heading home. She won't do this when he's here. But, if you call the police, or social services, and they see me, then they will put me in foster care. Since the little ones are not bruised, there is a chance they would leave them in her care and take me, then who would be there to protect them? And, if they took us all, we likely wouldn't stay together. If you call anyone, I won't have any other choice but to leave."

"No, don't leave, Marie. I'm not trying to hurt you. I'm just afraid that one of these days she will kill you."

"I'm probably tougher than you think. I've lived like this my whole life."

"No, you're probably tougher than any of us. That's a fact. But, you shouldn't have to be. You know we are here for you, and you're welcome to stay as long as you want."

"I know, Boss. You've been great. I don't know how I would have survived this past year without you and all your kindness. But, I'll just get my work done and get home, so I don't make her anymore mad than she already is. Don't worry. I'll be fine."

When Marie and the kids arrived home the door was open and Mom was gone. Puzzled, but relieved, she went inside and pulled the door shut. Settling everyone down with their homework assignments, she started preparing supper."

Monday morning dawned bright and cold. The sergeant crawled out of a stack of uniforms he'd been using for blankets in his truck camper. Shivering, he relieved himself on the gravel under the bridge, and crawled into the front cab's driver's seat. First stop would be the gas station down the highway. He would wash up, shave, and brush his teeth before he changed into some clean clothing. He'd been told the woman he needed to see would be in at nine a.m., and he intended to be her first appointment.

After making himself presentable; he only had uniforms with him, as all of his civvies were still located in his mother's basement, a situation that would be resolved as soon as possible; he picked up breakfast at Millie's and made his way to the shelter.

Ms. Stellar did not disappoint. She was stellar indeed. After the sergeant explained his situation, and his mother's lack of empathy, she agreed to help. Once she pulled the file for that fateful day, she remembered his wife and kids, and, in fact, the entire ordeal. She would take him to the trailer park where his family was living.

The children finished their homework, and packed their backpacks for the next school day and their time at the service station. Spaghetti with meatballs, a nice salad, and garlic toast was the menu for tonight. It was dark outside, and just as they were about to sit down for supper, Marie heard a vehicle pull up on the cement slab in front, and her stomach tightened. It was probably her mom with some guy, and a bottle of booze. She didn't know if she could take any more of the same abuse she'd endured this morning. "Just sit here and eat guys. I'll see who it is."

When she reached the door, it opened, and she couldn't believe her eyes. "Daddy! Oh my gosh, Daddy! When did you get here? Are you home for good? You must be hungry. I made supper." Then, as he stepped inside she saw her mother right behind him, and stepped back. As the full light of the entryway hit him, she gasped. He'd lost weight, quite a bit actually, and it changed his appearance dramatically. His hair had gone from a little gray at the temples, to completely ancient gray. But, his eyes. His eyes held the biggest change. Those eyes that had always been filled with hope and compassion whenever he looked at her were now filled with fear and anguish. Looking deep into the troubled depths, she could see that much of the man she'd known before his long absence had been left on the battlefield in that far away land, and her heart felt as if it was being crushed in a vise. What had happened to him that would have so completely broken him and left him in this much pain?

"Marie! It's so good to see you girl! What happened to you?" The look on her mother's face was life threatening, to say the least.

"Oh, it's nothing. I tripped and fell down the steps is all. You know what a klutz I am." Her mom's face relaxed a little, and her dad gave her a big hug. The kids squealed and piled on Dad, each waiting for a hug. "So, when did you get here? Are you home for good?"

"I got stateside on Friday night, and in town on Saturday. Imagine my surprise when I got to mom's house and found out you were all gone. I went to the police, and to the shelter, but since it was a holiday no one could tell me where you were. I had to wait until today to get more information. As soon as I had an address, I came right away. Your mom was sure surprised. And, as soon as we had a chance to say a proper hello, we got in the truck and headed over to my mom's to get some of our things from her basement. I have a truckload outside. After supper, which smells absolutely fantastic, by the way, maybe you could all help me bring things inside?'

"Sure. But, let's eat, before everything gets cold. Then we'll organize a work brigade."

"Good. I'm going back for more tomorrow. And once we have it all, I don't ever plan to go back to that house again."

"I'm sorry about Pops, Daddy."

"Me too. I can't believe she wouldn't let anyone call."

"Mom wanted to, but she put her foot down." Marie thought she saw a brief look of grateful relief flash across her mother's face. Maybe even a 'thank you' in her eyes.

"Well, I know how hateful my mother can be. I just

wish I'd gotten a chance to say good bye to my dad. I miss him already. I guess she even had a funeral for him. There were very few people there."

"You know we would have been there, Daddy. But she didn't tell us anything."

"I know you would have been. It's all pretty sad if you ask me. And now, she has brought all this on herself."

Marie happily set two more places, they pulled up a couple stools, and everyone dug in. "I can see you've been working on your cooking skills, Marie. These are the best meatballs I've ever eaten!"

"Thanks Daddy. It's the bread crumbs. I take the left-over bread, when I bake, and grate it into crumbs to use later."

"Well, imagine that. I would have never thought of it, Marie. The student is instructing the teacher. Well done."

Marie's heart swelled with pride and gratitude. He was home. Her daddy was home.

Blood curdling screams from the back bedroom woke Marie from a dead sleep. At first she thought it might have been a nightmare, but then she heard her mother's raised voice, "What was that? You nearly scared me to death."

"I'm sorry. I didn't mean to wake you. It was just a dream."

"A dream? What kind of a dream makes you scream like that? My heart is almost beating out of my chest. I don't know if I'll even be able to go back to sleep now. Thanks a lot."

"Really sweetheart, I'm sorry. I'm going to get a drink of water. You try to get back to sleep. Maybe I'll just hang out on the sofa for tonight."

"That's fine with me."

Marie watched from her bedroom as her dad walked shakily to where his parka hung near the door. She was just about ready to head to the living room to comfort him and give him a little company if he wanted it, when he reached in the pocket, and pulled out a bottle of vodka. She watched in horror as he took a long, deep draw from the bottle, and tucked it back in his coat pocket. He sat on the couch with his head in his hands and rocked. Tears slid from her eyes as she tried to decide what to do. She wanted to support him, to help him get through whatever might be bothering him, but she didn't want to encourage drinking as a way to overcome his problems. Should she pretend she hadn't seen the bottle? Not able to see him in such pain without reaching out, she walked quietly from her room and sat next to him on the sofa.

"Hey Daddy, are you okay? I heard you screaming. Is everything alright?"

"I'm fine, Marie. I've just got a lot on my mind. Don't worry. Now, you want to tell me what really happened to your face?"

"I, I told you already, Daddy."

"Yeah, that's what I thought. You're a terrible liar. But, I'm home now, so things will be settling down some. How has school been going for you?"

"Good. And I have a job too."

"A job? what do you mean? Who hired an eleven year old girl?"

"I'm twelve now Dad. A lot happened while you were gone." They talked until the wee hours of the morning; about her job, the guys at the service station, the accident, Frank, Angela, and anything else she could think of; and Marie didn't even feel tired when it was time to rise for school. She didn't feel like he'd shared any of his past year with her, but perhaps he'd open up more as the days went on.

Over the next few days she introduced her dad to her boss, and they cleared out Bernice's basement. It was hard for Marie to look her in the eyes, since she'd kept them from Pop's funeral, but she also felt badly that the old woman might never have a chance to speak to her son again. True, she'd brought it on herself, but no good could ever come from so much anger. Maybe Daddy would forgive her in time, that remained to be seen.

"When they are diminished and brought low through oppression, evil and sorrow, He pours contempt on princes and makes them wander in trackless wastes; but He raises up the needy out of affliction and makes their families like flocks."

Psalm 107:39-41

CHapter 13

He'd been trying with all his might, to get back to normal, since his return from overseas. Sleepless night after sleepless night, and endless bloody nightmares, taking him further down a road that his family simply couldn't travel with him. The terminology, 'PTSD', didn't arrive in the common vernacular until decades after the Vietnam war, and many soldiers came home trying unsuccessfully to fit back in to their old lives as they were expected to do. However, it was an exercise in futility for many, like trying to pound a square peg into a round hole. It didn't help that society held them in contempt, as if it had been their idea to fight in this meaningless conflict.

His mind had literally been altered by horrors unimaginable. Memories he couldn't erase, no matter how much vodka he downed. Mom didn't mind his drinking, because, if he was drinking, it gave her an excuse to continue on her drunken path. She'd imagined the party would be over once her husband returned, but this, this suited her just fine. Now they could pickle their perspective livers together.

Marie was devastated. The man who returned to her from a war far away, was a different man than the one who'd left her. He embodied that war. And he became more distant with each passing day, even resorting to random acts of cruelty toward his loyal daughter, playing right along with his twisted wife when she pressured him. Clearly, he was terrified that his wife would leave him if he didn't humor her, and his mind wouldn't have been able to tolerate that after all the months of being alone. He was on the very brink of madness every moment.

Marie reached out every chance she got, but it was clear to see he was having a hard time remembering who he was. She thought this was the cruelest trick God ever played. To bring the perfect dad into her life, and then rip him from her after so short a time. There was no question in her mind that the God who seemed so real to her boss, or to Richard for that matter, was simply not interested in her.

Her older sister had come home in February, after her stint in a teen corrections facility, and if anything, she was more defiant and mentally unstable than ever. Her absolute desire to self destruct didn't add any positive energy to the family dynamic.

School would be ending for the year in only a month, and Marie was looking forward to getting in more hours at the station, with Daddy's blessing of course. He thought it was great that she was so eager to help the family and to do extra things for her siblings. After all, sergeants didn't make a lot of money, so every little bit helped. Marie had one problem with this thinking. She didn't want to be subsidizing the family's finances, only to give Mom and Dad more money to spend on booze. It was a slippery slope.

Dad had been reporting to West Point since returning stateside. His bi-weekly trips to the base were supposed to be an opportunity for him to assimilate back into American life, and further, to determine if he was still fit for duty. Several reports had followed him from the base in Nam, and the powers that be were concerned. However, the sergeant had become a master of disguise. He'd learned to function under some pretty serious conditions, even filled with vodka, and he could certainly pull the wool over the eyes of these doctors. After several months of visits to the base, he was cleared and issued new orders to Nellis Air

Force Base outside of Las Vegas. They would be leaving New York, for his new duty station, only days after school let out for the summer.

Marie let her boss, and Richard, know about their imminent departure and they were both saddened, but promised to write.

"Marie, you'll do well no matter where you go. You're strong, and smart, and you are the hardest worker I've ever known. That's not my concern. I just worry about you. I've seen what your parents have done to you, and I know what could happen. You'll have to keep in touch and let me know how you are. Do you promise?"

"Of course I will. You've been like a big brother to me, Boss. There have been times, since I moved here, that I don't think I would have made it without you. I consider you my friend. But, I'll still be here for the next month, until school lets out, so if you want me to train someone else on how to do the books, I'd be happy to teach them."

"Actually, do you think you could train me? I've always wanted to learn, but never really had a teacher. You don't think I'm too stupid, do you?"

"Of course not! I'm sure you can learn. I'll spend some time with you each week, and I'm sure you'll be fine by the time I leave."

"I probably should have had you teach me a long time ago. It was just easier to have you do it all. And, you have done it all young lady, that's for sure. This past year and a half would have been almost impossible without you. Thank you for stopping by to ask for a job all those months ago."

"Well, thank you for hiring me. It has been a great adventure."

For the next month, Marie packed, taught her boss, excelled at school, cooked and cleaned, which was her escape from the escalating problems at home. Her sister was hanging out with her old group of friends again, and right back in trouble.

One evening there was a knock at the door and standing there, with his hand holding the arm of her wayward and very high sibling, was a certain vice officer. Marie answered the door, but she could feel the energy exchange between her mother and the officer, right through the empty space and across the room to where the woman was sitting. Daddy was oblivious, which was a good thing. It was also a good thing that they would be leaving this place of illicit relationships and trouble waiting to happen. Perhaps when the family had an opportunity to make a fresh start, a peace, of sorts, could be reached.

One day before their departure Marie took the kids to say goodbye to their friends at the service station. A moving van had arrived to take their boxes of belongings on to Vegas. They would take only necessities with them on their trip back West. When she arrived back at the trailer, Richard was waiting for her. "May I talk to you for a minute?"

"Of course. You kids go on inside. I'll be along in a minute."

"I wanted to tell you that I'll miss you."

"I'll miss you too, Richard. You've been a friend."

"I'm afraid not a very good one."

"Nonsense, we had our differences, but you were there for me when I really needed you. Thank you for that."

"I wish you didn't have to go."

"Actually, I'm looking forward to it. I don't mean that to hurt you, but I think this might just be what our family needs. If we can get my sister away from her friends here, and my mother away from unnecessary temptations, if you know what I mean, it might make a real difference. I think I'll be fine no matter where I am. I'm a survivor. And, it is warmer there."

"I agree. It is warmer. And, I'm sure you'll be fine wherever you go. I brought you a gift."

"You didn't have to do that."

"I know. But I wanted to." He held out a crudely wrapped package and Marie took and opened it. Inside was a lovely silver necklace with a delicate cross.

"It's beautiful. I don't know what to say."

"I know you've been struggling with the whole idea of a loving God, Marie. And I don't blame you after all the things that have happened to you in your life. I just wanted you to have a reminder that He really does love you. Will you wear it?"

"I'll consider it, Richard. I don't want people to get the wrong impression when they see it. I'm still not sure how I feel about all of this. God hasn't given me much confidence that He cares about me, or my family. Don't get me wrong. I'm pretty sure He exists. I just don't know if I exist for Him. I feel like a bit of a hypocrite because I asked Him to move into my heart. My problem is that I don't think he took me up on the invitation."

"I know He did, Marie. You'll be able to see that someday. My address is in the box. I hope you'll write to me.

I won't be able to write to you until I get an address, so remember that, okay?"

"I will. But we're going to be clear across the country from one another, so please don't expect much."

"Well, you're talking to the wrong person, if you're asking me not to expect much from you. I have discovered that you are the person I can expect the most from. Travel safely. I will keep you in my prayers."

"Thank you. I will always remember you, Richard."

A new home.

When the family arrived at Daddy's new duty station, the first order of business was to get settled in to their four bedroom apartment. Dad left them at their new quarters to begin setting up a household, while he reported to the administrative wing at the airbase.

Summer was certainly not the best position from which to view a new desert life. After a long drive from New York all they wanted was to rest. However, the heat was unbearable, and no one could figure out how to work the unfamiliar cooling system in the ceiling, so getting a few things organized seemed the best alternative.

Their unit was on the third floor and that added to the accumulation of heat, but they also had a small balcony which might be nice on cool evenings.

Marie was busy unpacking in the sweltering heat of the kitchen when she heard Mother call the other children. Curious, she sought them out, discovering that her siblings had been pressed into service as human fans for the purpose of cooling their mom. Taking turns, holding sheets of cardboard, they stood in the stifling heat and moved the air about as she lounged. The younger children were so terrified of the woman, that they would do whatever ridiculous things she asked, just to avoid being beaten. "Mother. What are you doing?"

"I'm resting."

"And the children?"

"They're helping me rest. This heat is exhausting."

"Yes, Mother. The heat is exhausting for everyone. You're going to give these kids a heat stroke using them like this. They are no more used to this terrible heat than you are. Why don't you try to be useful and figure out the cooling system?"

"You know I'm not mechanical, Marie. It will just have to wait for your dad. I simply can't move. I'm too miserable."

"Fine, but I need the kids to help me, unless you want to do the unpacking?"

"No, go ahead and take them. But get done as quickly as you can."

"Of course we will. I'm going to try figuring out something for supper that won't require the use of the oven. I don't think any of us will feel very hungry at this rate anyway."

"Do whatever you want, Marie. I know I'm not hungry. And, I'm not sure what time your dad will be home. Boy, I can't believe how hot it is here."

"Well, it is the desert. I understand it cools off considerably at night, because the air is so dry. I can survive this if I will at least be able to sleep at night."

When Dad arrived home he got the ceiling unit going. It was simply a huge fan in the hallway ceiling, that sucked hot air from the room and out the roof vents, providing air flow. It helped considerably during the day. At night the air cooled significantly, and most nights all that was required was to open the windows. Apartments on lower floors had simple fans in the windows, which were not nearly as effective as the ceiling unit.

They ate salads the first few evenings, until Marie began inventing meals which could be made entirely on the top of the stove. She'd gotten to be quite the cook: goulash, spaghetti, chicken and noodles, stew, soups, etc. Though she had to admit that cooking was much more rewarding in the cool winter months.

The one huge disadvantage of living on the third floor was that the laundry rooms in the base housing complexes were in the basement. It was a long walk carrying full baskets of dirty clothes, but someone had to do it.

Marie helped out these days by taking in laundry, baby sitting, baking and selling cookies, and walking dogs. She'd applied at the base theater, but was turned down due to her age. Even glowing recommendations from her boss at the service station in New York hadn't swayed the manager's opinion. Though, she was told that if she was still interested when she was fourteen, he would hire her gladly. So, that was her goal.

Mom and Dad were still drinking, but Dad was working the night shift on base, and didn't get home until seven a.m. Somehow he managed to stay sober during his shift, which was more than she could say for her mother. But, after he arrived home and ate the breakfast Marie had prepared for him, he did all within his power to catch up to his lush of a wife.

Marie's schedule became very important to the structure of their family life. She rose in the morning and got the kids up and dressed; prepared breakfast for the family; packed lunches and cleaned up; and then got the kids to school.

After school she rushed home to arrive before the children, because the scene when she arrived was not something she wanted them to witness. She usually found her mom and dad passed out in the living room, surrounded by empty bottles, and often not completely clothed. She would get them to their room, normally with much protesting, and clean up the room before her siblings made it home. Then homework, supper and baths.

At this point she would do a few loads of laundry; some for her family and some for profit; iron her dad's uniform for the night's work shift; and usually bake a few dozen cookies. Some of the cookies were for lunches, and some were to sell, as her cookies were the talk of the town, and everyone wanted a dozen or two when they smelled the fragrance of baking coming from her building. On weekends her baby sitting skills were widely sought after, though all of her regulars knew that meant she would necessarily bring her brother and sisters along. She was quite a busy girl, and time sped by as the kids all grew.

At fourteen she was hired to work at the base theater, which caused her to give up her side jobs, but didn't diminish at all the amount of work she was expected to do at home. She simply prepared supper before leaving, got the children involved in doing their homework, and made sure her dad's uniform was ready.

Usually, now that she didn't arrive home until ten p.m., she was doing laundry into the wee hours of the morning. Somehow she managed to keep up her 4.0 grade average, which would be essential to her future plans. Her aspirations were to go on to college, as she was told she would have her choice of scholarships at a number of very good universities, but she realized that would leave her brother and sisters with no one to care for them. Guilt at the thought of leaving them alone ate at her. Decisions would need to be made.

Rather than wait until her senior year to graduate, and with more than enough credits to achieve the goal, Marie decided to test out in her junior year. She passed all of her tests with perfect scores, which didn't surprise her instructors a single bit. She was a high school graduate at fourteen. There was no graduation ceremony, but that was okay, because she had a feeling her parents wouldn't have attended anyway. No party. No gifts. No congratulations. But, now she could work extra hours and help out at home even more than before. All she wanted was to be there for her siblings. Her sister Anne was rarely home these days, and she just wanted to be sure the kids were safe.

That summer she turned fifteen, with no fanfare. Little did she know, or imagine, what her future held.

" I said in my alarm, "All mankind are liars."

Psalm 116:11

CHAPTER 14

It was as if he'd read her mind and knew all of her newly hatched plans to escape. His mother would be so angry if their time table of separation did not match hers, which included an appropriate time of mourning. So, he was bound and determined to stay married to this constant thorn in his side, until his mom gave her nod of approval for initiating divorce proceedings.

Due to his astute revelation, and his continued desire to be out on the town, Marie was forced to go with him as he flitted about the city like a moth to flame. Every day when he arrived home from the base, he changed his clothing and made his way to the glitz and glitter that was the Vegas strip. He would no longer allow her to go to work at the nursing home, for fear that she might have people there who liked her well enough to help her achieve her plans to leave him. She was devastated. There were people in that nursing home that she cared about, and now they might think she no longer cared about them.

Marie wasn't old enough to drink, or gamble, and as a matter of fact shouldn't even be allowed in most of the establishments Jake frequented. But, because he had become such a common visitor to many of the casinos in Vegas, he obtained special permission from owners and managers to bring her along as a 'good luck charm'. So, he parked her on a stool, with a glass of root beer in her hand, and a look of pure disdain on her face.

Watching his activities at the tables, and his interactions with absolutely any skirt that ventured into his path, she grew ever more disgusted with him. How could she ever believe in a God who allowed monsters like this man to control her life. She had to figure out a way to flee. Her hatred of this man who'd been thrust upon her was all encompassing, and would soon cross a line into mindsets she didn't want to consider, if she couldn't get away.

She'd sent a letter to her family, weeks ago, telling them of the death of her baby. However, she never received a reply. Feeling very alone, she contemplated taking her own life. After all, she certainly didn't have much to live for. Now that her son was gone, could she ever love again? Was it even worth the effort? And, for that matter, who would love her back?

Sitting next to her husband, while he hooted and hollered over winnings at a Black Jack table, she observed the multitude of fake smiles and expertly painted faces walk by. As she watched, expressionless, the flashing and blinking lights in every corner of the room; her gaze met that of a gentleman standing in the casino's 'Pit'. His stare soon became uncomfortable, and she was forced to look away.

As the evening wound down she noticed the staring man walking toward them from the Pit. He introduced himself to her husband, and asked if he could speak to him privately. She was ordered to stay put while they spoke. Jake came away from that conversation with a huge smile on his face. She wondered what had put him in such good spirits, but knew better than to pry into his private affairs.

The following evening they arrived at Jake's favorite Black Jack table, and she noticed him right away. The man in the Pit was staring at her again. She spent most of the night trying to avoid the creepy, penetrating gaze which caused her to break out in gooseflesh.

Jake seemed especially chipper that evening, and she noticed the dealer replenishing his stack of chips several times throughout the night, without money changing hands. This seemed especially peculiar to her.

Usually her husband purchased one soft drink for her at the beginning of the evening, and she nursed it for the several hours he spent gambling and flirting. But, on this night, he was encouraging her to drink her beverage faster, so he could purchase another one. She was confused, but didn't want to upset him. So, she finished up about half way through the evening. Immediately, he bought another drink for himself, and a nice cold root beer for her. She accepted it with a confused and grudging look on her face. At least it didn't contain caffeine, so she would still be able to sleep tonight, if sleep came. Taking a long drink she thought it tasted a little funny, but not claiming to be a soft drink expert, assumed it might just be too much carbonation.

Waking in a strange room, she sat up abruptly. Too abruptly it seemed, because she felt as if she'd been struck in the back of the skull with a sledge hammer. She laid back down slowly, holding her head in her hands, with her eyes closed. But, closing her eyes caused a bout of dizziness so severe she thought she might vomit. Eventually, with eyes wide open and deep breaths, the nausea passed and she looked around the room from a prone position.

There were no windows in the room, and she had no earthly idea how long she'd been rendered unconscious, so she wasn't able to discern the time of day.

She sat up, slowly this time, head still swimming, and tried to stand. Still faintly nauseated and dizzy, she gazed around the room for any discernable signs of her possible whereabouts. So far she knew the queen sized bed, on which she sat, was covered in a purple spread. The walls were painted a light lavender, with pictures of unicorns and flying horses on practically every surface, and the ceiling was covered in stars; you know, the stick on kind that decorate the rooms of many young children. A neutral colored carpet covered the floor. But, right smack dab in the middle of it a rainbow was painted, as if by a childish amateur, across it's Berber surface. Besides the bed, a desk and chair were the only pieces of furniture in the place. She spied three doors, and as soon she felt able to walk without passing out, she made her way over to the first one. It was a closet. Inside were dresses in various pastel colors, all obviously designed for a young girl. The second door led to a nicely appointed bathroom. Though, again, the colors were all various shades of purple, and the theme of the room was pointedly directed to the tastes of a child.

When she tried the third door, she discovered it was locked. And, not just locked, but fastened with a dead bolt from the outside. Puzzled, but not quite ready to panic, at least just yet, she made her way around the room looking for any means of escape. Finding none, she put her hands to her head and tried to think. The last thing she remembered was sitting in the casino with Jake and drinking her odd tasting soda pop. Someone must have drugged her root beer. That was the only answer. Was Jake in on this? His private conversation with the casino Pit boss came flooding back to her, and his unexplained joyful mood after.

Just then, the lock began to rattle and the knob turned. She watched, as the door came slowly open. Panic set in as she watched the staring man from the casino entering with a tray on one arm. She backed up until the bed caught the backs of her knees, which took hers legs from underneath her and sat her abruptly on the purple spread.

"Who are you? Why am I here? I demand that you let me go. My husband will be looking for me. I promise, if you let me go right now, I won't tell the police."

"Oh, my sweet Marie. No one will be looking for you dear. Your husband is actually the one who sold you to me. Remember the conversation in the casino? Oh, I can see that you do. I find it quite sad really, that he found you of so little worth. A few stacks of casino chips were all the value he placed on your life. Actually, he told me he'd been looking for a way to get rid of you that wouldn't spark suspicion in his mother, who I happen to know by the way.

He's planning to tell her that you ran away. And, since there will be no signs of a struggle, and all your things will be gone, there should be no reason for his mother or the authorities to believe anything different than what he will tell them. Now, where are you? You are in the basement of my home. Who am I? I am your new owner. Why are you here? You are here to do my bidding and to serve at my pleasure. There is no place for you to go, as I live quite far from the city, in the middle of the desert in fact. And, the police won't be looking for you, as they do not believe you to be missing. So, I've brought you something to eat, and you will eat what I bring you. I have to leave for work, but I will be back later and we can spend some quality time together."

Marie sat stunned. "I, I don't understand. Sold me? You

can't buy another human being. That's slavery!"

"I'm very well aware of that my dear. And, yes, you are now my slave. And, I want to make this perfectly clear, you will do exactly as you are told. We will go over the rules when I return later."

"I will not! I will not do what you tell me to do. You can't make me. I'm not your property."

The slap came suddenly. And was brutal enough to snap her head sideways, hard. Marie's hand flew to her face, and she closed her eyes, trying to reestablish clear vision after the blow. She'd been slapped many times in her life, first by her mother, and later by Jake, but this man's blow had rendered her unable to even think.

"My dear, you are entirely mistaken. This is my house. You are my property. If you do not do the things I ask of you, exactly when, where and how I tell you to do them, I have ways of making you listen to reason. Now, again, I must run off to work, but I will be back later and we will have a more proper introduction. Have a good day."

He walked to the door, opened it, turned and smiled a condescending smile at her and left the room. She heard the dead bolt slide home and ran to the door. Putting her ear to the metal she strained to hear footsteps, or any indication of where her prison might be located in his house. He'd said the basement, but who knew? If this was indeed a basement room, then there would be no way to attract the attention of passersby, and attracting attention would likely be her only hope of getting help. He'd also said his property was a long way from the city, but that could be merely a diversionary tactic from this crazy man.

Clearly, others had lived in this room. From the looks of it, a young girl. Was she meant to take the place of a daughter? Was it possible he'd lost someone he loved and couldn't handle that loss? Or was this man more deviant than she'd imagined? Whatever the situation, she would find a way to freedom. And, when she did, she would find Jake and kill him.

"What do you mean she ran away? She doesn't have any friends, and doesn't own a car. How would she have run away."

"I told you Mother. I came home from work and her things were gone. I don't know where she went, or how she got there. All I know is that she's gone."

His mother looked at him suspiciously. She was agonizingly aware that her son hated his circumstances, the baby boy who was gone now, and the girl he blamed for his situation. And, he would likely do just about anything to be out from under them. When would he learn to take responsibility for his actions? The girl had merely been a victim of his selfishness. Her husband was right. Actually, he'd been right all along. He was able to see things from a different perspective, being Jake's step dad, and coming into the situation when Jake was older. Her son was a user, a cheat, a manipulator and a liar. He cared only about himself and how each and every situation might benefit him in some way.

Something was definitely amiss, she just knew it, but what to do about it now? It was true she'd never much cared for the girl, but that had nothing to do with Marie personally, if that made sense at all. It was more about stations. Marie had not been raised in a way that would allow her to fit in with proper society. But, she had to admit Marie tried in every way she knew, ever since she'd come into their lives, to gain her mother in law's approval. She was basically a good girl, who had been terribly wronged. And, just as her son had done, she'd held Marie somehow responsible for the entire situation too.

Oh, she knew better now, and felt terrible about the way she'd treated Marie. However, throughout it all, her husband, Mark, pointed out the actions of all parties involved. Helping her to see how wrong Jake was. And, looking back, she could see how Marie had tried to make the best of a dreadful situation, even while her son went about his philandering ways.

Marie proved herself to be an excellent mother, and a loyal wife to her son, which turned out to be much more than he deserved. She saw the appalling way Jake treated his young wife, the abhorrent way he acted toward his own son, and the way he reacted after the baby died. Marie was in so much pain right now, and she too felt that excruciating pain. After all, this baby, Johnny, was her only grandchild, and she'd grown very fond of him. For all she knew that might have been her only chance of ever being a grandmother.

No, she didn't believe her son. Not for a moment. But, she would contact Marie's family first. She would give him that much consideration before she jumped to any other conclusions. If the girl did leave on her own, her family would be her destination. She was sure of it. She hadn't wanted to leave them to marry Jake in the first place. That decision was made by the base commander and the judge. If she found that Marie wasn't with her family, she would use her trove of connections to sic the hounds of hell on her son, and figure out what happened to the poor child.

Marie was curled into a fetal position on the purple bed cover when the locks again began to rattle. She sat up and looked around the room for something she might be able to use as a weapon. But, he'd been smart in his choice of decorative items for the room. Nothing looked particularly deadly.

The door opened slowly, and the staring man came in once again carrying a tray. He set her supper on the desk, and moved her lunch tray to the side for later removal.

"Have you had a chance to look around, Marie?"

"There isn't much to see."

"You are correct. But, you do have all the necessaries, and I will make sure you have all you need to stay clean.'

"I don't know how I'm supposed to stay clean when I have no change of clothing."

"Haven't you looked in the closet? There are a number of lovely dresses for you right in there."

"Those dresses can't possibly be for me. They're made for a little girl."

"No, my dear. I specifically chose them for you. If you check, you will find that each one is in exactly your size."

"What is your deal? Did you lose a daughter? Is that what this is all about? I can't replace your daughter."

"This has nothing to do with a missing child. The clothing in the closet is simply what I enjoy seeing my young ladies wear."

"Well, I don't want to wear the dresses in that closet. They're ridiculous. Besides, there are no under things to wear with them. No, I'm not doing it. Do you hear me? I won't."

"Under garments won't be necessary. And, do you remember what I told you? You will do as I tell you to do, or you will pay the consequences."

"Do your worst mister. You will not change my mind."

He grabbed her by the hair and threw her to the floor. Slowly, he removed his belt, as she tried to slide her bottom backward toward the wall. Her heart pounded as she got up to run, but there was no place to hide from his attack. He beat her till she passed out. When she woke, sore, bruised and barely able to move, she found a note on her tray of cold supper. The note read: "Dear Miss Marie, I hope this behavior will not be a recurring theme. I would advise you to eat your supper, because you have angered me and therefore I shall not be bringing breakfast or dinner tomorrow. You will see me again at supper time. And, at that time you will be bathed and clothed in one of the dresses from your closet. I promise you that you will acquiesce, or face your own soon demise."

The next day she spent hours crawling around her room, looking for any small crack or opening that might be used to aid in an escape. She found nothing. She was hungry and miserable, and knew she'd lost. Finally she showered and dressed in a pink pastel baby doll dress, which fit her perfectly, other than the fact that is was ridiculously short. Scared and panicking, she cried out to God. "Where are you? If you're out there, God, if you're real, I need your help. Please don't leave me here alone. I'm frightened and alone. Please Lord, please."

"Where is she, Jake? I know she didn't run away. I called her family and she never showed up there."

"What makes you think she would have gone to her

family? She has a sister in town somewhere. Maybe she looked her up. I remember that sister. She was really something. Yeah, maybe she found her sister."

"I'm going to the police, Jake, and I'm going to have them search for her. If you are involved in this, in any way, you need to tell me now, before it's too late. I will not defend you if you've had anything to do with this girl's disappearance."

"I don't know what makes you think I've had anything to do with this girl disappearing. I didn't even have anything to do with her when she was my wife."

"She's still your wife, Jake. This doesn't change anything. But, much will change for you if you've done anything to that poor girl."

"You sound like you care more about her than you do about me, Mother. Nope, still don't know a thing. Search all you want. You won't find a thing."

His mother thought that last response sounded rather odd. How would he know that the girl would never be found?

Dorothy called the police; located Anne, who'd been arrested for prostitution twice since the rest of their family moved to the mid-west ; and determined that no one knew the whereabouts of Marie. Once again she confronted her son.

"Jake, I'm telling you now, that if you don't help us find Marie, and anything happens to her, I will see that you pay. If you know something, you need to come clean."

"You must really think I'm evil, Mother. I told you. She ran away. I don't know where she is, and I don't care."

"I'm going to find her, Jake. And, when I do, if she tells me that you have had anything to do with her disappearance, I will turn you over to the police myself."

When the lock again rattled, signaling the arrival of her persecutor, Marie was dressed as she'd been commanded to dress. Sitting on the purple bed cover wearing a look of weary defeat, but not wanting him to be able to claim victory over her, she quickly wiped her tears away and put on her best defiant face.

"Well, well, don't you look lovely my dear. Here, here, let's see. Come on now, stand up." When she didn't move, he began to unfasten his belt. She rose quickly, and stood before him. "Yes, that's it. Now, turn, so I can see you better. That's wonderful. A perfect color for your skin tones."

"I don't know what you want of me. Please let me go. So far you haven't really done much but beat me. I won't tell, I promise. Just let me go, please."

"That won't be possible my dear. I have plans for you. And, since it's Monday, and the beginning of my week end from the casino, we will have lots of time together."

For the next two days the staring monster used her in ways she would never be able to forget. By the time his week end had finished, she was numb with disgust and grief, and knew for a certainty that the God to whom she'd begged for help, didn't care.

Detectives tracked Marie's movements to the last place she'd been spotted with her husband, after constant pleas from Dorothy to the police commissioner. Folks had grown accustomed to seeing Marie at the casino with Jake for all those weeks before she went missing. This had been Jake's first major mistake. As they proceeded to question employees of the casino, and frequent visitors, a pattern began to emerge. Many employee testimonies fell in line with the pattern. Soon, some of his co-workers were remembering how the Pit boss seemed obsessed with the pretty young girl, staring at her endlessly; one young lady even referred to him as a 'complete creeper' and a 'perv'; and others, remembered a certain conversation which had taken place a few nights before Marie's disappearance, which left both the Pit boss and Jake walking away smiling oddly. Now the officers thought they might have a real lead. Since it was the Pit bosses week end off, those who would usually feel endangered or intimidated by his odd and menacing presence, were free to share information without threat of reprisal. Police were getting closer to an answer, and no longer believed Jake's story of a fleeing wife. Dorothy was making headway.

Marie knew she couldn't live through another of the staring man's weekends off. If she didn't do as he told her to do, he would beat her to death. But the humiliation of those dresses and the lack of under things, so that access to his property would be undeterred, was more degradation than she could stand. Was she being ridiculous? She'd been molested and beaten before, as a child and later by Jake, and lived through it all. Why was this so different? She'd always thought of herself as a survivor. But, that was when she had something worth living for, wasn't it?. When she had sisters and a brother to care for. When Johnny was still alive.

Now, with nothing to tether her to this earth, no one to love or be loved by, the idea of simply ceasing to exist began to sound rather attractive. She wondered where she would go if she died? She'd asked Jesus into her heart at the revival meeting in New York, but that preacher had turned out to be a con man, so what proof did she have that this Jesus wasn't part of the con? She'd begged God for help on so many occasions, only to be disappointed by His total lack of care and attention. Was there a heaven, or a hell? She'd certainly done her share of evil, and didn't want to burn forever, if there was indeed a hell to fear. But, if God was a con, then there was certainly no heaven. And if there was no heaven, then, it stood to reason there was no hell. Perhaps if she left this earthly plane, she would simply become a speck in the cosmos. Go back to the giant ball of cosmic dust where it all started. Or, maybe, she would just cease to be. If she couldn't have Johnny, there was really no point anymore anyway, was there? She shook her head at the idea of just giving up. That simply wasn't who she was!

She pushed and slid the heavy mattress of her purple

topped bed over just enough to get her arm through. A great idea had come to her. Tearing through the fabric lining on the inner edge of the box spring she saw the steel coils inside and grabbed one. Moving it from side to side, over and over multiple times, she was able to weaken the metal enough to break it from the frame. Moving the mattress back to its previous place, she made everything look exactly as it had before.

She'd have to be very careful that the staring man didn't find her new tool, or he'd likely get very angry and kill her. The metal was strong and unyielding, but she worked on it endlessly, looking to straighten it enough to insert into the locks on the door. She thought, with just the right finesse, she might be able to pick the locks.

She'd have to be shifty in order to know when to put things away, so as not to be discovered. Without a clock she was never quite sure when her persecutor would return. As she worked on her idea over the next few days; dealing with regular assaults by her 'owner' every night; she plotted. And, once she put her mind to it, she began to keep time by her own body's timepiece. Paying attention to signs of hunger and exhaustion, she kept track of the pervert's comings and goings, and spent a good deal of time working on the way out of her prison.

By the time the staring man came that night, she was very close to having a usable tool for her escape. She'd never picked a lock before, but thought she just might be able to pull it off. Her tool was hidden, each day when he arrived from town, in the water tank of the toilet; and with a tiny bit more intensive labor, she thought she just might have it, and was going to give it a go the next day while he was at work.

He was angry when he set her tray on the desk. He wouldn't tell her why, but one of his co-workers confessed to him he'd been questioned by the police. The confession was probably made for no other reason than fear. Fear that if the Pit Boss got away with murder; but still held his position at the casino, he might fire anyone who hadn't been upfront about the investigation. The fellow who sang like a canary was nothing but a pansy, and by revealing the police questioning to the Pit Boss, he practically guaranteed the man's escape from prosecution.

Now the staring man would be prepared for whatever the detectives set in motion. That confession by his co-worker got him thinking. Perhaps he should move the girl. He owned some property further out in the desert, and that property was almost inaccessible by most modes of transportation. He would make preparations, and to-morrow after work he would move her. At least until things cooled off a bit. He didn't touch her that night, which was a bonus, but she guessed something was up. Somehow she knew that the following day would be her last chance to make good her escape, before he followed through on the plan she could tell was spinning around in his head.

"Is everything okay?"

"That is sweet of you, Marie, to pretend that you care if something is wrong with me."

"Forget it. It's not as if I have a lot of friends out here. I was just making conversation. Clearly something is wrong."

"Don't worry about it, Marie. As of tomorrow, all will be well again."

This conversation confirmed in her mind that she had one day to make good her plans. She ate her supper and went straight to bed. She would be rested for whatever to-morrow brought.

In the morning she rose, showered, and waited for him to come with her breakfast. He seemed preoccupied.

"When I arrive home tonight I want you to be ready to go. Pack up a few things, enough to keep you for a week or so. There is a suitcase in the top of the closet."

"Where am I going?"

"Never mind. Just do as I say."

"Fine, but I need to know what to pack. Will it be hot or cold?"

"Don't be a smart mouth. Just do as you're told. We are taking a little trip to one of my other properties. I've decided we need a little rest."

Marie's heart began to pound. The scenario playing out looked very bad for her. Were the police on to him? Was he planning to kill her and hide her body in the desert? But why the suitcase and the packing? Was it just to throw her off? Perhaps he wasn't planning to kill her, but just trying to hide her more securely? Maybe someone had given him up? Marie was sure she wasn't his first victim, not by a long shot. All one had to do was look around at this room to know that. What had happened to the rest of the girls he'd kidnapped? Anyone's guess was as good as hers, and she didn't even want to think about it.

As soon as he left Marie made a B line for the bathroom and took her tool from the water tank. Just a little more bending and finagling, and she might actually be able to use the thing. By lunch time she thought it might work. For well over an hour she tried picking the lock, until she finally realized he'd taken the precaution of installing the dead bolt upside down to dissuade this sort of mischief. Sinking to her knees on the Berber carpet, she allowed the despair that had been dogging her since morning wash over her, and began to sob.

It was obvious now. One of his previous victims must have managed to escape, at least from the room where she was kept. And he'd taken precautions, because he wasn't about to go through that again. The proverbial clock was ticking, and it was getting closer to the time her captor would be arriving home. She hadn't even packed yet. But, she'd already decided she wasn't going anywhere with him. She knew the minute she left this place her chances of survival would drop dramatically, and she couldn't take that chance. She fought tears. What to do? He was bigger and stronger than she, but she had surprise on her side. He didn't know her plans. She retrieved the suitcase and threw a few things inside, just to throw him off the scent. Now she would wait for his arrival. She was formulating plan B in her mind, as the time ticked away.

"And you will be brought low; from the earth you shall speak, and from the dust your speech will be bowed down; your voice shall come from the ground like the voice of a ghost, and from the dust your speech will whisper."

Isaiah 29:4

CHapter 15

Detectives were using a room at the casino to conduct some final interviews, and the Pit Boss was trying not to look interested in the goings on. His insides were churning. He couldn't leave work early without sparking suspicion, so he would bide his time. As those who were being interviewed left the room, they avoided his gaze. That didn't bode well for his tenuous position. He was surprised, and worried, about the fact that he hadn't been called in for an interview by the police. Was he beyond reproach, or did they already have information implicating him? It would all be fine. Marie would be packed up and ready to move when he got home, and all would be well.

They were finishing up the last few interrogations when his shift ended. He moved as inconspicuously as possible, and left by the back employees entrance.

Detectives thought this last interview was particularly interesting. "Do you know the Pit Boss very well?"

"Not terribly well."

"So, you wouldn't consider him a friend?"

"Not really. He's just my boss is all."

"So, not worth risking your job over?"

"No. Why are you asking me that?"

"Well, a couple of your co-workers told us that the last night Jake was here with his wife; the night she disappeared; you were seen placing stacks of chips at his position on your table, without taking money for the chips. That's a direct violation of casino rules, isn't it?"

"Who said that. I've never broken casino rules. I would never risk my job like that. I have a wife and two kids at home. I need this job."

"No, no, we understand perfectly. But it's the word of two of your co-workers against yours. Are you sure you want to continue to deny what we already know, or are you willing to come clean?"

"Fine. But, he's my boss. He told me to do it. What am I supposed to do? He's crazy, and you absolutely do not want to be on the wrong side of him when he flips out!"

"We've heard the same thing from more than one of your co-workers. But, we don't want you to worry. We will protect you. And, if this all goes down the way we expect it will, you won't have to worry about him anymore anyway. Now, tell us exactly what happened."

"He told me he was conducting the best business deal of his life, and then he laughed. He told me to keep the chips coming for this Jake guy, for the rest of the night, or until the girl passed out. I gave the jerk over ten thousand dollars before all was said and done, but he's got more than one problem, and he rarely leaves the table with any money in his pockets. He just doesn't know when to quit."

"Okay, go back a bit. What did he mean by, "until the girl passed out"?"

"I'm guessing he drugged her drink. She's just a kid, so she always drinks root beer. She usually nurses the same soda all night, but this Jake guy kept telling her to hurry and drink the first one. When they brought another round, the boss took the drinks over to them himself, which is pretty strange anyway. Pretty soon the girl was tipping over in her chair, and Jake left carrying her, with the boss following close behind."

"So, you saw all that, and it didn't occur to you to call someone?"

"Hey, I told you the guy is crazy. And, I'm not suggesting just a little crazy, I mean bonkers if you get my drift.

I've got a family. I'm not going to risk my family's safety to keep a couple of guys from having a little fun."

"A little fun? This girl is missing. And, if she turns up dead, you, my friend, are going to be looking at accessory to murder charges."

"Hey, wait a minute. I came clean, didn't I? I told you I got a family."

"Yeah, Marie does too."

With this new evidence at their disposal, the detectives obtained the address of their suspect, and headed out to the desert.

The lock began to rattle and Marie tensed up. She was sitting on the purple bed spread with her hastily packed suitcase on her lap. The staring man entered, a look of unveiled panic on his face, and told her to follow him, quickly. He moved to take the suitcase from her lap and she leapt to her feet. With six inches of straight, hard metal extended from the spring in her hand, she went for his eye. He was caught totally unaware, and unprepared for her attack. The metal pierced his eye, and entered his brain. She pulled back and stabbed him again, over and over. Blood sprayed from his wounds, covering the front of her lavender baby doll dress and hands, and speckling her face. She let go of the weapon in her hand as if burned, and watched him fall to one knee. His arms flailed up and down, as if he was trying to fly, and he said, "Gahhhaggahhh". She ran.

His house was huge! She had not been kept in the basement, but in a soundproofed room in the back of the house. Running like she was being pursued by demons, she dashed through the house, vaguely recognizing rooms for their use, and wondering where the front door was located. An indoor pool, a chef's kitchen that belonged in a magazine, bathroom after bathroom, master bedroom suite, living room, movie room, family room, dining room, would it ever end? Finally she happened upon the formal entry, which boasted a waterfall and fish pond, indoors, and an enormous carved mahogany door. She burst through the door in her bloody baby doll dress, just as the detectives, followed by police cars with lights and sirens blazing, sped up the drive.

The first detective to the entryway caught Marie as she passed out cold.

She woke in the hospital. Two detectives, a nurse, and her mother-in-law, stood over her. "Oh my God, oh my God, I stabbed him. His blood, it was everywhere. I can't get it off. Help me get it off. She was hysterical and crying. Dorothy attempted to calm her and the nurse injected her with a sedative. "Jake. It was Jake. The staring man. He said it was Jake. He sold me to the staring man from the casino."

"So It was Jake, Marie? You're sure?" She was beginning to calm down.

"Yes, he told me that he felt sorry for me, sorry that my husband thought me of so little worth. Just a few stacks of casino chips. They put something in my root beer and I woke up in that house. I know I hurt him. I stabbed him with the spring from the bed frame. Is he dead?"

"Yes, Marie, he's very dead. He'll never be able to hurt anyone else again. We found evidence of seven other girls who disappeared before you over the years. He'd kept each one of them hostage until he grew tired of them. We used cadaver dogs and found all seven of the girls buried on his property. They had all been brutally murdered. All of their families have been waiting a long time to find out about their girls. Now we will have news for them. It isn't good news, but at least it's closure. You are very lucky to be alive."

"Why are you here, Dorothy?"

"She is the one who called us. She insisted you had not run away. She was sure Jake had something to do with your disappearance. She called us, and harassed us every single day until you were found. You have her to thank for us arriving when we did. But, it looked like you already had things pretty much under control."

"Well, you can call it that if you like. I call it desperation. Thank you Dorothy. Thank you for caring enough to do something. What are you going to do now?"

"Well Marie, I promised Jake that if he had anything to do with this, I would turn him over to the police myself. It sounds like he was up to his elbows in this, and I'm going to be true to my word. I will be testifying against Jake myself."

"I promised myself that if I made it out of there alive, I was going to kill him. But, you were always so much better at getting results from him than I was. Thank you."

"I want you to come stay with us until you're better, Marie. I feel like I owe you so much for putting up with my son for this long. There were so many times I saw how unfairly, and even cruelly you were being treated, and I did nothing. I know you always wanted to attend university, and that you are a very intelligent young woman. My husband and I would like to pay for your schooling."

"Oh, Dorothy, I can't let you do that. None of this was your fault."

"No, Marie, we insist. After all you've been through, you need a break, and we want to do this for you. You deserve so much more than this, but this is the least we can do."

"Then, I accept. I appreciate all you've done, and I promise I will not let you down, Dorothy."

"Mom, Marie. It's Mom, and I'm sure you won't. I've never known a young person who works so hard, or is so loyal and dedicated as you. And, I'm sure you'll do wonderfully well. We will look forward to having you around. I believe the company will be good for all of us. We miss Johnny too you know."

"I know you do. You were always very sweet with him. I don't think my life will ever be the same without that baby boy. Everywhere I look, everything I do, reminds me of the little guy."

"He was my only grandchild. And, now that Jake will be in prison, he will likely be the only grandchild I will ever have. I'm hoping we can help each other get through this difficult time."

"I don't mean to interrupt, ladies, but we need to get a statement from the witness. Are you up to that, Marie?"

"Oh, I thought I already did that when I was spilling my guts."

"Except this time we will record what you say, with your permission of course. Once we have your statement on tape we will have a transcriber type it up and you can sign it. Does that work for you?"

"Sure, that's fine. You don't have to stay, Dorothy, I mean Mom. Thank you for coming. I appreciate all you've done, and your lovely offer."

"I will stay in touch, dear, and we will make arrangements to get your things over to the house. Rest and get well. I look forward to having you around. I don't think I ever really took the time to get to know you, and I'd like to do that. I believe we never really know what we've got, until it's gone. I'm just glad we didn't have to lose you, to value you and all you have been to our family. I'll be back."

"Thank you. I will look forward to it, Mom.

Officers arrested Jake on the base where he worked.

The charges were assault, kidnapping, unlawful detention, and attempted murder. His mother would be subpoenaed, though that wouldn't have been necessary. And, that, along with Marie's testimony, should put him away for quite some time. Marie wasn't sure how to react to all of that. For a time she'd wanted him dead, but she was one to forgive quickly, or she'd never have survived her life up till now; and now that she was feeling like her old self, and excited about her upcoming college classes, she really didn't know if it was necessary.

"What do you mean you don't want to see him go to jail?"

"I'm not sure, Mom. I'm fine now, and I'm really excited about school. I just feel as though I should live and let live."

"Well, then I will be the one to protect you from yourself. You have to testify. You will simply tell the truth as you know it, and I will do the same. We will let the judge and jury make the determination about what should be done with him. I simply don't want him to ever be able to do this to anyone else."

"I agree with you there. I certainly don't want anyone else to go through all of that. Fine. I'll testify, but I'm going to tell the truth and nothing but the truth."

"No one expects anything else, Marie."

She was very excited about her new adventure. They were going today to sign her up for classes at the University of Nevada, Las Vegas. She'd thought about the University of Nevada, Reno, since it was almost a century old tradition in that area, and a very well respected institution, (her mother-in-law had attended there); but she decided it might be nice to be closer to Mom, and be able to stay at the house. She was really looking forward to getting to know this woman who'd been distant for so long. It would be comforting to be close to a mother figure, since she'd never had a particularly close relationship with her own mom.

The University of Nevada, Las Vegas, was not much more than a decade old, having been founded in 1957. But, what it lacked in old fashioned character, it more than made up for in the latest technology and information. Hers would be a Business Administration degree. And, she'd already checked into the 'Fast Track' program, to help her get through as quickly as possible. Wanting to get out into the business world, to forge her own path, she was anxious to get all the tedium of professors and classes out of the way. The campus was located in a desert landscape, and was a beautifully modern collection of buildings, but she missed the spectacular scenery of Northern California, and upper state New York. Someday she would make it out of the desert and to places abounding with life again.

True to her word, Dorothy set up an account for Marie. She'd already talked to the school and made arrangements to pay for four years of tuition and books in advance. But, the additional account was meant for extraneous expenses, and was much more than generous. Dorothy also took Marie shopping for new clothes. It was agreed that she didn't really own anything a woman of business would wear, so they concentrated on a lovely collection of business suits, blouses, and matching pumps. New under things, nightgowns, jeans and sweaters helped for times of leisure, and a jacket for those cold winter nights in the desert was a must. Pampered to a degree she'd never known, she was thankful beyond measure.

They'd discovered, after Jake was arrested, upon searching the house where they'd lived as a couple; that he'd disposed of all her personal belongings to shore up his story of a fleeing wife. She hadn't owned much, and certainly nothing of value, but the idea that he'd been so ready to be rid of her that he could be so cold and callused was disheartening to say the least. Mom replaced all of her personal hygiene items, handbag, and make up. Marie felt like a princess with all the attention she received. "I'm so grateful, Mom, but you really need to stop. You are spoiling me, and I'll never be able to repay you."

"Well, first of all I don't want you to repay me. After all my son put you through, it's the least I can do. And, for your information, I find that the longer I'm around you, the more I like you. I think we will be great friends. Perhaps, someday, when you meet the right man and have babies, I could be a part of their lives too. Unless that makes you feel uncomfortable."

"Not at all. Though, I'm not planning to remarry any time in the near future. I think I've had enough of men in my life, at least for now. They've never been much of a benefit to me, and have caused me much more grief than they're worth. If the years of my life have taught me any lessons at all, it is that I'm perfectly capable of taking care of myself. I don't need a man, any more than I need the God everyone continues trying to shove down my throat. No man, and no God, has ever been there for me when I needed Him."

"I can certainly see how you would come to that conclusion after all you've been through. Especially about men. But, you can see that I'm married to a good man, so they do exist. And, I wouldn't be so quick to close the book on God either, Marie. Sometimes the things we go through prepare us for events which are yet to come."

"All I know is that I can trust myself. I've become strong and independent through my experiences. And, I don't have to worry about me stabbing myself in the back, or leaving myself in the lurch, for any amount of money. No, I wouldn't plan on any relationships for me in the foreseeable future."

"Well then, for now we'll just concentrate on your present. You're all set for school to start in a few months. And, I can't wait to see what you make of it. For now you should relax and enjoy some time off."

"I have a better idea, Mom. I'm going to spend some time with the folks at the nursing home where I worked before Jake made me give up my job. They really need me there. Sitting around is not my style, and there are still too many pictures of Johnny floating around in my head. If I try to relax, I'll just end up feeling sorry for myself. I'm better off staying busy."

Marie wasn't used to having much help with anything.

Every place she'd ever lived she was the maid, laundress, and cook. Dorothy had a 'lady', a very nice one, who came in and did housework and laundry, and even some cooking for her. Having someone around doing the menial tasks left Marie with time on her hands that she'd never enjoyed before, and not too many ways to fill it until school started.

"Okay, but save some time for me too. I want us to get to know each other better. Is it a deal?"

"It's a deal. And, any time you'd like to come with me to the nursing home, I'm sure they'd love to have your company too. And, you can play the piano. They love music, so you'd be a regular celebrity!"

"Maybe I'll do that. It might be fun."

Jake's trial date came and went. Dorothy and Marie both testified, Jake glared at them both, and the Judge and jury sent him away for twenty years. Dorothy was sad about it, but also felt it was justified under the circumstances. Marie could see that Dorothy would need some serious companionship to get through this, so she urged her again to come to the nursing home. One beautiful summer day they picked flowers to fill vases and took off to entertain the loneliness out of the elderly. Once they arrived they passed out beautiful gifts of blooms to all the ladies. Excited, by the idea of a real piano player among them, they all shuffled to the great room. Dorothy could really play, and proceeded to take requests. Marie sang along, and before they knew it practically everyone in the home was joining in. By the time the afternoon was complete, they were laughing and joking and having the best time ever.

"I had no idea this would be so much fun!"

"I always enjoy myself here. These folks are so appreciative of any little bit of attention. And, even though I come here to cheer up others. I always find that I am the one cheered up the most before I leave."

"Well, now that I know the secret, I believe I will come along much more often."

The two became chums and spent two days a week entertaining the residents of Shady Pines Nursing Home. Dorothy wondered how she'd not been able to see what a delight her daughter in law was, and what a big heart she had, before this. Marie could feel the closeness developing between Dorothy and herself. Too bad it took something like a the death of a baby, and a kidnapping, for them to find each other.

School would be starting day after tomorrow. Marie might be too busy with class hours and homework to spend much time with Dorothy and their friends at Shady Pines for awhile, so Dorothy was going to take on that effort by herself until school took off for holiday break. She was enjoying herself so thoroughly. And, because of who she was, the local paper had done a wonderful article about her work at the nursing home bringing joy to others. Marie was overjoyed to see her loosening up a bit, and allowing herself to have some real fun.

Dorothy was usually bogged down with being prim and proper, and involved in what the social elite considered acts of charity; you know, like attending art galas and fund raisers; instead of spending time with real members of the community, and she'd never really seemed to be having any fun before. So, it was nice to see her enjoying herself.

Once she was a regular at the nursing home, her husband came along sometimes too. He had a wonderful baritone voice, and their duets were amazing. But the best thing was the way they worked together. The way they looked at each other as they entertained the troops warmed Marie's heart. Mark and Dorothy were made for each other, and Marie wondered if she would ever find that special someone to spend the rest of her life with. So far, it didn't look that way.

Mom and her husband found it odd that they'd first decided to come to Marie's aid, because she'd looked so lost after the passing of baby Johnny, and out of guilt, because of all the abuse she'd endured at the hands of Jake. But, it turned out it was actually Marie who was saving them. What an amazing young woman she was. It was too bad they hadn't seen it sooner. And it was sad too that the world had thrown her so many curve balls in her young life.

Marie tried several times to get in touch with her family, but never heard back. They'd never responded to her letter telling them of Johnny's passing. Had they even received it? She knew that at the very least the children would care. But, perhaps that information hadn't been passed along to the kids. More recently she'd tried to contact them to tell them she was back in school. She wanted them to be proud of her, but she also wanted them to know she was doing okay after losing her baby. Why they hadn't responded was a mystery. But she would plug on. She'd never really had any support from them anyway, so why would she expect that now?

The holidays arrived with a flourish that year. Dorothy's house was expertly decorated by a leading florist in the city, and looked like something out of 'Good Housekeeping' magazine. Nothing like the handmade mess she and the kids put together, in New York, for 'the best Christmas ever'. But no amount of expert enhancement could replace the feeling she'd had when she was attempting to give her siblings a perfect Christmas. No, there would never be another Christmas like that one.

She still hadn't heard a word from her family, and grew more concerned about her brother and sisters with each passing day. Her older sister lived in Las Vegas, but never got in touch, except for the one time she showed up at Dorothy's door wanting money. Of course Dorothy wouldn't give it to her, as it was clear she was using drugs. Marie hoped her sister was okay, after all, she was a mess because of the environment in which they'd been brought up.

However, Dorothy was quick to point out to her, when she was letting her feelings get the best of her, that her sister Anne had grown up in exactly the same circumstances she'd endured, and she'd turned out pretty well in spite of all that.

School was going great. She was on the Dean's list again and enjoying the fast track program to its fullest. And, though she'd never liked people very much, she was getting ever closer to Dorothy who began to resemble the mom she always wished she'd had. None of them had been out to see Jake, and she was actually trying to convince her mother-in-law that she should visit her son. After all, we never know what the universe has planned, and if something were to happen to him in prison, how would that make her feel? And, actually, dreams of an impending death had begun to haunt her sleep again. She'd heard how likely it was for inmates at federal penitentiaries to be killed while incarcerated. And, though she'd never cared for Jake, she knew his mom would regret it if she allowed hard feelings to keep her from seeing him.

Marie started divorce proceedings the previous month,

and the judge decided to wave the waiting period due to the circumstances of her husband's incarceration. Her divorce would be final by the end of the week.

It was surprising how quickly the news of her abduction and torture, and Jake's subsequent imprisonment, got into the news. No doubt due to the notoriety of the case and the celebrity status of her mother-in-law. And, even though the picture of her in the local paper; that was used to accompany the article; was an ancient one, people still seemed to recognize her wherever she went. She soon became oblivious to the stares and even the misguided, rude comments. She actually had an economics professor who commented that she deserved whatever she'd gotten, due to the fact that she was a rich brat from a rich family. Obviously he didn't know her, her circumstances, or where she'd come from, but he led one of the radical left wing organizations on campus that seemed to rally against anything establishment, or capitalist. She was pretty sure if he'd had the opportunity he would have given her a failing grade, just because he disagreed with her so called family. Thankfully, her reputation, and grade point average, were so stellar that there was no way he could pull that one off.

Over the holiday break she was once again visiting

Shady Pines with Mom. Her mother-in-law had become quite the superstar there. Some folks recognized Marie when she arrived, but many others were new residents. And, a couple of her favorites had passed on since her last visit, which made her feel especially sad. When they walked in the door, the residents were already assembled en mass; in a room decorated with a beautiful tree, wreaths and holly, and handmade snow men in every window sill; and they began to clap and cheer for Dorothy. She gave a little curtsy and headed for the piano. It was clear that she loved what she was doing, and extremely clear that the people loved her. The smile on her face was contagious, and she had everyone, including Marie, smiling and singing along in no time. They spent two hours with the residents, singing every Christmas carol in the book, and then passing out corsages to the women and boutonnieres to the men. Marie was glad she'd come. This was the closest she'd felt to any kind of Christmas spirit since putting burnt cotton on the heat register and candy on the floor at the old trailer in New York.

The new semester began and Marie was up to her eyeballs in homework again.

"Hey, little book worm, do you want to come with me to the nursing home this afternoon?"

"I can't, Mom, I have so much to do."

"You should take a break. You work too hard and you're going to give yourself a heart attack. The people there love it when you accompany me. Please come."

"I wish I could, Mom, but I have a big test in Economics tomorrow, and I really need to study. This is the class with the professor who hates me because I'm a spoiled rich kid."

"Should I talk to him? He really doesn't know you at all Honey. And, if he knew the real you he might lighten up a little."

"No, I'll handle it. I'd rather get great grades because I deserve them, than because someone feels sorry for me. You go on. I'll see you when you return."

"Okay, but you're going to miss all the fun."

"I'm sure I'll live. You go and have a good time for me."

"I will. Love you, Marie."

"Love you too, Mom."

"Blessed are those who mourn, for they shall be comforted."

Matthew 5:4

CHAPTER 16

With her nose in a book, as usual, Marie didn't hear the doorbell as it rang several times. When she heard rustling at the room's portal and looked up, Dorothy's 'lady' stood on the threshold, of her office, ashen faced and shaking.

"Miss, Marie. I'm not sure what to do."

"What's the matter, Georgia?"

"There's a policeman at the door. He says there's been an accident. But he wants to talk to the lady of the house."

Marie's blood froze in her veins. She rose slowly and made her way to the front door; knowing already the news she might hear.

"Ma'am, are you Marie?"

"Yes, what can I do for you officer?"

"I'm afraid there's been an accident. Your mother has been taken to Mercy Hospital. I can drive you if you'd like."

"Yes, officer, I'll just grab my handbag. I'll call you when I get there, Georgia."

The ride to hospital seemed never ending, as if they were moving in extreme slow motion, and Marie felt she would vomit if it didn't end soon. "Okay, God. I will give you one more chance. If you save her, I will try my best to be good enough for You. I will try not to break any of Your Commandments and rules. I will do my best to be kind to everyone, and be the kind of person the Bible says I should be. I will even quit school, if You want me to, to do your work. Just please save her."

They arrived in the hospital's Emergency Room dock, with lights flashing, and she flew from the cruiser into the main hall. At the reception desk she blurted out her mother-in-law's name, and watched as the nurse's face contorted into what she could only assume was a look of sorrowful compassion. "I'm sorry. Are you family?"

"Yes, I'm her daughter."

"Here, I'm going to take you to a conference room. The doctor will be in with you shortly."

"Can't you just tell me where she is, or how she is, so I can at least prepare the people I have to contact?" She didn't even know if Mom's husband, Mark, who was on another business trip, had been called. She decided to take care of that right now. Except that she didn't know where he was staying. That old familiar feeling of total panic was setting in, again.

The nurse interrupted her confusion. "I'm so sorry. I know the doctor will be right in, but in the meanwhile, would you like coffee, or a glass of water?"

"No, really, I just want to see my mom." When the nurse left, she was in a family waiting room, alone. Light grey walls, televisions on all four sides of the room, and a refreshment station with fruit, cookies, donuts, coffee, and other assorted beverages stretching along an entire wall. She sat, tapping her foot, until she couldn't stand it anymore. And, when she decided she was fed up, and was just about to leave the waiting area to search for Dorothy's whereabouts on her own, a man who she could only assume was the doctor, entered the room carrying a clipboard.

"Are you Marie?"

"Yes, yes I'm Marie. How is she?"

"I'm afraid the news isn't very good. She was hit head on by an interstate mail delivery truck. It seems the truck driver was tired and fell asleep at the wheel. He was killed instantly. When the ambulance brought your mom in she was still coherent, in and out of consciousness. She mentioned your name several times. I have to admit that I never knew your mother had a daughter. I've known her for years. She's done a number of fund raising events for the hospital. Anyway, she never mentioned a daughter, only a son."

"Well, I'm actually her daughter-in-law. I mean, I was her daughter-in-law. Her son and I were married. He is in prison, and I've been staying with them, going to school. We're divorced now. Her son and I, I mean. You said she was in and out of consciousness. So how is she now?"

"I've sent her for a C.T. scan. As I said, when she arrived she was in and out of awareness, but she has since fallen into a coma. I am concerned that there might be bleeding on the brain, and I want to get that contained while there is still a chance."

"What do you mean, "While there is still a chance?""

"What I mean, Marie, is that your mom has been gravely injured, and what we do in these first few hours will make the difference between life and death. We must determine what is going on inside her head."

"Well, so do whatever you have to do. I'm still trying to figure out how to contact her husband. He's out of town on a business trip."

"Have you tried calling his employer? They usually have numbers by which they can contact those employees who are traveling for business."

"That's a great idea. I'll do that right now. After I contact them, can I see her?"

"Just let the nurse know. If your mom's back from her scan, I'm sure that can be arranged. I just don't want you to expect very much. She won't know you're there. But, hearing the voice of a loved one, or feeling the touch of someone who cares can be very significant, so I will never tell you not to spend time with her."

Marie made some calls and got word to Mark. He would be in on the next flight. After her calls she let the nurse know she was ready to see Mom. But, the scans were done and just as the doctor feared, there was significant bleeding and swelling on the brain. He would need to do an emergency craniotomy, so her visit would have to wait.

The doctor hastily explained that the surgery was needed to lessen the pressure on her brain, which, if not reversed, would at the very least cause severe brain damage, if that was not already an issue to be addressed, and could even kill her. He would remove a portion of her skull and suction off the extraneous blood there. The removal of a flap of bone from her cranium would provide room for the swelling brain to expand without doing further damage. "If you are a praying woman, Marie, now would be the time to do that."

"I'll be happy to do that. I just hope someone is listening this time."

Marie waited. After what seemed like eons a nurse came out to tell her the surgery was successful, and that the doctor would once again be in to see her. This time she was shown to his office, and she sat facing his desk, waiting for him to return. She watched as a Newton's cradle device clicked back and forth on his desktop. Metal balls hitting metal balls, click, click, click, reminding her of high heels on cement.

She was exhausted from the day, and being lulled into a sense of calm by the device, when the doctor entered. Looking up, she saw an expression that did not give her as much hope as she'd anticipated. "I'm sorry to have kept you waiting, Marie. I want you to know that we've done all we can. The rest will be up to your mother and the universe. The next forty eight hours or so will be critical, and I can't make any promises. Once the swelling diminishes, if it does, we will be able to tell more about the damage that has been done. I will never tell a family member not to hope, but I'm afraid I don't have a lot of confidence that the outcome will be a good one. Were you able to get in contact with her husband?"

"Yes, he'll be on the next flight in. Will you be here to talk to him when he arrives?"

"Yes, I'll make a point of it."

"May I see her now?"

"Yes you may, but I fear you will not like what you see. She's been through a lot of trauma."

"I don't care. I just want to see her." Marie was led to a very bright, and very cold room in the ICU, and when she breached the door she gasped at the visage before her. If she'd not been absolutely sure that the woman laying in that bed was Dorothy, she wouldn't have believed it coming from anyone. Her face and head were swollen to twice the size of normal, and covered with so many bruises and lesions that a person wouldn't be able to tell where one ended and the next began, for all the purple and black. A large piece of her skull was removed and that area covered lightly with gauze, which moved ever so slightly with the pulsations of her brain. Forced air, through a light blue tube down her throat, which was taped to her dry cracked lips, was causing her lungs to expand and contract rhythmically. Her body was swollen, so swollen that the skin seemed ready to burst, from the fluids being dripped into her system by an IV hanging nearby. Machines showed an almost non-existent blood pressure and pulse, but there was still a faint heartbeat.

"God, I asked You to save her, and this is what I see? How can she live like this? Is this Your way of telling me that my prayers to You are not even worth considering? I was begging you before, God. But now I'm telling You. If You do not save her, I won't give you the time of day for the rest of my life, and that's a promise!"

Dorothy hung on until Mark arrived. He sat by her bed and wept. Marie placed her hand on his shoulder and tried to comfort him, but she was in shock herself, and had little by way of compassion to share. Once the nurses came in and removed the tubes, wires and IV lines, they were given time to say goodbye. But, how do you say goodbye to a corpse?

So many things she wanted to tell this woman who had fought to be her champion, after she thought everyone had given up on her. She was the only other person on the earth who had loved Johnny. The only person who shared her pain.

She'd saved her from the staring man, and from further

attacks by her own son, Jake. And, she'd given her a second chance to make something of herself, by paying for her schooling. How could she ever thank her enough now? The folks at the nursing home would miss her, Georgia would miss her, and her husband would miss her. But, most of all, Marie would miss her. Few people in her life had affected her the way this woman had, and she didn't even get the chance to say goodbye. Why hadn't she gone with her to the nursing home that day? Perhaps her presence might have saved her mom, but if not, at least they could have died together. She was saddened to the point of numbness; and angry enough to scream at the heavens, to this uncaring, meaningless God who would never have a place in her heart again.

The house was quiet. So very quiet. She'd considered moving out, as Mark was almost never there, and with Mom gone she felt she was just being an imposition to Georgia. But, Mark insisted she stay until she was finished with her schooling. "This was a promise we made to you. Mom wanted you to be here and be comfortable while you were studying for your degree. Besides, what will Georgia do if you're not here? You wouldn't want me to have to let her go, would you?"

The funeral was not a simple, intimate affair. Not by any stretch of the imagination. Not with Dorothy's status and celebrity. It came off more like a state sponsored event. Dignitaries from every branch of the state's government, military, casino owners, celebrities, mobsters, regular people and friends from the Shady Pines nursing home came to pay their respects. Marie had never seen so many flowers in one place in her life. She shuddered from head to toe as she walked through the doors of the familiar mortuary reception hall. And, memories of Johnny's funeral, in conjunction with this one, threatened to undo her. For obvious reasons she and Mark had opted for a closed casket service.

At the cemetery she took a deep breath of cold air and tried to stop the shaking which was consuming her entire body. A mound of earth, next to the waiting grave, was covered by a large swath of green outdoor carpet; in an attempted effort to hide the fact that the dirt there would soon cover their loved one. The customary green tent and velvet covered folding chairs were set up to accommodate family. But with only Mark and herself present, in that role, the row seemed rather empty. Dorothy was being laid to rest next to Johnny. There was also a place for Mark, one for Jake, and one for her to use, if she chose to do so when the time came. There was a lovely maple tree very close to the family plot, which Marie had not noticed in her previous grief, with a nice bench underneath. Marie hadn't spent much time at the cemetery. So far the prospect of seeing the place where her dead son lay had been too painful. But, she might have to change that. And if she did, she would utilize that bench for her upcoming visits.

Interment proceedings began and, as usual, the priest droned on much too long, blah, blah, blah, about the need for repentance and confession and all that. Marie was in even more pain now that God had ignored her pleas once again. She hoped there was a heaven for the sake of her baby, and now for Dorothy, but wouldn't have made any bets on it. They certainly deserved to be in a peaceful place. But, if God was as quick to disregard her after death, as He appeared to be in her present life, she would probably not have much chance of getting there anyway, by herself.

Someone brought her a rose. She was supposed to place it on the coffin, but she threw it into the grave. No one said anything. Tears ran from her eyes as workers lowered the beautiful, carved, cherry wood, casket into the ground.

Mark grabbed her arm when she got weak in the knees and looked ready to pass out. She gave him a fragile smile and noticed how frail he looked in the bright sun of his wife's burial day. Suddenly she felt terrible about the amount of time she'd been spending feeling sorry for herself, when Mom's husband was obviously struggling. After the funeral there was a reception in the church hall. The thought of food made her nauseous, and the last thing she wanted was to stand around shaking hands with a bunch of strangers. So, she and Mark gave hugs to the folks from Shady Pines and excused themselves to head home.

A week after the funeral Mark was still a mess, and Marie was worried about him. He seemed forgetful and depressed, and it was clear the trauma of his wife's death was seriously affecting his health. He'd been going to work, since way before anyone thought it appropriate. But his answer to that was, he couldn't just sit around. For when he did, he could think of nothing but his dead wife. This made Marie glad he'd talked her out of leaving, because now she could be there for him, as he'd been there for her. She might be the only other person in the world who knew exactly how he was feeling right now.

Marie and Georgia became great friends, as they banded together to keep Mark well. He seemed to be going downhill more each day after losing Dorothy. He had a son, from a previous marriage, but they weren't close, so, though he'd been notified of his father's failing health, he still didn't show up to be a part of the solution.

Soon Mark wasn't even going in to work, and he'd shut himself almost completely away from the world. The only persons allowed in his space were Marie and Georgia. Marie called the doctor in, who did tests and exams, trying to figure out what was going on. He could find no reasons for such a dramatic change in Mark's health. His best professional diagnosis was that Mark was slowly dying of a broken heart. Marie thought of praying for her friend, but hadn't had much success with that approach in the past, so she simply tried to be there for him.

After so much time off school she was finally back to her studies, but spending less time by herself, and more time trying to cheer Mark up. Her grades were still stellar, so her professors were willing to do whatever they could to work with her.

One Friday, when she arrived home from classes, to find that Georgia had left a note and gone shopping, she found Mark alone in his bedroom. He'd simply given up, and given into the desire to be with his beloved wife. He was laying on his bed, the same bed he'd shared with Dorothy for so many years. He was holding a wedding picture of the two of them, taken in Aruba on their wedding day. In the picture they were smiling and happy, and it seemed to her that the look on his face now, as he imagined himself going to meet her, was one of quiet joy. He couldn't live without her any longer, so he would try to find her in death. Marie sincerely hoped that they would really truly find each other. She still didn't know where people went when they left the earth in death, but for his sake, and the sake of all the suffering he'd gone through losing her, she hoped they were together again.

She called the police and Mark's attorney. They could sort things out from here.

Packing the last of her things she looked around to make sure she wasn't missing anything. She'd found a house to rent not far from the college, where she could live comfortably as she finished up her degree, and was thankful she'd chosen the fast track program for its quicker results. Dorothy had left her way more than enough money in the special account set up for her when she'd started school, so she'd be fine financially until then. It was a good thing too, because since that money had been left specifically in an account for her, Mark's arrogant son couldn't take it away.

Mark's funeral hadn't been nearly as well attended as Dorothy's. Some business associates, a few friends, and some of Dorothy's oldest associates; and, of course, the great folks from Shady Pines; were present when his polished mahogany casket was lowered into the earth next to his wife's, even before the earth around her remains had settled. His passing was a shock to everyone except Marie and Georgia. Dorothy's 'lady' would be moving back to her family, as Marie had no further need for her services, but they would remain friends.

Ever the responsible one, Marie had been tasked with making arrangements for the memorial service and interment all by herself, as Mark's son still hadn't bothered to show up in any meaningful way. Mark's attorney contacted his people and when his dad was buried he arrived on the scene afterward to take possession of his father's estate. Everything was to be sold. Even though most of the property and holdings belonged to Dorothy since long before she'd married Mark, the laws of the state had awarded everything she owned to her husband the moment she died. Jake would get nothing when he finally paid his dues to society and was released from prison. That would create a whole new set of problems for many people down the road.

She'd received a rather formal notice to vacate, from the son's attorney, right in the middle of her grief. She was floored at the brashness of his demands under the circumstances, but didn't want to make waves. The letter was very specific that she shouldn't take anything but her own personal effects with her. That all items on the property were now his, and that she would be prosecuted for theft if anything was missing when he arrived. She was angered and ashamed that anyone would assume she had any intention of trying to profit from the death of these people who had been so good to her.

Again she made an attempt to contact her family, only to find that her siblings weren't doing well under the drunken raging of her parents. She offered to take them in, and the offer was gladly accepted by both parents and children.

When she went to collect them, and bring them home, they clung to her as if to a life raft on stormy seas. She felt thankful to have them with her, because even though she didn't care much for people in general, she loved her family very much. Their presence would help in her particular need to feel useful again, and would go a long way to alleviating the vast loneness in which she was drowning after the deaths of so many who were close to her. It was truly good to see them again.

After having their transcripts transferred and enrolling them in school, she set about purchasing a few items they would need, including appropriate clothing for the climate. She even broke down and bought them each a couple pairs of the stylish and coveted 'bell bottomed' pants, and a few tie dyed, and paisley print shirts, so they would fit in with their new classmates. They'd all grown so much since the last time she'd seen them, and there was so much catching up to do. Now that they would be going to school at the same time again, they settled into a comfortable routine.

Two and a half years went by so quickly, she hardly had time to register the passing. Marie was graduating with honors from the Master's in Business fast track program, in May, and then would be turning twenty one in July. Old enough to drink or gamble if she'd wanted to, but knowing she certainly never would.

Her younger sister was eighteen, and had graduated mid-term just months ago. Marie planned a special day for her graduation and they'd all gone out to eat at a fancy restaurant. The girl was working at Shady Pines now. She held a special affinity for the elderly, just as Marie did. She could have gone on to college for free, with help from the state, but had no desire to further her education, at least not yet. Marie bought her a nice used car as a graduation gift, with money from her special Dorothy account. She'd been extremely frugal over the years and the funds had lasted quite nicely.

Her brother was turning fifteen, and was every bit the man of the family. Very protective and willing to help anyone of his loved ones at any time. Marie often paid him to do mowing and other chores around the property.

The littlest one was fourteen. Occasionally, when Marie opened her bedroom door to check on her late at night, she would still find her sucking her thumb in her sleep, but she just chuckled, kissed her forehead, and tucked her in a little tighter.

They were all good kids. All teenagers, but so grateful to Marie for taking them in and saving them from the monsters that were their parents that they would never be disrespectful to her or cause her any trouble. Marie petitioned for guardianship of the kids six months after they moved to Nevada, and her parents didn't fight it at all. Marie just shook her head when she thought of them. Her parents. They were the ones who should have been protecting them. Yet they turned out to be the very ones the kids grew to fear the most. They could have all been so happy together, if only selfish desires hadn't taken over their lives and their sense of reason.

Christmases over the past couple of years had been great, filled with surprises and fun, but none would ever be as wonderful as that long ago Christmas in New York, when the little ones still believed in magic.

Marie had evolved into an amazingly self sufficient, independent woman. She didn't need help from anyone. She didn't need a man in her life, and she certainly didn't need God. She'd already been offered a job in upper management, at a large marketing firm in New York state, actually quite close to where they'd lived as children, and she and the kids would be moving shortly after graduation. They were all anxious for a fresh start, and spring. It would be wonderful to have four separate seasons again, instead of Nevada's typical hot, hotter and hottest.

One last visit to Johnny's, Dorothy's and Mark's graves before they left. That was the only thing that gave her pause when she was offered the very lucrative position in New York. After all, who would visit them now? Who would keep their small parcels of land clean and neat? Well, she supposed, it wasn't as if they knew when she was there to visit anyway. She'd surely done all of that more for her own piece of mind than for the sake of anyone who'd passed on to whatever realm came next. What she knew and remembered of each of them would live on in her heart. That would have to be enough.

"You will say to me then, "Why does He still find fault? For who can resist His will?" But who are you, O man, to answer back to God? Will what is molded say to its molder, "Why have You made me like this?"

Romans 9:19-20

CHAPTER 17

"Hey, you two, let's get a move on. You don't want to be late, and neither do I."

"You know, you wouldn't have to drive us if I had a car."

"We already talked about this. I like our time together in the morning, and there's always the bus if you're tired of the scenery."

"But all my friends are driving. I've saved up almost a thousand dollars from work at the pizza place. Can't we just look?

"Fine, perhaps we'll go out and look around a bit this weekend. But you have to remember that the friends you are referring to are already sixteen, so that makes a difference. You, sir, are still fifteen."

"I don't want to ride with him if he has a car. I'd be afraid.'

"Why would you be afraid if I was driving?"

"'Cause you don't know how to drive!"

"I do too know. And, they make you learn before you

get your license anyway. Then I would know how to drive you goof ball."

"Marie, he called me a goof ball."

"I know, dear. I heard him. Please don't call your sister a goof ball. And, why is it that you think you know how to drive already?"

"Well, I'll be sixteen next month, and I wanted to be ready, so Jeff, you know, my friend from work, has been letting me practice in his car. But don't be mad, Marie, we go clear out to the country on the back roads. There's no traffic there."

"I don't know whether to be angry, or to encourage you for your ingenuity, but I'm upset that you were doing that behind my back. What if you'd been hurt? And, what about Jeff? I wonder if he knows it's against the law for him to let you drive his car without a license, or even an adult in the car? I don't know if I will ever be ready for you to be that grown up. It seems like just yesterday that you were taking off to go get candy at the little mom and pop shop down the back road from the trailer court."

"Yeah, that was a really long time ago. But I am growing up, whether anyone likes it or not, and I'd really like to help out more around here. With sis gone, I could drive us to school, and you wouldn't have to worry about being late for work."

"I do agree that you are growing up. Sometimes I believe all too fast. And, I believe you are very responsible for your age. And, I will even admit, it would help if you were transporting your sister, but you have to give me time to get used to the idea. So, okay. We will look for a car this weekend, for sure."

"All right! That's great. Thanks Marie."

"You're welcome. Now, let's get a move on. We're really going to be late."

Marie's younger sister had begun working at a local nursing home right after they moved to the New York area, and she'd met a nice young man who worked as an orderly in the same facility. They fell in love and were married by a justice of the peace several months ago. They seemed genuinely happy; poor, but happy. And, just last week she'd given Marie the wonderful news that she was expecting a baby, so Marie would be an aunt. She was glad for her sister, but the odd mixture of feelings the news evoked in her, especially when she thought of her own Johnny, were ones of sadness and not joy. Would she ever get to a point where it didn't hurt so much?

She'd also received some sad news about her sister, Anne. She died of an overdose shortly after her siblings moved from Las Vegas, and she was already buried in a pauper's grave supplied by the county where she'd lived in Nevada. The news made Marie feel sad, and a little guilty too. Perhaps if they'd stayed; but no, her sister rarely came around to see them, and then only to 'borrow' money.

Oddly, their mother had been the one to receive the information, and to deliver the bad news. The information came In a random and completely frightening phone call, where she was stuttering and stammering drunk as usual. Where the sound of her voice on the other end of the phone caused Marie to stop and look behind her to be sure the woman hadn't snuck in to her house somehow. How she'd gotten Marie's phone number was a mystery, as she'd signed up for the unlisted registry for this very reason.

Somehow; probably through base records; the authorities in Nevada tracked their mother down after Anne's 'accident'. And, as per her mother's usual selfishness, she didn't ask a single question about the kids during the entire phone call. Marie didn't offer any information either, as she figured the woman forfeited the right to know anything about them when she so willingly gave them up. A small nagging piece of her wanted to ask how Daddy was doing, but knew that if he cared at all he would have been in touch. He'd lived in his own little world of monsters and nightmares for a long time now. It broke her heart to think of the relationship they'd had before he left for Vietnam, and how utterly broken and destroyed he was when he returned. She would defy anyone to explain to her a loving God who would let that kind of madness happen. She was glad there was still a significant amount of distance between them, at least until the children were grown. There was just too much water under the bridge after all.

Marie was extremely respected at her place of employment. Not too many people in upper management, for any company anywhere, are indispensible, but Marie was exactly that. She knew the company from top to bottom and inside out. Everyone knew if you needed something done, or needed to find out how to do it, you went to Marie. But, she was also feared. She was strict and by the book. Loyal to a fault, she owed her fealty to the company that hired her, and that could never be questioned.

Her serious outlook on life in general, and her need to

control those aspects of her life that affected her employment and her family, had a great deal to do with having lived an existence filled with great tragedy. But the people who signed her paychecks, and those who answered to her, needn't know that. She was almost completely devoid of sense of humor, which was somewhat odd in someone so young, and was never one to share a joke. She couldn't remember the last time she'd laughed. What was there to laugh about? As a matter of fact, if you were to try and share a joke with her, you were likely to receive a look that could melt glass, as many would be willing to attest.

She was sharp, organized, efficient, punctual, intelligent, and beautiful. Though, she didn't think of herself as beautiful, and she dressed in a way that caused her to appear much older than her, almost, twenty two years. She still didn't like people, and she did her job well, in part, in an effort to limit her necessary dealings with them.

She considered it her duty, but also her joy, to finish raising her brother and sister, to keep them out of the destructive hands of their parents. So, there was never a feeling of resentment for the years she spent caring for them, any of them. But, they too loved her for the sacrifices she'd made for their safety and well being. Knowing full well the life they would have been subjected to had it not been for her interjection. They were a family, a real family, and their love was deep and abiding.

Graduation day for Marie's youngest sister came as a blow to her older sister. One minute she was fourteen, and the next she was almost eighteen and graduating from high school. Of course Marie was proud of her accomplishments, graduating at the head of her class, but soon that would mean off to college. Her last baby chick was leaving the nest. Her emotions, vacillating between joy and sadness, took her for a wild ride that day. The littlest one's future was secure. All she had to do now was choose which of the five full-ride scholarships she would accept; and then try to hide her thumb sucking from her dorm roommate.

Her younger sister had three children now, two girls and a boy, and was an even better mommy than Marie could have ever hoped. Visiting her nieces and nephew was always a joy, as the children were very well behaved. And when she witnessed the look in their parent's eyes, as her sister and her husband exchanged glances across the room, she knew they would spend the rest of their lives happily ever after.

Her brother was working as a medical tech, and doing quite well for himself, after taking a course at the local community college. He shared a small apartment with a friend, but would be moving after his wedding. Yes, he had met, 'The One', and proposed just last week. Presenting his future wife with a lovely engagement ring at a holiday family get together just recently.

Surprisingly, to many who knew the family's story, Marie had made peace with her parents some time ago. Being a person who tended to forgive, and learning over the past few years how tenuous a grasp we mere humans have on life, she'd thought it best to unite the family before it was too late. Now that the children were grown, and had matured into healthy, intelligent, strong adults, there wasn't much the parents could do to hurt them.

She'd also been experiencing some menacing dreams once again, and that usually meant something bad would be happening soon. She never knew what, when, or to whom, but that didn't matter. She wouldn't have been able to forgive herself if something happened to her parents and she'd still been on bad terms with them, not to mention how she would feel if she'd kept the kids from seeing them. She'd even gone so far as taking the children to visit a couple of times recently, since moving back to New York, though when they visited they stayed at motels, refusing to inconvenience their folks.

She'd invited their parents to each of the significant events in their children's lives: graduations, births and proposals, even offering to pay their passage to the events, but they hadn't made a single appearance. Always excusing themselves for reasons of ill health. Daddy's physical well being, and mental health had deteriorated little by little as the years wore on, and though he still worked part time, his temperament was even more erratic now, than when he first returned from the war.

Mom's health, due to years and years of drinking, had slipped away. On their last visit Marie was shocked at how bloated and discolored her mother was. Obvious signs of advanced liver disease. The change was like a slap in the face. She'd been such a beautiful woman once. The change in her own appearance was even difficult for her to take, as she'd been used to the lingering glances of men her whole life. No one looked anymore. Even Daddy wasn't interested. Unwisely, she'd stayed in touch with her lover from the time her husband was away in Vietnam, and he had accidently intercepted some of the correspondence between them a couple of years back. He was so hurt over the betrayal that he wouldn't give her the time of day. They merely occupied the same space now, for reasons of convenience. It was a sad lot.

Marie felt much older than her twenty six years. More like a crotchety old lady most of the time. And, if you'd asked any of the hundreds of employees who answered to her at work, they would agree to that assessment, or at least the crotchety part. Her demeanor, if anything, had become even more serious over the past few years. After all, she'd been involved in the very serious endeavor of raising teenagers to be responsible adults; along with the thankless task of managing hundreds of workers at the marketing firm. And now that the last of her charges had flown from the proverbial nest, she didn't know what to do with herself. So, she began to fill the lonely hours with more work. Before too long she'd adopted the habit of arriving at work before eight in the morning and staying past eight in the evening. She was making everyone nervous, as it seemed she practically lived in her office. Some of her management associates tried to reach out.

"Hey Marie, we're having a get together at our house this Saturday evening. We'd love it if you could come."

"Oh, Judy, I'm not much for partying. And, in case you hadn't noticed, I'm really not much of a people person. I'd probably just bring everyone down."

"Nonsense. And, it's not that kind of a get together. We have a new pastor at our church. He's a young guy, only twenty eight, and we were getting together to have a Bible study. He's got some really radical ideas that we want to discuss more."

"Oh, then you really don't want to have me around. I've never been much for all that Bible stuff."

"Well, then there's no better time than the present. You can't continue to work seventy two hours a week, and not expect to get sick. Besides, you're making the rest of us look bad. Just come and spend some time with us. If it turns out that it's not your thing, then nobody's dragging you to a second meeting. Sound like a plan?"

"Fine. I'll come check it out. It's not like I have anyone to go home to anymore, now that the baby of the family has flown the coop. I'll tell you what. I'll come along, just to play devil's advocate. How does that sound?"

"Anything that trips your trigger, Marie. We're getting together at six on Saturday evening. Just dress casual. We all get tired of skirts and heels during the week. We're going to have a meal first, pot luck; I'm making the cheesy ham casserole; so if you want to bring something, a salad or dessert would be great. But don't feel pressured."

"I haven't made my dad's maple, cinnamon twist bread in a long time, so maybe I'll whip up a batch."

"Good, see you Saturday?"

"Yes, I'll see you Saturday."

As soon as she accepted the invitation, she regretted her decision and began trying to come up with an excuse. But anything she might say now, by way of apology, would simply sound like a way to avoid her peers. And if she did that, what kind of message would she be sending? No, she would make her dad's maple, cinnamon twist bread, and take her chances with the group. Maybe she could fake a headache and excuse herself early. It might be worth a try.

Saturday evening rolled around, and Marie was nervous. She hated meeting new people, and didn't feel comfortable in crowds, unless she was in complete control of the situation. She'd spent her life dealing with feelings of inadequacy and low self esteem, feelings that were exacerbated by being married to a verbally abusive and philandering husband. These were also some of the reasons she insisted on presenting herself as a strong woman who didn't need help from anyone. By taking control of the situation, such as leading training seminars and meetings at work, she was able to put on a front. One that didn't allow the people watching to see the trembling, shaking mess she was on the inside.

Her twist bread turned out perfectly golden brown and when finished was dripping with maple glaze, and when she knocked on the door of her co-worker's house, holding the platter of gooey goodness, her progress to the buffet table was followed by Oohs and Ahhs from everyone watching. "Wow, Marie, I didn't know you could bake?"

"There are probably many things you don't know about me. I've tended to stay pretty closed up to all of you, haven't I?"

"To put it mildly."

"Well, for those of you who don't know, I've been raising my brother and sisters for years. I guess it was just a self defense mechanism to pull away the way I did. And, no offense to any of you, but I took the responsibility of caring for them pretty seriously. I just wanted to keep them safe, and away from anything that might hurt them. That included any of you who might be into things I wasn't familiar with at the time. But, now they're grown and the last one is gone, so I guess I have to take the time to figure out who I am all over again."

"Oh Marie, no offense here either, but we all know how seriously you take everything you do. And, we're sure, that if you had anything to say about it, they have all grown up to be great young people. You do tend to do everything that you do very well."

"Okay, okay, so here I am. I'm usually in bed and asleep by ten, so let's get started. Where is this great and mighty pastor you've been bragging about?"

Just then, a tall, well built man with slightly graying temples and the greenest, most beautifully, compassionate eyes she'd ever seen stepped toward her with his hand out. "Hi, I'm Pastor Joseph. Brother Joe to my friends."

With a face turning crimson, due to her previous, vaguely, uncharitable comment, she held out her small hand to be completely engulfed in his larger one, and stammered, "Hi, I, I'm Marie." She pulled her hand away as if his touch had burned her skin and stepped back, looking side to side.

His look was one of complete confusion, but he stepped back also, and made his way over to another more congenial group of guests. From there he shot her occasional wondering glances. He had found the lovely young woman completely enchanting, and wondered why she pulled away so quickly. Was it something he said or did? Well, she was avoiding him now, shunning even his glances, so it didn't make much difference how captivating he might find her. Obviously she found him less than charming.

Marie was now even more sorry she'd consented to come. The feeling she'd experienced in the pit of her stomach when the pastor held her hand was disconcerting. She was not a fan of any situation that left her feeling so out of control. She tried her best, as the gathering's hosts and guests mingled, to stay across the room and out of the pastor's field of vision. She waited until each person had filled their plates, before she approached the buffet table to select her meal.

When everyone had eaten their fill of the ample pot luck dishes, and Marie's twist bread was nothing more than a fond memory, Judy clapped her hands to get the attention of the crowd, "Okay everyone. If you've all had enough to eat we'll wait to clear away until after our Bible study. We have chairs set up in the great room, if you'd like to follow me."

Joe took a seat facing the rather large group, looking completely at ease. He had an easy smile that showed off a dimple on his left cheek and a mouth full of beautiful teeth. "Hi everyone. For anyone whose hand I've not shaken, or ear I've not talked off, I'm Brother Joe. I want everyone to feel comfortable, so please know that I don't think there are any stupid questions. Everyone's comments will be heard, and I will answer all of them to the best of my ability."

The questions began sporadically, and a bit benign. Subjects such as: If Adam and Eve were the first two people on earth, where did Cain's wife come from? Was the piece of fruit Eve offered Adam really an apple? Did Adam and Eve have belly buttons? If we all come from Adam and Eve, why are there so many different colors and kinds of people now? Was Abraham really going to kill his son Isaac as a sacrifice, just because God told him to? How did Noah get all the animals on the Ark? How old is the universe, really? And others. But, before they knew it, the conversation had turned to the subject of sin, and salvation.

Several of those attending gave their testimonies, and

talked about how they used to be sinners, but now they were saved. Finally, annoyed by the mundane and goody two shoes answers to many of the questions, Marie spoke up, "It's really hard for me to listen to you all talking about salvation. The God I know is obviously not the same God you know. I have begged and pleaded to your God to save the lives of people I've loved; only to have them taken; and to save me from circumstances you can't even begin to understand. And He has turned His back on me more times than I care to count. I've tried my whole life to be good enough to ask for His forgiveness and salvation, but no matter how hard I've worked, no matter how much I've tried, I've never felt good enough. I've never been good enough for Him to answer my prayers. Just not good enough." Her voice faded away at this last comment.

"Of course you're not." Marie's head snapped around and she gave that preacher a look, that if looks could kill, should have dropped him to the ground.

"And, I suppose, Mr. Pastor, that you are?"

"No. Of course I'm not, Marie. None of us is good enough. That's why Jesus died on the cross to take our sins upon Himself, and then rose again to overcome death. He suffered for us, and in our place, so we wouldn't have to. He paid a debt He didn't owe, so that we could have eternal life we didn't deserve. It really doesn't have anything to do with you or me. It's all about Him. From what I heard you say, it seems like maybe you've spent your life trying to earn His Grace. Grace isn't something that can be earned, Marie. It's a free gift. None of us deserves it. Does that make sense?"

Marie stopped in her tracks. The scowl on her face softened, and her lip began to tremble. She looked toward Joe and began to cry. In front of co-workers and strangers alike. Softly at first. But then she cried like she'd never cried before. No one in her entire life had ever said that to her. No one had ever told her she didn't have to be good enough. That it wasn't just her, but that no one was good enough on their own. That God would accept her exactly as she was, with all her flaws, just because Jesus paid the price for her. "I, I didn't know. No one has ever told me that before." That night, after the group disbanded, she talked to Joe for hours, and was up way past her bedtime. She had years worth of questions, and was hungry for answers. The next day she made her way to the little church where Joe preached. And, when he gave the invitation, she went forward to recommit her life to the Lord. This time, knowing full well what that meant concerning her life and eternity.

Joe and Marie quickly became an item, and spent hours praying together and studying the Bible. She was learning things about the Lord, and about herself, she'd never known before. It was as if she'd been born again. She felt like a completely different person. A person who wasn't afraid anymore, and wasn't hesitant to approach the throne of God with her praises and petitions. She'd never felt so free. And after many conversations, some lasting until the wee hours of the morning, she began to feel like God had deliberately brought her together with this amazing man, for such a time as this. Joe became her best friend, staunchest ally, and most trusted confidant. She shared all the details of her childhood and previous marriage with him, and he still wanted to be her friend. She was truly blessed.

There was just one problem. Since she'd begun seeing Joe, her nightmares had grown worse. She wasn't exactly sure what that meant, but she didn't want to see him hurt. She became nervous about getting too much closer to this man she'd grown to respect, and dare she say it, love? Knowing that each time her nights became a jumble of terrible dreams and premonitions, someone she loved was bound to suffer sooner or later. If only she had more control over interpreting her dreams. For now, at least, Marie decided she must dissuade this wonderful man from his interest in her. He must not get any closer. She would be devastated if anything were to happen to him.

Joe felt the same way about her. He knew he loved her. Had grown to love her rather quickly. She was the woman of his dreams, and his soul mate. He'd watched her develop in faith, and become a woman strong in the Lord, instead of one who is dependent on her own strength. He was certain their meeting had been by divine appointment, and that God intended for them to be together. But, every time it seemed they were growing close enough for him to approach her with certain questions, she backed off. He was very aware he'd not had much of a love life to speak of, and wondered if he was just going about this thing the wrong way. Gosh, how to make romantic overtures to a skittish woman. That was a question he hadn't discovered the answer to quite yet. He was also aware, after all the conversations they'd shared, that her life had been filled with horrible, damaging relationships. Perhaps she was just afraid of being hurt again. That was alright. He had all the time in the world, and he would wait as long as it took to gain her confidence.

"The kids are growing so fast! I don't know how you keep up with them."

"Probably the same way you kept up with us, Marie. I wondered, when I got older, how you did it all. I mean, for crying out loud, you worked a job and studied and kept the house clean and the laundry washed, and you still managed to love us and be there for us."

"Well, the loving part was easy. I don't know how the rest got done either. I guess I was walking around in a daze most of the time. But you know very well that we do what we must."

"In case I haven't told you lately, I love you very much, Marie."

"Then that makes it all worthwhile, doesn't it? I love you too, and I'm very proud of you. And now that you have these little ones to care for, you can see for yourself how rewarding it is to be there for someone you love. You are a very good mommy."

"Well, I had the best example in the world. So, what's on your mind?"

"What do you mean?"

"I can always tell when something is bothering you. You are my big sister you know."

"I'm struggling a little."

"With what?"

"I've met a man."

"Oh Marie, that's wonderful! Who is it?"

"His name is Joseph, and he is pastor of a wonderful church. I've been attending again, which is something I never thought I would do, but he's explained things to me in such a way that I feel I have a whole new beginning. I've rededicated my life to Jesus, and I've been attending Bible studies where I'm learning things I just never knew before."

"That's great, so what's the problem?"

"The problem is that I've begun to have nightmares again. You know when I start having bad dreams something always goes wrong. I've lost so many people I love, and I don't feel comfortable getting any closer to him. What if we started dating seriously and then something terrible happened to him. How would I live with myself?"

"Well, first of all, if something is going to go wrong, it might go wrong with any number of people. After all, he is not the only loved one you have left. Besides, your dreams are always so random, and so far removed from any actual events, that it could just be coincidence. Who knows. It's not as if your nightmares create some sort of voodoo curse or something, is it?. You can't walk around scared all the time, Marie. If you do that you might as well go live in a cave. You have to grab opportunities when they knock, or pretty soon they will quit knocking."

"You are very wise sister. Thank you. I just might have to take your advice."

"I'm glad to hear that you've been going to church and Bible study, because we've been talking about starting to go as well. I didn't want to mention it to you before, because you seemed so dead set against all of that. You know, with children and everything, it seems like a good thing to do. We just haven't known where to go. Perhaps we could join you?"

"That would be great!"

"Then you can introduce us to your boyfriend!"

"Oh, don't call him that. It sounds so silly."

"Well, what would you call him? I would like to meet him, that's all."

"Okay, why don't you join me this Sunday? Maybe we can all go get lunch after?"

"I'd love that. We don't spend nearly enough time together anymore. You're always working."

"Okay, then it's settled. And, I will introduce you to Joe."

"I can't wait!"

When Sunday rolled around Marie arrived at church a little early, and stood outside waiting for her sister. But, when her sister's family drove up in their van, she saw her brother and his new wife pull in right behind them. She was so elated she felt tears of joy spring to her eyes.

"I didn't know you two were coming along as well! This is great. Let's go inside everyone. The church provides a nursery, if you'd like the little ones to go downstairs, but you don't have to. I will leave that up to you."

"That would be great. They're all so young, I'm not sure how much they'd get out of the service, so it's probably better if they have toys to play with for awhile."

Marie showed her sister to the nursery and introduced her to the lovely young ladies who made the care of the church's children their personal ministry. The kids seemed thrilled when they saw all the new toys, and didn't even wait around for the tearful goodbye their mother was expecting.

"Well, that proves it. I am just chopped liver!"

"Hey, welcome to parenthood. You wouldn't rather have

them crying, would you?"

"No, but they could've at least said goodbye."

"Let's go upstairs. I want to introduce you to Joe before services begin."

When Marie brought her sister and brother, along with their families, forward Brother Joe greeted them with a broad smile, handshakes and hugs. They all loved him immediately. But, he was a bit puzzled. After all the attempts he'd made to get closer to Marie, and all the times she'd backed off, here she was bringing her family to meet him. He would never understand women. But, maybe he wasn't supposed to.

The service was beautiful, and when Brother Joe gave the alter call Marie's brother-in-law, her brother and his wife went forward to accept Jesus into their hearts and lives. And her sister rededicated herself to the Lord. Marie couldn't contain herself and wept for the joy of it all. Things were really beginning to turn around for their family, and she couldn't be happier.

Lunch was a free for all. With three tiny ones they couldn't go to a real restaurant, so they decided on pizza. They laughed and talked and passed kids around; spending time getting to know one another. Marie's brother decided he really liked Brother Joe, and gave Marie the thumbs up when his back was turned, which made her smile. "I love it when you smile."

"Thank you. You make it sound like I don't do it very often, Joe."

"Well, maybe you do it when you're other places, but I don't see it very often."

"I'm sorry, I'll try to change that. I've had so much on my mind, including what to do about you, and I Just didn't have many smiles in me."

"What do you mean, what to do about me?"

"I was trying to decide whether to stop seeing you, or not."

"What did you decide?"

"Well, I brought my family to meet you, so that should be a clue."

"Yes, I wondered about that. I'm really glad you decided not to break my heart."

"Oh, don't be ridiculous. Your heart would not have been broken if I decided to stop seeing you."

"Obviously I haven't made my feelings for you very clear then. I absolutely would have been heartbroken. I really care about you, Marie. I don't want to scare you, but I believe I love you.”

“Oh my. Well, just so you don’t step out on that limb alone, Joe. I believe I love you too. I was just afraid that having me in your life might bring you disaster. So many people that I love have seen tragedy, and I can’t help but think it has something to do with me.”

“So far, Marie, all you’ve brought me is joy. Well, maybe a little bit of confusion now and then. But mostly joy.”

“Good. I don’t ever want to bring you anything but joy. My brother gave me the thumbs up, and my sister really likes you too. You haven’t met the youngest one yet, but she’ll be home for the holidays, so you’ll have a chance to meet her then. I would like to have you meet my parents too, but that would require taking a trip. And, you’d have to be prepared. They are both very broken people.”

“We’re all broken people, Marie. I’d be pleased to meet them.”

A trip to meet Marie’s parents came just a few weeks down the road. Marie was embarrassed and a little ashamed when they arrived, having given plenty of advanced notice, when her parents were still in their pajamas. “Well”, she thought, "At least they aren't naked."

As she watched Joe with her folks, she remembered all over again why she was falling more and more in love with this unique and wonderful man. He was patient and kind, and he acted as though he didn't know they were falling down drunk, though it was abundantly clear to see, or still in their night clothes. He talked to them of Jesus, and of his love for Marie, and she was sure she saw a tear in her dad's eye. So, Daddy was still in there somewhere. He was simply trapped in the nightmares that had turned him into a monster. Her mother listened, but visibly struggled with the idea of putting anything, including the Lord, above her need for alcohol. But, as Joe always said, it wasn't his job to force people to surrender to Jesus; it was only his job to introduce them.

On the way back home they talked. "I'm sorry."

"Sorry about what?"

"About my parents. I really did tell them, days in advance, that we were coming. You know I pay someone to come in and clean for them and check on them, so I don't know why the place was such a mess. I send them money for food also, and it clearly gets spent on things they find more important. I'm just afraid that if I don't help, they won't eat."

"Marie."

"What?"

"You don't have to keep apologizing for your parents. They are broken people, just like you said. And God can meet them right where they are. They have been introduced. Now let's see where the Lord takes it from here. Of course they have to be open to the change. But, they have been extended an olive branch; now all they have to do is grab hold."

"Thank you for coming with me. And thank you for talking to them. I've actually tried to talk to them about the Lord before, but I think I'm too close to the situation, and I get so impatient with them. After all the years of watching them destroy lives; their own, and those of the children; it's hard to remain objective."

"It is. I know. But, I don't see the children's lives destroyed. They had a great older sister who took care of them and shielded them from the horror as much as she could, and now they are coming, one by one, to Jesus. So, I'd say you've done a pretty good job. And I know exactly what you are talking about. I lost my only sister to a drug overdose a number of years ago. Both of my parents seemed to just fade away after that, and within a year and a half they were both gone too."

"Oh, Joe, I'm so sorry. I didn't know. Here I've been so focused on my own family, and the mess that we are, I guess I never really thought to ask you very many questions about yours. Please forgive me."

"There's nothing to forgive, Marie. To be honest, I think most people don't really think of pastors as having a life before ministry. Both of my parents were saved. I'm still not sure about my sister. Though, I'd bugged, bothered and nagged her for several years, trying to share Jesus. It was hard for her to take me seriously, because I was a hell raiser for such a long time, before the Lord saved me from myself. She just couldn't see me as an authority on Grace and salvation, when, for so long, I clearly wasn't listening myself. I like to think that when she was dying, perhaps the Lord came to her. We had shared His love with her so often, that I have to believe she opened her eyes and her heart right at the last, and that I will see her someday in heaven."

"My older sister died of a drug overdose too."

"I'm sorry, Marie. I didn't know that. I guess I thought I knew just about everything concerning your family."

"On the other hand, I don't think Anne knew anything

about Jesus. I've felt so guilty since my mom called and told me she was dead. She used to come around sometimes and I wouldn't let her near the kids. I quit giving her money too. After she died, I wondered if things might have been different if I'd tried harder to be her friend. Maybe she would have quit using if I'd been more accepting of her."

"You can't take that on. If you'd been more 'accepting' of her, she might have interpreted that as acceptance of her habit. Drug addiction is a disease, and the person afflicted must be the one to seek help, or they won't take it seriously. It isn't your fault she was using. And, you had the welfare of your younger brother and sisters on your mind when you wouldn't let her come around. You did the right thing for them. God works in mysterious ways, and you don't know that she hadn't met someone out there on the streets who shared the Lord with her. Let's just believe the best about the situation."

"Agreed, now, let's put the past few days behind us and concentrate on having a good trip home."

"I'm all for that. We are going to need to stop somewhere for supper pretty soon. What would you like to eat my love."

Marie blushed. She wasn't used to anyone speaking to her in endearing terms. "It really doesn't make any difference to me. As long as they can make a good salad."

"And I, on the other hand, would love a nice thick, juicy steak. So, let's look for a steak house that has great salads."

At supper Joe kept sneaking glances at Marie, and finally she started giggling. "What are you doing?"

"I'm just assessing your mood."

"My mood?"

"Yes, my love, your mood. I have a question I would like to ask you, but I want to be sure you're in a good mood. And I know the past few days have been hard on you."

"Well, just the fact that you know the past few days have been difficult, makes me more accepting of anything you might have to say to me. Just please, don't tell me you don't want to see me any longer. I'm not sure I could take that right now."

"What in the world would ever make you think I didn't want to see you any longer? Actually, I was about to tell you that I would love to see you every moment of ever day for the rest of my life. I was about to do this." He got out of his chair, and slowly dropped to one knee in front of her, while pulling a small black box from his pocket. When he opened the box, a glittering diamond ring caught light from the chandelier above, and sparkled beautifully. She gasped, caught completely unaware, and reached to touch his shoulder. "Marie, would you do me the honor of becoming my wife? I promise to spend my life serving God with you by my side, and loving you to the best of my ability. I will protect you, watch over you, guide you, and cherish you, all the days of my life."

"Oh, Joe, are you sure you want to? I mean the mess that I am, the mess that my family is. Are you sure you want to take that on?"

"I've never been more sure of anything in my life. So, please don't leave me down here forever."

"Then yes. Of course I will marry you. And I promise to spend my life serving God by your side as well. I will honor you, and look up to you as the head of my family. I love you Joe."

The restaurant erupted in applause, and Marie blushed again. They held hands the rest of the way home, and Marie, feeling as if this might be a dream, but wanting to be sure she didn't wake if it was, kept sneaking glances at her new fiancé. "What are you doing?"

"I'm just keeping an eye on you. I don't want you to disappear. Somehow this all feels too good to be true."

"No, my beautiful wife to be, this is all very real. And, I'm not going anywhere."

"An excellent wife who can find? She is far more precious than jewels. The heart of her husband trusts in her, and he will have no lack of gain. She does him good, and not harm, all the days of her life."

Proverbs 31:10-11

CHAPTER 18

Back at home Marie was nervous. Joe planned to tell his church of their recent engagement on Sunday before services. All she had to do was call her parents and siblings. They had talked about her cutting back a little on her hours at work, so she could spend more time with her husband and with the various Bible study and women's groups, but she wasn't ready to quit completely, at least not yet.

Her parents congratulated her. It seemed they liked Joe, and hoped to get to know him a little better on their next visit. Her mother didn't sound quite as drunk as she would normally be by this late in the day, and Marie was surprised. On Friday evening Marie made supper for Joe, her sister's family, and her brother's family. While they were visiting Marie made a call to her youngest sister and while the littlest one was on the phone, she and Joe announced their engagement. She knew the ones who'd met Joe liked him, but didn't know what her youngest sister's reaction would be. Evidently one of the other siblings had already called her and prepared her for what might be coming up. Everyone was thrilled and began talking about possible dates for the wedding.

"Whoa, wait just a minute. We don't even know how the people at church will react. They might not want me to be their pastor's wife."

"Well, just a minute, Marie. First of all, I want you to be my wife, so we aren't worried about what anyone else thinks or wants. But, past that, Everyone at the church loves you, and I don't think that's going to be a problem at all."

"Okay, Marie, what do you think about a Christmas wedding? The little one would be home for the holidays, and the colors and ambiance would be perfect. I can help you plan it, and I know it would be perfect! I can even help with flowers and a cake. I'm getting pretty good with most of that stuff, and I've been doing a little professional baking for people right from my house. It's a great way to make extra money when you have little ones at home.""

"I would listen to your sister, my love. Sounds like you'd have some pretty great help and I know you want all your sisters and brother there for the wedding. Maybe we could even talk your parents into coming."

"Well, I guess it's settled then. Christmas it is. That's always been a special time for the kids and I anyway, so this will give us one more reason to celebrate. Let's see how well this goes over on Sunday, before we start firming up any plans, and then I'll call Mom and Dad. How does that sound?"

"I think it sounds great. What about everyone else?"

From the cheers all around, it was clear they were all on board.

The next couple of months were a flurry of activity. Even though Marie cut back significantly on her hours at the marketing firm, she was constantly in demand for functions at the church and associated women's group meetings. And, yes, the congregation not only accepted her with open arms, they cheered as one when Brother Joe made the announcement.

Many women in the congregation wanted to help with the wedding in any way they could, so Marie and her sister had more help than they needed.

Marie had chosen to go for it on the wedding dress

and accessories. After all, when she'd married Jake she'd been deprived of all the hoopla that should accompany a bride's important day. However, her dress would be a pale cream color instead of white, which should be reserved for first timers.

Joe was choosing to stay back a few steps, so that Marie and her sister could make plans. He told someone during Bible study that it was like trying to harness a whirlwind, to try and tie those girls down while they were making plans.

Marie and her sister were becoming closer than ever during the process, and it made her heart glad. Her sister would also be her matron of honor, so they were working on that dress as well. Her brother would be standing up for Joe, as his best man, and her youngest sister would be a bride's maid. Some of the ladies and men of the church would complete the wedding party, and others would head up the refreshment table. There were some pretty amazing cooks and bakers in their church family. Her sister was handling the cake, but the meal would consist of baked ham; roast beef; chicken; cheesy potatoes; a vegetable medley; a variety of salads and homemade breads; a fruit and cheese plate; two kinds of punch; nut bowls; handmade mints; and hand churned ice cream, to accompany the wedding cake.

One of the women's groups was handling the decorations. They'd approached Marie to get her choice of colors for the reception theme, and they were busy as bees making pew decorations; corsages and boutonnieres; table enhancements; wall decorations; and flower arrangements. One lovely older gal was even handling the creation of the women's bouquets, including Marie's bridal bouquet. Everything was coming right along.

At home, two weeks before the wedding, Marie's phone rang. "Hi, Marie."

"Daddy?"

"Yes, Honey. It's your dad." Marie was shocked. Her dad didn't sound drunk. She almost hadn't recognized his voice; but for the hopeful little girl living somewhere in the back of her heart, who'd always hoped he'd come back to her someday. "I wanted you to know that your mom and I have been doing a lot of thinking, since you and Joe came to visit. We found a local church that offers a program for people with addiction problems, and we've been attending church and wellness programs. We've both asked Jesus into our hearts, and we've been working on forgiving each other for a multitude of things. We've stopped drinking too, and I have to say that I don't think either of us has ever felt so good. I wanted to tell you I'm sorry for all the pain I've caused you since I returned from Vietnam. I know it doesn't make it okay, but I was pretty sick for a long time. Learning about God's love for me has really helped me heal from all the monsters that were haunting me. You and Joe coming here and talking about Jesus' Grace has saved our lives. Marie, we'd like to come to your wedding, if that's okay. I'd really like to walk my girl down the aisle."

"Oh, Daddy, I can't think of anything I'd love more."

"Well, hey, your mom is sitting right here, and she'd like to talk to you too."

Marie's jaw clenched, and her body tensed, as her dad handed the phone to her mom. "Hi Marie. It's your mom."

"Hi mom. Dad was just saying that you two have quit drinking."

"Yes, we have. We've been going to church and Bible studies, and we're feeling much better. I wanted to tell you that I've been doing a lot of thinking, and I don't know how you managed to deal with me for all those years. I've been a terrible mother, and I'd like to ask you for your forgiveness. Do you think you can do that, Marie?"

Marie was sobbing quietly, but so hard that she almost couldn't get the words out of her mouth. "Of course I forgive you Mom. And I would love it if you came to my wedding. I'll get the girls working on a mother's corsage, and Daddy's boutonniere. I would also love it if you could light some special candles at the ceremony. If you come a couple days early we could spend some time together before the day, and I'm sure the other kids would love to see you. I have plenty of room at my house. I'm going to send someone to retrieve you so that you don't have to drive in inclement weather. It is December after all. Oh, Mom, we can all spend Christmas together too, I mean if you want to."

"That would be great, Honey. We would love that. Do you need us to bring anything?"

"Just yourselves. The ladies of the church have got everything pretty well covered. I can't wait to see you both."

"We can't wait either." Marie couldn't believe how wonderful her mother sounded. And the fact that she'd called her, Honey. Marie didn't remember a time, ever in her life, being referred to by her mother with any terms of endearment. Her heart was so full she was fairly floating on air. And, she couldn't wait to call Joe to tell him of the Christmas miracle which had just occurred.

Marie told all the kids about the phone call, and though

they were all a little leery, for good reason, they were excited about the prospect of spending the holidays as a complete family.

Joe and Marie bought a tree. Their first one together. It was almost too big for her living room, and she had a very large living room. Things had been so hectic this year, she just hadn't gotten around to it yet. Thanksgiving had been full of great food and plans for the upcoming nuptials, and the decorating which usually took place on the following day just never began. Well, now they wanted everything to be special, with Marie's parents coming, so they spent a full day decorating the tree, assembling a brand new manger set, and decking the halls with pine boughs, holly, and various Christmassy adornments.

Marie put fresh sheets on the guest bed upstairs, and filled vases with fresh pine and great big red carnations. She wasn't quite sure how things would unfold during the upcoming visit with her parents, but it felt good to be expecting to have a blessed time with people she'd feared and dreaded most of her life. Maybe this was the one time that all her frightening nightmares would mean nothing.

It was three days before the wedding, and Marie was picking up the watch she'd purchased as a wedding gift for her future husband. The words, "No, In all these things we are more than conquerors through Him who loved us." Romans 8:37, My heart forever, inscribed on the back. Her parents would be arriving later that day, as a member of the church was picking them up and driving them in for the festivities, and she wanted to be able to spend as much time as possible with them before the ceremony.

As she walked out of the quaint shop on Main Street a beat up old white van pulled up. A woman with brightly dyed red hair pulled back in a messy ponytail motioned to her. "I'm so sorry, but I'm lost. Can you help me?"

"Certainly. Where is it you're trying to go?" As Marie came along the driver's side of the van, the door slid open, and she was grabbed from behind. Something hit her, hard, in the back of the head, and she blacked out.

Several pedestrians witnessed the kidnapping, but weren't quick enough to stop it. However, one ran in to the store Marie just exited, yelling frantically for the owner to call the police. Another citizen found the small bag Marie had been holding when she left the shop, laying on the side of the street. And a third, one of the member's of Joe's church, stood crying on the curb, as she kicked herself for not being quicker in her assessment of the situation.

Police arrived and cordoned off the area. One detective started taking statements, while another checked the area for clues. The congregant from Joe's church, still crying, insisted that someone drive her to Joe, so they could tell him, in person, of the current, terrible situation.

Calls were made, and Marie's brother and sisters met Joe at the church to evaluate the state of affairs, and to try and come up with a way to save Marie. The police were adamant that they stay out of the way, stating that they might get themselves hurt, or even killed, but they couldn't just sit around doing nothing. She was the one person in their lives who had always been there for them, and they wouldn't leave her hanging.

Joe was calm on the outside, ever the people's pastor, but on the inside he was falling apart. Oh, he knew God loved Marie, just like he did. And, he knew that he could pray for good results. But, he didn't know what God's specific plans were in all of this, and hoped they didn't include Marie dealing with any more pain than she'd already been forced to endure in her life.

Yes, she was strong, but there was a limit to the amount

any human being could tolerate. And, just as her relationship with her parents was beginning to heal; just as she, and all the rest of her family, was finally coming to know the Lord; just as they would be starting their new life together, was not the time to test her ability to stay the course, was it?

As the minister, he was supposed to have the answers, wasn't he? Or, at least that seemed to be the general consensus. But, for the life of him, he couldn't figure any of this out. Perhaps they'd all brushed off Marie's nightmares too quickly? God uses even dreams as a way to warn us of harm to come. When she talked about the bad dreams from her past, and her fear that something terrible was about to happen; even though she was afraid the harm would be coming to him, he'd shrugged it off like it was nothing.

Well, they knew that the description of the vehicle was a beat up old white van. His parishioner said that it was a woman in her twenties, very thin, with bright red, dyed, hair who was driving. She also told them that the person who grabbed Marie was a man, probably in his thirties, well built, wearing a white tee shirt, with brown hair, and what looked like a prison tattoo on his upper left arm. She'd only gotten a quick look, and it was partially covered by the arm of his tee, but it looked like a skull with a snake crawling through the eye sockets.

The authorities quickly put a report out, and flashed a likeness of the perpetrators on television all throughout the state, but so far there were no calls. When Marie's younger sister saw the male likeness she said, to her brother, "I hate to say this, but doesn't that look like Marie's ex-husband Jake?"

"I was so young, I don't remember very much about him, but I think you might be right."

"I'm going to call the prison, and find out if he's been released."

After a few calls, and a long conversation with prison officials, they found that Jake had escaped from the Nevada penitentiary a week ago, supposedly with the help of a female he'd been corresponding with for some time. They would have notified Marie, if they'd known where she'd moved, but they weren't provided with that information.

So, it seemed they were dealing with a very angry ex-husband who thought he had an axe to grind. Joe called the police, who contacted the prison to get a name on the accomplice. They were able to come up with her name, and the fact that she owned an old white Volkswagen van, so the license plate was added to the current information given out to the police force and media.

The church was praying, and the family was coming together, but so far, they had heard nothing. In the midst of the turmoil the parents arrived. Joe took them to Marie's house, and set up a new command center there, so they wouldn't have to feel left out. The siblings and their families all pitched in, cooking and running errands. The grandparents met their three small grandchildren for the first time, and Marie's younger sister was especially touched when her mom asked to hold the baby.

She'd never seen her mother with tears in her eyes, or being so gentle with anyone. She only wished Marie was here to see the miraculous change in them. She'd been leery when Marie contacted them and made arrangements to go visit when they were younger, and even more so when she'd taken Joe along. She'd been disbelieving when she'd heard that the parents had asked Jesus into their hearts. And she'd been floored when she found out that Marie had forgiven them both, even after all the hell they'd put her through for her entire life. But, this was proof, that God could do anything. Now they just had to get Marie back, before that crazy person could do anything to hurt her.

Marie heard yelling coming from somewhere in the fog, when she broke through and woke in the back of a bouncing, rattling van. Opening her eyes she was shocked to see Jake sitting in the passenger seat, caddy corner from where she lay, and the woman who'd asked her for directions in the driver's seat. They were arguing, and her head was pounding.

She didn't make a sound, and when Jake turned to check on her, she quickly closed her eyes to avoid detection. She peeked, and saw that he was again facing forward, so she used the opportunity to assess her surroundings. The inside of the van was a mess. She was dumped on a dirty, smelly old mattress, which she assumed had been serving as Bonnie and Clyde's bed for whatever undetermined period of time they'd been on the run. She knew they must be on the run, because, even with good behavior (and what was the likelihood of that) he wasn't due to be released for another seven years or so. She'd intended to leave her address, so she could be informed of his impending release date, but thought she had plenty of time to accomplish that task. Obviously not so.

Looking around she saw a mixed pile of clothing that she guessed was dirty from the looks of it; a plastic bag containing a few toiletries, like toothpaste, deodorant, and soap, though she wasn't sure either of them bothered to use any of it, since the inside of the van smelled like a junior high school, boys, locker room after practice; several food items such as: crackers, cereal, beef jerky, and other non perishables; a couple of big jugs of water; and a large, beat up, red toolbox. Her mind was racing with ideas, and if they left the van long enough for any reason, that tool box would be her go to for a weapon or way to release her bindings.

"Lord, I know you love me, and I need help. Please Father, help me find a way so that I can get back to Joe." She whispered under her breath. She had no way of knowing that the entire congregation of their church was praying, and that members there had reached out to sister churches in the city and state, until there were thousands petitioning the Lord on her behalf.

Jake looked back again, and she quickly closed her eyes. "She ought to be awake by now. Do you suppose I hit her too hard? I don't want her to be dead, because I plan on taking care of that slowly. I want her to suffer a long time for everything she's put me through. You know, that would be just like her to ruin all the fun." His girlfriend let loose with a tittering giggle that was enough to make Marie's stomach turn.

At her Daddy's suggestion, the whole family joined hands around the dining room table to pray. He began, "Heavenly Father, I know that you love us, and that you love Marie. Thank you first of all for the knowledge of your love that has plucked us out of the miry muck and welcomed us into Your Kingdom by Your Grace. And then secondly, has placed us tenderly around this table with the ones we love. Lord, please keep our girl safe and bring her back into our arms. In Jesus' Holy and perfect Name. Amen." When he finished he wiped away the tears that had begun to track down his cheeks. He had to remind himself not to continue berating himself for all the wasted years. Grace had healed and that same Grace would save his daughter.

"That was a beautiful prayer. I didn't know you even knew how to pray, Daddy. I'm so glad you're here. That both of you are here."

"We're glad too, daughter. Thank you for allowing us back into your lives, all of you, after the things we've done to make your lives miserable in the past."

"That's all water under the bridge, Dad. I'm glad we have the chance to begin again. Now we just need to figure out how to get Marie back."

"Thank you Son. And, yes, just tell us what to do."

"Well, for now, until we get some kind of direction, we're going to stay right here and pray. That's the most powerful tool we have. And, our Lord is the most powerful force in the universe. We will trust in Him."

"Okay, Joe. Perhaps we should pray in shifts. That way there will always be someone lifting our girl up to the Lord."

"That's a great idea, Dad. Would you and Mom start?"

"We'd be glad to."

Now that the entire family was working together, and praying in the Name of Jesus, there was no enemy in the world that could withstand the power of the Word of God.

They'd driven for awhile when the van veered off the road and began a steep assent. From her position on the floor of the van she couldn't see much. Just the green of pines flashing past the windshield and passenger seat. When they stopped she continued to feign unconsciousness, so Jake pulled her out of the van and threw her roughly over his shoulder. There was something familiar about the property where they walked. And, when they neared the house Marie suddenly knew where they were. Angela's boarded up old house. It was still standing. From her angle she could see that it was pretty much as she remembered. But, since it was December, there was a fair amount of snow on the ground.

Jake's girlfriend pushed past the back door into the kitchen, and Marie saw, after being dumped unceremoniously on the floor of the main room, that they'd obviously found the place at some point earlier, because they'd hauled numerous supplies in and piled them against the living room wall.

It was cold. There would be no way to heat the house, since the power lines had been disconnected for years. Marie remembered that from their trip to the homestead to find Angela all those years ago. There was a wood burning stove in the corner, but the exhaust venting was torn from the wall, so lighting it would mean suffocation within hours. Drafts blew in from cracks around window frames, a broken piece of glass by the front door, and the hole in the wall where the vent should have been attached.

Jake looked over and caught Marie with her eyes open. "Well, well, well. If it isn't Miss Marie. How ya doing missy?"

"Jake, what are you doing? You don't want to do this. What will you accomplish?"

"What will I accomplish? I will get even with you for all the years of trouble you've caused me."

"Trouble that I've caused you, Jake?"

"Yeah. First you and your brat wreck my life in the Air Force, and make my mom hate me; then the prison term. I would call that trouble, wouldn't you Marie?"

"Jake, you would never have been in trouble with the Air Force, or your mom, if you hadn't raped me and gotten me pregnant." His girlfriend looked at him sharply. This must be new information for her. "And, if you hadn't sold me to the Pit Boss at the casino, you wouldn't have been in prison. I would say you've caused me a lot more trouble than I've ever caused you." His girl looked angry now, so he kicked Marie, hard, in the gut. And then he just kept kicking her until she passed out.

She woke freezing, teeth chattering, and her whole body

shaking from the extreme cold. Jake and his girl were sleeping. They'd dragged the mattress in from the van, and were sleeping under a pile of blankets, while she lay in the middle of the floor in her underwear. Someone had relieved her of her coat and clothing. She looked around the room again. It was a small room, so she wasn't far from the door, but she was bound hand and foot. To get outside, especially in her condition, would mean certain death. "Lord, I need a way out. I am trusting You."

Morning came and Jake woke stretching and farting. He shoved his girl. "Hey, knock it off." He slapped her. "What did you do that for?"

"Go get me a drink of water and something to eat." She rose, naked, and walked to their pile of supplies rubbing her cheek. Marie noticed quite a number of bruises, old and new, and was so grateful she wasn't married to him anymore. Soon she would be married to her love. She had to continue believing that, or she would lose her mind.

They satisfied themselves with some beef jerky and a handful of crackers, then he yanked her down by the hair and they had sex while Marie closed her eyes and tried not to hear. "What's the matter, Marie. You need a little of this too?" His girlfriend smacked him on the arm, and he turned and punched her in the face and she screamed. Marie could only shake her head.

As Jake and his girl dressed, and he settled his handgun in the back of his belt, she reasoned. Reminding him, last night, that he was responsible for his own misfortune, had not gone over well. Perhaps this morning she would try a different approach. Still shaking from the cold she spoke. "I'm sorry, Jake. I really am. I know I ruined your life and I'm really sorry. I should never have told the police anything. It's all my fault that they put you in jail. All I can do is beg for your forgiveness." He looked at her suspiciously, then nodded. "So, you admit it? You know it was your fault?"

"Yes. And, if you let me go, I will tell the police that it was all my fault. They can cancel your sentence, and you'll probably even get some kind of compensation for the time you've spent in jail."

"I don't need their compensation. They told me my mom died, so I have a huge inheritance waiting for me. All I have to do is clear my name." So, no one had told him that his inheritance had gone to his step dad, and then to his step dad's son. She didn't want to be around when he found that out.

"Right. I forgot. Just think of it, Jake. Once your name is cleared you'll be able to go anywhere you want. You can travel and gamble, and party to your heart's content. You and your girlfriend can have anything you desire. All you have to do is let me go, and we'll go to the police right now to clear all this up."

"She isn't my girlfriend."

"What do you mean I'm not your girlfriend? You wouldn't even be out of the joint if it wasn't for me."

"Well, let's just say you've served your purpose."

"Hey, I don't have to put up with this. I didn't have to help you escape and drive all the way across the country for this."

"No, I imagine there were plenty of losers right there in Vegas who would have been happy to have you. So, why don't you leave."

"Give me my keys, and I will."

"You're not getting your keys, now go."

"I'm not going out in the cold without my van. I'll freeze to death. Now give me my keys, or I'll go to the police myself." At that point Jake pulled the nine millimeter out of his belt and shot her between the eyes. Her head flipped back and she hit the floor with a thud. Marie, in shock from what she'd just seen, watched as blood pooled around the poor girl's head. She had to keep her wits about her, and act like she was on his side, so she couldn't show him how stunned she was at this brazen act of violence. "Good, now we don't have to put up with her anymore. You're going to need to get dressed."

"That's fine. If you'll untie me I'll take care of that."

"Do I look stupid? I'll untie your legs and get your slacks on, then I'll tie your legs and we'll figure out your blouse."

"Okay, Jake. Whatever you need to do." She was terrified. She'd always known he was evil, but she'd never actually seen him kill anyone. And, she knew deep down inside that if she wasn't careful she would be next.

Somehow they managed to dress her, but then Jake decided he needed to go for more supplies before they decided what to do about the police.

"Aren't you going to take me with you? I can go in the store, and that way you don't have to risk being seen."

"And have you tell them I'm in the van? You really must think I'm a fool. No, you're going to stay right here until I get back. Then we'll head back to Vegas."

"Do we really need to go all the way back to Vegas? Why can't we just go to the police here? I'm sure they can take care of it."

"No, no, no, The people in Vegas will remember us. It will be easier for them to remember you, and all the trouble you caused me. You'll be able to make them see how you framed me. No, we'll leave as soon as I get back." He hog tied her and left her on the floor.

She was still cold, but with her clothing and coat on it wasn't nearly as bad. He'd trussed her up like a pig, with her hands and feet nearly touching in back, so comfort would not be an option.

After a couple of hours she began to wonder where he was. No errands should have taken this long. She even began to wonder if he'd been stopped and arrested by the police. If so, perhaps they would be coming to get her. But no, he wouldn't tell them where she was, or he'd have to explain the dead body of his girl friend. If they sent him back to jail now, it would just be to serve out the rest of his time, and probably a penalty for escaping. If he was found guilty of murder, he'd likely be in prison for the rest of his life. "Oh, Lord, I really need you now. No one knows I'm here, Lord, and it's pretty cold in this place. So, whatever You can do to help me out would be greatly appreciated."

What Marie didn't know was that Jake had never in his

life driven on icy, snow covered roads, which is why his girlfriend had been doing the driving for most of their trip out east. So, when he left the house and got in the van, to head down the winding road to the river highway, he'd slid most of the way. Trying his best to stop as he got to the main road, he stomped on the brake and sent himself into a deadly spin. The spin, which took him across the road and through the guard rails overlooking the Hudson river embankment, sent him flying into the freezing cold water below. As the water engulfed him, numbing him and filling his lungs, he tried to scream. He was dead within minutes. No one would ever find his body.

"Behold, God is my salvation; I will trust, and will
not be afraid; for the Lord God is my strength and
my song, and He has become my salvation."

Isaiah 12:2

CHAPTER 19

Marie had been missing for three days, and her family was trying desperately not to lose hope. The wedding day was here, but there was no bride, and the groom was heartbroken. Reminding himself over and over to trust God for her life, he prayed nonstop. Her mom and dad had actually been a great comfort throughout the past few days, and he could see that their children were getting closer to them by the minute.

The ladies at the church were still getting together to provide intercessory prayer for Marie and the situation, but they'd taken down all the pew decorations, and stored all the wedding fixtures. Best not to rub salt in the wound. They saw how desolate their pastor seemed without his beloved, and they wanted to comfort him as much as possible. The police were following every lead, but no one had seen the van, and it seemed there hadn't been any recent calls claiming sightings of the perpetrators.

Marie wasn't sure how long she'd been alone in the old house. Perhaps two or three days. But she knew she was very thirsty, and she'd lost feeling in her arms and legs long ago. She didn't know if she could even walk anymore if she was rescued. Hunger had sapped her of any latent energy reserves, and she wondered if she would ever see her loved ones again. This house had been hidden away for so long. There was no reason for anyone to come up the icy, dangerous driveway now.

The girl's body didn't smell, she was sure, in part, to the freezing temperatures, but if they were locked away in here for too long, she had no doubt animals would find them. And, she imagined, if they began to eat the girl, she would probably end up on the menu as well. She just hoped she'd be dead at that point in time. She couldn't think of very many things more gruesome than to be eaten alive.

Going in and out of consciousness, due to her extreme hunger and thirst, she began to think she was seeing things skittering across the floor. Suddenly, sitting cross legged before her, was her old friend Angela. It was odd. She hadn't aged a bit since Marie's accident all those years before.

"Hi Angela."

"Hello Marie. How are you doing my child?"

"Well, as you can see, I'm trussed up pretty good, and I can't get free."

"I can see that. I want you to know that God is watching, Marie. He will never leave you."

"Okay, but unless someone unties me, I'm not getting out of here."

"Do you believe He loves you, Marie?"

"Yes, I believe, please help my unbelief. I will, Angela. I will trust in Him."

"You're such a brave girl. Always remember that God loves you, Marie." Then as quickly as she'd appeared, she was gone.

It was dark again. Marie thought she remembered something, and then she wasn't sure. Was today her wedding day? She was sad for Joe. She hoped her family was doing alright. she knew that if no one found her and she died in this place she would be with the Lord, but she was saddened by the fact that she knew her family would be devastated. She'd really wanted to be Joe's wife, and she'd just begun a whole new relationship with her parents, but if this was how her life would end she would be fine with that. She couldn't take much more of the cold, the numbness in her arms and legs, and the thirst that had caused her tongue to stick to the back of her throat, which was making it difficult to even take a breath.

Marie's brother was tossing in his sleep. As the hours and days ticked away since Marie's disappearance, he'd grown more depressed. It was great that their parents had come into their lives again, and that their lives had been changed by the presence of the Lord, but Marie was the one who had raised him. She was more of a mom to him than anyone else in the world had ever been. He didn't know what he would do if she was never found. The idea that this monster from her past might be torturing her, or doing who knows what to her, was tearing him up inside. Just then, an old friend appeared to him in his sleep.

"Hi Angela."

"Hello my dear."

He sat up in his bed and knew immediately and instinctively where Marie had been taken. He called the family together, and they contacted the police. He and Joe headed out, not willing to wait for the detectives to figure out where the boarded up old house was located. Her brother knew innately that she didn't have much time left. "It was Angela, Joe. She came to me."

"Who is Angela?"

"She's an angel that Marie and I met after a terrible accident when we were kids. She was there when we needed her then, and she showed up when we needed her now. God is good, Joe, all the time.

"And, all the time, God is good."

Marie was close to death when the men arrived and loosed her bonds, with the detectives following close behind. Attendants put her gently on a gurney and out to the waiting ambulance. There wouldn't be enough room for both the men in the bus, so her brother would follow in his car, after answering some questions from the officers. Joe held her hand, which was cold as ice, and paid very close attention to everything the medics were doing. They were pumping her full of fluids, and trying to get the circulation going in her extremities, to see if they could be saved.

"Father. Thank you for sending an angel, and saving her life. Now I'm asking for more. Please save all of her. I love her more than my own life, and I'll do anything you ask of me, but I know how much she wants to help people. Let her be your hands and feet, Lord. And, let's face it Father. In order to be Your hands and feet, she will need hers."

At the hospital she was rushed to ICU. Doctors were working feverishly to restore blood flow to her hands and feet, when suddenly, all of her vital signs were completely normal. She opened her eyes, and Joe began to sob. "Thank you, Lord. Thank you."

"Where am I?"

"You're in the hospital, Marie. Angela came to your brother and told him where you were. I'm pretty sure we all arrived just in the nick of time."

"My hero. Thank you for coming for me."

"I would do anything for you, Marie. But, it was God who touched you. He sent Angela, and He got your circulation going again too, so it looks like you won't lose your hands and feet."

"Yes, Angela came to me too. Just like she did when I was a child. She kept telling me that God loves me, and calling me brave. Do they have Jake? It was him. He broke out of prison with the help of some girl he'd met through correspondence."

"No, they haven't found Jake. They found the body of the girl who helped him. She had a bullet in her head."

"It was awful. The way he treated her. It was just like he used to treat me. I couldn't even be angry with her. She was every bit as much a victim as I was. If they don't have him, how do we know he won't try this again?"

"All we know my love is that God is watching over us. He has proved that abundantly today. So, we're not going to worry about any of it, okay?"

"Agreed. So, I missed my wedding."

"Well, I think we can talk the ladies into getting everything set up again, under the circumstances. I would wait a thousand years for you, Marie. I can't imagine my life without you. And, thanks be to God, I don't have to."

"God is good, all the time."

"And, all the time, God is good."

"Who told you where she was?"

"I've already told you. Angela. She's an angel."

"So, you expect me to believe that an angel appeared to you and told you where your sister was being held?" As he spoke with the detectives, the coroner's office collected the body of Jake's accomplice.

"I don't expect you to believe anything officer. You're entitled to believe, or not believe, anything you'd like. But, explain to me how I knew where to come?"

"Okay. But, if you think of anything else, I mean something that might actually help us find your sister's ex husband, call." This was said while the detective handed him a business card.

"Do you believe him? I mean about the angel and all?"

"I don't know what to believe. He sure seems to believe it though."

"I mean, I don't not believe in angels. I'm just glad we got here before it was too late. It sure seems like she didn't have much time left. Now, maybe the city will do the right thing and tear down this old house."

Marie healed quickly. And, once she was well the ladies at the church were once again buzzing like a hive of very industrious bees. Her sister baked the cake, as she'd promised. French vanilla with butter cream frosting. None of that tasteless fondant stuff. Joe and Marie talked, and she gave the marketing firm notice. She really wanted to have time to focus on the church. The pews were again decorated. And, though it was past Christmas, all the decorations had been left up for the wedding. Her family, too, had left the house in all its holiday glory, including gifts under the tree. They planned to open them tonight, right before tomorrow's long awaited nuptials, so the couple could leave right away on their honeymoon.

One of her sister's little ones passed out the gifts, and excitedly pasted the bows on her head as the presents were opened. Marie received a Bible from Joe. White, with gold embossed lettering and her name inscribed on the cover. Inside was this very profound and timely inscription: "I can do all things through Christ who strengthens me." Philippians 4:13. She loved it. And, the watch she'd been picking up on the day she was abducted was also wrapped and under the tree. Joe loved it as well.

With the fireplace lit, and coffee brewing in the kitchen; after all the gifts were open, and children were playing in the corner; Marie sat wrapped in Joe's arms, talking about tomorrow's big day with her family. With ALL of her family. She'd never felt so cradled in love.

The church was packed to the rafters. Marie was nervous. Not about marrying Joe, but about walking down the aisle in front of so many people. What if she tripped, in spite of all her precautions?

Her dress had turned out perfectly, though she'd lost some weight during her unexpected absence. Slightly form fitting, from shoulder to hip, with long sleeves, and a flared skirt; the dress was cream colored, satin, with small red roses along the neckline and sleeves. She wore ballet slippers, so she wouldn't trip. And, a beautiful up do, with red roses, and baby's breath, worked into her shining auburn tresses, in lieu of a traditional veil.

Her matron of honor and bride's maids wore pink satin, with red roses, and the men wore red cummerbunds with their black tuxes. Corsages and boutonnieres were bits of pine, with red roses, carnations, and small sprays of baby's breath. Two of her sister's kids would be in the ceremony; one as the flower girl, and one as the ring bearer. They looked so adorable in their pink lacy dress, and tiny black tux, respectively. But, they were starting to get grumpy, and there went the girl's thumb, right into her mouth, while the little guy began making car noises with the pillow, which was meant to carry their rings. Her sister got a worried look on her face, but Marie just laughed. These would be things they could remember and talk about for years.

At the altar two candles had been placed to represent Joe's absent parents. And, there were also two candles that Marie's mom would light at the beginning of the ceremony, for the later lighting of the unity candle. Mom looked beautiful. Since quitting drinking, her skin had begun to lose the yellowish cast that covered her for so long. Her hair was fixed nicely and she even had a little eye makeup on. She'd chosen a pink satin dress, with embroidered red roses on the hem and sleeves, which fit in nicely with the day's theme.

Downstairs the ladies had gone all out. Tables were covered in white satin cloths and each table was decorated with candles and red roses. The head table was scattered with rose petals, and the cake was set up in the corner with plates of mints and bowls of nuts. There was so much food, Marie thought she might just gain back any weight she'd lost, and she felt almost faint from the delicious smells rising up into the sanctuary.

Joe's best friend from college would be performing the ceremony, and the moment he met Marie, he knew why his confirmed bachelor friend had changed his mind. One of the ladies from the church would sing a solo, while they lit the unity candle, and her youngest sister would play the violin.

Guests were seated, the men stood at the altar with Joe and his best man, and the music began. As the bride's maids made their way down the aisle, Daddy looked at his daughter. "I've never been more proud of you, than I am today, daughter. You are beautiful."

"Thank you, Daddy. I'm pretty proud of you too. Thank you for making my day complete. It would have been pretty sad without you and Mom here."

"Are you ready?"

"Absolutely."

When Joe saw his lovely bride approaching, tears of joy began to stream down his face. And the moment Marie saw that he was crying, she began to weep too. Pretty soon, sisters, her brother, parents and friends were all bawling. They would all laugh afterward, when they watched the wedding video, as the entire congregation was a sobbing mess. They had witnessed the miracle of Marie being saved and brought back to them, and they all knew that God was good.

Vows and kisses were exchanged, and the minister introduced them as man and wife. Then, as they walked back down the aisle, into their bright new life together, Marie caught sight of something out of the corner of her eye. She turned and saw Angela. They smiled affectionately at one another. But when she turned to get Joe's attention, and then looked back again, her friend was gone. Yes, God is good all the time, and all the time God is good.